PENGUIN BOOKS

FELUDA'S LAST CASE

Satyajit Ray was born on 2 May 1921 in Calcutta. After graduating from Presidency College, Calcutta, in 1940, he studied art at Rabindranath Tagore's university, Shantiniketan. By 1943, Ray was back in Calcutta and had joined an advertising firm as a visualizer. He also started designing covers and illustrating books brought out by the Signet Press. A deep interest in film led to his establishing the Calcutta Film Society in 1947. During a six-month trip to Europe, in 1950, Ray became a member of the London Film Club and managed to see ninety-nine films in only four-and-a-half months.

In 1955, after innumerable difficulties had been overcome, Satyajit Ray completed his first film, *Pather Panchali*, with financial assistance from the West Bengal Government. The film was an award-winner at the Cannes Film Festival and established Ray as a director of international stature. Together with *Aparajito* (The Unvanquished, 1956) and *Apur Sansar* (The World of Apu, 1959), it forms the *Apu* trilogy—perhaps Ray's finest work to date. Ray's other films include *Jalsaghar* (The Music Room, 1958), *Charulata* (1964), *Aranyer Din Ratri* (Days and Nights in the Forest, 1970), *Shatranj Ke Khilari* (The Chess Players, 1977), *Ghare Baire* (The Home and the World, 1984), *Ghanashatru* (Enemy of the People, 1989), *Shakha Proshakha* (Branches of a Tree, 1990), and *Agantuk* (The Stranger, 1991). Ray also made several documentaries, including one on Tagore. In 1987, he made the documentary *Sukumar Ray*, to commemorate the birth centenary of his father, perhaps Bengal's most famous writer of nonsense verse and children's books. Satyajit Ray won numerous awards for his films. Both the British Federation of Film Societies and the Moscow Film Festival Committee named him one of the greatest directors of the second half of the twentieth century. In 1992, he was awarded the Oscar for Lifetime Achievement by the Academy of Motion Picture Arts and Science and, in the same year, was also honoured with the Bharat Ratna.

Apart from being a film-maker, Satyajit Ray was a w iter of repute. In 1961, he revived the children's magazine, *Sandesh*, which his grandfather, Upendrakishore Ray, had started and to which his father used to contribute frequently. Satyajit Ray contributed numerous poems, stories and essays to *Sandesh*, and also published several novels in Bengali, most of which became best sellers. In 1978, Oxford University awarded him its D.Litt degree.

Satyajit Ray died in Calcutta in April 1992.

*

Gopa Majumdar was born in Delhi in 1956. She graduated in English Literature from Delhi University. Her first translations of Bengali short stories (including one by Ray) were published in the *Namaste* magazine. This was followed by more stories by Ray (*Twenty Stories, The Emperor's Ring* and *The Mystery of the Elephant God*), which were published by Penguin.

She has also translated and edited a collection of Bengali short stories titled *In the Same Boat—Golden Tales from Bengal*. She is currently translating the works of two leading women writers of Bengal, Ashapurna Debi and Nabaneeta Dev Sen and hopes to start working soon on the remaining stories by Satyajit Ray.

In 1995, she was given the *Katha* award for translation.

Satyajit Ray

Feluda's Last Case

Translated from the Bengali by
Gopa Majumdar

PENGUIN BOOKS

Penguin Books India (P) Ltd., 210 Chiranjiv Tower, Nehru Place, New Delhi 110 019, India
Penguin Books Ltd., 27 Wrights Lane, London W8 5TZ, UK
Penguin Books USA Inc., 375 Hudson Street, New York, New York 10014, USA
Penguin Books Australia Ltd., Ringwood, Victoria, Australia
Penguin Books Canada Ltd., 10 Alcorn Avenue, Suite 300, Toronto, Ontario M4V 3B2, Canada
Penguin Books (NZ) Ltd., 182-190 Wairau Road, Auckland 10, New Zealand

First published in English by Penguin Books India (P) Ltd. 1995

Typeset in Palatino by Digital Technologies and Printing Solutions, New Delhi

Contents

Translator's Note

When, in 1965, Satyajit Ray wrote 'Feludar Goendagiri' ('Danger in Darjeeling') for the children's magazine called *Sandesh*, neither he nor his readers could have foreseen the enormous impact Feluda and his young cousin Tapesh would make on every household in Bengal.

The Adventures of Feluda (published by Penguin in 1988) was the first collection that introduced these two central characters and their friend, Lalmohan Ganguli (alias Jatayu) to non-Bengali readers. Their response was as enthusiastic as those who had read the originals. This led to *The Emperor's Ring: Further Adventures of Feluda* (1994) and *The Mystery of the Elephant God: More Adventures of Feluda* (1995). It would perhaps not be wrong to say that Feluda and his team no longer need to be formally presented to readers.

This collection starts at the very beginning, going back thirty years, when the two cousins are in Darjeeling on a summer holiday. They are certainly not looking for a mystery, but when an amiable old gentleman begins to receive strange threats, Feluda feels obliged to step in.

This was followed, over the years, by 'Trouble in Gangtok' ('Gangtokey Gondogol', 1970), 'The Anubis mystery' ('Sheyal Debota Rahasya', 1970), 'The Key' ('Samaddarer Chabi', 1973), 'The Gold Coins of Jehangir ('Jehangirer Swarnamudra', 1983),

'The Mystery of Nayan' ('Nayan Rahasya', 1990) and 'Robertson's Ruby' ('Robertsoner Ruby', 1992).

It is interesting to note Feluda's development from a totally unknown amateur detective to a famous professional private investigator. Like all well-known figures, he had to pay the price of fame, as the opening chapter of 'The Mystery of Nayan' reveals. Tapesh (affectionately called Topshe), his faithful Watson, stays with him throughout, alert, watchful and of immense help at all times. Lalmohan Babu appears in three of the seven stories in this book, all written after 1973. He made his debut in 1971 ('The Golden Fortress', translated by Chitrita Banerjee and included in 'The Adventures of Feluda'), chiefly to act as a foil to Feluda. But he soon became an important member of the team.

Translating these novellas has been a deeply fulfilling experience for me. Some of the early stories took me back to my early teens, when a ride in a taxi could cost one the princely sum of one rupee and seventy paisa, and a bearded foreigner in colourful clothes was likely to be labelled a 'hippie' ('The Anubis Mystery' and 'Trouble in Gangtok'). But, more importantly, it gave me a new insight into the author's mind and a chance to rediscover his varied interests—magic, hypnotism, music, history, ancient art and antiques.

I am grateful to Penguin for giving me another opportunity to share my experiences with the readers; and to Sandip Ray for giving his permission for the translation. My thanks go also to my brother, Jyotirmoy, and sisters, Ishani and Indrani, for all their help and support.

Finally, I dedicate this translation to my nephew, Ayan.

London   *Gopa Majumdar*
May 1995

Danger in Darjeeling

I saw Rajen Babu come to the Mall every day. He struck me as an amiable old man. All his hair had turned grey, and his face always wore a cheerful expression. He generally spent a few minutes in the corner shop that sold old Nepali and Tibetan things; then he came and sat on a bench in the Mall for about half-an-hour, until it started to get dark. After that he went straight home. One day, I followed him quietly to see where he lived. He turned around just as we reached his front gate and asked, 'Who are you? Why have you been following me?'

'My name is Tapesh Ranjan,' I replied quickly.

'Well then, here is a lozenge for you,' he said, offering me a lemon drop. 'Come to my house one day. I'll show you my collection of masks,' he added.

Who knew that this friendly old soul would get into such trouble? Why, he seemed totally incapable of getting involved with anything even remotely sinister!

Feluda snapped at me when I mentioned this. 'How can you tell just by looking at someone what he might get mixed up with?' he demanded.

This annoyed me. 'What do *you* know of Rajen Babu?' I said. 'He's a good man. A very kind man. He has done a lot for the poor Nepali people who live in slums. There's no reason why he should be in trouble. I *know*. I see him every day. You haven't seen him even once. In fact, I've hardly seen you go out at all since we came to Darjeeling.'

'All right, all right. Let's have all the details then. What would a little boy like you know of danger, anyway?'

Now, this wasn't fair. I was not a little boy any more. I was thirteen and a half. Feluda was twenty-seven.

To tell you the truth, I came to know about the trouble Rajen Babu was in purely by accident. I was sitting on a bench in the Mall today, waiting for the band to start playing. On my left was Tinkori Babu, reading a newspaper. He had recently arrived from Calcutta to spend the summer in Darjeeling, and had taken a room on rent in Rajen Babu's house. I was trying to lean over his shoulder and look at the Sports page, when Rajen Babu arrived panting and collapsed on the empty portion of our bench, next to Tinkori Babu. He looked visibly shaken.

'What's the matter?' asked Tinkori Babu, folding his newspaper. 'Did you just run up a hill?'

'No, no,' Rajen Babu replied cautiously, wiping his face with one corner of his scarf. 'Something incredible has happened.'

I knew what 'incredible' meant. Feluda was quite partial to the word.

'What do you mean?' Tinkori Babu asked.

'Look, here it is,' Rajen Babu passed a piece of folded blue paper to Tinkori Babu. I could tell it was a letter, but made no attempt to read it when Tinkori Babu unfolded it. I looked away instead, humming under my breath to indicate a complete lack of interest in what the two old men were discussing. But I heard Tinkori Babu remark, 'You're right, it *is* incredible! Who could possibly write such a threatening letter to you?'

4

'I don't know. That's what's so puzzling. I don't remember having deliberately caused anyone any harm. As far as I know, I have no enemies.'

Tinkori Babu leant towards his neighbour. 'We'd better not talk about this in public,' he whispered. 'Let's go home.'

The two gentlemen left.

*

Feluda remained silent for a while after I had finished my story. Then he frowned and said, 'You mean you think we need to investigate?'

'Why, didn't *you* tell me you were looking for a mystery? And you said you had read so many detective novels that you could work as a sleuth yourself!'

'Yes, that's true. I could prove it, too. I didn't go to the Mall today, did I? But I could tell you which side you sat on.'

'All right, which side was it?'

'You chose a bench on the right side of the Radha restaurant, didn't you?'

'That's terrific. How did you guess?'

'The sun came out this evening. Your left cheek looks sunburnt but the right one is all right. This could happen only if you sat on that side of the Mall. That's the bit that catches the evening sunshine.'

'Incredible!'

'Yes. Anyway, I think we should go and visit Mr Rajen Majumdar.'

*

'Another seventy-seven steps.'

'And what if it's not?'

'It has to be, Feluda. I counted the last time.'

'Remember you'll get knocked on the head if you're wrong.'

'OK, but not too hard. A sharp knock may damage my brain.'

To my amazement, seventy-seven steps later, we were still at some distance from Rajen Babu's gate. Another twenty-three brought us right up to it. Feluda hit my head lightly, and asked, 'Did you count the steps on your way back?'

'Yes.'

'That explains it. You went down the hill on your way back, you idiot. You must have taken very big steps.'

'Well . . . yes, maybe.'

'I'm sure you did. You see, young people always tend to take big, long steps when going downhill. Older people have to be more cautious, so they take smaller, measured steps.'

We went in through the gate. Feluda pressed the calling bell. Someone in the distance was listening to a radio.

'Have you decided what you're going to say to him?' I asked.

'That's my business. You, my dear, will keep your mouth shut.'

'Even if they ask me something? You mean I shouldn't even make a reply?'

'Shut up.'

A Nepali servant opened the door. '*Andar aaiye,*' he said.

We stepped into the living room. Made of wood, the house had a lovely old charm. All the furniture in the room was made of cane. The walls were covered with strange masks, most showing large teeth and wearing rather unpleasant expressions. Some of them frightened me. Apart from these, the room was full of old weapons—shields and swords and daggers. Beside these hung pictures of the Buddha, painted on cloth. Heaven knew how old they were, but the golden colour that had been used had not faded at all.

We took two cane chairs. Feluda rose briefly to inspect the walls. Then he came back and said, 'All the nails are new. So Rajen Babu's passion for antiques must have developed only recently.'

Rajen Babu came into the room. Feluda sprang to his feet and said, 'Do you remember me? I am Joykrishna Mitter's son, Felu.'

Rajen Babu looked a little taken aback at first. Then his face broke into a smile. 'Felu? Of course I remember you. My word, you have become a young man! How is everyone at home? Is your father here?'

As Feluda answered these questions, I sat trying to hide my astonishment. How unfair the whole thing was—why hadn't Feluda told me that he knew Rajen Babu?

It turned out that Rajen Babu had worked in Calcutta for many years as a lawyer. He had once helped Feluda's father fight a case. He had come to Darjeeling and settled here ten years ago, soon after his retirement.

Feluda introduced me to him. He showed no sign of recognition. Perhaps the matter of offering me a lozenge a week ago had slipped his mind completely.

'You're fond of antiques, I see,' said Feluda conversationally.

'Yes. It's turned almost into an obsession.'

'How long—?'

'Over the last six months. But I've managed to collect quite a lot of things.'

Feluda cleared his throat. Then he told Rajen Babu what he had heard from me, and ended by saying, 'I still remember how you had helped my father. If I could do anything in return . . . .'

Rajen Babu looked both pleased and relieved. But before he could say anything, Tinkori Babu walked into the room. From the way he was breathing, it appeared that he had just come back after his evening walk. Rajen Babu made the introductions. 'Tinkori Babu happens to be a neighbour of Gyanesh, a friend of mine. When this friend heard that I was going to let one of my rooms, he suggested that I give it to Tinkori Babu. He would have gone to a hotel otherwise.'

Tinkori Babu laughed. 'I did hesitate to take up his offer,

I must admit, chiefly because of my special weakness for cheroots. You see, Rajen Babu might well have objected to the smell. So I wrote to him first to let him know. He said he didn't mind, so here I am.'

'Are you here simply for a change of air?'

'Yes, but the air, I've noticed, isn't as cool and fresh as one might have expected.'

'Are you fond of music?' asked Feluda unexpectedly.

'Yes, but how did you guess?' Tinkori Babu gave a startled smile.

'Well, I noticed your finger,' Feluda explained. 'You were beating it on top of your walking-stick, in keeping with the rhythm of that song from the radio.'

'You're quite right,' Rajen Babu laughed, 'he sings Shyamasangeet.'

Feluda changed the subject. 'Do you have the letter here?' he asked.

'Oh yes. Right next to my heart,' said Rajen Babu and took it out of the inside pocket of his jacket. Feluda spread it out.

It was not handwritten. A few printed words had been cut out of books or newspapers and pasted on a sheet of paper. 'Be prepared to pay for your sins,' it read.

'Did this come by post?'

'Yes. It was posted in Darjeeling, but I'm afraid I threw the envelope away.'

'Have you reason to suspect anyone?'

'No. For the life of me, I cannot recall ever having harmed anyone.'

'Do certain people visit you regularly?'

'Well, I don't get too many visitors. Dr Phoni Mitra comes occasionally if I happen to be ill.'

'Is he a good doctor?'

'About average, I should say. But then, my complaints have always been quite ordinary—I mean, no more than the usual coughs and colds. So I haven't had to look for a really good doctor.'

'Does he charge a fee?'

'Of course. But that's hardly a problem. I've got plenty of money, thank God.'

'Who else visits you?'

'A Mr Ghoshal has recently started coming to my house . . . look, here he is!' A man of medium height wearing a dark suit was shown into the room.

'Did I hear my name?' he asked with a smile.

'Yes, I was just about to tell these people that you share my interest in antiques. Allow me to introduce them.'

After exchanging greetings, Mr Ghoshal—whose full name was Abanimohan Ghoshal—said to Rajen Babu, 'I thought I'd drop by since you didn't come to the shop today.'

'N-no, I wasn't feeling very well, so I decided to stay in.'

It was clear that Rajen Babu did not want to tell Mr Ghoshal about the letter. Feluda had hidden it the minute Mr Ghoshal had walked in.

'All right, if you're busy today, I'll come back another time . . . actually, I wanted to take a look at that Tibetan bell,' said Mr Ghoshal.

'Oh, that's not a problem at all. I'll get it for you.' Rajen Babu disappeared into the house to fetch the bell.

'Do you live here in Darjeeling?' Feluda asked Mr Ghoshal, who had picked up a dagger and was looking at it closely. 'No,' he replied, turning the dagger in his hand. 'I don't stay in any one place for very long. I have to travel a lot. But I like collecting curios.' Feluda told me afterwards that a curio was a rare and ancient object of art.

Rajen Babu returned with the bell. It was really striking to look at. Its base was made of silver, the handle was a mixture of brass and copper, which was studded with colourful stones. Mr Ghoshal took a long time to examine it carefully. Then he put it down on a table and said, 'You got yourself a very good deal there. It's absolutely genuine.'

'Ah, that's a relief. You're the expert, of course. The man at the shop told me it came straight out of the household of the Dalai Lama.'

9

'That may well be true. But I don't suppose you'd want to part with it? I mean . . . suppose you got a handsome offer?'

Rajen Babu shook his head, smiling sweetly.

'No. You see, I bought that bell simply because I liked it. I have no wish to sell it only to make money.'

'Very well,' Mr Ghoshal rose. 'I hope you'll be out and about tomorrow.'

'Thank you. I hope so, too.'

When Mr Ghoshal had gone, Feluda said to Rajen Babu, 'Don't you think it might be wise not to go out of the house for the next few days?'

'Yes, you're probably right. But this business of an anonymous letter is so incredible that I cannot really bring myself to take it seriously. It just seems like a foolish practical joke!'

'Well, why don't you stay in until we can be definite about that? How long have you had that Nepali servant?'

'Right from the start. He is completely reliable.'

Feluda now turned to Tinkori Babu. 'Do you stay at home most of the time?'

'Yes, but I go for morning and evening walks, so I'm out of the house for a couple of hours every day. In any case, should there be any real danger, I doubt if I could do anything to help. I am sixty-four, younger than Rajen Babu by only a year.'

'Don't involve poor Tinkori Babu in this, please,' Rajen Babu said. 'After all, he's come here to relax, so let him enjoy himself. I'll stay in if you insist, together with my servant. You two can come and visit me every day, if you so wish.'

'All right.'

Feluda stood up. So did I. It was time to go.

There was a fireplace in front of us. Over it, on a mantelshelf, were three framed photographs. Feluda moved closer to the fireplace to look at these. 'My wife,' said Rajen Babu, pointing at the first photograph. 'She died barely five years after our marriage.'

The second photo was of a young boy, who must have been about my own age when the photo was taken. A handsome boy indeed. 'Who is this?' Feluda asked.

Rajen Babu began laughing. 'That photo is there simply to show how time can change everything. Would you believe that that is my own photograph, taken when I was a child? I used to go to a missionary school in Bankura in those days. My father was the magistrate there. But don't let those angelic looks deceive you. I might have been a good-looking child, but I was extremely naughty. My teachers were all fed up with me. In fact, I didn't spare the students, either. I remember having kicked the best runner in our school in a hundred-yards race to stop him from winning.'

The third photo was of a young man in his late-twenties. It turned out to be Rajen Babu's only child, Prabeer Majumdar.

'Where is he now?' Feluda asked.

Rajen Babu cleared his throat. 'I don't know,' he said after a pause. 'He left home sixteen years ago. There is virtually no contact between us.'

Feluda started walking towards the front door. 'A very interesting case,' he muttered. Now he was talking like the detectives one read about.

We came out of the house. It was already dark outside. Lights had been switched on in every house nestling in the hills. A mist was rising from the Rangeet valley down below. Rajen Babu and Tinkori Babu both walked up to the gate to see us off. Rajen Babu lowered his voice and said to Feluda, 'Actually, I have to confess that despite everything, I do feel faintly nervous. After all, something like this in this peaceful atmosphere was so totally unexpected . . . .'

'Don't worry,' said Feluda firmly. 'I'll definitely get to the bottom of this case.'

'Thank you. Goodbye!' said Rajen Babu and went back into the house. Tinkori Babu lingered. 'I am truly impressed by your power of observation,' he said. 'I, too, have read a large number of detective novels. Maybe I can help you with this case.'

'Really? How?'

'Look at the letter in your hand. Take the various printed words. Do they tell you anything?'

Feluda thought for a few seconds. 'The words were cut out with a blade, not scissors,' he said.

'Very good.'

'Second, each word has come from a different source—the typeface and the quality of paper vary from each other.'

'Yes. Can you guess what those different sources might be?'

'These two words—'prepared' and 'pay'—appear to be a newspaper.'

'Right. *Ananda Bazar.*'

'How can you tell?'

'Only *Ananda Bazar* uses that typeface. And the other words were taken out of books, I think. Not very old books, mind you, for those different typefaces have been in use over the last twenty years, and no more. Apart from this, does the smell of the glue tell you anything?'

'I think the sender used Grippex glue.'

'Brilliant!'

'I might say the same for you.'

Tinkori Babu smiled. 'I try, but at your age, my dear fellow, I doubt if I knew what the word "detective" meant.'

We said namaskar after this and went on our way. 'I don't yet know whether I can solve this mystery,' said Feluda on the way back to our hotel, 'but getting to know Tinkori Babu would be an added bonus.'

'If he is so good at crime detection, why don't you let *him* do all the hard work? Why waste your own time making enquiries?'

'Ah well, Tinkori Babu might know a lot about printing and typefaces, but that doesn't necessarily mean he'd know everything!'

Feluda's answer pleased me. I bet Tinkori Babu isn't as clever as Feluda, I thought. Aloud, I said, 'Who do you suppose is the culprit?'

'The culp—'Feluda broke off. I saw him turn around and glance at a man who had come from the opposite direction and had just passed us.

'Did you see him?'

'No, I didn't see his face.'

'The light from that streetlamp fell on his face for only a second, and I thought—'

'What?'

'No, never mind. Let's go, I feel quite hungry.'

*

Feluda is my cousin. He and I were in Darjeeling with my father for a holiday. Father had got to know some of the other guests in our hotel fairly well, and was spending most of his time with them. He didn't stop us from going wherever we wished, nor did he ask too many questions.

I woke a little later than usual the next day. Father was in the room, but there was no sign of Feluda.

'Felu left early this morning,' Father explained. 'He said he'd try to catch a glimpse of Kanchenjunga.'

I knew this couldn't be true. Feluda must have gone out to investigate, which was most annoying because he wasn't supposed to go out without me. Anyway, I had a quick cup of tea, and then I went out myself.

I spotted Feluda near a taxi stand. 'This is not fair!' I complained. 'Why did you go out alone?'

'I was feeling a bit feverish, so I went to see a doctor.'

'Dr Phoni Mitra?'

'Aha, you're beginning to use your brain, too!'

'What did he say?'

'He charged me four rupees and wrote out a prescription.'

'Is he a good doctor?'

'Do you think a good doctor would write a prescription

for someone in perfect health? Besides, his house looked old and decrepit. I don't think he has a good practice.'

'Then he couldn't have sent that letter.'

'Why not?'

'A poor man wouldn't dare.'

'Yes, he would, if he was desperate for money.'

'But that letter said nothing about money.'

'There was no need to ask openly.'

'What do you mean?'

'How did Rajen Babu strike you yesterday?'

'He seemed a little frightened.'

'Fear can make anyone ill.'

'Oh?'

'Yes, seriously ill. And if that happened, he'd naturally turn to his doctor. What might happen then is something even a fathead like you can figure out, I'm sure.'

How clever Feluda was! But if Dr Mitra had really planned the whole thing the way Feluda described, he must be extraordinarily crafty, too.

By this time, we had reached the Mall. As we came near the fountain, Feluda suddenly said, 'I feel a bit curious about curios.' We were, in fact, standing quite close to the Nepal Curio Shop. Rajen Babu and Mr Ghoshal visited this shop every day. Feluda and I walked into the shop. Its owner came forward to greet us. He had a light grey jacket on, a muffler round his neck, and wore a black cap with golden embroidery. He beamed at us genially.

The shop was cluttered with old and ancient objects. A strange musty smell came from them. It was quiet inside. Feluda looked around for a while, then said, sounding important, 'Do you have good tankhas?'

'Come into the next room, sir. We've sold what was really good. But we're expecting some fresh stock soon.'

'What is a tankha?' I whispered.

'You'll know when you see one,' Feluda whispered back.

The next room was even smaller and darker. The owner

of the shop brought out a painting of the Buddha, done on a piece of silk. 'This is the last piece left, but it's a little damaged,' he said. So this was a tankha! Rajen Babu had heaps of these in his house. Feluda examined the tankha like an expert, peering at it closely, and then looking at it from various angles. Three minutes later, he said, 'This doesn't appear to be more than seventy years old. I am looking for something much older than that, at least three hundred years, you see.'

'We're getting some new things this evening, sir. You might find what you're looking for if you came back later today.'

'This evening, did you say?'

'Yes, sir.'

'Oh, I must inform Rajen Babu.'

'Mr Majumdar? He knows about it already. All my regular customers are coming in the evening to look at the fresh arrivals.'

'Does Mr Ghoshal know?'

'Of course.'

'Who else is a regular buyer?'

'There's Mr Gilmour, the manager of a tea estate. He visits my shop twice a week. Then there's Mr Naulakha. But he's away in Sikkim at present.'

'All right, I'll try to drop in in the evening . . . Topshe, would you like a mask?' I couldn't resist the offer. Feluda selected one himself and paid for it. 'This was the most horrendous of them all,' he remarked, passing it to me. He had once told me there was no such word as 'horrendous'. It was really a mixture of 'tremendous' and 'horrible'. But I must say it was rather an appropriate word for the mask.

Feluda started to say something as we came out of the shop, but stopped abruptly. I found him staring at a man once again. Was it the same man he had seen last night? He was a man in his early forties, expensively dressed in a well-cut suit. He had stopped in the middle of the Mall to light his pipe. His eyes were hidden behind dark glasses. Somehow he looked vaguely familiar, but I couldn't recall ever having met him before.

Feluda stepped forward and approached him. 'Excuse me,' he said, 'are you Mr Chatterjee?'

'No,' replied the man, biting the end of his pipe, 'I am not.'

Feluda appeared to be completely taken aback. 'Strange! Aren't you staying at the Central Hotel?'

The man smiled a little contemptuously. 'No, I am at the Mount Everest; and I don't have a twin,' he said and strode off in the direction of Observatory Hill.

I noticed he was carrying a brown parcel, on which were printed the words 'Nepal Curio Shop'.

'Feluda!' I said softly. 'Do you think he bought a mask like mine?'

'Yes, he may well have done that. After all, those masks weren't all meant for your own exclusive use, were they? Anyway, let's go and have a cup of coffee.' We turned towards a coffee shop. 'Did you recognize that man?' asked Feluda.

'How could I,' I replied, 'when you yourself failed to recognize him?'

'Who said I had failed?'

'Of course you did! You got his name wrong, didn't you?'

'Why are you so stupid? I did that deliberately, just to get him to tell me where he was staying. Do you know what his real name is?'

'No. What is it?'

'Prabeer Majumdar.'

'Yes, yes, you're right! Rajen Babu's son, isn't he? We saw his photograph yesterday. No wonder he seemed familiar. But of course now he's a lot older.'

'Even so, there are a lot of similarities between father and son. But did you notice his clothes? His suit must have been from London, his tie from Paris and shoes from Italy. In short, there's no doubt that he's recently returned from abroad.'

'But does that mean Rajen Babu doesn't know his own son is in town?'

'Perhaps his son doesn't even know that his father lives here. We should try to find out more.'

The plot thickens, I told myself, going up on the open terrace of the coffee shop. I loved sitting here. One could get such a superb view of the town and the market from here.

Tinkori Babu was sitting at a corner table, drinking coffee. He waved at us, inviting us to join him.

'As a reward for your powerful observation and expertise in detection, I would like to treat you to two cups of hot chocolate. You wouldn't mind, I hope?' he said with a twinkle in his eye. My mouth began to water at the prospect of a cup of hot chocolate. Tinkori Babu called a waiter and placed his order. Then he took out a book from his jacket pocket and offered it to Feluda. 'This is for you. I had just one copy left. It's my latest book.'

Feluda stared at the cover. 'Your book? You mean . . . *you* write under the pseudonym Secret Agent?' Tinkori Babu's eyes drooped. He smiled slightly and nodded. Feluda grew more excited. 'But you're my favourite writer! I've read all your books. No other writer can write mystery stories the way you do.'

'Thank you, thank you. To tell you the truth, I had come to Darjeeling to chalk out a plot for my next novel. But I've now spent most of my time trying to sort out a real life mystery.'

'I do consider myself very fortunate. I had no idea I'd get to meet you like this!'

'The only sad thing is that I have to go back to Calcutta. I'm returning tomorrow. But I think I may be of some help to you before I leave.'

'I'm very pleased to hear that. By the way, we saw Rajen Babu's son today.'

'What!'

'Only ten minutes ago.'

'Are you sure? Did you see him properly?'

'Yes, I am almost a hundred per cent sure. All we need to

do is check with the Mount Everest Hotel, and then there won't be any doubt left.'

Suddenly, Tinkori Babu sighed. 'Did Rajen Babu talk to you about his son?' he asked.

'No, not much.'

'I have heard quite a lot. Apparently, his son had fallen into bad company. He was caught stealing money from his father's cupboard. Rajen Babu told him to get out of his house. Prabeer did leave his home after that and disappeared without a trace. He was twenty-four at the time. A few years later, Rajen Babu began to regret what he'd done and tried to track his son down. But there was no sign of Prabeer anywhere. About ten years ago, a friend of Rajen Babu came and told him he'd spotted Prabeer somewhere in England. But that was all.'

'That means Rajen Babu doesn't know his son is here in Darjeeling.'

'I'm sure he doesn't. And I don't think he should be told. After all, he's already had one shock. Another one might . . .' Tinkori Babu stopped. Then he looked straight at Feluda and shook his head. 'I think I am going mad. Really, I should give up writing mystery stories.'

Feluda laughed. 'You mean it's only just occurred to you that the letter might have been sent by Prabeer Majumdar himself?'

'Exactly. But . . . I don't know . . .' Tinkori Babu broke off absent-mindedly.

The waiter came back and placed our hot chocolate before us. This seemed to cheer him up. 'How did you find Dr Phoni Mitra?' he asked.

'Good Heavens, how do you know I went there?'

'I paid him a visit shortly after you left.'

'Did you see me coming out of his house?'

'No. I found a cigarette stub on his floor. I knew he didn't smoke, so I asked him if he'd already had a patient. He said yes, and from his description I could guess that it was you. However, I didn't know then that you smoked. Now, looking at your slightly yellowish fingertips, I can be totally sure.'

'You really are a most clever man. But tell me, did you suspect Dr Mitra as well?'

'Yes. He doesn't exactly inspire confidence, does he?'

'You're right. I'm surprised Rajen Babu consults him rather than anyone else.'

'There's a reason for it. Soon after he arrived in Darjeeling, Rajen Babu had suddenly turned religious. It was Dr Mitra who had found him a guru at that time. As followers of the same guru, they are now like brothers.'

'I see. But did Dr Mitra say anything useful? What did you talk about?'

'Oh, just this and that. I went there really to take a look at the books on his shelves. There weren't many. Those that I saw were all old.'

'Yes, I noticed it, too.'

'Mind you, he might well have got hold of different books from elsewhere, just to get the right printed words. But I'm pretty certain that is not the case. That man seemed far too lazy to go to such trouble.'

'Well, that takes care of Dr Mitra. What do you think of Mr Ghoshal?'

'I don't trust him either. He's a crook. He pretends to be interested in art and antiques, but I think what he really wants to do is sell to foreign buyers at a much higher price what he can buy relatively cheaply here.'

'But do you think he might have a motive in sending a threatening letter to Rajen Babu?'

'I haven't really thought about it.'

'I think I might have stumbled onto something.'

I looked at Feluda in surprise. His eyes were shining with excitement.

'What do you mean?'

'I learnt today,' Feluda said, lowering his voice, 'that the shop they both go to is going to get some fresh supplies this evening.'

19

Tinkori Babu perked up immediately. 'I see, I see!' he exclaimed. 'A letter like that would naturally frighten Rajen Babu into staying at home for a few days. In the meantime, Abani Ghoshal would go in and make a clean sweep.'

'Exactly.'

Tinkori Babu paid for the chocolate and rose. We went out together. My heart was beating fast. Abani Ghoshal, Prabeer Majumdar and Dr Phoni Mitra. As many as three suspects. Who was the real culprit?

Tinkori Babu went home. Feluda and I walked over to the Mount Everest Hotel. They confirmed that a man called Prabeer Majumdar had checked in five days ago.

*

We were supposed to visit Rajen Babu in the evening. But it began to rain so heavily at around 4 p.m. that we were forced to stay in. Feluda spent that whole evening scribbling in a notebook. I was dying to find out what he was writing, but didn't dare ask. In the end, I picked up the book Tinkori Babu had given Feluda and began reading it. It was so thrilling that in a matter of minutes, all thoughts of Rajen Babu went out of my mind.

The rain stopped at 8 p.m. But by then it was very cold outside. Father, for once, stood firm and refused to allow us to go out.

Feluda shook me awake the next morning. 'Get up, Topshe. Quick!'

'What—what is it?' I sat up.

Feluda whispered into my ear, speaking through clenched teeth. 'Rajen Babu's Nepali servant was here a few moments ago. He said Rajen Babu wants to see us, and it's urgent. Do you want to come with me?'

'Of course!'

We got ready and were in Rajen Babu's house in less than

twenty minutes. We found him lying in his bed, looking pale and haggard. Dr Mitra was by his side, feeling his pulse; and Tinkori Babu was standing before him, fanning him with a hand-held fan, despite the cold.

Dr Mitra released his hand as we came in. Rajen Babu spoke with some difficulty. 'Last night . . . after midnight . . . I woke suddenly and there it was . . . in this room . . . I saw a masked face!' Rajen Babu continued. 'I can't tell you . . . how I spent the night!'

'Has anything been stolen?'

'No. But I'm sure he bent over me . . . only to take the keys from under my pillow. Oh, it was horrible . . . horrible!'

'Take it easy,' said the doctor. 'I'm going to give you something to help you sleep. You need complete rest.' He stood up.

'Dr Mitra,' said Feluda suddenly, 'did you go to see a patient last night? Your jacket's got a streak of mud on it.'

'Oh yes,' Dr Mitra replied readily enough. 'I did have to go out last night. Since I *have* chosen to dedicate my life to my patients, I can hardly refuse to go out when I'm needed, come rain or shine.'

He collected his fee and left. Rajen Babu sat up in his bed. 'I feel a lot better now that you're here,' he admitted. 'I did feel considerably shaken, I must say. But now I think I might be able to go and sit in the living room.' Feluda and Tinkori Babu helped him to his feet. We made our way to the living room.

'I rang the railway station to change my ticket,' said Tinkori Babu. 'I don't want to leave today. But they said if I cancelled my ticket now, they couldn't give me a booking for another ten days. So I fear I've got to go.' This pleased me. I wanted Feluda to solve the mystery single-handedly.

'My servant was supposed to stay in yesterday,' Rajen Babu explained, 'but I myself told him to take some time off. His father is very ill, you see. He went home last night.'

'What did the mask look like?' Feluda asked.

'It was a perfectly ordinary mask, the kind you can get

anywhere in Darjeeling. There are at least five of those in this room. There's one, look!' The mask he pointed out was almost an exact replica of the one Feluda had bought me yesterday.

Tinkori Babu spoke again. 'I think we ought to inform the police. We can no longer call this a joke. Rajen Babu may need protection. Felu Babu, you can continue with your investigation, nobody will object to that. But having thought things over, I do feel the police should know what's happened. I'll go myself to the police station right away. I don't think your life's in any danger, Rajen Babu, but please keep an eye on that Tibetan bell.'

We decided to take our leave. But before we left, Feluda said, 'Since Tinkori Babu is leaving today, you're going to be left with a vacant room, aren't you? Would you mind if we came and spent the night in it?'

'No, no, why should I mind? You're like a son to me. I'd be delighted. To tell you the truth, I'm beginning to lose my nerve. Those who are reckless in their youth generally tend to grow rather feeble in their old age. At least, that's what has happened to me.'

'I'll come and see you off at the station,' Feluda said to Tinkori Babu.

We passed the curio shop on our way back. Neither of us could help look inside. We saw two men looking around and talking. From the easy familiarity with which they were talking, it seemed as if they had known each other for a long time. One of them was Abani Ghoshal. The other was Prabeer Majumdar. I glanced at Feluda. He didn't seem surprised at all.

We went to the station at half-past ten to say goodbye to Tinkori Babu. He arrived in five minutes. 'My feet ache from having walked uphill,' he said. I noticed he was walking with a slight limp. 'Besides,' he added, 'it took me a while to buy this. I know Rajen Babu couldn't go to the curio shop but they really did get a lot of good stuff yesterday. So I chose something for him this morning. Will you please give it to him with my good wishes?'

'Certainly,' said Feluda, taking a brown packet from Tinkori Babu. 'There's one thing I meant to ask you. If I solve this mystery, I'd like to tell you about it. Will you give me your address, please?'

'You'll find the address of my publisher in my book. He'll forward all letters addressed to me. Goodbye . . . good luck!'

He climbed into a blue first-class carriage. The train left.

'That man would have made a lot of money and quite a name for himself if he had lived abroad. He has a real talent for writing crime stories,' Feluda remarked.

*

We returned to our hotel from the station. But Feluda went out again and, this time, refused to take me with him. When he finally came back, it was time to go to Rajen Babu's house to stay the night. As we set off, I said to him, 'You might at least tell me where you were during the day.'

'I went to various places. Twice to the Mount Everest Hotel, once to Dr Mitra's house, then to the curio shop, the library and one or two other places.'

'I see.'

'Is there anything else you'd like to know?'

'Have you been able to figure out who is the real cul—?'

'The time hasn't come to disclose that. No, not yet.'

'But who do you suspect the most?'

'I suspect everybody, including you.'

'*Me?*'

'Yes. Anyone who has a mask is a suspect.'

'Really? In that case, why don't you include yourself in your list?'

'Don't talk rubbish.'

'I'm not! You didn't tell me that you knew Rajen Babu, which means you were not totally honest with me. Besides, you could have easily used that mask. I did not hide it anywhere, did I?'

'Shut up, shut up!'

Rajen Babu seemed a lot better when we arrived at his house, although he still looked faintly uneasy. 'I felt fine during the day,' he told us, 'but I must say I'm beginning to feel nervous again now it's getting dark.'

Feluda gave him the packet from Tinkori Babu. Rajen Babu opened it quickly and took out a beautiful statue of the Buddha, the sight of which actually moved him to tears.

'Did the police come to make enquiries?' asked Feluda.

'Oh yes. They asked a thousand questions. God knows if they'll get anywhere, but at least they've agreed to post someone outside the house during the night. That's a relief, anyway. In fact, if you wish to go back to your hotel, it will be quite all right.'

'No, we'd rather stay here, if you don't mind. It's too noisy in our hotel. I need peace and quiet to think about this case.'

Rajen Babu smiled. 'Of course you can stay. You'll get your peace and quiet here, and I can promise you an excellent meal. That Nepali boy is a very good cook. I've asked him to make his special chicken curry. The food in your hotel could never be half as tasty, I'm sure.'

We were shown to our room. Feluda stretched out on his bed and lit a cigarette. I saw him blow out five smoke rings in a row. His eyes were half-closed. After a few seconds of silence, he said, 'Dr Mitra did go out to see a patient last night. I found that out this morning. A rich businessman who lives in Card Road. He was with his patient from eleven-thirty to half-past twelve.'

'Does that rule him out completely?'

Feluda did not answer my question. Instead, he said, 'Prabeer Majumdar has lived abroad for so long and has such a lot of money that I can't see why he should suddenly arrive here and start threatening his father. He stands to gain very little, actually. Why, I learnt that he recently made a packet at the local races!'

I sat holding my breath. It was obvious that Feluda hadn't finished. I was right. Feluda stubbed out his cigarette and continued, 'Mr Gilmour has come to Darjeeling from his tea estate. I met him at the Planters' Club. He told me there was only one Tibetan bell that had come out of the palace of the Dalai Lama, and it is with him. The one Rajen Babu has is a fake. Abani Ghoshal is aware of it.'

'You mean the bell that we saw here isn't all that valuable?'

'No. Besides, both Abani Ghoshal and Prabeer Majumdar were at a party last night, from 9 p.m. to 3 a.m. They got totally drunk, I believe.'

'That man wearing a mask came here soon after midnight, didn't he?'

'Yes.'

I began to feel rather strange. 'Well then, who does that leave us with?'

Feluda did not reply. He sighed and rose to his feet. 'I'm going to sit in the living room for a minute,' he said. 'Do not disturb me.'

I took his place on the bed when he left. It was getting dark, but I felt too lazy to get up and switch on the lights. Through the open window I could see lights in the distance, on Observatory Hill. The noise from the Mall had died down. I heard the sound of hooves after a while. They got louder and louder, then slowly faded away.

It soon grew almost totally dark. The hill and the houses on it were now practically invisible. Perhaps a mist was rising again. I began to feel sleepy. Just as my eyes started to close, I suddenly sensed the presence of someone else in the room. My blood froze. Too terrified to look in the direction of the door, I kept my eyes fixed on the window. But I could feel the man move closer to the bed. There, he was now standing right next to me, and was leaning over my face. Transfixed, I watched his face come closer . . . oh, how horrible it was . . . a mask! He was wearing a mask!

I opened my mouth to scream, but an unseen hand pulled the mask away, and my scream became a nervous gasp. 'Feluda! Oh my God, it's you!'

'Had you dozed off? Of course it's me. Who did you think . . .?' Feluda started to laugh, but suddenly grew grave. Then he sat down next to me, and said, 'I was simply trying on all those masks in the living room. Why don't you wear this one for a second?' He passed me his mask. I put it on.

'Can you sense something unusual?'

'Why, no! It's a size too large for me, that's all.'

'Think carefully. Isn't there anything else that might strike you as odd?'

'Well . . . there's a faint smell, I think.'

'Of what?'

'Cheroot?'

'Exactly.'

Feluda took the mask off. My heart started to beat faster again.

'T-t-t-inkori Babu?' I stammered.

Feluda sighed. 'Yes, I'm afraid so. It must have been extremely easy for him. He had access to all kinds of printed material; and you must have noticed he was limping this morning. That might have been the result of jumping out of a window last night. But what I totally fail to understand is his motive. He appeared to respect Rajen Babu a lot. Why then did he do something like this? What for? Perhaps we shall never know.'

*

The night passed peacefully and without any further excitement. In the morning, just as we sat down to have breakfast with our host, his Nepali servant came in with a letter for him. It was once again a blue envelope with a Darjeeling post-mark.

Rajen Babu went white. He took out the letter with a trembling hand and passed it to Feluda. 'You read it,' he said in a low voice.

Feluda read it aloud. This is what it said:

Dear Raju,

When I first wrote to you from Calcutta after Gyanesh told me you had a house in Darjeeling, I had no idea who you really were. But that photograph of yours on your mantelshelf told me instantly that you were none other than the boy who had once been my classmate in the missionary school in Bankura fifty years ago.

I did not know that the desire for revenge would raise its head even after so many years. You see, I was the boy you kicked at that hundred-yards race on our sports day. Not only did I miss out on winning a medal and setting a new record, but you also managed to injure me pretty seriously. Unfortunately, my father got transferred to a different town only a few days after this incident, which was why I never got the chance to have a showdown with you then; nor did you ever learn just how badly you had hurt me, both mentally and physically. I had to spend three months in a hospital with my leg in a cast.

When I saw you here in Darjeeling, leading such a comfortable and peaceful life, I suddenly thought of doing something that would cause you a great deal of anxiety and ruin your peace of mind, at least for a short time. This was my way of settling scores, and punishing you for your past sins.

With good wishes,

Yours sincerely,
Tinu
(Tinkori Mukhopadhyaya)

Trouble in Gangtok

Chapter 1

Even a little while ago it had been possible to stare out of the window and look at the yellow earth, criss-crossed with rivers that looked like silk ribbons and sweet little villages with tiny little houses in them. But now grey puffs of cloud had blocked out that scene totally. So I turned away from the window and began looking at my co-passengers in the plane.

Next to me sat Feluda, immersed in a book on space travel. He always read a lot, but I had never seen him read two books—one straight after the other—that were written on the same subject. Only yesterday, back at home, he had been reading something about the Takla Makan desert. Before that, he'd finished a book on international cuisine, and another of short stories. It was imperative, he'd always maintained, for a detective to gain as much general knowledge as possible. Who knew what might come in handy one day?

There were two men sitting diagonally opposite me. One of them was barely visible. All I could see was his right hand and a portion of his blue trousers. He was beating one of his fingers on his knee. Perhaps he was singing quietly. The other gentleman sitting closer to us had a bright and polished look about him. His greying hair suggested he might be in his mid-forties, but apart from that he seemed pretty well-preserved. He has reading *The Statesman* with great concentration. Feluda might have been able to guess a lot of things about the man, but I couldn't think of anything at all although I tried very hard.

'What are you gaping at?' Feluda asked under his breath, thereby startling me considerably. Then he cast a sidelong glance at the man and said, 'He's not as flabby as he might have been. After all, he does eat a lot, doesn't he?'

Yes, indeed. Now I remembered having seen him ask the air hostess for two cups of tea in the past hour, with which he'd eaten half-a-dozen biscuits.

'What else can you tell me about him?' I asked curiously.

'He's used to travelling by air.'

'How do you know that?'

'Our plane had slipped into an air pocket a few minutes ago, remember?'

'Oh yes. I felt so strange! My stomach began to churn.'

'Yes, and it wasn't just you. Many other people around us had grown restless, but that gentleman didn't even lift his eyes from his paper.'

'Anything else?'

'His hair at the back is tousled.'

'So?'

'He has not once leant back in his seat in the plane. He's sat up straight throughout, either reading or having tea. So obviously at Dum Dum—'

'Oh, I get it! He must have had some time to spare at Dum Dum airport, at least time enough to sit back against a sofa and relax for a while. That's how his hair got tousled.'

'Very good. Now you tell me which part of India he comes from.'

'That's very difficult, Feluda. He's wearing a suit and he's reading an English newspaper. He could be a Bengali, a Punjabi, a Gujarati or a Maharashtrian, anything!'

Feluda clicked his tongue disapprovingly. 'You'll never learn to observe properly, will you? What's he got on his right hand?'

'A news—no, no, I see what you mean. He's wearing a ring.'

'And what does the ring say?'

I had to screw up my eyes to peer closely. Then I saw that in the middle of the golden ring was inscribed a single word: Ma. The man had to be a Bengali.

I wanted to ask Feluda about other passengers, but at this moment there was an announcement to say that we were about to reach Bagdogra. 'Please fasten your seat-belts and observe the no-smoking sign.'

We were on our way to Gangtok, the capital of Sikkim. We might have gone to Darjeeling again, where we had been twice already to spend our summer holidays. But at the last minute Feluda suggested a visit to Gangtok, which sounded quite interesting. Baba had to go away to Bangalore on tour, so he couldn't come with us. 'You and Felu could go on your own,' Baba told me. 'I'm sure Felu could take a couple of weeks off. Don't waste your holiday in the sweltering heat of Calcutta.'

Feluda had suggested Gangtok possibly because he had recently read a lot about Tibet (I, too, had read a travelogue by Sven Hedin). Sikkim had a strong Tibetan influence. The King of Sikkim was a Tibetan, Tibetan monks were often seen in the gumphas in Sikkim, many Tibetan refugees lived in Sikkimese villages. Besides, many aspects of Tibetan culture—their music, dances, costumes and food—were all in evidence in Sikkim. I jumped at the chance to go to Gangtok. But then, I would have gone anywhere on earth, quite happily, if I could be with Feluda.

Our plane landed at Bagdogra at 7.30 a.m. Baba had arranged a jeep to meet us here. But before climbing into it, we went to the restaurant at the airport to have breakfast. It would take us at least six hours to reach Gangtok. If the roads were bad, it might take even longer. However, since it was only mid-April, hopefully heavy rains hadn't yet started. So the roads ought to be in good shape.

I had finished an omelette and just started on a fish-fry, when I saw the same gentleman from the plane rise from the next table and walk over to ours, grinning broadly. 'Are you Kang, or Dang, or Gang?' he asked, wiping his mouth with a handkerchief.

I stared, holding a piece of fish-fry a few inches from my mouth. What on earth did this man mean? What language was he speaking in? Or was it some sort of a code?

But Feluda smiled in return and replied immediately, 'We're Gang.'

'Oh good. Do you have a jeep? I mean, if you do, can I come with you? I'll pay my share, naturally.'

'You're welcome,' said Feluda, and it finally dawned on me that Kang meant Kalimpong, Dang was Darjeeling, and Gang was Gangtok. I found myself laughing, too.

'Thank you,' said the man. 'My name is Sasadhar Bose.'

'Pleased to meet you, Mr Bose. I am Pradosh Mitter and this is my cousin, Tapesh.'

'Hello, Tapesh. Are you both here on holiday?'

'Yes.'

'I love Gangtok. Have you been there before?'

'No.'

'Where will you be staying?'

'We're booked somewhere, I think the hotel is called Snow View,' Feluda replied, signalling at the waiter for our bill, and offering a Charminar to Mr Bose. Then he lit one himself.

'I know Gangtok very well,' Mr Bose told us. 'In fact, I've travelled all over Sikkim—Lachen, Lachung, Namche, Nathula, just name it! It's really beautiful. The scenery is just out of this world, and it's all so peaceful. There are mountains and rivers and flowers—you get orchids here, you know—and bright sunshine and rain and mist . . . nature in all her glory. The only thing that stops this place from being a complete paradise is its roads. You see, some of the mountains here are still growing. I mean, they are still relatively young, and therefore restless. You know what youngsters are like, don't you . . . ha ha ha!'

'You mean these mountains cause landslides?'

'Yes, and it can really be a nuisance. Halfway through your journey you may suddenly find the road completely blocked. That then means blasting your way through rocks, rebuilding the road, clearing up the mess . . . endless problems. But the army here is always on the alert and it's very efficient. Besides, it hasn't yet started to rain, so I don't think we'll have any problem today. Anyway, I'll be very glad of your company. I hate travelling alone.'

'Are you here on holiday as well?'

'Oh no,' Mr Bose laughed, 'I am here on business. But my job is rather a peculiar one. I have to look for aromatic plants.'

'Do you run a perfumery?'

'Yes, that's right. Mine's a chemical firm. Among other things, we extract essences from plants. Some of the plants we need grow in Sikkim. I've come to collect them. My business partner is already here. He arrived a week ago. He's got a degree in Botany and knows about plants. I was supposed to travel with him, but a nephew's wedding came up. So I had to go to Ghatshila to attend it. I returned to Calcutta only last night.'

Feluda paid the bill. We picked up our luggage and began walking towards our jeep with Mr Bose.

'Where are you based?' Feluda asked.

'Bombay. This company is now twenty years old. I joined it seven years ago. S. S. Chemicals. Shivkumar Shelvankar. The company is in his name.'

We set off in a few minutes. From Bagdogra we had to go to Siliguri, to find Sewak Road. This road wound its way through the hills, going up and down. It would finally take us to a place called Rongpo, where West Bengal ended, and the border of Sikkim began.

On our way to Rongpo, we had to cross a huge bridge over the river Tista. On the other side was a market called Tista Bazaar. We stopped here for a rest. By this time the sun had come up, and we were all feeling a little hot.

'Would you like a Coca-Cola?' asked Mr Bose. Feluda and I both said yes, and got out of the jeep. Two years ago, said Mr Bose, this whole area had been wiped out in a devastating flood. All the buildings and other structures, including the bridge, were new.

By the time I finished my own bottle of Coca-Cola, Mr Bose had emptied two. When we went to return the bottles, we noticed a jeep parked near the stall selling cold drinks. A few men were standing near it, talking excitedly. The jeep had come from the other side, and was probably going to Siliguri. Suddenly, all of us caught the word 'accident', and went across to ask them what had happened. What they told us was this: it had rained heavily in Gangtok a week ago. Although there had been no major landslide, somehow a heavy boulder had rolled off a mountain and fallen on a passing jeep, killing its passenger. The jeep had fallen into a ravine, five hundred feet below. It was totally destroyed. None of these men knew who the dead man was.

'Fate,' said Feluda. 'What else can you call this? The man was destined to die, or else why should just a single boulder slip off a mountain and land on his jeep? Such accidents are extremely rare.'

'One chance in a million,' said Mr Bose. As we got back into the jeep, he added, 'Keep an eye on the mountains, sir. One can't be too careful.' However, the scenery became so incredibly beautiful soon after we crossed Tista that I forgot all about the accident. There was a brief shower as we were passing through Rongpo. As we climbed up to three thousand feet, a mist rose from the valley just below, making us shiver in the cold. We stopped shortly to pull out our woollens from our suitcase. I saw Mr Bose dig out a blue pullover from an Air India bag and slip it on.

Slowly, through the mist, I began to notice vague outlines of houses among the hills. Most houses appeared to be Chinese in style. 'Here we are,' said Mr Bose. 'It took us less than five hours. We're very lucky.'

The city of Gangtok lay before us. Our jeep made its way carefully through its streets, past a military camp, sweet little houses with wooden balconies and flower-pots, groups of men and women in colourful clothes, and finally drew up before Snow View Hotel. The people in the streets, I knew, were not from Sikkim alone. Many of them were from Nepal, Bhutan or Tibet.

Mr Bose said he was staying at the Dak Bungalow. 'I'll make my own way there, don't worry,' he said. 'Thank you so much. No doubt we shall meet again. In a small place like this, it is virtually impossible to avoid bumping into one another every day.'

'Well, since we don't know anyone in Gangtok except you, I don't think we'd find that a problem. If you don't mind, I'll visit your Dak Bungalow this evening,' said Feluda.

'Very well. I'll look forward to it. Goodbye.'

With a wave of his hand, Mr Bose disappeared into the mist.

Chapter 2

Although our hotel was called Snow View and the rooms at the rear were supposed to afford a view of Kanchenjunga, we didn't manage to see any snow the day we arrived, for the mist didn't clear at all. There appeared to be only one other Bengali gentleman among the other guests in the hotel. I saw him in the dining hall at lunch time, but didn't get to meet him until later.

We went out after lunch and found a paan shop. Feluda always had a paan after lunch, though he admitted he hadn't expected to find a shop here in Gangtok. The main street outside our hotel was quite large. A number of buses, lorries and station wagons stood in the middle of the road. On both sides were shops of various kinds. It was obvious that business people from almost every corner of India had come to Sikkim. In many ways it was like Darjeeling, except that the number of people out on the streets was less, which helped keep the place both quiet and clean.

Stepping out of the paan shop, we were wondering where to go next, when the figure of Mr Bose suddenly emerged from the mist. He appeared to be walking hurriedly in the direction of our hotel. Feluda waved at him as he came closer. He quickened his pace and joined us in a few seconds.

'Disaster!' he exclaimed, panting.

'What happened?'

'That accident . . . do you know who it was?'

I felt myself go rigid with apprehension. The next words Mr Bose spoke confirmed my fears. 'It was SS,' he said, 'my partner.'

'What! Where was he going?'

'Who knows? What a terrible disaster, Mr Mitter!'

'Did he die instantly?'

'No. He was alive for a few hours after being taken to a hospital. There were multiple fractures. Apparently, he asked for me. He said, "Bose, Bose" a couple of times. But that was all.'

'How did you find out?' Feluda asked, walking back to the hotel. We went into the dining hall. Mr Bose sat down quickly, wiping his face with a handkerchief. 'It's a long story, actually,' he replied. 'You see, the driver survived. What happened was that when the boulder hit the jeep, the driver lost control. I believe the boulder itself wasn't such a large one, but because the driver didn't know where he was going, the jeep tilted to one side, went over the edge and fell into a gorge. The driver, however, managed to jump out in the nick of time. All he got was a minor cut over one eye. But by the time he could scramble to his feet, the jeep had disappeared with Shelvankar in it. This happened on the North Sikkim Highway. The driver began walking back to Gangtok. On his way he found a group of Nepali labourers who helped him to go back to the spot and rescue Shelvankar. Luckily, an army truck happened to be passing by, so they could take him to a hospital almost immediately. But . . . well . . .'

There was no sign of the jovial and talkative man who had accompanied us from Bagdogra. Mr Bose seemed shaken and deeply upset.

'What happened to his body?' Feluda asked gently.

'It was sent to Bombay. The authorities here got through to his brother there. SS had married twice, but both his wives are dead. There was a son from his first marriage, who fought

39

with him and left home fourteen years ago. Oh, that's another story. SS loved his son; he tried very hard to contact him, but he'd vanished without a trace. So his brother was his next of kin. He didn't allow a post mortem. The body was sent to Bombay the next day.'

'When did this happen?'

'On the morning of the eleventh. He'd arrived in Gangtok on the seventh. Honestly, Mr Mitter, I can hardly believe any of this. If only I was with him . . . we might have avoided such a tragedy.'

'What are your plans now?'

'Well, there's no point in staying here any longer. I've spoken to a travel agent. I should be able to fly back to Bombay tomorrow.' He rose. 'Don't worry about this, please,' he added. 'You are here to have a good time, so I hope you do. I'll see you before I go.'

Mr Bose left. Feluda sat quietly, staring into space and frowning. Then he repeated softly the words Mr Bose had uttered this morning: 'One chance in a million . . . but then, a man can get struck by lightning. That's no less amazing.'

The Bengali gentleman I had noticed earlier had been sitting at an adjacent table, reading a newspaper. He folded it neatly the minute Mr Bose left, and came over to join us. 'Namaskar,' he said to Feluda, taking the chair next to him. 'Anything can happen in the streets of Sikkim. You arrived only this morning, didn't you?'

'Hm,' said Feluda. I looked carefully at the man. He seemed to be in his mid-thirties. His eyes were partially hidden behind tinted glasses. Just below his nose was a small, square moustache, the kind that was once known as a butterfly moustache. Not many people wore it nowadays.

'Mr Shelvankar was a most amiable man.'

'Did you know him?' Feluda asked.

'Not intimately, no. But from what little I saw of him, he seemed very friendly. He was interested in art. He bought a Tibetan statue from me only two days before he died.'

'Was he a collector of such things?'

'I don't know. I found him in the Art Emporium one day, looking at various objects. So I told him I had this statue. He asked me to bring it to the Dak Bungalow. When I showed it to him there, he bought it on the spot. But then, it was a piece worth having. It had nine heads and thirty-four arms. My grandfather had brought it from Tibet.'

'I see.' Feluda sounded a little stiff and formal. But I found this man quite interesting, especially the smile that always seemed to hover on his lips. Even the death of Mr Shelvankar appeared to have given him cause for amusement.

'My name is Nishikanto Sarkar,' he said.

Feluda raised his hands in a namaskar but did not introduce himself.

'I live in Darjeeling,' Mr Sarkar continued. 'We've lived there for three generations. But you'd find that difficult to believe, wouldn't you? I mean, just look at me, I am so dark!'

Feluda smiled politely without saying anything. Mr Sarkar refused to be daunted. 'I know Darjeeling and Kalimpong pretty thoroughly. But this is my first visit to Sikkim. There are quite a few interesting places near Gangtok, I believe. Have you already seen them?'

'No. We're totally new to Sikkim, like yourself.'

'Good,' Mr Sarkar grinned. 'You're going to be here for some time, aren't you? We could go around together. Let's visit Pemiangchi one day. I've heard it's a beautiful area.'

'Pemiangchi? You mean where there are ruins of the old capital of Sikkim?'

'Not just ruins, dear sir. According to my guide book, there's a forest, old dak bungalows built during British times, gumphas, a first class view of Kanchenjunga—what more do you want?'

'We'd certainly like to go, if we get the chance,' said Feluda and stood up.

'Are you going out?'

'Yes, just for a walk. Is it necessary to lock up each time

41

we go out?'

'Well, yes, that's always advisable in a hotel. But cases of theft are very rare in these parts. There is only one prison in Sikkim, and that's here in Gangtok. The total number of criminals held in there would be less than half-a-dozen!'

*

We came out of the hotel once more, only to find that the mist hadn't yet cleared. Feluda glanced idly at the shops and said, 'We should have remembered to buy sturdy boots for ourselves. These shoes would be no good if it rained and the roads became all slushy and slippery.'

'Couldn't we buy us some boots here?'

'Yes, we probably could. I'm sure Bata has a branch in Gangtok. We could look for it in the evening. Right now I think we should explore this place.'

The road that led from the market to the main town went uphill. The number of people and houses grew considerably less as we walked up this road. Most of the passers-by were schoolchildren in uniform. Unlike Darjeeling, no one was on horseback. Jeeps ran frequently, possibly because of the army camp. Sixteen miles from Gangtok, at a height of 14,000 feet, was Nathula. It was here that the Indian border ended. On the other side of Nathula, within fifty yards, stood the Chinese army.

A few minutes later, we came to a crossing, and were taken aback by a sudden flash of colour. A closer look revealed a man—possibly a European—standing in the mist, clad from head to foot in very colourful clothes: yellow shoes, blue jeans, a bright red sweater, through which peeped green shirt cuffs. A black and white scarf was wound around his neck. His white skin had started to acquire a tan. He had a beard which covered most of his face, but he appeared to be about the same age as Feluda—just under thirty. Who was he? Could he be a hippie?

He gave us a friendly glance and said, 'Hello.'

'Hello,' Feluda replied.

Now I noticed that a leather bag was hanging from his shoulder, together with two cameras, one of which was a Canon. Feluda, too, had a Japanese camera with him. Perhaps the hippie saw it, for he said, 'Nice day for colour.'

Feluda laughed. 'When I saw you from a distance, that's exactly what I thought. But you see, colour film in India is so expensive that one has to think twice before using it freely.'

'Yes, I know. But I have some in my own stock. Let me know if you need any.' I tried to work out which country he might be from. He didn't sound American; nor did he have a British or French accent.

'Are you here on holiday?' Feluda asked him.

'No, not really. I'm here to take photographs. I'm working on a book on Sikkim. I am a professional photographer.'

'How long are you going to be here for?'

'I came five days ago, on the ninth. My original visa was only for three days. I managed to have it extended. I'd like to stay for another week.'

'Where are you staying?'

'Dak Bungalow. See this road on the right? The Dak Bungalow is on this road, only a few minutes from here.'

I pricked up my ears. Mr Shelvankar had also stayed at the same place.

'You must have met the gentleman who died in that accident recently—' Feluda began.

'Yes, that was most unfortunate,' the hippie shook his head sadly. 'I got to know him quite well. He was a fine man, and—' he broke off. Then he said, more or less to himself, 'Very strange!' He looked faintly worried.

'What's wrong?' Feluda enquired.

'Mr Shelvankar acquired a Tibetan statue from a Bengali gentleman here. He paid a thousand rupees for it.'

'One thousand!'

'Yes. He took it to the local Tibetan Institute the next day.

43

They said it was a rare and precious piece of art. But—' the man stopped again and remained silent for a few moments. Finally, he sighed and said, 'What is puzzling me is its disappearance. Where did it go?'

'What do you mean? Surely his belongings were all sent back to Bombay?'

'Yes, everything else he possessed was sent to Bombay. But not that statue. He used to keep it in the front pocket of his jacket. "This is my mascot," he used to say, "it will bring me luck!" He took it with him that morning. I know this for a fact. When they brought him to the hospital, I was there. They took out everything from his pockets. There was a notebook, a wallet and his broken glasses in a case. But there was no sign of the statue. Of course, it *could* be that it slipped out of his pocket as he fell and is probably still lying where he was found. Or maybe one of those men who helped lift him out saw it and removed it from the spot.'

'But I've been told people here are very honest.'

'That is true. And that is why I have my doubts—' the man seemed lost in thought.

'Do you know where Mr Shelvankar was going that day?'

'Yes. On the way to Singik there's a gumpha. That is where he was going. In fact, I was supposed to go with him. But I changed my mind and left a lot earlier, because it was a beautiful day and I wanted to take some photographs here. He told me he'd pick me up on the way if he saw me.'

'Why was he so interested in this gumpha?'

'I'm not sure. Perhaps Dr Vaidya was partly responsible for it.'

'Dr Vaidya?'

This was the first time anyone had mentioned Dr Vaidya. Who was he?

The hippie laughed. 'It's a bit awkward, isn't it, to chat in the middle of the road? Why don't you come and have coffee with me in the Dak Bungalow?'

Feluda agreed readily. He was obviously keen to get as

44

much information as possible about Shelvankar.

We began walking up the road on our right. 'Besides,' added the hippie, 'I need to rest my foot. I slipped in the hills the other day and sprained my ankle slightly. It starts aching if I stand anywhere for more than five minutes.'

The mist had started to clear. Now it was easy to see how green the surroundings were. I could see rows of tall pine trees through the thinning mist. The Dak Bungalow wasn't far. It was rather an attractive building, not very old. Our new friend took us to his room, and quickly removed piles of papers and journals from two chairs for us to sit. 'Sorry, I haven't yet introduced myself,' he said. 'My name is Helmut Ungar.'

'Is that a German name?' Feluda asked.

'Yes, that's right,' Helmut replied and sat down on his bed. Clearly, he didn't believe in keeping a tidy room. His clothes (all of them as colourful as the ones he was wearing) were strewn about, his suitcases were open, displaying more books and magazines than clothes, and spread on a table were loads of photographs, most of which seemed to have been taken abroad. Although my own knowledge of photography was extremely limited, I could tell those photos were really good.

'I am Pradosh Mitter and this is my cousin, Tapesh,' said Feluda, not revealing that he was an amateur detective.

'Pleased to meet you both. Excuse me,' Helmut went out of the room, possibly to order three coffees. Then he came back and said, 'Dr Vaidya is a very interesting person, though he talks rather a lot. He stayed here in this Dak Bungalow for a few days. He can read palms, make predictions about the future, and even contact the dead.'

'What! You mean he can act as a medium?'

'Yes, something like that. Mr Shelvankar was startled by some of the things he said.'

'Where is he now?'

'He left for Kalimpong. He was supposed to meet some Tibetan monks there. But he said he'd return to Gangtok.'

'What did he tell Mr Shelvankar? Do you happen to know anything about it?'

'Oh yes. They spoke to each other in my presence. Dr Vaidya told Mr Shelvankar about his business, the death of his wives, and about his son. He even said Mr Shelvankar had been under a lot of stress lately.'

'What could have caused it?'

'I don't know.'

'Didn't Shelvankar say anything to you?'

'No. But I could sense something was wrong. He used to grow preoccupied, and sometimes I heard him sigh. One day he received a telegram while we were having tea on the front veranda. I don't know what it said, but it upset him a good deal.'

'Did Dr Vaidya say that Mr Shelvankar would die in an accident?'

'No, not in so many words; but he did say Mr Shelvankar must be careful over the next few days. Apparently, there was some indication of trouble and bad times.'

The coffee arrived. We drank it in silence. Even if Mr Shelvankar's death had been caused truly by a freak accident, I thought, there was something wrong somewhere. It was evident that Feluda was thinking the same thing, for he kept cracking his knuckles. He never did this unless there was a nasty suspicion in his mind.

We finished our coffee and rose to take our leave. Helmut walked with us up to the main gate.

'Thank you for the coffee,' Feluda told him. 'If you're going to be here for another week, I'm sure we shall meet again. We're staying at the Snow View. Please let me know if Dr Vaidya returns.'

In reply, Helmut said just one thing: 'If only I could find out what happened to that statue, I'd feel a lot happier.'

Chapter 3

Although the mist had lifted, the sky was still overcast, and it was raining. I didn't mind the rain. It was only a faint drizzle, the tiny raindrops breaking up into a thin, powdery haze. One didn't need an umbrella in rain like this; it was very refreshing.

We found a branch of Bata near our hotel. Luckily, they did have the kind of boots we were looking for. When we came out clutching our parcels, Feluda said, 'Since we don't yet know our way about this town, we'd better take a taxi.'

'Where to?'

'The Tibetan Institute. I've heard they have a most impressive collection of tankhas, ancient manuscripts and pieces of Tantrik art.'

'Are you beginning to get suspicious?' I asked, though I wasn't at all sure that Feluda would give me a straight answer.

'Why? What should I be getting suspicious about?'

'That Mr Shelvankar's death wasn't really caused by an accident?'

'I haven't found a reason yet to jump to that conclusion.'

'But that statue is missing, isn't it?'

'So what? It slipped out of his pocket, and was stolen by someone. That's all there is to it. Killing is not so simple. Besides, I cannot believe that anyone would commit murder simply for a statue that had been bought for a thousand rupees.'

47

I said nothing more, but I couldn't help thinking that if a mystery did grow out of all this, it would be rather fun.

A row of jeeps stood by the roadside. Feluda approached one of the Nepali drivers and said, 'The Tibetan Institute. Do you know the way?'

'Yes sir, I do.'

We got into the jeep, both choosing to sit in the front with the driver. He took out a woollen scarf from his pocket, put it round his throat and turned the jeep around. Then we set off on the same road which had brought us into town. Only this time, we were going in the opposite direction.

Feluda began talking to the driver.

'Have you heard about the accident that happened recently?'

'Yes, everyone in Gangtok has.'

'The driver of that jeep survived, didn't he?'

'Yes, he's very lucky. Last year there had been a similar accident. The driver got killed, not the passenger.'

'Do you happen to know this driver?'

'Of course. Everyone knows everyone in Gangtok.'

'What is he doing now?'

'Driving another taxi. SKM 463. It's a new taxi.'

'Have you seen the accident spot?'

'Yes, it's on the North Sikkim Highway. Three kilometres from here.'

'Could you take us there tomorrow.'

'Yes, sure. Why not?'

'Well then, come to the Snow View Hotel at 8 a.m. We'll be waiting for you.'

'Very well, sir.'

A road rose straight through a forest to stop before the Tibetan Institute. The driver told us that orchids grew in this forest, but we didn't have the time to stop and look for them. Our jeep stopped outside the front door of the Institute. It was a large two-storey building with strange Tibetan patterns on its walls. It was so quiet that I thought perhaps the place was closed, but then we discovered that the front door was open. We stepped into a big hall. Tankhas hung on the walls. The floor was lined with huge glass cases filled with objects of art.

As we stood debating where to go next, a Tibetan gentleman, clad in a loose Sikkimese dress, came forward to meet us.

'Could we see the curator, please?' Feluda asked politely.

'No, I'm afraid he is away on sick leave today. I am his assistant. How may I help you?'

'Well, actually, I need some information on a certain Tibetan statue. I do not know what it's called, but it has nine heads and thirty-four arms. Could it be a Tibetan god?'

The gentleman smiled. 'Yes, yes, you mean Yamantak. Tibet is full of strange gods. We have a statue of Yamantak here. Come with me, I'll show it to you. Someone brought a beautiful specimen a few days ago—it's the best I've ever seen—but unfortunately, that gentleman died.'

'Oh, did he?' Feluda feigned total surprise.

We followed the assistant curator and stopped before a tall showcase. He brought out a small statue from it. I gasped in horror. Good heavens, was this a god or a monster? Each of its nine faces wore a most vicious expression. The assistant curator then turned it in his hand and showed us a small hole at the base of the statue. It was customary, he said, to roll a piece of paper with a prayer written on it and insert it through that little hole. It was then called the 'sacred intestine'!

He put the statue back in the case and turned to us once more. 'That other statue of Yamantak I was talking about was only three inches long. But its workmanship was absolutely exquisite. It was made of gold, and the eyes were two tiny rubies. None of us had ever seen anything like it before, not even our curator. And he's been all over Tibet, met the Dalai Lama—why, he's even drunk tea with the Dalai Lama, out of a human skull!'

'Would a statue like that be valuable? I mean, if it was made of gold—?'

The assistant curator smiled again. 'I know what you mean. This man bought it for a thousand rupees. Its real value may well be in excess of ten thousand.'

We were then taken on a little tour down the hall, and the assistant curator told us in great detail about some of the other exhibits. Feluda listened politely, but all I could think of was Mr Shelvankar's death. Surely ten thousand rupees was enough to tempt someone to kill? But then, I told myself firmly, Mr Shelvankar had not been stabbed or strangled or poisoned. He had died simply because a falling rock had hit his jeep. It had to be an accident.

As we were leaving, our guide suddenly laughed and said, 'I wonder why Yamantak has created such a stir. Someone else was asking me about this statue.'

'Who? The man who died?'

'No, no, someone else. I'm afraid I cannot recall his name, or his face. All I remember are the questions he asked. You see, I was very busy that day with a group of American visitors. They were our Chogyal's guests, so . . .'

When we got back into the jeep, it was only five to five by my watch; but it was already dark. This surprised me since I knew daylight could not fade so quickly. The reason became clear as we passed the forest and came out into the open again. Thick black clouds had gathered in the western sky. 'It generally rains at night,' informed our driver. 'The days here are usually dry.' We decided to go back to the hotel as there was no point now in trying to see other places.

Feluda did not utter a single word on our way back. He simply stared out of the jeep, taking in everything he saw. If we went up this road again on a different day, I was sure he'd be able to remember the names of all the shops we saw. Would I ever be able to acquire such tremendous powers of observation, and an equally remarkable memory? I didn't think so.

We saw Mr Bose again as we got out of our jeep in front

of our hotel. He appeared to be returning from the market, still looking thoughtful. He gave a little start when he heard Feluda call out to him. Then he looked up, saw us and came forward with a smile. 'Everything's arranged. I am leaving by the morning flight tomorrow.'

'Could you please make a few enquiries for me when you get to Bombay?' asked Feluda. 'You see, Mr Shelvankar had bought a valuable Tibetan statue. We must find out if it was sent to Bombay with his other personal effects.'

'All right, I can do that for you. But where did you learn this?'

Feluda told him briefly about his conversation with Mr Sarkar and the German photographer. 'Yes, it would have been perfectly natural for him to have kept the statue with him. He had a passion for art objects,' Mr Bose said. Then he suddenly seemed to remember something, and the expression on his face changed. He looked at Feluda again with a mixture of wonder and amusement.

'By the way,' he said, 'you didn't tell me you were a detective.'

Feluda and I both gave a start. How had he guessed? Mr Bose began laughing. Then he pulled out his wallet and, from it, took out a small visiting card. To my surprise, I saw that it was one of Feluda's. It said: Pradosh C Mitter, Private Investigator.

'It fell out of your pocket this morning when you were paying the driver of your jeep,' Mr Bose told us. 'He picked it up and gave it to me, thinking it was mine. I didn't even glance at it then, but saw it much later. Anyway, I'm going to keep it, if I may. And here's my own card. If there is any development here . . . I mean, if you think I ought to be here, please send me a telegram in Bombay. I'll take the first available flight . . . . Well, I don't suppose I'll meet you tomorrow. Goodbye, Mr Mitter. Have a good time.' Mr Bose raised his hand in farewell and began walking briskly in the direction of the Dak Bungalow. It had started to rain.

*

Feluda took his shoes off the minute we got back into our room and threw himself down on his bed. 'Aaaah!' he said. I was feeling tired, too. Who knew we'd see and hear so many different things on our very first day?

'Just imagine,' Feluda said, staring at the ceiling, 'what do you suppose we'd have done if a criminal had nine heads? No one could possibly sneak up to him and catch him from behind!'

'And thirty-four arms? What about those?'

'Yes, we'd have had to use seventeen pairs of handcuffs to arrest him!'

It was raining quite hard outside. I got up and switched on the lights. Feluda stretched out an arm and slipped his hand into his handbag. A second later, he had his famous blue notebook open in front of him and a pen in his hand. Feluda had clearly made up his mind that there was indeed a mystery somewhere, and had started his investigation.

'Can you tell me quickly the name of each new person we have met today?'

I wasn't prepared for such a question at all, so all I could do for a few seconds was stare dumbly at Feluda. Then I swallowed and said, 'Today? Every new person? Do I have to start from Bagdogra?'

'No, you idiot. Just give me a list of people we met here in Gangtok.'

'Well . . . Sasadhar Datta.'

'Wrong. Try again.'

'Sorry, sorry. I mean Sasadhar Bose. We met him at the airport in Bagdogra.'

'Right. Why is he in Gangtok?'

'Something to do with aromatic plants, didn't he say?'

52

'No, a vague answer like that won't do. Try to be more specific.'

'Wait. He came here to meet his partner, Shivkumar Shelvankar. They have a chemical firm. Among other things, they . . . .'

'OK, OK, that'll do. Next?'

'The hippie.'

'His name?'

'Helmet—'

'No, not Helmet. It's Helmut. And his surname?'

'Ungar.'

'What brought him here?'

'He's a professional photographer, working on a book on Sikkim. He had his visa extended.'

'Next?'

'Nishikanto Sarkar. Lives in Darjeeling. No idea what he does for a living. He had a Tibetan statue which he—'

I was interrupted by a knock on the door. 'Come in!' Feluda shouted.

The man I was just talking about walked into the room. 'I hope I'm not disturbing you?' asked Nishikanto Sarkar. 'I just thought I'd tell you about the Lama dance.'

'Lama dance? Where?' Feluda offered him a chair. Mr Sarkar took it, that same strange smile still hovering on his lips.

'In Rumtek,' he said, 'just ten miles from here. It's going to be a grand affair. People are coming from Bhutan and Kalimpong. The chief Lama of Rumtek—he is number three after the Dalai Lama—was in Tibet all this while. He has just returned to Rumtek. And the monastery is supposed to be new and worth seeing. Would you like to go tomorrow?'

'Not in the morning. Maybe after lunch?'

'OK. Or if you wish to have a darshan of His Holiness, we could go the day after tomorrow. I could get hold of three white scarves.'

'Why scarves?' I asked.

Mr Sarkar's smile broadened. 'That is a local custom. If

you wish to meet a high class Tibetan, you have to present him with a scarf. He'll take it from you, and return it immediately. That's all, that takes care of all the formalities.'

'No, I don't think we need bother about a darshan,' said Feluda. 'Let's just go and see the dance.'

'Yes, I would actually prefer that myself. The sooner we can go the better. You never know what might happen to the roads.'

'Oh, by the way, did you tell anyone else apart from Shelvankar about that statue?'

Mr Sarkar's reply came instantly, 'No. Not a soul. Why do you ask?'

'I was curious, that's all.'

'I did think of taking it somewhere to have it properly valued, but I met Mr Shelvankar before I could do that, and he bought it. Mind you, he didn't pay me at once. I had to wait until the next day.'

'Did he pay you in cash?'

'No, he didn't have that much cash on him. He gave me a cheque. Look!' Mr Sarkar took out a folded cheque from his wallet and showed it to Feluda. I leant over and saw it, too. It was a National and Grindlays Bank cheque. Feluda returned it to Mr Sarkar.

'Did you notice anything sus-suspicious?' Mr Sarkar asked, still smiling. I realized later that he had a tendency to stammer if he was upset or excited. 'No, no.' Feluda yawned. Mr Sarkar rose to go. At this precise moment, there was a bright flash of lightning, followed almost immediately by the ear-splitting noise of thunder. Mr Sarkar went white. 'I can't stand thunder and lightning, heh heh. Good night!' he went out quickly.

It continued to rain throughout the evening. Even when I went to bed after dinner, I could hear the steady rhythm of the rain, broken occasionally by distant thunder. Despite that, it didn't take me long to fall asleep.

I woke briefly in the middle of the night and saw a figure

walk past our window. But who would be mad enough to go out on a night like this? Perhaps I wasn't really awake. Perhaps the figure wearing a red garment that I saw only for a few seconds in the flash of lightning was no more than a dream . . . a figment of my imagination.

Chapter 4

I woke at 6.30 a.m. the next morning, to find that the rain had stopped and there was not a single cloud in the sky. The sun shone brightly on the world, and behind the range of mountains, now easily visible from our room, stood Kanchenjunga. The view from here was different from that in Darjeeling, but it was still unmistakably the same Kanchenjunga, standing apart from all the other mountains—proud, majestic and beautiful.

Feluda had risen before me and already had a bath. 'Be quick, Topshe. We have lots to do,' he said. It took me less than half an hour to get ready. By the time we went down for breakfast, it was only a little after 7 a.m. To our surprise, we found Mr Sarkar already seated in the dining hall.

'Good morning. So you're an early riser, too,' Feluda greeted him.

Mr Sarkar smiled, but seemed oddly preoccupied, even somewhat nervous. 'Er . . . did you sleep well?' we asked.

'Not too badly. Why, what's the matter?'

Mr Sarkar glanced around briefly before taking out a crumpled yellow piece of paper from his pocket. Then he handed it over to Feluda and said, 'What do you make of this?'

Feluda spread it out. There were some strange letters written with black ink. 'It looks like a Tibetan word. Where did you get it?'

'Last night . . . in the . . . I mean, d-dead of night . . . someone threw it into my room.'

'What!' My heart gave a sudden lurch. Mr Sarkar's room was next to ours.

The same stretch of the veranda that ran in front of our room went past his. If the man I saw last night was real, and not something out of a dream, why, he might have—! But I chose not to say anything.

'I wish I knew what it said,' added Mr Sarkar.

'That shouldn't be a problem, surely? Dozens of people here can read Tibetan. You could go to the Tibetan Institute, if no one else will help you. But why are you assuming this is some sort of a threat? It could simply mean 'may you live long', or 'God be with you', or something like that. Is there a specific reason to think this is a warning or a threat?'

Mr Sarkar gave a little start, then smiled and said, 'No, no, certainly not. I do nothing but mind my own business. Why should anyone threaten me? But then again, why should anyone send me their good wishes? I mean, purely out of the blue like this?'

Feluda called a waiter and ordered breakfast. 'Stop worrying. We're right next to you, aren't we? We'll both look after you. Now, have a good breakfast, relax and think of the Lama dance this afternoon.'

Our jeep arrived on time. Just as we were about to get into it, I saw another jeep coming from the direction of the Dak Bungalow. As it came closer, I could read its number plate. SKM 463, it said. Why did it seem familiar? Oh, of course, this was the new jeep that Mr Shelvankar's driver was now driving. I caught a glimpse of the blue jacket the driver was wearing, and then, to my utter surprise, I saw Mr Bose sitting in the passenger's seat. He stopped his jeep at the sight of ours. 'I was waiting for information from the army,' he told us, leaning out. 'All that rain last night made me wonder if the roads were all right.'

'And are they?'

'Yes, thank God. If they weren't, I'd have had to go via Kalimpong.'

'Didn't Mr Shelvankar use the same driver?'

Mr Bose laughed. 'I can see you've started making enquiries already. But yes, you're right. I chose him deliberately, partly because his jeep is new, and partly because . . . lightning doesn't strike the same place twice, does it? Anyway, goodbye again!'

He drove off and soon disappeared. We climbed into our own jeep. The driver knew where he was supposed to take us, so we were off without wasting another minute. I glanced up as we approached the Dak Bungalow to see if I could see Helmut, but there was no one in sight. There was a slope to our left, leading to another street lined by buildings. One of them looked like a school for there was an open square ground in front of it with two tiny goal posts. A little later, we reached a crossing where four roads met. We drove straight ahead and soon came across a large sign that said, 'North Sikkim Highway.'

Feluda had been humming under his breath. Now he broke off and asked the driver, 'How far has this road gone?'

'Up to Chungtham, sir. Then it splits into two—one goes to Lachen, and the other to Lachung.'

I had heard of both these places. They were both at a height of nearly 9,000 feet and reported to be very beautiful.

'Is it a good road?'

'Yes, sir. But it gets damaged sometimes after heavy rain.'

The few buildings that could be seen by the road soon disappeared altogether. We were now well out of town, making our way through hills. Looking down at the valley below, I could only see maize fields. It seemed as though someone had cut steps in the hillside to plant the maize. It looked most attractive.

After driving in silence for another ten kms, our driver slowed down suddenly and said, 'Here's the spot. This is where the accident took place.' He parked the jeep on one side and we got out. The place was remarkably quiet. I could hear nothing but the faint chirping of a bird, and the gurgling of a small river in the far distance.

On our left was a slope. The hill rose almost in a straight line on our right. It was from the top of this hill that the boulder had fallen. Pieces of it were still strewn about. The thought of the accident suddenly made me feel a little sick.

Feluda, in the meantime, had finished taking a few quick photos. Then he passed his camera to me and walked over to the edge of the road on the left. 'It may be possible to climb down this slope, if I go very carefully. Wait for me. I shouldn't take more than fifteen minutes,' he said. Before I could say or do anything to stop him, he had stepped off the road and was climbing down the slope, clutching at plants, bushes and rocks, whistling nonchalantly. But the sound of his whistling faded gradually, and in just a few minutes there was silence once more. Unable to contain myself, I moved towards the edge of the road and took a quick look. What I saw made me give an involuntary gasp. I could see Feluda, but he had climbed such a distance already that his figure looked like that of a tiny doll.

'Yes, he's found the right spot,' said the driver, joining me. 'That's where the jeep had fallen.'

Exactly fifteen minutes later, I heard Feluda climbing up, once again clutching and grasping whatever he could lay his hands on. When he came closer, I stretched an arm and helped him heave himself up on the road.

'What did you find, Feluda?'

'Just some nuts and bolts and broken parts of a vehicle. No Yamantak.'

This did not surprise me. 'Did you find nothing else?' I asked. In reply, Feluda took out a small object from his pocket. It was a white shirt button, possibly made of plastic. Feluda put it away, and made his way to the hill that rose high on the other side of the road. I heard him mutter 'rocks and boulders, rocks and boulders' a couple of times. Then he raised his voice and said, 'Felu Mitter must now turn into Tenzing.'

'What do you mean? Why Tenzing? Hey Feluda, wait for me!'

This time, I was determined not to be left behind. The hill that had looked pretty daunting at first turned out to have little clefts and hollows one could use as footholds. 'All right, you go before me,' Feluda said. I knew he wanted to be right behind me so that he could reach out and catch me if I slipped and fell. Luckily, that did not happen. A few minutes later, I heard Feluda say, 'Stop!' We had reached a place that was almost flat. I decided to sit on a small rock and rest for a while. Feluda began pacing, examining the ground carefully. I paid no attention until he stopped and said, 'Hm. This is where that boulder must have slipped from. Look at those bushes over there—and that small fern—see how they've been crushed?'

'How big do you think it was?'

'You saw the pieces, didn't you? It need not have been very big. A rock the size of a dhobi's bundle would be enough to kill, if it fell from such a height.'

'Really?'

'Yes. It's a matter of momentum, you see. Mass x velocity. If you stood at the bottom of Qutab Minar and someone from its top threw a pebble aimed at your head, you might end up with a fractured skull. Haven't you noticed when you play cricket that the higher the cricket ball is thrown in the air, the more difficult and painful it is for a fielder to catch it?'

'Yes, I see what you mean.'

Feluda turned and started to stare at a certain spot that looked more barren than its surroundings. There were grassy patches everywhere else.

'Topshe, do you want to find out how that stone slipped out? Come and have a look.' Feluda pointed at something in that barren portion of the hill. I got up and peered. There was a small hole. What could it mean?

'As far as I can see,' Feluda said slowly, 'yes, I am almost a hundred per cent sure about this—someone forced the rock out of the ground, using either a strong iron rod, or something like that. Otherwise there wouldn't be an empty space here. Which means—'

I knew what his next words were going to be. But I held my breath and let him finish.

'—which means the accident that took Mr Shelvankar's life was caused by man, not nature. Someone killed him . . . someone incredibly cruel, and clever.'

Chapter 5

When we returned to the hotel from the place of the murder (I am not going to call it an accident any more), Feluda told me to wait in the hotel. He had to go out on some work. I didn't ask him for details for I knew he wouldn't tell me.

On our way back, we had met Helmut near the big crossing. When he heard we were going to Rumtek later in the afternoon, he said he'd like to join us. Nobody had told him about the Lama dance. I wondered where Mr Sarkar was. Had he managed to find out what that Tibetan word meant?

I found him in the dining hall, looking morose and depressed. However, my arrival seemed to cheer him up. 'Where's your cousin?' he asked with his usual smile.

'He's gone out for a while. He should be back soon.'

'Er . . . he's very strong, isn't he?'

I looked up in surprise at this question, but Mr Sarkar continued, 'You see, I am staying on in Gangtok only because he said he'd help me, if need be. Or else I'd have gone back to Darjeeling today.'

'Why?'

Mr Sarkar began looking nervous again. Then he slowly took out the same yellow paper from his pocket. 'I've ne-never done anyone any harm. Why should anyone try to threaten me?'

'Did you find out what that word means?'

'Ye-es. I took it to the Tibetan Institute. And they said . . . they said it means "death". Giangphung, or something like that. The Tibetan word for death. It's got me really worried. I am thirty-seven now, you see, and once an astrologer had told me my stars were all going to fall into unfavourable positions after I turned thirty-seven . . . '

This irritated me somewhat. 'I think you are jumping to conclusions,' I said a little sternly. 'All it says is "death". Does it say *you* have to die?'

'Yes, yes, you're right. It could be anybody's death, couldn't it? Even so . . . I don't know . . . ' I thought of the figure in red I had seen last night. But obviously it was far better not to mention it to Mr Sarkar. He was upset enough as it was. After a few moments of silence, he seemed to pull himself together with an effort. 'I mustn't brood,' he said. 'Your cousin's there to help me. The very sight of him inspires confidence. Is he a sportsman?'

'He used to play cricket. Now he does yoga.'

'I knew it! One doesn't often get to see a man looking so fit. Anyway, would you like a cup of tea?'

I was feeling quite tired after all that climbing. So I said yes, and Mr Sarkar ordered tea for both of us. Feluda arrived just as the waiter placed two steaming cups before us. Mr Sarkar told him of his problem at once. Feluda looked at the Tibetan word again and asked, 'Can you figure out why anyone should want to do this to you?'

'No, sir. I've thought a great deal, but I can't think of a reason at all.'

'Very well. If you're sure there's no one to bear you a grudge, then there's nothing to be worried about. I am sure that was dropped into your room by mistake. What is the point in threatening someone in a language he doesn't know? That warning must have been meant for someone who can read Tibetan. You were not the real target.'

'Yes, that makes a lot of sense. Besides, I can rely on you, can't I, if there's any trouble?'

'Yes, but perhaps there's something I should tell you here and now. Trouble follows me around wherever I go.'

'R-really?'

Feluda went up to our room without another word. I knew he couldn't stand people who were given to frequent attacks of nerves. If Mr Sarkar wanted his support, he'd have to stop whining all the time.

When I returned to our room after finishing my tea, Feluda was writing something in his blue notebook. 'I knew most people in telegraph offices were illiterate, but this is too much!' he exclaimed upon seeing me.

'Why, what happened?'

'I sent a telegram to Mr Bose. He will get it as soon as he reaches Bombay.

'What did you tell him?'

'Have reason to suspect Shelvankar's death not accidental. Am investigating.'

'But why are you so cross with the telegraph office?'

'That's another matter. You see, I went to find out if Shelvankar had received any telegrams while he was here. It wasn't easy to get this information, of course, but in the end they told me there had been two. One was from Mr Bose, saying, "Am arriving fourteenth."'

'And the other?'

'Here, read this,' Feluda offered me his notebook. I saw what was written in it: YOUR SON MAY BE IS A SICK MONSTER. PRITEX.

I stared. What on earth did it mean? Were we now going to deal with demons and monsters?

'Some words have clearly been misspelt. But what could they be?' Feluda muttered.

'What is Pritex?'

'That probably refers to a private detective agency.'

'You mean Shelvankar had appointed a detective to trace his son?'

'Quite possibly. But "sick monster"? Dear God!'

'This is getting increasingly complicated, Feluda. How many mysteries will you solve all at once?'

'I was thinking the same thing. There is no end to the questions. In fact, it might not be a bad idea to write them down.' He bent over his notebook, pen in hand.

'Go ahead,' he invited.

'Number one—sick monster.'

'Yes. Next?'

'Who threw that boulder?'

'Good.'

'Number three—where did that statue disappear?'

'Carry on. You're doing quite well.'

'Number four—who threw that piece of paper into Mr Sarkar's room?'

'And why? All right, next?'

'Number five—whose shirt button did you find at the site of the murder?'

'Yes, although that might well have dropped from the shirt of the murder victim.'

'Number six—who, apart from ourselves, went to the Tibetan Institute to ask about Yamantak?'

'Splendid. If you keep going like this, in about ten years you'll become a full-fledged detective yourself!'

I knew Feluda was joking, but I felt quite pleased to think I'd passed the test.

'There is only one person we haven't yet met and I feel we ought to.'

'Who is that?'

'Dr Vaidya. If he can make predictions for the future, speak to departed souls, and perform other tricks, he's got to be an interesting man.'

Chapter 6

We left for Rumtek as planned, taking the road to Siliguri. The same road turned right to join a new road that went straight up to Rumtek. Both roads passed through picturesque villages and green and gold maize fields. I found the ride thoroughly enjoyable, despite the fact that the sun had disappeared and the sky had started to turn grey.

Our driver was driving very cautiously. Feluda and I sat with him in the front. Helmut and Mr Sarkar sat at the back, facing each other. Helmut's foot, he said, was now a lot better. The pain had gone, thanks to a German pain balm he had used. Mr Sarkar seemed much more cheerful. I could hear him humming a Hindi song. Only Feluda was totally silent and withdrawn. I knew he was trying very hard to find answers to those six questions. If we hadn't already planned this trip, he would have spent the afternoon scribbling in his notebook.

Our jeep turned right, bringing into view new houses and buildings, and rows of what looked like bunting. I learnt later that Tibetans hung square pieces of cloth from ropes outside their houses in the belief that they ward off evil spirits.

A few minutes later, a faint noise that had already reached my ears grew louder. It was a mixture of the deep and sombre sound of a horn, clanking of cymbals and a shrill note from a flute. This must be the music for the Lama dance, I thought, as our jeep pulled up outside the huge gate of the monastery. 'The lamas are dan-dancing,' informed Mr Sarkar, possibly for Helmut's benefit. All of us climbed out.

Passing through the gate, we found ourselves in a large open courtyard. A beautiful blue and white embroidered shamiana stood over it. The audience sat under the shamiana. About ten men, wearing bright costumes and rather grotesque masks, were dancing before this audience, jumping and swaying to the music. The musicians were all dressed in red. Small boys—barely ten years old—were blowing the horns, each one of which was several feet long. I had never seen anything like it.

Helmut started taking photos. He was carrying three cameras today.

'Would you like to sit down?' asked Mr Sarkar.

'What do you want to do?' Feluda said.

'I have seen this kind of thing before, in Kalimpong. I'm going to have a look at the temple behind this courtyard. Its inside walls are supposed to be beautifully carved.'

Mr Sarkar left. Feluda and I sat down on the floor. 'Tradition is a strange thing,' remarked Feluda. 'A traditional dance like this can make you forget you're living in the twentieth century. I don't think this form of dance has changed at all in the last thousand years.'

'Why is this place called a gumpha?'

'No, this isn't a gumpha. A gumpha is a cave. This is monastery. See those little rooms on the other side? That's where the monks stay. All these little boys with shaved heads, wearing long Tibetan robes are being trained to become monks. In a monas—' Feluda broke off. I looked at him quickly to find him frowning, his mouth hanging open. Now what was the matter? What had he suddenly thought of? 'It's this mountain air,' he said finally, shaking his head. 'It's affecting my brain. I've stopped thinking. Why did it take me so long to work out what that telegram meant? It's so simple!'

'How is it simple? I still can't—.

67

'Look, it said "sick". That means Sikkim. And monster" is monastery.'

'Hey, that makes sense! What does the whole thing say?'

'YOUR SON MAY BE IS A SICK MONSTER. If you read "IN" for "IS", it says YOUR SON MAY BE IN A SIKKIM MONASTERY.'

'Does that mean Mr Shelvankar's son, who left home fifteen years ago, is here right now?'

'That's what Pritex said. If Shelvankar had managed to figure out the meaning of this telegram, he might well have started to feel hopeful. From what I've heard, he loved his son and wanted him back.'

'Perhaps he was going to that gumpha the day he died only to look for his son.'

'That's entirely possible. And if his son was really somewhere in Sikkim, the chances of . . .' Feluda broke off again. Then I heard him mutter under his breath, 'Will . . . will . . . if Shelvankar made a will leaving everything to his son, he stood to gain a lot.' Feluda rose and made his way out of the crowd. I followed quickly. He was obviously feeling restless, having just discovered what the telegram had really meant. I saw him look around. Was he looking for an Indian among the Tibetans?

We began walking in the direction of the temple, where Mr Sarkar had disappeared a few minutes ago. There were fewer people on the other side of the courtyard. As we passed the rooms in which the monks lived, we saw a couple of very old monks sitting outside in the corridor, turning a prayer wheel silently, their eyes closed. If their heavily wrinkled faces were anything to go by, they must have been a hundred years old.

Behind the rooms was a long veranda. Its walls were covered with pictures depicting scenes from the Buddha's life. The veranda led to a dark hall. Inside it, flickering oil lamps stood in rows. A huge wooden door, painted red, had been thrown open, but there was no one at the door. Feluda and I stepped in quietly.

The dark, damp hall was filled with a strange scent of incense. Incredibly long lengths of bright silk, heavily embroidered, hung from the high ceiling. Benches, draped in colourful fabrics, stood in corners, as did what looked like very large drums. These were supported by bamboo rods. Behind these, in the darkest corner of the hall, were a number of tall statues, chiefly of the Buddha. Flowers had been arranged in a number of vases, and the oil lamps I had seen from outside were placed under the statues.

I was totally engrossed in looking at these things when suddenly Feluda placed a hand on my shoulder. I looked up swiftly and found him staring at a side entrance to the hall. A much smaller door on one side was open.

'Let's get out of here,' he said, speaking through clenched teeth, and started to move towards the door.

We emerged from the hall to find a flight of stairs going up. 'I can't tell where he went, but let's go upstairs, anyway,' Feluda said.

'Where who went?' I whispered, running up the stairs.

'A man in red. He was peeping into the hall. Ran away the moment he realized I had seen him.'

'Did you see his face?'

'No, it was too dark.'

We found a room on the first floor, but its door was closed. Perhaps this was the senior lama's room, who had recently returned from Tibet. On the left was an open terrace. Here again, pieces of cloth hung from ropes. Strains of the music from the courtyard down below reached my ears. A dance like this could go on for seven or eight hours.

We walked across the terrace and stood by a railing, overlooking a green valley. A mist had started to rise, slowly engulfing everything that was visible. 'If Shelvankar's son was here—' Feluda began, but was interrupted by a loud scream.

'Help me! Oh God . . . save! . . . help . . . help!'

It was Mr Sarkar's voice.

We ran back to the stairs. It took us less than a minute to

get down and find the rear exit from the monastery. We rushed out to find that the shrieks for help were coming from the bottom of a hill. The area was uneven, dotted with bushes and shrubs, one end leading to a steep drop of about a hundred feet. It was here that Mr Sarkar was hanging from a bush, right at the edge of the hill. Our appearance made him shout even louder. 'I am d-d-dying . . . save me, please save me!'

It wasn't too difficult to pull him up to safety. But the instant his feet touched solid ground, he rolled his eyes and fainted. Then we had to carry him back to the jeep and splash cold water on his face. He came round in a few moments and sat up slowly.

'What happened?' asked Feluda.

'D-don't remind me!' Mr Sarkar whimpered. 'After that long journey, I n-n-needed to . . . I mean . . . relieve myself, you see . . . so I thought I'd better go out of the monastery, and I found this place that seemed quite suitable, but . . . but who knew I had been followed?'

'Did someone give you a push from the back?'

'Absolutely. It was h-horrible! If I hadn't found that bush to hang on to, that Tibetan warning would have come t-true, in no t-time!'

'Did you see the man?'

'No, of course not! He stole up behind me, didn't he?'

*

There was no point in staying on in Rumtek after an incident like this. We decided to go back to Gangtok immediately. Helmut, who had seen us coming back to the jeep, agreed to return with us, although I suspect he was disappointed at not being able to take more photos.

Feluda had sunk into silence once more. But he spoke suddenly as our driver started the jeep. 'Mr Sarkar,' he said, surely you realize you have a certain responsibility in this whole business?'

'Res-responsibility?' croaked Mr Sarkar.

'There's no way we can figure out who's trying to frighten you unless you tell us what—or who—*you* are after.'

Mr Sarkar sat up, looking profoundly distressed. 'I swear, sir—I promise—I've never caused anyone any harm. Not knowingly, anyway.'

'You don't happen to have an identical twin, do you?'

'No, no. I am the only child of my parents.'

'Hm. I assume you're telling the truth. Mind you, if you tell me a lie, it is you who is going to be in trouble.'

The rest of the journey was made in total silence. Feluda spoke again only when our jeep stopped at the Dak Bungalow and Helmut tried to pay his share.

'No, no,' Feluda said, 'we invited you, didn't we? Besides, you are a guest in our country. We cannot allow you to pay a single paisa.'

'All right.' Helmut smiled. 'Will you at least allow me to offer you a cup of tea?'

This seemed like a very good idea, so all of us got out. Feluda and Mr Sarkar paid the driver. Helmut then took us to his room.

We had just found three chairs for ourselves, and Helmut had placed his cameras on the table, when a strange man walked into the room and greeted Helmut with a smile. A thick beard—flecked with grey—covered most of his face. Long hair came down to his shoulders. He was clad in loose flannel trousers and a shapeless orange jacket with a high neck. In his hand was a stout walking-stick.

Helmut smiled back, and turned to us. 'Allow me to introduce you,' he said. 'This is Dr Vaidya.'

Chapter 7

'Are you from Bengal?' Dr Vaidya asked. He spoke with a funny accent.

'Yes,' Feluda replied. 'Helmut has told us about you.'

'Helmut is a nice boy,' Dr Vaidya nodded, 'but I've had to warn him about one thing. People here don't normally like being photographed. You see, it is their belief that if a part of a person is represented somewhere else in a different form, it reduces the vital force—the ability to live—of that person.'

'Do you believe this yourself?'

'What I believe is of no consequence, at least not to Helmut. He hasn't stopped taking pictures, has he? Why, I have been captured in his camera, too! What I say is this: one cannot disregard anything in life without studying it, or examining it thoroughly. I still have a lot to learn.'

'But there's such a lot you know already! I've heard you can see the future and even speak to the dead.'

'No, not always.' Dr Vaidya gave a slight smile. 'A lot depends on the immediate surroundings. But there are certain things that are fairly easy to tell. For instance, I can tell that this gentleman here is under a lot of stress,' he pointed at Mr Sarkar, who licked his lips nervously.

'Yes, you're right,' Feluda said. 'Somebody is trying to threaten him. He thinks his life is in danger. Can you tell us

72

who's doing this?'

Dr Vaidya closed his eyes. He opened them a few seconds later and stared out of the window absently. 'Agent,' he said.

'Agent?'

'Yes. A man must be punished for his sins. Sometimes he is punished by the Almighty. At other times, God sends His agents out to do this job.'

'Enough!' shouted Mr Sarkar. His voice shook. 'I don't want to hear any more.'

Dr Vaidya smiled again. 'I am saying all this only because your friend asked me. If you can learn something yourself, there's no need to go looking for a teacher. But one thing I must tell you. If you wish to live, you will have to tread most carefully.'

'What does that mean?' asked Mr Sarkar.

'I can't say anything more than that.'

The tea arrived. Helmut poured it out and passed the cups around.

'I believe you met Mr Shelvankar,' said Feluda, sipping his tea.

'Yes. It's all very sad. I did warn him about a rough patch he might have to go through. But death? No, that's a different matter altogether, and no one has any control over it.'

No one spoke after this. We drank our tea in silence. Helmut sorted a few papers out on his table. Mr Sarkar stared absently into space, apparently unaware that his tea was getting cold. Only Feluda seemed totally at ease, happily finishing the biscuits that had arrived with the tea. After a while, Helmut rose to switch on a light. Daylight had almost gone by this time. But it turned out that there was a power cut. 'I'll get some candles,' said Helmut and went out to look for the bearer.

Feluda turned to Dr Vaidya again. 'Do you really believe Mr Shelvankar's death was accidental?'

Dr Vaidya took a moment to reply. Then he said, 'Only one person knows the answer to that question.'

73

'Who?'

'The person who died. Only he knows the truth. We who are living look upon this world and this life through eyes that take in every irrelevant and unnecessary detail. Just look out of that window. All those mountains and trees and rivers are irrelevant. They stand as a screen between ourselves and the truth. But death opens an inner eye that sees nothing but what is real and of true significance.'

Most of this speech went over my head, but I was sure Feluda had understood every word. 'You mean it is only Mr Shelvankar who could tell how he died?' Feluda asked.

'Yes. He couldn't have known the truth when he died. But now . . . yes, now he knows exactly what happened.'

I shivered suddenly. There was something eerie in the atmosphere, in so much talk about death, and the way Dr Vaidya smiled in the dark. It gave me goose-pimples.

The bearer came in at this moment. He cleared the table and placed a candle on it. Feluda took out a packet of Charminar, offered it to everyone else in the room, then lit one himself. 'It may be a good idea to consult Mr Shelvankar and see what he thinks,' he remarked, blowing out a smoke ring. I knew he had read a lot on seances and most things supernatural. He kept an open mind on every subject, never hesitating to read or hear about other people's views, even if he didn't believe in something himself.

Dr Vaidya closed his eyes. A few moments later, he opened them and said, 'Shut the door and windows.' There was something authoritative in his tone. Mr Sarkar got up like a man hypnotized and obeyed silently. We were left sitting around the table in the faint flickering light of the candle. On my right was Dr Vaidya. On my left sat Feluda. Mr Sarkar sat next to him. Helmut finished the circle.

'Place your hands, palms down, on this table. Your fingers must touch your neighbour's,' commanded Dr Vaidya. We did as we were told. Dr Vaidya placed his own hands between mine and Helmut's, and said, 'Look straight at that candle and

74

think of the death of Shelvankar.'

The candle was burning steadily. A few drops of wax had fallen on the table. A small insect, trapped in the room, began buzzing around the flame. God knows how long we sat in silence. I did cast a few sidelong glances at Dr Vaidya, but he couldn't have seen me for his own eyes were closed.

After a long time, he spoke. His voice sounded very faint as though he was speaking from a great distance. 'What do you want to know?' he asked. Feluda answered him. 'Did Mr Shelvankar die in an accident?'

'No,' said that faint, strange voice.

'How did he die?'

Silence. All of us were now gazing at Dr Vaidya. He was leaning back in his chair. His eyes were shut tight. Lightning flashed outside, lighting up our room for a second. Feluda's question was answered the same instant.

'Murder,' said Dr Vaidya.

'Mu-h-h-u-rder?' Mr Sarkar gasped.

'Who killed him?' Feluda wanted to know. He was staring at Dr Vaidya's hands. Dr Vaidya sighed. Then he began breathing hard, as though the act of breathing was causing him a great deal of pain. 'Virendra!' he finally whispered. Virendra? Who was he? Feluda started to speak, but Dr Vaidya opened his eyes unexpectedly and said, 'A glass of water, please.'

Helmut rose and poured him water from his flask. Feluda waited until Dr Vaidya had finished drinking it. Then he asked, 'I don't suppose there's any chance of finding out who this Virendra is?'

Helmut answered him this time. 'Virendra is Mr Shelvankar's son. He told me about him.'

It was now time for us to leave. All of us stood up. Helmut opened the door and windows. The power came back a second later.

'You get nervous rather easily, don't you?' said Dr Vaidya, placing a hand on Mr Sarkar's shoulder. Mr Sarkar tried to smile. 'Anyway, I don't think you are in any danger now,' Dr Vaidya told him reassuringly. This time, Mr Sarkar smiled more naturally, looking visibly relieved.

'How long are you here for?' Feluda asked Dr Vaidya.

'I'd like to go to Pemiangchi tomorrow, if it doesn't rain. I've heard they've got some ancient valuable manuscripts in the monastery there.'

'Are you making a study of Tibet and the Tibetan culture?'

'Yes, you might call it that. It's the only ancient civilization that's left in the world. Egypt, Iraq, Mesopotamia . . . each one of those got destroyed. But for that matter, what is left in India, tell me? It's all a great hotch-potch. It's only Tibet that's managed to retain most of what it had. Luckily, some of the old monasteries in Sikkim have got pieces of their art and culture, so one doesn't have to go all the way to Tibet to find them.'

We came out, to find that the sky was covered by thick, dark clouds, being frequently ripped by lightning. It was certain that it would start raining again.

'Why don't you go to Pemiangchi as well?' Dr Vaidya asked.

'Yes, we might do that. I've heard a lot about the place.'

'If you do, don't forget to take a bag of salt with you.'

'Salt? Whatever for?'

'Leeches. There's nothing like salt to get rid of them.'

Chapter 8

Feluda, Mr Sarkar and I were back in our hotel, sitting down to our dinner. Although the hotel was pretty average in may ways, it had an excellent cook.

'A most decent fellow, I must say,' remarked Mr Sarkar, trying to get the marrow out of a bone. A delicious lamb curry was on the menu tonight.

'Who? You mean Dr Vaidya?'

'Yes. What a remarkably gifted man, too. He seemed to know everything.'

'Yes, you should be pleased,' Feluda said, laughing. 'Didn't he tell you you were no longer in danger?'

'Why, didn't *you* believe what he said?'

'If what he said turns out to be true, then of course I shall believe him. But, right now, I think we should be careful in what or whom we believe. There are so many cheats in this line.' Feluda was frowning again. Something was obviously bothering him a great deal. I wish I knew what it was.

'Do you believe what he said about the murder?' Mr Sarkar persisted.

'Yes, I do.'

'Really? Why?'

'There is a reason.' Feluda refused to say anything more.

The two of us went out after dinner again to buy paan. It

hadn't yet started to rain, but there was virtually no breeze. Feluda put a paan in his mouth and began pacing. After only a few minutes, however, he stopped and said, 'I'm only wasting my time like this. Tell you what, Topshe, why don't you go for a walk for half an hour? I'd like to work alone in our room, undisturbed.'

I agreed, and Feluda walked away. I ambled across to the opposite pavement and made my way slowly down the road that led to the main town. All the shops were closed. A few men were sitting in a circle in front of a shop and gambling. I heard someone rattle the dice, which was followed by a great shout and loud laughter.

The street lights were dim, but even so I didn't fail to notice the figure of a man coming from the opposite direction, walking very fast. As he came closer, I realized it was Helmut. Something stopped me from calling out to him. But he was so preoccupied that even when he passed me by, he didn't seem to notice me at all. I stared foolishly at his receding back, until it vanished from sight. Then I looked at my watch and returned to the hotel.

Feluda was lying flat on his back, resting his notebook on his chest.

'I brought the list of suspects up to date,' he told me as I came in.

'Well, Virendra Shelvankar was already a suspect, wasn't he? It's just that we didn't know his name. Have you added Dr Vaidya's name to your list?'

Feluda grinned. 'The man put up a jolly good show, I must admit. Yet, the whole thing could be genuine, who knows? But we mustn't forget that he and Shelvankar had talked to each other. There's no way of making sure whether Dr Vaidya is a fraud or not unless we can find out what exactly the two had discussed.'

'But he was right about Mr Sarkar, wasn't he?'

'That was easy enough. Mr Sarkar was biting his nails constantly. Anyone could have guessed he was tense.'

'And what about the murder?'

'He may have said that only to create an effect. A natural death, or death by a real accident, is too tame. Call it a murder, and it sounds so much more dramatic.'

'So who's on your list of suspects?'

'Everyone, as always.'

'Everyone including Dr Vaidya?'

'Yes. He may have known about the statue of Yamantak.'

'And Helmut? He walked past me just now, but didn't seem to see me.'

This did not appear to surprise Feluda. 'Helmut struck me as a mysterious character right from the start. He's supposed to be taking photographs for a book on Sikkim, and yet he didn't know about the Lama dance in Rumtek. That's reason enough to feel suspicious about him.'

'Why? What can it mean?'

'It can mean that he hasn't told us the real reason why he is here in Sikkim.' I began to feel quite confused, so I stopped asking questions. Feluda went back to scribbling in his notebook.

At a quarter to eleven, Mr Sarkar knocked on our door to say good-night. I tried to read a book after that, but couldn't concentrate. Feluda spent his time either sitting silently or studying the entries in his notebook. I do not know when I fell asleep. When I woke, the mountains outside were bright with sunshine.

Feluda was not in the room. Perhaps he was having a shower. I noticed a piece of paper on his bed, placed under an ashtray. Had he left a message for me? I picked it up and found a Tibetan word staring at me. I knew what it meant.

Death.

Chapter 9

Feluda was not in the bathroom. I learnt later that he had risen early that morning to make a trunk call to Bombay. When I came down for breakfast, I found him speaking to someone on the telephone.

'I couldn't get Mr Bose,' he told me, putting the receiver down. 'He left very early this morning. Perhaps he got my telegram.'

We ordered breakfast. 'I'll have to conduct an experiment today,' Feluda revealed a few minutes later. 'I think I made a mistake somewhere. I have to make sure.'

'Where will you carry out this experiment?'

'I need a quiet spot.'

'You mean an empty room?'

'No, no, you idiot. I could use our hotel room if that's what I needed. I have to be out on the road, but I must not be seen. If anyone saw me, they'd definitely think I was mad. Let's go towards Nathula Road after breakfast.' We hadn't yet seen any of the other large streets of Gangtok. The prospect of doing a little more exploration on foot was quite exciting.

We ran into Dr Vaidya as we came out of the hotel. He was wearing sun glasses today. 'Where are you off to?' he asked.

'Just for a walk. We haven't really seen much of the city.

We were thinking of going towards the palace.'

'I see. I am going to look for a jeep. It's a good day to make that trip to Pemiangchi. If you don't go there, you really will miss a lot.'

'We do intend going there one day.'

'Try to make it while I'm there. Gangtok isn't a very safe place, particularly for you.'

Dr Vaidya left with a smile and a friendly wave.

'Why did he say that?' he asked.

'He's a very clever man. He wanted to startle us, that's all. Clearly he's seen I am involved in a complex matter, so he decided to say something odd for more effect.'

'But you really have been threatened, haven't you? I saw that piece of paper.'

'That's nothing new, is it?'

'No, but—'

'But nothing. If you think I'll give up now simply because someone wrote a Tibetan word on a piece of paper, you don't know me at all.'

I didn't say anything, but thought to myself how well I did know him. Hadn't I seen him work wonders in the case of the Emperor's ring in Lucknow, despite being showered with threats and warnings?

We had been walking uphill and had now reached a point where the road spread out, almost like the Mall in Darjeeling. There was a small roundabout with yellow roadsigns. The one pointing right said 'Palace'. There was a large, heavily decorated gate at the end of this road, which was obviously the gate of the palace. The sign on the left said 'Nathula Road'. It seemed a quiet enough road. The few people we could see all appeared to be tourists, heading for the palace. 'Let's take this left turn. Quick!' Feluda said.

We turned left and took the road that led to the Chinese border. There was no one in sight. Feluda kept looking up at the hills through which the road had been built. We had now come to the eastern side of Gangtok. Kanchenjunga was on the west. I couldn't see any of the snow-capped peaks from here, but what I could see was a ropeway.

It seemed so interesting that I stopped and stared at it, losing all track of time. I had to look up with a start a few minutes later, when I heard Feluda calling out to me. While I had been gazing at the busy ropeway, Feluda had climbed up the side of a hill, and was shouting from several feet above the road. 'Hey, Topshe, come here!'

I left the road and joined him. Feluda was standing near a rock, nearly as large as a football. 'I'm going down,' he said. 'I'll come walking past the hill. Push this stone down when I tell you to. Just a little push will make it roll off the hill. Is that clear?'

'Yes, sir. No problem!'

Feluda climbed down and disappeared in the direction from which I had come.

Then I heard him call, 'Ready?'

'Ready!' I replied.

Feluda started walking. I couldn't see him, but I heard his footsteps. A few moments later, he came vaguely within my line of vision, but before I could see him properly, I heard him shout, 'Go!' I pushed the rock, and it began to roll down. Feluda did not stop walking. By the time the rock landed on the road, he had crossed that area and gone ahead by at least ten steps.

'Wait right there!' he shouted again.

He then came back with the rock in his hand. It was still intact. 'Now you go down, and walk past this hill exactly as you saw me do. I will throw this stone at you, but you must continue walking. If you can see it rolling down at enormous speed and feel that it might hit you, you'll have to jump aside. Can you do that?'

'Sure.'

I scrambled down, and started walking, keeping an eye on Feluda. I saw him standing still, waiting for the right moment. Then he kicked the stone. I kept on walking. The stone hit the ground a few seconds before I could reach the spot. Then it rolled down the slope on the left and disappeared.

Feluda sat down, slapping his forehead. I didn't want to stand around like a fool, so I climbed up again.

'What an ass I've been, Topshe! What a perfect idiot. This simple—'

'Feluda!' I screamed, quickly pulling him to one side. In the same instant, a huge boulder came crashing from the top of the hill and went down, missing us by inches and crushing a large flowering bush on the way. By the time it struck the road and vanished from sight, my breathing was starting to return to normal. Thank God I had looked up when Feluda was speaking. Thank God I had seen the boulder. If I hadn't . . . I shuddered to think of the consequences. 'Thanks, Topshe,' Feluda said. 'This place really appears unsafe. Let's go back.'

We got down to the road and walked as fast as we could to the next crossing. There were benches on one side, placed under a canopy. We threw ourselves down on one of these. 'Did you see anyone?' asked Feluda, wiping his face.

'No. That boulder came from quite a height. I couldn't have seen who threw it even if I'd had the time to look.'

'I've got to move faster now. I've *got* to find a final solution!'

'But there are so many questions that need to be answered.'

'And who told you I haven't found some of the answers already? Do you know what time I went to bed last night? At two a.m. I did a lot of thinking. And now this experiment merely confirmed every suspicion I had. Mr Shelvankar's jeep had not been hit by a falling rock. One cannot commit a murder banking on a chance that's one in a million. What really happened, I'm sure, was this: Mr Shelvankar was knocked unconscious. Then he was dropped into that ravine, along with the jeep. Someone pushed that boulder afterwards, just to make it look an accident.'

'But the driver? What about him?'

'He had been bribed. I'm sure of it.'

'Or the driver himself might have killed him?'

'No, that's unlikely. He wouldn't have had a sufficiently strong motive.'

Feluda rose. 'Let's get back, Topshe. We must find SKM 463.'

But SKM 463 was not in Gangtok, as it turned out. It had left for Siliguri the day before. 'I think people want to hire it because it's a new jeep,' Feluda remarked.

'What do we do now?'

'Wait, let me think. I'm getting muddled.

We returned to the hotel from the jeep stand. Feluda ordered cold drinks in the dining hall. His hair was dishevelled and he seemed greatly perturbed.

'When did we arrive here?' he asked suddenly.

'Fourteenth April.'

'And when was Shelvankar killed?'

'On the eleventh.'

'Apart from Shelvankar, Mr Sarkar was here in Gangtok, and Helmut and Dr Vaidya.'

'And Virendra.'

'All right, let us make that assumption. When did Mr Sarkar get that Tibetan warning?'

'On the night of the fourteenth.'

'Right. Who was in town that day?'

'Helmut, Mr Bose, Virendra, and . . . and . . .'

'Mr Sarkar.'

'Yes, of course.'

'He may well have committed a crime. Maybe he is trying to remove suspicion from himself by showing us a piece of paper with a Tibetan word written on it. He may have written it himself. His shrieks for help in Rumtek could have been a clever piece of acting.'

'But what can he have done?'

'I don't know that yet, though I don't think he killed Shelvankar.'

'Well then, who is left?'

'Dr Vaidya. Don't forget him. We don't know for sure whether he did go to Kalimpong or not.'

Feluda finished a glass of Sikkim orange in one gulp. Then he continued, 'The only person whose movements cannot be questioned is Mr Bose, because he came with us and went to Bombay the next day. Someone in his house confirmed that he had indeed returned to Bombay. But he's not there now. Maybe he's on his way here. Perhaps our trip to Pemiangchi—' Feluda stopped speaking. Someone had walked into the dining hall and was talking to the manager. It was our German friend, Helmut Ungar. The manager pointed at us. Helmut wheeled around. 'Oh sorry, I didn't realize you were here,' he said, adding rather hesitantly, 'There's something I'd like to discuss with you. Do you think we could go up to your room?'

Chapter 10

'May I close the door?' asked Helmut as we walked into our room. Then he shut the door without waiting for an answer. I looked at him and began to feel vaguely uneasy. He was tall and strong, taller than Feluda by at least an inch. What did he want to do that required such secrecy? I had heard that some hippies took drugs. Was Helmut one of them? Would he—?

By this time, Helmut had placed his camera on my bed, and was opening a large red envelope with Agfa written on it.

'Would you like a cup of tea?' Feluda offered.

'No, thanks. I came here only to show you these photos. I couldn't get them printed here. So I had sent them to Darjeeling. I got the enlargements only this morning.'

Helmut took out the first photograph. 'This was taken from the North Sikkim Highway. The road where the accident took place goes right across to the opposite hill. You can get a wonderful view of Gangtok from there. That is where I was that morning, taking photos of this view. Mr Shelvankar had offered to pick me up on his way. But his jeep never got to the spot where I was standing. I heard a noise as I was clicking, which made me turn around. What I saw from where I was standing has been captured in these photos that I took with my telephoto-lens.'

It was a strange photo. Most of the details were clear,

although it had been taken from a distance. A jeep was sliding down a hill. A few feet above it, a man was standing on the road, looking at the falling jeep. This was probably the driver. He was wearing a blue jacket. His face couldn't be seen.

Helmut took out the second photo. This was even stranger. Taken a few seconds after the first one, it showed the jeep lying wrecked by the side of the hill. Next to it, behind a bush, there was a partially hidden figure of a man in a dark suit, lying on the ground. The driver was still standing on the road, this time with his back to the camera, looking up at the hill. Right on top of the hill was another man, bending over a rock. His face was just as unclear, but he was wearing red clothes.

In the third photograph, this man in red could not be seen at all. The driver was running—in fact, he had nearly shot out of the frame. The jeep and the man in the dark suit were still lying on the ground. And the rock that was on top of the hill was now lying on the road, broken to pieces.

'Remarkable!' Feluda exclaimed. 'I have never seen photographs like these!'

'Well, it isn't often that one gets such an opportunity,' Helmut replied dryly.

'What did you do after taking these pictures?'

'I returned to Gangtok on foot. By the time I could walk across to the spot where the jeep had fallen, Mr Shelvankar had been taken away. All I could see was the broken jeep and the shattered rock. I heard about the accident the minute I reached Gangtok. I then went straight to the hospital where Mr Shelvankar had been taken. He remained alive for a couple of hours after I got there.'

'Didn't you tell anyone about the photographs?'

'No. There was no point, at least not until I could have the film developed, and use it as evidence. Yet, I knew it was not an accident, but murder. Had I been a little closer, the face of the murderer might have been clearer in the picture.'

Feluda took out a magnifying glass and began examining

the large prints again. 'I wonder if that man in red is Virendra?' he said.

'That's impossible!' Helmut declared. There was something in his voice that made us both look at him in surprise.

'Why? How can you be so sure?'

'Because *I* am Virendra Shelvankar.'

'What!' For the first time, I saw Feluda go round-eyed. 'What do you mean? How can you be Virendra? You are white, you have blue eyes, you speak English with a German accent, your name . . .'

'Please let me explain. You see, my father married twice. My mother was his first wife. She was a German. She met my father in Heidelburg when he was a student. That was where they got married. Her maiden name was Ungar. When I left India and settled in Germany, I started using this name, and changed my first name from Virendra to Helmut.'

My head started reeling. Helmut was Shelvankar's son? Of course, if he had a German mother, that would explain his looks.

'Why did you leave home?' Feluda asked after a brief pause.

'Five years after my mother died, my father married again. I couldn't bring myself to accept this. I loved my mother very much. It's not that I did not care for my father, but somehow when he remarried, I began to hate him. In the end, I thought leaving home was the only thing I could do to solve my problems. It wasn't easy to travel to Europe on my own, and make a new beginning. For about eight years, I moved from place to place, and job to job. Then I studied photography, and finally started to make money. A few years ago, I happened to be in Florence working on an assignment. A friend of my father's saw me there and recognized me. He came back and told my father about it, after which he approached a detective agency to track me down. When I came to know about this, I grew a beard and changed the colour of my eyes.'

'Contact lenses?'

Helmut smiled and took the lenses out of his eyes. His real eyes were brown, just like my own. He then put the lenses back and continued, 'A year ago, I came to India with a group of hippies. I hadn't stopped loving this country. But then I realized that the detective agency was still trying to trace me. I went to a monastery in Kathmandu. When someone found me even there, I came over to Sikkim.'

'Wasn't your father pleased to see you?'

'He did not recognize me at all. I have lost a lot of weight since he last saw me. Besides, my long hair, my beard and blue eyes must have all worked together to stop him from recognizing his own son. He told me about Virendra, and how much he missed him. By this time, I, too, had forgotten my earlier dislike of my father. After all, whatever happened between us was now in the past. But when he failed to recognize me, I did not tell him who I was. I probably would have told him eventually, but . . . well, I never got the chance.'

'Do you have any idea who the murderer might be?'

'May I speak frankly?'

'Of course.'

'I don't think we should let Dr Vaidya escape.'

'I agree with you,' said Feluda, lowering his voice.

'I began to suspect him the minute he mentioned the name of Virendra that evening in my room. Obviously, he didn't know I was the same person. I think he is a first class cheat, and I bet it was he who took that statue.'

'When Mr Shelvankar set out that morning, was he alone?'

'I don't know. I left quite early, you see. Dr Vaidya may well have stopped the jeep on the way and asked for a lift. Naturally, at that stage, my father had no reason to suspect him. In any case, he was a simple man. He trusted everyone.'

Feluda stood up and began pacing. Then he stopped

abruptly and said, 'Would you like to go to Pemiangchi with us?

'Yes. I am prepared to go anywhere to catch my father's killer.'

'Do you know how far it is?'

'About a hundred miles from here. If the roads are good, we can get there in less than six hours. I think we should leave today, as soon as possible.'

'Yes, you're right. I'll try to find a jeep.'

'OK, and I'll get rooms booked at the Dak Bungalow in Pemiangchi. By the way—' Helmut turned back from the doorway, 'a dangerous man like him may well be armed. I have nothing except a flashgun. Do you—?'

Without a word, Feluda slipped a hand inside his suitcase and brought out his revolver. 'And here's my card,' he said, handing one of his cards of Helmut. 'Pradosh C Mitter, Private Investigator', it said.

*

Unfortunately, we couldn't get a jeep that day. The few there were had all been hired by American tourists for a day trip to Rumtek. We booked one for the next morning and spent the day walking around in the streets of Gangtok.

We ran into Mr Sarkar near the main market. 'We're going to Pemiangchi tomorrow,' Feluda told him. 'Would you like to join us?'

'Oh sure. Thanks!'

In the evening, he came to our room carrying a strange object. A small white bundle was tied at the end of a stick. 'I bet you can't guess what this is,' he said, beaming. 'This is actually used to get rid of leeches. This small bundle contains salt and tobacco. If a leech attaches itself to your foot, just rub it once with this stick and it's bound to drop off.'

'But how can a leech attack anyone through heavy leather

boots and nylon socks?'

'I don't know, but I've seen leeches slip through even very thick layers of clothes. The funny thing about leeches is that they can't see. Suppose a number of people were walking in a single file, no leech would attack the person at the head of the file. It would simply pick up the vibrations created by his movements. Then it would get ready to strike as the second person passed it by; and for the third, there would be no escape at all. He would definitely get bitten.'

We decided to take four similar sticks with us the next day.

'It's Buddha Purnima the day after tomorrow,' Feluda remarked as we were getting ready for bed. 'There will be a big celebration here.'

'Shall we get to see it?'

'I don't know. But if we can catch the man who killed Mr Shelvankar, that will make up for everything we miss seeing.'

The sky remained clear that night. I spent a long time looking at a moon that was nearly full. Kanchenjunga gleamed in its light.

The next day, the four of us left for Pemiangchi at five in the morning, with just a few essentials. Mr Sarkar did not forget the 'leech-proof' sticks.

Chapter 11

There were two routes to Pemiangchi. Unfortunately, we couldn't take the shorter one as the main road had been damaged. Taking the longer route meant spending at least eight hours on the journey. Pemiangchi was a hundred and twenty-seven miles away. But it couldn't be helped. Our hotel had given us packed lunches, and we had two flasks. One was full of hot coffee, the other had water. So there was no need for us to stop anywhere for lunch, which would have taken up a lot of time.

Helmut was carrying only one camera today. Mr Sarkar, I noticed, had packed a pair of galoshes. 'No point in taking risks,' he told me. 'This is cent per cent safe.'

'Cent per cent? What if a leech fell on your head from a tree?'

'No, that's not likely. That happens in July and August. Leeches are normally to be found on the ground at this time of the year.'

Mr Sarkar didn't know we were going in search of a criminal. He was therefore perfectly happy and relaxed.

We reached Singtham at a quarter past six. We had passed through this town on our way to Gangtok. A left turn brought us to the river Tista again. We crossed it and found ourselves on a road none of us knew. This led straight to Pemiangchi.

The jeep we were in wasn't new, but was in reasonably good condition. Its driver looked like a bandit from a Western film. He was dressed purely in black—the trousers, shirt and the leather jerkin he wore were all black. Even the cap on his head was dark enough to qualify as black. He was too tall to be a Nepali, but I couldn't figure out where he was from. Feluda asked him his name. 'Thondup,' he replied.

'That's a Tibetan name,' said Mr Sarkar, looking knowledgeable.

We drove in silence for about twenty kilometres. The next town on the way to Pemiangchi was Namchi. Just as we got close to it, a jeep behind us started blowing its horn loudly. Thondup made no attempt to let it pass.

'Why is he in such a hurry?' Feluda asked.

'No idea, sir. But if we let it go ahead, it'll only blow up clouds of dust.'

Thondup increased his speed. But the sound of the horn from the other jeep got more insistent. Mr Sarkar turned around irritably to see who it was. Then he exclaimed, 'Why, look, it's that same gentleman!'

'Who?' Feluda and I turned and saw, to our amazement, that Mr Bose was in the other jeep, still honking and waving madly.

'You'll have to stop for a minute, Thondupji,' Feluda said. 'That's a friend of ours.'

Thondup pulled up by the side of the road. Mr Bose came bounding out of the other jeep. 'Are you deaf or what?' he demanded. 'I yelled myself hoarse in Singtham, but none of you heard me!'

'Sorry, very sorry, Mr Bose. If we knew you were back, we wouldn't have left without you,' Feluda apologized.

'I could hardly stay on in Bombay after receiving your telegram. I've been following your jeep for miles.'

Thondup was absolutely right about the dust. Mr Bose was covered with it from head to foot, like an ash-smeared sadhubaba, thanks—no doubt—to the wheels of our own jeep.

93

'In your telegram you said you were suspicious about something. So where are you off to now? Why did you leave Gangtok?'

Instead of giving him a straight answer, Feluda asked, 'Do you have a lot of luggage?'

'No, just a suitcase.'

'In that case, why don't we move our own luggage into your jeep, and you can climb in with us? I'll fill you in.'

It took only a couple of minutes to transfer all the luggage. Mr Bose climbed in at the back with Mr Sarkar and Helmut, and we set off again. Feluda told Mr Bose briefly what had happened over the last two days. He even revealed that Helmut was Mr Shelvankar's son. Mr Bose frowned when Feluda finished. 'But who is this Dr Vaidya? He's bound to be a fraud. You should not have allowed him to get away, Mr Mitter. You could have—'

Feluda interrupted him. 'My suspicions fell on him when I learnt about Helmut's true identity. You are partly to blame, Mr Bose. You should have told us your partner's first wife was a German.'

'How was I to know that would matter? Besides, all I knew was that she was a foreigner. I had no idea about her nationality. Shelvankar married her about twenty-five years ago. Anyway, I just hope that Vaidya hasn't left Pemiangchi. Or our entire journey will come to nothing!'

*

We reached Namchi a little after ten. Here we stopped for a few minutes, to pour cold water into the engine, and hot coffee into ourselves. I could see clouds gathering in the sky, but wasn't unduly worried since I'd heard Namchi was considered by many to be the driest and cleanest place in Sikkim. Helmut was taking photographs, more out of habit than any real interest. He had hardly spoken since we left.

Now that Mr Sarkar had learnt the real reason for going to Pemiangchi, he seemed faintly uneasy; but the prospect of having an adventure was obviously just as appealing. 'With your cousin on one side, and the German Virendra on the other, I see no reason to worry,' he declared to me.

We left Namchi after ten minutes. The road went down from here, towards another river called Rangeet. This river was very different from the Tista. Its water was clear, with a greenish tinge, and it flowed with considerable force. Pools of foam formed where it struck against stones and rocks. I had never seen such a beautiful river in the hills. We had to cross another bridge and climb up the hill again to get to Pemiangchi, which was at a height of 9,000 feet.

As we wound our way up, I could see evidence of landslides almost everywhere. The thick green foliage on the hills had large gaps here and there. Great chunks of the hill had clearly slid down towards the river. Heaven knew how long it would take nature to repair the damage caused by these 'young mountains'!

We passed a gumpha on the way. Outside its entrance were a lot of flags strung from a thin rope, to ward off evil spirits. Each of them looked clean and fresh. 'Preparations for Buddha Purnima,' explained Mr Bose.

'When is it?' asked Feluda absent-mindedly.

'Buddha Purnima? Tomorrow, I think. On seventeenth April.'

'Seventeenth April . . . on the Indian calendar that would be the fourth of Baisakh . . . hmm . . . Baisakh . . . .'

I looked at Feluda in surprise. Why was he suddenly so concerned about dates? And why was he looking so grim? Why was he cracking his knuckles?

There was no opportunity to ask him. Our jeep had entered a forest. The road here had been badly damaged by the recent rains. Thondup crawled along with extreme care, despite which there were a few nasty bumps. One of these resulted in Mr Sarkar banging his head against the roof of the jeep. 'Bloody hell!' I heard him mutter.

The forest grew thicker and darker. Helmut pointed at a tall tree with dark green leaves and a light bark, and said, 'That's a birch. If you ever went to England, you'd get to see a lot of them.' There were trees on both sides. The road coiled upwards like a snake. It wasn't just dark inside the forest, but also much more damp. From somewhere came the sharp cry of a strange bird.

'Th-thrilling, isn't it?' said Mr Sarkar. Suddenly, without any warning, the trees cleared. We found ourselves in front of a hillock, under an overcast sky. A few moments later, the tiled roof of a bungalow came into view, followed by the whole building.

This was the famous Dak Bungalow of Pemiangchi. Built during British times, it stood at a spot that was truly out of this world. Rows and rows of peaks rose behind the bungalow, their colours ranging from lush green to a hazy blue.

Our jeep stopped outside the front door. The chowkidar came out. On being told who we were, he nodded and confirmed that rooms had been booked for us.

'Is there anyone else staying here?' asked Mr Bose.

'No, sir. The bungalow's empty.'

'Empty? Why, did no one come here before us?' Feluda asked anxiously.

'Yes, but he left last night. A man with a beard, and he wore dark glasses.'

Chapter 12

The chowkidar's words appeared to disappoint Helmut the most. He sat down on the grass outside, placing his camera beside him.

Mr Bose said, 'Well, there's nothing we can do immediately, can we? Let's have lunch. I'm starving.'

We went into the bungalow carrying our luggage. It was obvious that the bungalow had been built several decades ago. The wooden floor and ceiling, the wide verandas with wooden railings and old-fashioned furniture all bore evidence of an era gone by. The view from the veranda was breathtaking. If the sky wasn't cloudy, we would have been able to see Kanchenjunga, which was twenty-two miles away. There was no noise anywhere except the chirping of birds.

We crossed the veranda and went into the dining hall. Mr Bose found an easy chair and took it. He said to Feluda, 'I wasn't too sure about Vaidya before, although you did tell me you had your suspicions. But now I'm convinced he's our man. SS should never have shown him such a valuable object as that statue.'

Helmut had risen to his feet, but hadn't joined us. I could see him pacing in the veranda outside. Mr Sarkar went inside, possibly to look for a bathroom. Feluda began to inspect the other rooms in the bungalow. I sat quietly in the dining hall, feeling most depressed. Was our journey really going to turn out to be a complete waste to time?

There were two doors on one side, leading to two bedrooms. Feluda came out of one of these with a walking-stick in his hand. 'Dr Vaidya most certainly visited this place,' Feluda said, 'and he left this stick to prove it. How very strange!' Feluda's voice sounded different. I looked up quickly, but said nothing. Mr Sarkar returned, wiping his face with a handkerchief. 'What a weird place!' he exclaimed, taking the chair next to mine, yawning noisily. Feluda did not sit down. He stood before the fireplace, tapping the stick softly on the ground. His mouth was set in a grim line.

'Mr Sarkar!' called Mr Bose. 'Where are those packed lunches your hotel gave you? Let's eat.'

'No!' said Feluda, his voice sounding cold and remote. 'This is not the time to eat.'

Mr Sarkar had started to rise. He flopped back in his chair at Feluda's words. Mr Bose and I both looked at him in surprise. But Feluda's face remained without expression.

Then he sat down, lit a Charminar and inhaled deeply. 'Mr Bose,' he said conversationally, 'you know someone in Ghatshila, you said. Isn't that where you were before you caught a flight from Calcutta?'

'Yes. A nephew of mine got married.'

'You are a Hindu, aren't you, Mr Bose?'

'Why? What do you mean?'

'You heard me. What are you? A Hindu, or a Muslim, or a Christian, or what?'

'How does that—?'

'Just tell me.'

'I'm a Hindu, of course.'

'Hm.' Feluda blew out two smoke rings. One of them wafted towards Mr Bose, getting larger and larger, until it disappeared in front of his face.

'But—' Feluda frowned, 'you and I travelled together in

the same plane. You had just got back from Ghatshila, hadn't you?'

'Yes, but why is that causing you such concern? I can't understand this at all, Mr Mitter. What has my nephew's wedding in Ghatshila got to do with anything?'

'It has plenty to do with things, Mr Bose. Traditionally, no Hindu would get married in the month of Chaitra. We left Calcutta on 14 April, which was the first of Baisakh. Your nephew's wedding took place before that, so it must have been in the preceding month, which was Chaitra. How did you allow this to happen?'

Mr Bose was in the middle of lighting a cigarette. He stopped, his hands shaking a little. 'What are you implying, Mr Mitter? Just what are you trying to say?'

Feluda looked steadily at Mr Bose, without giving him an immediate answer. Then he said, slowly and deliberately, 'I am implying a lot of things, Mr Bose. To start with, you are a liar. You never went to Ghatshila. Secondly, you betrayed someone's trust—'

'What the hell is that supposed to mean?' Mr Bose shouted.

'We have all heard how depressed Mr Shelvankar had been before he died. He had even mentioned it to Helmut, though he did not specify the reason. It is easy enough to get totally broken in spirit if one is betrayed by a person one has trusted implicitly. I believe you were that person. You were his partner, weren't you? Mr Shelvankar was a simple, straightforward man. You took full advantage of this and cheated him endlessly. But one day, he came to know of what you'd done. When you realized this, you decided to get him out of the way forever. That wasn't possible in Bombay, so you had to wait until he came to Sikkim. You were not supposed to be here. But you came—possibly the next day—disguised as Dr Vaidya. Yes, *you* were Dr Vaidya! You met Shelvankar and impressed him a great deal by telling him a few things about his life that you knew already. Then you told him about the possibility of finding Virendra in a gumpha, and left with him that morning in the same jeep. On the way, you hit his head with this heavy stick. This made him unconscious, but he did not die. You went ahead with your plan, and had the jeep pushed into the gorge. The driver had, no doubt, been bribed; that must have been easy enough to do. Then you threw that stone from the hill, using the same heavy stick to dislodge it from the ground. In spite of all this, Mr Shelvankar remained alive for a few hours, long enough to mention your name. Perhaps he had recognized you at the last minute.'

'Nonsense! What utter rubbish are you talking, Mr Mitter?' shouted Mr Bose. 'Where is the proof that I am Dr Vaidya?'

In reply, Feluda asked him a strange question. 'Where is your ring, Mr Bose?'

'My ring?'

'Yes, the one with "Ma" engraved on it. There's a white mark on your finger, but you're not wearing your ring. Where did it go?'

'Oh, that . . .' Mr Bose swallowed. 'I took it off because . . . because it felt too tight.' He took the ring out of his pocket to show us he still had it with him.

'When you changed your make-up and your costume, you forgot to put it back on. I had noticed that mark that evening when you were supposed to be talking to the departed soul of Shelvankar. I found it odd then, but did not pay enough attention at the time.'

Mr Bose began to rise, but Feluda's voice rang out again, cold as steel, 'Don't try to move, Mr Bose. I haven't finished.' Mr Bose quickly sat down again, and began wiping his face. Feluda continued, 'The day after Mr Shelvankar died, Dr Vaidya said he was going to Kalimpong. He didn't. He shed his disguise, became Sasadhar Bose and returned to Calcutta. He had already sent a telegram to Shelvankar saying "Arriving Fourteenth". This upset him very much since Mr Bose wasn't supposed to be in Sikkim at all. Anyway, he came here on the fourteenth just to create an alibi for himself. Then he pretended to be greatly distressed by his partner's death and said he would go back to Bombay the next day. Again, he didn't. He remained in hiding somewhere near Gangtok. He returned as Dr Vaidya just to add to the confusion, and pretend he could speak to the dead. But by then he had come to know that I was a detective. So he tried to remove me from the scene, too, by throwing another boulder at me. He must have seen me walking towards Nathula Road, and had probably guessed what I was going to do. And it was he who had followed us to Rumtek—' Feluda was interrupted suddenly by a highpitched wail. To my surprise, I discovered it was coming from Mr Sarkar.

'All right, Mr Sarkar,' said Feluda. 'Out with it! And I want the truth. Why did you go to the spot where the murder had taken place?'

Mr Sarkar raised his hands as though someone had shouted, 'Hands up!' Then he croaked, 'I d-didn't know, you see, how val-valuable that statue was. When they t-told me—'

'Was it you who went to the Tibetan Institute?'

'Yes. They s-said it was totally unique. So I th-thought—'

'So you thought there was no harm in stealing from a dead man if the statue was still lying at the accident site? Especially when it had once belonged to you?'

'Y-yes, something like th-that.'

'But didn't you see anyone at that particular spot?'

'No, sir.'

'All right. But it appears that someone did see you and was afraid that you had seen *him*. Hence the threats you received.'

'Yes, that explains it.'

'Where's the statue?'

'Statue? But I didn't find it!'

'What? You—?' Feluda was interrupted again, this time by Mr Bose. He jumped to his feet, overturning his chair, and rushed out of the room. Helmut, who was standing at the door, was knocked down by him. Since there was only one door that led to the veranda outside, and this exit was blocked for a few moments by Helmut, who had fallen to the ground, we were delayed by about ten seconds.

By the time all of us could get out, Mr Bose had climbed back into his jeep, and its engine had already roared into life. No doubt his driver had been warned and prepared for such an eventuality. His jeep made a quick about turn and began moving towards the forest. Without a word, Thondup, who was standing by our own jeep, threw himself back in it and started the engine, assuming we would want to follow Mr Bose. As it turned out, however, there was no need to do that. Feluda took out his revolver from his pocket and fired at the rear wheels of Mr Bose's jeep. The tyres burst instantly, making the jeep tilt to one side, run into a tree, and finally come to a halt. Mr Bose jumped out, and vanished among the trees. His driver came out, too, clutching the starting handle of his jeep. Feluda ignored him completely. He ran after Mr Bose, with Helmut, Mr Sarkar and me right behind him. Out of the corner of my eye, I saw Thondup pick up his own starting handle and move forward steadily, to deal with the other driver.

The four of us shot off in different directions to look for Mr Bose. I heard Helmut call out to us about ten minutes later. By the time I found him, Feluda and Mr Sarkar had joined him already. Mr Bose was standing under a large tree a few feet away. No, he wasn't just standing. He was actually hopping around, stamping his feet and wriggling in what appeared to be absolute agony.

The reason became clear as we got closer to him. He had been attacked by leeches. At least two hundred of them were clinging to his body, some on his legs, others on his neck, shoulders and elbows. Helmut pointed at a thick root that ran across the ground near the tree. Obviously, Mr Bose had stumbled against it and fallen flat on the ground.

Feluda caught him by his collar and pulled him out in the

open. 'Get those sticks with the bundles of salt and tobacco,' he said to me. 'Quick!'

*

We had finished eating, and were sitting on the veranda of the Dak Bungalow. Helmut was taking photographs of orchids. Thondup had gone and informed the police in the nearest town. Mr Bose had been handed over to them. The statue of Yamantak had been found amongst his belongings. He had forgotten to take it from Mr Shelvankar on the day of the murder. He went back later to look for it where the jeep had fallen, and found it behind a bush. As he was climbing up the hill, he saw Mr Sarkar going down, with the same purpose in mind. Fearing that he might have been seen, he started threatening and frightening Mr Sarkar.

It also turned out that Mr Bose had an accomplice in Bombay, with whom he had stayed in touch. It was this man who had answered Feluda's call, received his telegram and informed Mr Bose in Gangtok.

Having explained these details, Feluda turned to Mr Sarkar. 'You are a small time crook yourself, aren't you? You're lucky you couldn't retrieve that statue. If you had, we'd have had to find a suitable punishment for you.'

'I've been punished adequately, believe me!' Mr Sarkar said, looking profusely apologetic. 'I found as many as three leeches in one of my socks. They must have drunk gallons of my blood. I feel quite weak, as a matter of fact.'

'I see. Anyway, I hope you'll have the sense not sell anything else that belonged to your grandfather. And look, here's your button.'

I noticed for the first time that the last button on Mr Sarkar's shirt was missing. Mr Sarkar took the button from Feluda and, after a long time, smiled his old smile.

'Th-thanks,' he said.

The Anubis Mystery

'Who rang you, Feluda?' I asked, realizing instantly that I shouldn't have, for Feluda was doing yoga. He never spoke until he had finished every exercise, including sheershasan. He had started this about six months ago. The result was already noticeable. Feluda seemed a lot fitter, and openly admitted that yoga had done him a world of good.

I glanced at the clock. Feluda's reply came seven and a half minutes later. 'You don't know him,' he said, rising from the floor. Really, Feluda could be most annoying at times. So what if I didn't know the man? He could tell me his name, surely?

'Do *you* know him?' I asked impatiently. Feluda began chewing chick-peas which had been soaked overnight. This was a part of his keep-fit programme.

'I didn't know him before,' he replied, 'but I do now.'

Our Puja holidays had started a few days ago. Baba had gone to Jamshedpur on tour. Only Ma, Feluda and I were at home. We didn't plan to go out of town this time. I didn't mind staying at home as long as I could be with Feluda. He had become quite well-known as an amateur detective. So it shouldn't be surprising at all, I thought, if he got involved in another case. My only fear was that he might one day refuse to take me with him. But that hadn't happened so far. Perhaps there was an advantage in being seen with a young boy. No one could guess easily that he was an investigator, if we travelled together.

'I bet you're dying to know who made that phone call,' Feluda added. This was an old technique. If he knew I was anxious for information, he never came to the point without beating about the bush and creating a lot of suspense. I tried to be casual. 'Well, if that phone call had anything to do with a mystery, naturally I'd be interested,' I said lightly.

Feluda slipped on a striped shirt. 'The man's called Nilmoni Sanyal,' he finally revealed. 'He lives on Roland Road, and wants to see me urgently. He didn't tell me why, but he sounded sort of nervous.'

'When do you have to go?'

'I told him I'd be there by nine. It's going to take us at least ten minutes by taxi, so let's go!'

*

On our way to Roland Road, I said to Feluda, 'But suppose this Mr Sanyal is a crook? Suppose he's called you over to his house only to cause you some harm? You've never met him before, have you?'

'No,' said Feluda, looking out of the window. 'There is always a risk in going out on a case like this. But mind you, if his sole intention was to cause me bodily harm, he wouldn't invite me to his house. It would be far more risky for *him* if the police came to know. A hired goonda could do the job much more simply.'

Last year, Feluda had won the first prize in the All India Rifle Competition. It was amazing how accurate his aim had become after only three months of practice. Now he possessed a revolver, although he didn't carry it in his pocket all the time, unlike detectives in books.

'Do you know what Mr Sanyal does for a living?' I asked.

108

'No. All I know about the man is that he takes paan, is probably slightly deaf and tends to say "Er..." before starting a sentence.' I asked no more questions after this.

We soon reached Nilmoni Sanyal's house. The meter showed one rupee and seventy paisa. Feluda gave a two-rupee note to the driver and made a gesture indicating he could keep the change. We climbed out of the taxi and walked up to the front door. Feluda pressed the bell. The house had two storeys. It didn't appear to be very old. There was a front garden, but it looked a bit unkempt and neglected. A man who was probably the chowkidar opened the door and took Feluda's card from him. We were then ushered into the living room. I was surprised to see how well-furnished it was. It was obvious that a lot of money had been spent on acquiring the furniture and paintings, flower vases, and old artefacts displayed in a glass case. Someone had arranged these with a great deal of care.

Mr Sanyal entered the room a few minutes later. He was wearing a loose kurta over what must have been his sleeping-suit pyjamas. His fingers were loaded with rings. He was of medium height, clean-shaven and looked as if he had been sleeping. I tried to guess his age. He didn't seem to be more than fifty. 'You are Mr Pradosh Mitter?' he asked. 'I had no idea you were so young.' Feluda smiled politely. Then he pointed at me and said, 'This is my cousin. He's a very intelligent boy, but if you'd rather speak to me alone, I can send him out.'

I cast an anxious glance at Mr Sanyal, but he said, 'No, no, I don't mind at all. Er... would you like some tea or coffee?'

'No, thanks.'

'Very well then, allow me to tell you why I asked you to come here. But before I do so, I think I ought to tell you something about myself. I'm sure you've already noticed that I am reasonably wealthy, and am fond of antiques and other beautiful things. What you may find difficult to believe is that I wasn't born rich. I did not inherit any money; nor have I got a job, or a business.'

Nilmoni Babu stopped, and looked at us expectantly.

'Lottery?' said Feluda.

'Pardon?'

'I said, did you win a lottery?'

'Exactly, exactly!' Nilmoni Babu shouted like an excited child. 'I won two hundred and fifty thousand rupees in the Rangers Lottery eleven years ago. I have managed—pretty well, I must admit—all these years on the strength of that. I built this house eight years ago. Now you may wonder how I fill my time, do I not have an occupation at all? The thing is, you see, I have only one main occupation. I spend most of my time going to auction houses and buying the kind of things this room is filled with.' He waved his arms about to indicate what he meant. Then he continued, 'What happened recently may not have a direct connection with these objects of art in my collection, but I cannot be sure about that. Look—' he took out a few pieces of paper from his pocket and spread them out. There were three pieces in all, with something scribbled on them. A closer look showed me that instead of words, there were rows of little pictures. Some of them I could recognize—there were pictures of owls, snakes, the sun and the human eye. Others were more difficult to figure out. But the whole thing seemed familiar somehow. Where had I seen something like this before? In a book?

'These look like hieroglyphics,' said Feluda.

'What?' Nilmoni Babu sounded amazed.

'The form of writing used in ancient Egypt. That's what it looks like.'

'Really?'

'Yes, but it is extremely doubtful that we can find someone in Calcutta who might be able to tell us what it means.'

Nilmoni Babu's face fell. 'In that case, what shall I do? Someone has been mailing a note like that to me fairly regularly over the last few days. If I cannot have these read or decoded, it's going to be really worrying . . . what if these are warnings? What if it's someone threatening to kill me?'

Feluda thought for a while. Then he said, 'Is there anything from Egypt in your collection?'

Nilmoni Babu smiled slightly. 'I wouldn't know, and that's the truth. I bought these things only because they were beautiful, rare and expensive. I have very little idea of where they originally came from before they reached the auction house.'

'But all these things appear to be perfectly genuine. No body'll believe you're not a true connoisseur!'

'Er . . . that is simple enough. Most auction houses do their homework properly and have every item valued by an expert. So if something is expensive, you can safely assume that it is genuine. My greatest pleasure lies in outbidding my rivals, and why not, since I do have the means? If, in the process, I happen to collect something really valuable, so much the better.'

'But you wouldn't know if any of this stuff is Egyptian?'

Nilmoni Babu rose and walked over to the glass case. He brought out a statuette from the top shelf and gave it to Feluda. It was about six inches long. Made of some strange green stone, it was studded with several other colourful stones. What was most striking was that although its body had a human shape, its head was that of a jackal.

'I bought this only ten days ago at an auction. Could this be Egyptian?'

Feluda glanced briefly at the statuette, and said, 'Anubis.'

'Pardon?'

'Anubis. The Ancient Egyptian god of the dead. It's a beautiful piece.'

'But,' Nilmoni Babu sounded apprehensive, 'do you think there's a connection between this . . . this Anubis and those notes I've been receiving? Did I make a mistake by buying it? Is someone threatening to snatch it away from me?'

Feluda shook his head, returning the statuette to Nilmoni Babu. 'That is difficult to say. When did the first letter arrive?'

'Last Monday.'

'You mean just after you bought it?'

'Yes.'

'Did you keep the envelopes?'

'No, I'm afraid not. Perhaps I should have kept them, but they were ordinary envelopes and the address was typewritten. The post mark said Elgin Road. That I did notice.'

'All right,' Feluda rose. 'I don't think we need do anything right now. But just to be on the safe side, I suggest you keep that statue somewhere else. Someone I know got burgled recently. Let's not take any chances.'

We came out of the living room and stood on the landing. 'Can you think of anyone who might wish to play a practical joke on you?' Feluda wanted to know.

Nilmoni Babu shook his head. 'No. I've lost touch with all my friends.'

'What about enemies?'

'Well . . . most wealthy people have enemies, but of course it's difficult to identify them. Everybody behaves so well in my presence. What they might do behind my back, I cannot tell.'

'Didn't you say you bought that piece at an auction?'

'Yes. At Aratoon Brothers.'

'Was anyone else interested in it?'

Nilmoni Babu suddenly grew agitated at this question. 'Mr Mitter,' he said excitedly, 'you have just opened a whole new aspect to this case. You see, I have a particular rival with whom I clash at most auctions. He was bidding for this Anubis, too.'

'Who is he?'

'A man called Pratul Datta.'

'What does he do?'

'I think he was a lawyer. Now he's retired. He and I were the only ones bidding for that statue. He stopped when I said twelve thousand. When I was getting into my car afterwards,

I happened to catch his eye. I did not like the look in it, I can tell you!'

'I see.'

By this time, we had come out of the house and were walking towards the gate.

'Do a lot of people live in this house?' Feluda asked.

'Oh no. I am quite alone in this world. I live here with my driver, mali and two old and trusted servants, that's all.'

'Isn't there a small child in this house?' Feluda asked totally unexpectedly.

Nilmoni Babu stared for a few seconds, then burst out laughing. 'Just look at me! I forgot all about my nephew. Actually, I was thinking only of adults in this house. Yes, my nephew Jhuntu happens to be visiting me. His parents are away in Japan. His father runs a business. Jhuntu has been left in my charge. But the poor child has been suffering from influenza ever since he arrived. But what made you think there might be a child in my house?'

'I noticed a kite peeping out from behind a cupboard in your living room.'

A taxi arrived for us at this moment, crunching gravel under its tyres. It was thoughtful of Nilmoni Babu to have sent his servant out to fetch it. 'Thank you,' said Feluda, as we got in. 'Please let me know if anything suspicious occurs. But at this moment there's nothing to be done.'

On our way back, I said, 'There's something rather sinister about that statue of Anubis, isn't there?'

'If you replace a human head with the head of an animal, any statue would look sinister.'

'It's dangerous to keep statues of old Egyptian gods and goddesses.'

'Who told you that?'

'Why, you did! A long time ago.'

'No, never. All I told you was that some of the archaeologists who dug up old Egyptian statues ran into a lot of trouble afterwards.'

'Yes, yes, I remember now . . . there was a British gentleman, wasn't there . . . what was his name?'

'Lord Carnarvon.'

'And his dog?'

'The dog wasn't with him. Lord Carnarvon was in Egypt. His dog was in England. Soon after he helped dig the tomb of Tutankhamen, he fell ill and died. It was discovered later that his dog, who was thousands of miles away, died mysteriously at the same time as his master. He had been in perfect health, and no one could ever figure out the cause of his death.'

Any mention of Egypt always reminded me of this strange story I had heard from Feluda. That figure of Anubis might well have come from the tomb of some Egyptian pharaoh. Didn't Nilmoni Babu realize this? Why did he have to take such a big risk?

*

At a quarter to six the next morning, the phone rang just as I heard our newspaper land on our balcony with a thud. I picked up the receiver quickly and said 'hello', but before I could hear anything from the other side, Feluda rushed in and snatched it from me. I heard him say, 'I see' three times, then he said, 'Yes, all right,' and put the phone down.

'Anubis disappeared last night,' he told me, his voice sounding hoarse. 'We've got to go there, at once!'

Since there was a lot less traffic so early in the morning, it took us only seven minutes to reach Nilmoni Babu's house. He was waiting for us outside his gate, looking thoroughly bemused. 'What a nightmare I've been through!' he exclaimed as we jumped out of our taxi. 'I've never had such a horrible experience.'

We went into the living room. Nilmoni Babu sank into a sofa before either of us could sit down, and showed us his wrists. It was obvious that his hands had been tied. The rope had left red marks on his skin.

'Tell me what happened,' said Feluda.

Nilmoni Babu took a deep breath and began, 'I took your advice and kept that Egyptian statue with me last night, right under my pillow. Now I feel it might have been simpler if I'd left it where it was. At least I might have been spared this physical pain. Anyway, I was sleeping peacefully enough, when suddenly I woke—no, I couldn't tell you the time—feeling quite breathless. I realized instantly that I had been gagged. I tried to resist my assailant with my arms, but he was far too strong for me. He tied my hands behind my back, took the statue of Anubis from under my pillow and disappeared—in just a few minutes! I didn't get to see his face at all.' Nilmoni Babu stopped for breath. After a brief pause, he resumed, 'When my bearer came in with my morning tea, he found me in my room, my hands still tied behind my back, my mouth gagged. By that time I had pins and needles all over my body. Anyway, he untied me, and I rang you immediately.'

Feluda heard him in silence, looking rather grim. Then he said, 'I'd like to inspect your bedroom, and then take some photographs of your house, if I may.' Photography was another passion he had developed recently.

Nilmoni Babu took us upstairs to see his bedroom. 'What!' exclaimed Feluda the minute he stepped into the room. 'You didn't put grills on your window?'

'No, I'm afraid not,' Nilmoni Babu shook his head regretfully. 'This house was built on the same pattern as foreign bungalows. So the windows were left without grills. And sadly, I have never been able to sleep with the windows closed.' Feluda took a quick look out of the window and said, 'It must have been very simple. There's a parapet, and a pipe. Any able-bodied man could climb into the room with perfect ease.'

Feluda took out his camera and began taking pictures. Then he said, 'Many I see the rest of your house?'

'Yes, of course.' Nilmoni Babu took us to the next room.

Here we found a bundle lying on the bed, completely wrapped in a blanket. A small boy's face emerged as he removed part of the blanket and peered at us through eyes that seemed unnaturally large. The boy was obviously unwell.

'This is my nephew, Jhuntu,' said Nilmoni Babu. 'I had to call Dr Bose last night. He gave him a sleeping pill. So Jhuntu slept right through, without seeing or hearing anything at all.'

We glanced briefly into the other rooms on the first and the ground floor, and then we came down to look at the garden and its surrounding areas. There were three flower-pots just below the window of Nilmoni Babu's bedroom. Feluda began peering into these. The first two yielded nothing. In the third, he found an empty tin. 'Does anyone in this house take snuff?' he asked, lifting its lid. Nilmoni Babu shook his head. Feluda put the tin away in his pocket.

'Look, Mr Mitter,' said Nilmoni Babu, sounding openly desperate, 'I don't mind losing that statue so much. Maybe one day I'll be able to buy another. But what I can't stand is that an intruder should get into my house so easily and subject me to such . . . such . . . trauma! You've *got* to do something about this. If you can catch the thief I'll . . . I'll . . . give you . . . I mean . . . .'

'A reward?'

'Yes, yes!'

'Thank you, Mr Sanyal, that is very kind of you. But I was going to make further investigations, anyway, not because I expected to be rewarded, but because I find this case both interesting and challenging.' Now he was talking like famous detectives in well-known crime stories. I felt very pleased.

After this, Feluda spent the next ten minutes talking to Nilmoni Babu's driver, Govind, his servants (Nandalal and Panchu) and his mali, Natabar. Sadly, none of them could tell us anything useful. The only outsider who had come to the house, they said, was Dr Bose. He had come at around 9 p.m. to see Jhuntu. After he had gone, Nilmoni Babu had gone out to buy some medicines from the local chemist. That was all.

We left soon after this. On our way back, I suddenly noticed that our taxi was not going in the direction of home. Where was Feluda taking me? But he was looking so grave that I didn't dare ask him.

Our taxi stopped outside a shop in Free School Street. 'Aratoon Brothers—Auctioneers', said its signboard, each letter painted in gleaming silver. I had never seen an auction house before. The sight of this one astounded me. Who knew so many different things could be collected under one roof? Somewhere among these various objects, Nilmoni Sanyal had found his Anubis. Feluda finished his work in just two minutes. The auction house gave him Pratul Datta's address—7/1 Lovelock Street. Were we going to go there now? No, Feluda told the driver to take us home.

When we sat down to have lunch later in the afternoon, I was still trying to work things out, and getting nowhere. Please God, I prayed silently, let Feluda find a clue or something, so that he had something concrete to work on. Otherwise, he might well have to accept defeat, which I would find totally unbearable.

'What next, Feluda?' I asked him.

'Fish curry,' he replied, mixing his rice with dal, 'and then I shall have vegetables, followed by chutney and dahi.'

'And then?'

'Then I shall wash my hands, rinse my mouth and have a paan.'

'After that?'

'I shall make a phone call and then I intend having a siesta.'

I saw no point in asking anything further. All I could do was wait patiently for him to make the phone call. I knew he would call Pratul Datta, so I had already taken his number from the directory.

When Feluda finally made the call, I could hear only his side of the conversation. This is how it went:

Feluda (changing his voice and sounding like an old man):

Hello, I am speaking from Naktola.

. . . .

'My name is Joynarayan Bagchi. I am interested in antiques and ancient arts. In fact, I am writing a book on this subject.'

. . . .

'Yes. Yes, I've heard of your collection, you see. So I wondered if I might go and see what you've got?'

. . . .

'No, no, of course not!'

'Yes, thank you. Thank you very much indeed!'

Feluda put the receiver down and turned to me. 'He's having his house whitewashed, so he's had to move things around. But he's agreed to let us have a look this evening.'

'But,' I couldn't help asking, 'if he's really stolen the statue of Anubis, he's not going to show it to us, is he?'

'I don't know. If he's an idiot like you, he may. However, I am not going to visit him just to look for a stolen object. I simply want to meet the man.'

True to his word, Feluda went to his room after this to have a nap. He had this wonderful knack of catching a few minutes sleep whenever necessary. Apparently, Napoleon had had this knack, too. He could go to sleep even on horseback, and wake a few moments later, much refreshed. Or so I had heard. I decided to pass the afternoon by leafing through one of Feluda's books on Egyptian art. Only a few minutes later, however, the phone rang. I ran to the living room to answer it.

'Hello!' I said.

There was no immediate response from the other side, though I could make out that there was someone holding a receiver to his ear. I began to feel uneasy. 'Can I speak to Pradosh Mitter?' asked a harsh voice after a few moments.

'He is resting,' I replied, swallowing once. 'May I know who's calling?'

The man fell silent again. Then he said, 'All right. Just tell him that the Egyptian god is where he should be. Mr Mitter needn't concern himself with the movements of Anubis. If he continues to meddle in this matter, the consequences may well be disastrous.' With a click, the line went dead.

I sat foolishly—heaven knows for how long—still holding the receiver in my hand. I finally had the sense to replace it only when Feluda walked into the room. 'Who was on the phone?' he asked. I repeated what I had been told by the strange voice. Feluda frowned and clicked his tongue in annoyance.

'You should have called me.'

'How could I? You always get cross if I disturb your siesta.'

'Hm. What did this man's voice sound like?'

'Harsh and gruff.'

'I see. Anyway, it's time now to get ready for Pratul Datta. I was beginning to see light, but now things have got complicated again.'

*

We got out of a taxi in front of Pratul Datta's house at five minutes to six that evening. We were both dressed for our parts—so cleverly disguised that I bet even Baba could not have recognized us. Feluda looked like an old man, about sixty years of age, sporting a wide moustache (liberally sprinkled with grey), thick glasses perched on his nose. He was wearing a black jacket with a high neck, a white dhoti, long socks and brown tennis shoes. It took him about half-an-hour to get ready. Then he called me to his room and said, 'I have a few things for you. Put these on quickly.'

'What! Do *I* have to wear make-up as well?'

'Of course.' In two minutes, I had a wig on to cover my real hair and, like Feluda, a pair of glasses to hide my eyes. Then he took out an eyebrow pencil and worked on my neatly trimmed side-burns until they began to look untidy and overgrown. Finally, he said, 'You are my nephew. Your name is Subodh. Your only aim in life is to keep your mouth shut. Just remember that.'

We found Pratul Datta sitting in the veranda as we went in through the gate. His house must have been built thirty years ago, but the walls and doors and windows were gleaming after a new coat of paint.

Feluda bowed, his hands folded in a 'namaskar', and said in his thin, old-man voice, 'Excuse me, are you Mr Pratul Datta?'

'Yes,' Mr Datta replied without smiling.

'I am Joynarayan Bagchi, and this is my nephew Subodh.'

'Why have you brought him? You said nothing about a nephew on the phone!'

'N-no, but you see, he's recently started to paint and is very interested in art, so . . . .' Mr Datta said nothing more. He rose to his feet.

'I don't mind you looking at things. But I'd had to put everything away because of the whitewashing; and now every little piece has had to be dragged out. That wasn't easy, I can tell you. As it is, I've been going berserk with the workmen pushing and shoving all my furniture all day. The smell of paint makes me sick. I'll be glad when the whole thing's over. Anyway, come inside, please.'

I didn't like the brusque way in which he spoke, but once inside his drawing room on the first floor, my mouth fell open in amazement. His collection seemed larger than Nilmoni Babu's.

'You seemed to have gathered a lot of things from Egypt,' remarked Feluda.

'Yes. I bought some of these in Cairo. Others were bought locally.'

'Look, Subodh, my boy,' Feluda said, laying a hand on my back and giving me a sharp pinch quite unobtrusively, 'See all these animals? The Egyptians used to worship these as gods. This owl here, and that hawk over there—even these birds were gods for them.'

Mr Datta sat down on a sofa and lit a cheroot. I don't know what possessed me, but I suddenly found myself saying, 'Uncle, didn't they have a god that looked like a jackal?'

Mr Datta choked. 'This cheroot,' he said after a while, still coughing. 'You can't get good quality stuff any more. It never used to be so strong.'

Feluda ignored this remark. 'Heh heh,' he said in his thin voice, 'my nephew is talking of Anubis. I told him about Anubis only last night.'

Mr Datta flared up unexpectedly. 'Anubis? Ha! Stupid fool!'

Feluda stared at him through his glasses. 'I don't understand,' he complained. 'Why are you calling an ancient Egyptian god a stupid fool?'

'No, no, not Anubis. It's that man. I've seen him before at auctions. *He* is an idiot. His bidding makes no sense at all. There was a lovely statue, you see. But he quoted a figure so absurdly high that I had to withdraw. God knows where he gets that kind of money from.'

Feluda said nothing in reply. He glanced around the room once more, then said 'namaskar' again. 'Thank you very much,' he added, moving towards the door through which we had come. 'It was really very kind of you. It's given me a great deal of pleasure, and my nephew . . . heh heh . . . has learnt a lot.' On our way downstairs, Feluda asked one more question, very casually. 'Do you live alone in this house?'

'No,' came the reply. 'I live here with my wife. I have a son, but he doesn't live here.'

We came out of Mr Datta's house and began walking, in the hope of finding a taxi. It was remarkably quiet outside, although it was not even 7 p.m. There was no one in sight except two small boys who were out begging. One of them was singing Shyamasangeet; the other was playing a khanjani. As they came closer, Feluda began humming the same words:

> Help me, Mother
>   for I have no one
>   to turn to . . .

A few minutes later, we reached Ballygunj Circular Road and spotted an empty taxi. Feluda stopped singing and shouted, 'Taxi!' so loudly that it screeched to a halt almost immediately. As we got in, I caught the driver give Feluda a puzzled look. He was probably wondering how a shrivelled old man like him could possibly have such powerful lungs!

*

When the phone rang the next morning, I was brushing my teeth. So it was Feluda who answered it. When I came out of the bathroom, he told me that Nilmoni Babu had just called to say that Pratul Datta's house had been burgled last night. All the cash had been left untouched. What was missing was a number of old and precious statues and other objects of art, the total value of which would be in the region of fifty thousand rupees. The theft had been reported by the press, and the police had started their investigations.

By the time we reached Pratul Datta's house, it was past 7 o'clock. Needless to say, this time we went without wearing any make-up. Just as we stepped in, a man of rather generous proportions, wearing a policeman's uniform, emerged from the house. It turned out that he knew Feluda. 'Good morning, Felu babu,' he greeted us, grinning broadly and thumping Feluda on the back, 'I can see that it didn't take you long to find your way here!'

Feluda smiled politely, 'Well, I had to come, you see, since it's my job.'

'No, don't say it's your job. The job is ours. For you, it's no more than a pastime, isn't it?'

Feluda chose to ignore this. He said instead, 'Have you

been able to work anything out? Is it simply a case of burglary?'

'Yes, yes, what else could it be? But Mr Datta is very upset. He told us something about an old man and his nephew who came to visit him yesterday. He thinks they're responsible.'

My throat suddenly felt dry. Perhaps Feluda had been a bit too reckless this time. What if—? But Feluda remained quite unperturbed. 'Well then, all you need to do is catch this old man and his nephew. Simple!' he said.

'Well said!' returned the plump police officer. 'That's exactly the kind of remark an amateur detective in a novel might have made.'

'Can we go into the house?' Feluda asked, determined not to take any notice of the jibes made by the officer.

'Yes, yes, go ahead.'

Pratul Datta was sitting on the same veranda. But he was clearly far too preoccupied to pay any attention to us. 'Do you want to see the room where all the action took place?' asked our friend from the police.

'Yes, please.'

We were taken to the drawing room upstairs. Feluda went straight to the balcony and leant over its railing. 'Look, there's a pipe. So gaining access was not a problem at all.'

'True. In any case, the door couldn't be closed because the paint was still wet. So really it was something like an open invitation.'

'What time did this happen?'

'At 9.45 p.m.'

'Who was the first to realize—?'

'There is an old servant. He was making the bed in that other room over there. He heard a noise, apparently, and came here to have a look. The room was totally dark. But someone knocked him out even before he could switch on the light. By the time he recovered sufficiently to raise an alarm, the thief had vanished.'

Feluda frowned. I had come to recognize this frown pretty

123

well. It usually meant a new idea had occurred to him. 'I'd like to speak to this servant,' he said crisply.

'Very well.'

Mr Datta's servant was called Bangshalochan. He still appeared to be in a state of shock. 'Where does it hurt?' Feluda asked him, for he was obviously in pain.

'In the stomach,' he croaked.

'Stomach? The thief hit you in the stomach?'

'Yes, sir. And what a powerful blow it was—I felt as though a bomb had come and hit my body. Then everything went dark.'

'When did you hear the noise? What were you doing?'

'I couldn't tell you the exact time, Babu. I was making the bed in Ma's room. She was in the next room, doing her puja. There were two beggar boys singing in the street. Ma told me to give them some money. I was about to go, when there was a strange noise in this room. It sounded as though something heavy was knocked over. So I came to see what was going on, and . . .' Bangshalochan couldn't say anything more. It seemed that the thief had broken into the house only a couple of hours after we'd gone. Feluda said, 'Thank you' both to Bangshalochan and the officer, and we left.

Feluda began walking without saying a word. His face was set, his eyes had taken on a glint that meant he was definitely on to something.

But I knew he wasn't yet prepared to talk about it. So I walked by his side silently, trying to think things through myself. Sadly, though, I got nowhere. It was obvious that Mr Datta was not the burglar who had attacked Nilmoni Babu. He seemed strong enough—and he had a deep voice—but somehow I couldn't imagine him climbing a pipe. A much younger man must have done it. But who could it be? And what was Feluda thinking about?

We continued to walk, ignoring every empty taxi that sailed by. After sometime, I suddenly realized we were standing quite close to the boundary wall of Nilmoni Babu's house. Feluda began walking straight, with the wall on his left. After a few seconds, we realized the wall curved to the left. We made a left turn to follow it. About twenty steps later, Feluda stopped abruptly, and began inspecting a certain portion of the wall. Then he took out his small Japanese camera and took a photograph of that particular section. This time, I, too, peered closer and saw that there was a brown imprint of a hand. All that was visible was really two fingers and a portion of the palm, but it was clear that it was a child's hand that had left the mark.

We retraced our steps, making our way this time to the main gate. We pushed it open and went in. Nilmoni Babu rushed down to meet us. 'This may sound awful,' he told us when we were all seated in his living room, 'but I must confess today my heart is feeling a lot lighter. Yes, I do feel better knowing that my biggest rival has met with the same fate. But . . . where did my Anubis go? Who took him? You are a well-known detective, Mr Mitter. Are you still totally in the dark, even after two cases of burglary?'

Instead of replying, Feluda asked a seemingly irrelevant question. 'How is your nephew?'

'Who, Jhuntu? He's much better today, thanks. His temperature's gone down.'

'Do you know if he has any friends? I mean, is there a child who might climb over that boundary wall to come in here and play with Jhuntu?'

'Climb over the wall? Why do you say that?'

'I found the impression of a child's hand on the other side of the wall.'

'Was it a fresh mark?'

'That's difficult to say, but it can't be very old.'

'Well, I have never seen a child in this house. The only child who visits us occasionally is a small beggar boy. But he comes in through the gate, usually singing Shyamasangeet. He does have a good voice, I must say. However, there is a guava tree in my garden. So maybe that attracts little boys from time to time—I really couldn't say.'

'Hmm.'

Nilmoni Babu changed the subject. 'Did you learn anything new about the thief?'

'The man has extraordinary strength. Pratul Datta's servant was knocked unconscious with just one blow.'

'Then it must have been the same man who attacked me.'

'Perhaps. But I am concerned not so much with his physical strength but with the way his mind functions. He seems to have remarkable cunning.'

Nilmoni Babu began to look sort of helpless. 'I hope your own intelligence can match his cunning, Mr Mitter. Or else I must give up all hope of ever finding my Anubis again,' he said.

'Give me two more days. Felu Mitter has never been defeated. No, sir, not yet.'

We left soon after this. As we were walking down the driveway towards the front gate, we both heard a strange noise, as though someone was tapping on a glass pane. I turned around and saw a small boy standing at a window on the first floor. It was he who was tapping on the window pane. 'Jhuntu!' I said. 'Yes, I've seen him, too,' Feluda replied.

*

Feluda spent the afternoon scribbling in his famous blue notebook. I had learnt by now not to worry about what he was writing, for I knew whatever he wrote in his notebook was written in English, using Greek letters. I couldn't read it even if I tried; and certainly Feluda wouldn't tell me if I asked. In fact, he had stopped talking to me completely. I did not disturb him. He needed time to think. But he was humming a song under his breath. It was the same song that we had heard the beggar boy sing.

At about 5 p.m. Feluda broke his silence. 'I am going out

for a few minutes,' he said. 'I have to collect the enlargements of my photograph from the studio.'

I was left all alone. Days were growing shorter. It grew fairly dark in less than an hour after Feluda left. The studio wasn't far from where we lived. Why was Feluda taking so long to come back? I did hope he hadn't gone somewhere else without telling me. Maybe his photos weren't ready, and he was being made to wait at the shop.

The sound of a khanjani reached my ears, which was followed immediately by a familiar song:

> Help me, Mother
> for I have no one
> to turn to . . . .

The same boys were now singing in our street. I went and stood near the window. Now I could see both boys. One of them was playing the khanjani and the other was singing. He really did sing well. They were now standing in front of our house. The one who was singing stopped and raised his face. 'Ma, please give us some money, Ma!' he cried. I took out a fifty-paisa coin from my wallet and threw it out of the window. The boy picked it up just as it landed at his feet with a faint chink. Then he put it in his shoulder bag, and walked on, picking up the song where he had left it.

I stared after him, profoundly puzzled. Our street wasn't particularly well-lit. But when the boy had raised his face to beg for money, I had seen it quite clearly. There was an uncanny resemblance between his face and Jhuntu's. No, I must have made a mistake, I told myself. Even so, this was something I had to tell Feluda the minute he got back.

He returned at half past six, looking cross. I had been right in thinking he'd had to wait in the shop. 'I'll make a dark room of my own and develop my own prints from now on,' he declared. 'These studios simply cannot be trusted to deliver on time.'

He spread out all his enlarged prints on his bed and began studying them. I could wait no longer, so I told him about the beggar boy. Feluda's face did not register any surprise. 'There's nothing odd about that,' he said.

'Isn't there?'

'No.'

'In that case, this whole business is more complicated than I thought.'

'Yes, that's true.'

'But do you actually believe that that young boy is involved in the burglaries?'

'He may well be.'

'But how can a boy of his age and his size be strong enough to knock people out?'

'Who said it was a young boy who attacked Nilmoni Babu and Bangshalochan?'

'Wasn't it?'

Feluda did not answer me. He went back to examining his photos. I found him looking carefully at the enlarged version of the photograph he had taken only this morning of the imprint of a hand on Nilmoni Babu's boundary wall.

'You told me once you could read palms,' I said jokingly. 'Can you tell me how long the owner of that hand will live?'

Feluda didn't laugh, or make a retort. He was frowning again, deep in thought. 'What do you make of this?' he asked suddenly. His question startled me.

'What do I make of what?'

'What you saw this morning, and what you're seeing now.'

'In the morning? You mean when you took that photo?'

'Yes.'

'It was the impression of a child's hand. What else was there to see?'

'Didn't its colour tell you anything?'

'Colour? It was brown, wasn't it?'

'Yes, but what did that mean?'

128

'That the boy had something smeared on his hand?'

'Something? Try to think, try to be more specific.'

'Well, it might have been paint, mightn't it?'

'All right, but where could it have come from?'

'Brown paint? How should I know—no, wait, wait. I remember now. The doors and windows of Mr Datta's house were all painted brown!'

'Exactly. You caught some of it on your sleeve that day. If you look at your shirt, you'll probably still find it there.'

'But . . . ' I began to feel a bit dazed, 'does that mean the person who got paint on his hand was the burglar who stole into Pratul Datta's house?'

'Yes, there's a possibility. But look at the photo again. Can you spot anything else?'

I tried to think very hard, but had to shake my head in the end.

'It's all right,' Feluda comforted me, 'I knew you wouldn't be able to spot it. If you had, I would've been very surprised—no, in fact, I would have been shocked.'

'Why?'

'Because that would have proved that you are no less clever than me.'

'Oh? And what have *you* spotted, Mr Clever?'

'That this is more than just a complicated case. There is a sinister angle to it, which I have realized only recently. It is as horrific as Anubis himself!'

*

Feluda rang Nilmoni Babu the next day.

'Hello? Mr Sanyal? . . . Your mystery has been solved . . . No, I haven't actually got that statue, but I think I know where it is . . . Are you free this morning? . . . What? . . . He's worse, is he? . . . Which hospital? . . . All right. We'll meet later. Thank you.'

Feluda replaced the receiver and quickly dialled another number. I couldn't hear what he said for he lowered his voice and practically whispered into the telephone. But I could tell that he was speaking to someone in the police. Then he turned to me and said, 'Get ready quickly. We're going out. Yes, now.'

Luckily there wasn't much traffic on the roads since it was still fairly early. Besides, Feluda had told the driver to drive as fast as he could. It took us only a few minutes to reach Nilmoni Babu's street. Just as we reached his gate, we saw him driving out in his black Ambassador. There didn't seem to be anyone else in the car apart from Nilmoni Babu himself and his driver. 'Follow that car!' shouted Feluda. Excited, our driver placed his foot on the accelerator. I saw Nilmoni Babu's car take a right turn. At this moment, Feluda did something completely unexpected. He took out his revolver from the inside pocket of his jacket, leant out of the window and shot at the rear tyres of the Ambassador.

The noise from the revolver and the bursting of tyres was absolutely deafening. Then I saw the Ambassador lurch awkwardly, bump against a lamp-post and come to a standstill. Our taxi pulled up just behind it. From the opposite end came a police jeep and blocked the other side.

Nilmoni Sanyal climbed out his car and stood glancing around, looking furious. Feluda and I got out of our taxi and began walking towards him. From the police jeep, the same plump officer jumped out.

'What the hell is going on?' demanded Nilmoni Babu when he saw us.

'Who else is with you in the car apart from the driver, Mr Sanyal?' Feluda asked coldly.

'Who do you think?' Nilmoni Babu shouted. 'Didn't I tell you I was taking my nephew to the hospital?'

Without a word, Feluda stepped forward and pulled the handle of one of the rear doors of the Ambassador. The door opened, and a small child shot out from the car, promptly attaching himself to Feluda's throat.

Feluda might have been throttled to death. But he wasn't just an expert in yoga. He had learnt ji-jitsu and karate, too. It took him only a few seconds to twist the child's wrists, and swing him over his head, finally throwing him down on the road. The child screamed in pain, which made my heart jump into my mouth. The voice wasn't a child's voice at all. It belonged to a fully-grown adult. It sounded harsh and raucous. This was the voice I had heard on the telephone.

By this time, the police officer and his men had surrounded the car and arrested Nilmoni Babu, his driver and the 'child'.

Feluda straightened his collar and said, 'That imprint of his hand had made me wonder. It couldn't be a child's hand, for it had far too many lines on it. A child's hand would have been much more smooth. However, since the size of the palm was small, there could be just one explanation for it. The so-called 'child' was really a dwarf. How old is your assistant, Mr Sanyal?'

'Forty,' Nilmoni Babu whispered. His own voice sounded different.

'You thought you were being very clever,' Feluda went on. 'Your plan was flawless, and your acting good enough to win an award. You told me a weird tale of warnings in hieroglyphics, then staged a robbery, just to remove suspicion from yourself. Then you had Pratul Datta's house burgled, and some of his possessions became yours. Tell me, the boy we saw in your house was the other beggar boy, wasn't he? The one who used to sing?'

Nilmoni Babu nodded in silence. 'Yes, that boy used to sing,' Feluda continued, 'and the dwarf played the khanjani. You never had a nephew at all. That was another story you cooked up. You've kept that boy in your house by force, haven't you, to help you with your misdeeds? I know that now, but it took me a while to figure it out. The boy and the dwarf were sent out together. The dwarf disappeared into Pratul Datta's house, leaving the khanjani with the singer, who continued to play it. The dwarf was obviously powerful enough to tackle Bangshalochan. It was a wonderful plan, really. I've got to give you full marks for planning all the details, Mr Sanyal.'

Nilmoni Babu sighed. 'The truth is,' he said, 'that I had become obsessed with ancient Egypt. I have studied that period in some depth. I couldn't bear the thought of Pratul Datta hanging on to those pieces of Egyptian art. I had to have them, at any cost.'

'Well, Mr Sanyal, you have now seen where greed and temptation can lead you. There is just one more thing I need to ask you for.'

'What is it?'

'My reward.'

Nilmoni Babu stared at Feluda blankly.

'Reward?'

'Yes. That statue of Anubis is with you, isn't it?'

Nilmoni Babu slipped his hand into his pocket rather foolishly. Then he brought it out, clutching a four-thousand-year-old statue of Anubis, the Egyptian god of the dead. The stones it was studded with glittered in the sun.

Feluda stretched an arm and took the statue from Nilmoni Babu.

'Thank you,' he said.

Nilmoni Babu swallowed, quite unable to speak. The police officer pushed him gently in the direction of the jeep.

The Key

The Key

Chapter 1

'Do you know why the sight of trees and plants have such a refreshing effect on our eyes?' asked Feluda. 'The reason is that people, since primitive times, have lived with greenery all around them, so that their eyes have developed a healthy relationship with their environment. Of course, trees in big cities these days have become rather difficult to find. As a result, every time you get away from town, your eyes begin to relax, and so does your mind. It is mostly in cities that you'll notice people with eye disorders. Go to a village or a hill-station, and you'll hardly find anyone wearing glasses.'

Feluda himself had a pair of sharp eyes, didn't wear glasses, and could stare at any object for three minutes and fifteen seconds without blinking even once. I should know, for I had tested him often enough. But he had never lived in a village. I was tempted to point this out to him, but didn't dare. The chances of having my head bitten off if I did were very high.

We were travelling with a man called Monimohan Samaddar. He wore glasses (but then, he lived in a city), was about fifty years old and had sharp features. The hair around his ears had started to turn grey. It was in his Fiat that we were travelling, to a place called Bamungachhi, which was a suburb of Calcutta. We had met Moni Babu only yesterday.

135

He had turned up quite out of the blue in the afternoon, as Feluda and I sat in our living room, reading. I had been watching Feluda reading a book on numerology, raising his eyebrows occasionally in both amazement and appreciation. It was a book about Dr Matrix. Feluda caught me looking at him, and smiled. 'You'd be astonished to learn the power of numbers, and the role they play in the lives of men like Dr Matrix. Listen to this. It was a discovery Dr Matrix made. You know the names of the two American Presidents who were assassinated, don't you?'

'Yes. Lincoln and Kennedy, right?'

'Right. Now tell me how many letters each name has.'

'L-i-n-c-o-l-n—seven. K-e-n-n-e-d-y—also seven.'

'OK. Now listen carefully. Lincoln was killed in 1865 and Kennedy died in 1963, a little less than a hundred years later. Both were killed on a Friday, and both had their wives by their side. Lincoln was killed in the Ford Theatre. Kennedy was killed in a car called Lincoln, manufactured by the Ford company. The next President after Lincoln was called Johnson, Andrew Johnson. Kennedy was succeeded by Lindon Johnson. The first Johnson was born in 1808, the second in 1908, exactly a hundred years later. Do you know who killed Lincoln?'

'Yes, but I can't remember his name right now.'

'It was John Wilkes Booth. He was born in 1839. And Kennedy was killed by Lee Harvey Oswald. He was born in 1939! Now count the number of letters in both names.'

'Good Heavens, both have fifteen letters!'

Feluda might have told me of a few more startling discoveries by Dr Matrix, but it was at this point that Mr Samaddar arrived, without a prior appointment. He introduced himself, adding, 'I live in Lake Place, which isn't far from here.'

'I see.'

'Er . . . you may have heard of my uncle, Radharaman Samaddar.'

'Oh yes. He died recently, didn't he? I believe he was greatly interested in music?'

'Yes, that's right.'

'I read an obituary in the local newspaper. I hadn't heard about him before that, I'm afraid. He was quite old, wasn't he?'

'Yes, he was eighty-two when he died. I'm not surprised that you hadn't heard of him. When he gave up singing, you must have been a young boy. He retired fifteen years ago, and built a house in Bamungachhi. That is where he lived, almost like a recluse, until his death. He had a heart attack on 18 September, and died the same night.'

'I see.'

Mr Samaddar cleared his throat. After a few seconds of silence, he said a little hesitantly, 'I'm sure you're wondering why I've come to disturb you like this. I just wanted to give you a little background, that's all.'

'Of course. Don't worry, Mr Samaddar, please take your time.'

Moni Babu resumed speaking. 'My uncle was different from other men. He was actually a lawyer, and he made a lot of money. But he stopped practising when he was about fifty, and turned wholly to music. He didn't just sing, he could play seven or eight different instruments, both Indian and Western. I myself have seen him play the sitar, the violin, piano, harmonium, flute and the tabla, besides others. He had a passion for collecting instruments. In fact, his house had become a mini museum of musical instruments.'

'Which house do you mean?'

'He had started collecting before he left Calcutta. Then he transferred his collection to his house in Bamungachhi. He used to travel widely, looking for instruments. Once he bought a violin from an Italian in Bombay. Only a few months later, he sold it in Calcutta for thirty thousand rupees.'

Feluda had once told me that three hundred years ago, in Italy there had been a handful of people who had produced violins of such high quality that, today, their value was in excess of a hundred thousand rupees.

Mr Samaddar continued to speak. 'As you can see, my uncle was gifted. There were a lot of positive qualities in his character that made him different from most people. But, at the same time, there was an overriding negative factor which eventually turned him into a recluse. He was amazingly tightfisted. The few relatives he had stopped seeing him because of this. He didn't seem to mind, for he wasn't particularly interested in staying in touch with them, anyway.'

'How many relatives did he have?'

'Not a lot. He had three brothers and two sisters. The sisters and two of his brothers are no more. The third brother left home thirty years ago. No one knows if he's alive. Radharaman's wife and only child, a son called Muralidhar, are both dead. Muralidhar's son, Dharanidhar, is his only grandchild. Radharaman was very fond of him once. But when he left his studies and joined a theatre under a different name, my uncle washed his hands off him. I don't think he ever saw him again.'

'How are you related to him?'

'Oh, my father was one of his elder brothers. He died many years ago.'

'I see; and is Dharanidhar still alive?'

'Yes, but I believe he's moved on to another group, and is now doing a jatra. I tried contacting him when my uncle passed away, but he wasn't in Calcutta. Someone told me he was off on a tour, travelling through small villages. He's quite well-known now in the theatre world. He was interested in music, too, which was why his grandfather was so fond of him.'

Mr Samaddar stopped. Then he went on, speaking a little absently, 'It's not as if I saw my uncle regularly. I used to go and meet him, maybe once every two months or so. Of late, even that had become difficult as my work kept me very busy. I run a printing press in Bhawanipore, called the Eureka Press. We've had such frequent power cuts recently that it's been quite a job clearing all our backlog. Anyway, my uncle's neighbour, Abani Babu, telephoned me when he had a heart attack. I left immediately with Chintamoni Bose, the heart specialist. My uncle was unconscious at first, but opened his eyes just before he died, and seemed to recognize me. He even spoke a few words, but then . . . it was all over.'

'What did he say?' Feluda leant forward.

'He said, "In . . . my . . . name." Then he tried to speak, but couldn't. After struggling for sometime, he could get only one word out. "Key . . . key," he said. That was all.'

Feluda stared at Mr Samaddar, a frown on his face. 'Have you any idea what his words might have meant?'

'Well, at first I thought perhaps he was worried about his name, and his reputation. Perhaps he'd realized people called him a miser. But the word "key" seemed to matter to him. I mean, he sounded really concerned about this key. I haven't the slightest idea which key he was referring to. His bedroom has an almirah and a chest. The keys to these were kept in the drawer of a table that stood by the side of his bed. The house only has three rooms, barring a bathroom attached to his bedroom. There is hardly any furniture, and almost nothing that might require a key. The lock he used on the main door to his bedroom was a German combination lock, which didn't work with a key at all.'

'What did he have in the almirah and the chest?'

'Nothing apart from a few clothes and papers. These were in the almirah. The chest was totally empty.'

'Did you find any money?'

'No. In the drawer of the table was some loose change and a few two and five rupee notes, that's all. There was a wallet under his pillow, but even this had very little money in it. Apparently, he kept money for daily use in this wallet. At least, that's what his old servant Anukul told me.'

'What did he do when he finished spending what he had in his wallet or in his table drawer? Surely he had a bigger source to draw on?'

'Yes, that's what one has to assume.'

'Why do you say that? Didn't he have a bank account?'

Mr Samaddar smiled. 'No, he didn't. If he had had one, there would've been nothing unusual about him, would there? To tell you the truth, there was a time when he did keep his money in a bank. But many years ago, that bank went out of business, and he lost all he'd put in it. He refused to trust another bank after that. But—' Mr Samaddar lowered his voice, 'I *know* he had a lot of money. How else do you suppose he could afford to buy all those rare and expensive instruments? Besides, he didn't mind spending a great deal on himself. He ate well, wore specially tailored clothes, he maintained a huge garden, and had even bought a second hand Austin. He used to drive to Calcutta occasionally. So . . .' his voice trailed away.

Feluda lit a Charminar, and offered one to Mr Samaddar. Mr Samaddar took it, and waited until Feluda had lit it for him. 'Now,' he said, inhaling deeply, 'do you understand why I had to come to you? What will the key unlock? Where has all my uncle's money gone? Which key was he talking about, anyway? Shall we find any money or something else? Had he made a will? Who knows? If he had, we must find it. In the absence of a will, his grandson will get everything, but someone has to find out what that consists of. I have heard such a lot about your intelligence and your skill. Will you please help me, Mr Mitter?'

Feluda agreed. It was then decided that Mr Samaddar would pick us up today at 7 a.m. and take us to his uncle's house in Bamungachhi. I could tell Feluda was interested because this was a new type of mystery. Or perhaps it was more a puzzle than a mystery.

That is what I thought at first. Later, I realized it was something far more complex than a mere puzzle.

Chapter 2

We drove down Jessore Road, and took a right turn after Barasat. This road led straight to Bamungachhi. Mr Samaddar stopped here at a small tea shop and treated us to a cup of tea and jalebis. This took about fifteen minutes. By the time we reached Radharaman Samaddar's house, it was past eight o'clock.

A bungalow stood in the middle of a huge plot of land (it measured seven acres, we were told later), surrounded by a pink boundary wall and rows of eucalyptus trees. The man who opened the gate for us was probably the mali, for he had a basket in his hand. We drove up to the front door, passing a garage on the way. A black Austin stood in it.

As I was getting out of the car, a sudden noise from the garden made me look up quickly. I found a boy of about ten standing a few yards away, wearing blue shorts and clutching an air gun. He returned my stare gravely.

'Is your father at home?' asked Mr Samaddar. 'Go tell him Moni Babu from Calcutta has come back, and would like to see him, if he doesn't mind.'

The boy left, loading his gun.

'Is that the neighbour's son?' Feluda asked.

'Yes. His father, Abani Sen, is a florist. He has a shop in New Market in Calcutta. He lives right next door. He has his nursery here, you see. Occasionally, he comes and spends a few weeks with his family.'

An old man emerged from the house, looking at us enquiringly. 'This is Anukul,' Mr Samaddar said. 'He had worked for my uncle for over thirty years. He'll stay on until we know what should be done about the house.'

There was a small hall behind the front door. It couldn't really be called a room, all it had was a round table in the middle, and a torn calendar on the wall. There were no light switches on the wall as the whole area did not receive any electricity at all. Beyond this hall was a door. Mr Samaddar walked over to it, and said, 'Look, this is the German lock I told you about. One could buy a lock like this in Calcutta before the Second World War. The combination is eight-two-nine-one.'

It was round in shape, with no provision for a key. There were four grooves instead. Against each groove were written numbers, from 1 to 9. A tiny object like a hook stuck out of each groove. This hook could be pushed from one end of the groove to the other. It could also be placed next to any of the numbers. It was impossible to open the lock unless one knew exactly which numbers the hooks should be placed against.

Mr Samaddar pushed the four hooks, each to rest against a different number—8, 2, 9 and 1. With a faint click, the lock opened. It seemed almost as though I was in a magic show. 'Locking the door is even easier,' said Mr Samaddar. 'All you need to do is push any of those hooks away from the right number. Then it locks automatically.'

The door with the German lock opened into Radharaman Samaddar's bedroom. It was a large room, and it contained all the furniture Radharaman's nephew had described. What was amazing was the number of instruments the room was packed with. Some of these were kept on shelves, others on a long bench and small tables. Some more hung on the wall.

Feluda stopped in the middle of the room and looked around for a few seconds. Then he opened the almirah and the chest, and went through both. This was followed by a search of the table drawers, a small trunk he discovered under the bed (all it revealed was a pair of old shoes and a few rags) and all the instruments in the room. Feluda picked them up, felt their weight and turned them over to see if any of them was meant to be operated by a key. Then he stripped the bed, turned the mattress over, and began tapping on the floor to see if any part of it sounded hollow. It didn't. It took him another minute to inspect the attached bathroom. He still found nothing. Finally, he said, 'Could you please ask the mali to come here for a minute?' When the mali came, he got him to remove the contents of two flower-pots kept under the window. Both pots were empty. 'All right, you can put everything back into those pots, and thank you,' he told the mali.

In the meantime, Anukul had placed a table and four chairs in the room. He then put four glasses of lemonade on the table, and withdrew. Mr Samaddar handed two glasses to us, and asked, 'What do you make of all this, Mr Mitter?' Feluda shook his head. 'If it wasn't for those instruments, it would've been impossible to believe that a man of means had lived in this room.'

'Exactly. Why do you suppose I ran to you for help? I've never felt so puzzled in my life!' Mr Samaddar exclaimed, taking a sip from his glass.

I looked at the instruments. I could recognize only a few like the sitar, sarod, tanpura, tabla and a flute. I had never seen any of the others, and I wasn't sure that Feluda had, either. 'Do you know what each one of these is called?' he asked Mr Samaddar. 'That string instrument that's hanging from a hook on the wall over there. Can you tell me its name?'

'No, sir!' Mr Samaddar laughed. 'I know nothing of music. I haven't the slightest idea of what these might be called, or where they came from.'

There were footsteps outside the room. A moment later, the boy with the airgun arrived with a man of about forty. Mr

Samaddar made the introductions. The man was Abani Sen, the florist who lived next door. The boy was his son, Sadhan. 'Mr Pradosh Mitter?' he said. 'Of course I've heard of you!' Feluda gave a slight smile, and cleared his throat. Mr Sen took the empty chair and was offered the fourth glass of lemonade. 'Before I forget, Mr Samaddar,' he said, picking it up, 'do you know if your uncle had wanted to sell any of his instruments?'

'Why, no!' Mr Samaddar sounded quite taken aback.

'A gentleman came yesterday. He went to my house since he couldn't find anyone here. He's called Surajit Dasgupta. He collects musical instruments, very much like your uncle. He showed me a letter written by Radharaman Babu, and said he'd already been to this house and spoken to Radharaman Babu once. Anukul told me later he had seen him before. The letter had been written shortly before your uncle died. Anyway, I told him to come back today. I had a feeling you might return.'

'I have seen him, too.'

This came from Sadhan. He was playing with a small instrument that looked a bit like a harmonium, making slight tinkling noises. His father laughed at his words. 'Sadhan used to spend most of his time in or around this house. In fact, he still does. He and his Dadu were great friends.'

'How did you like your Dadu?' Feluda asked him.

'I liked him a lot,' Sadhan answered, with his back to us, 'but sometimes he annoyed me.'

'How?'

'He kept asking me to sing the sargam.'

'And you didn't want to?'

'No. But I can sing.'

'Ah, only songs from Hindi films.' Mr Sen laughed again. 'Did your Dadu know you could sing?'

'Yes.'

'Had he ever heard you?'

'No.'

'Well then, how do you think he knew?'

144

'Dadu often used to tell me that those whose names carry a note of melody are bound to have melodious voices.'

This made very little sense to us, so we exchanged puzzled glances. 'What did he mean by that?' Feluda asked.

'I don't know.'

'Did *you* ever hear him sing?'

'No. But I've heard him play.'

'What!' Mr Samaddar sounded amazed. 'Are you sure, Sadhan? I thought he had given up playing altogether. Did he play in front of you?'

'No, no. I was outside in the garden, killing coconuts with my gun. That's when I heard him play.'

'Could it have been someone else?'

'No, there was no one in the house except Dadu.'

'Did he play for a long time?' Feluda wanted to know.

'No, only for a little while.'

Feluda turned to Mr Samaddar. 'Could you please ask Anukul to come here?'

Anukul arrived in a few moments. 'Did you ever hear your master play any of these instruments?' Feluda asked him.

'Well . . . ' Anukul replied, speaking hesitantly. 'My master spent most of his time in this room. He didn't like being disturbed. So really, sir, I wouldn't know whether he played or not.'

'I see. He never played in your presence, did he?'

'No, sir.'

'Did you ever hear anything from outside, or any other part of the house?'

'Well . . . only a few times . . . I *think* . . . but I can't hear very well, sir.'

'Did a stranger come and see him before he died? The same man who came yesterday?'

'Yes, sir. He spoke to my master in this room.'

'When did he first come?'

'The day he died.'

'What! That same day?' Mr Samaddar couldn't hide his surprise.

'Yes, sir.' Anukul had tears in his eyes. He wiped them with one end of his chadar and said in a choked voice, 'I came in here soon after that gentleman left, to tell my Babu that the hot water for his bath was ready, but found him asleep. At least, I thought he was sleeping until I found I just couldn't wake him up. Then I went to Sen Babu's house and told him.'

'Yes, that's right,' Mr Sen put in. 'I rang Mr Samaddar immediately, and told him to bring a doctor. But I knew there wasn't much that a doctor could do.'

A car stopped outside. Anukul left to see who it was. A minute later, a man entered the room, and introduced himself as Surajit Dasgupta. He had a long and drooping moustache, broad side-burns and thick, unruly hair. He wore glasses with a very heavy frame. Mr Sen pointed at Mr Samaddar and said, 'You should speak to him, Mr Dasgupta. He's Radharaman Babu's nephew.'

'Oh, I see. Your uncle had written to me. So I came to meet—'

'Can I see that letter?' Mr Samaddar interrupted him.

Surajit Dasgupta took out a postcard from the inside pocket of his jacket and passed it on to Mr Samaddar. Mr Samaddar ran his eyes over it, and gave it to Feluda. I leant across and read what was written on it: 'Please come and meet me between 9 and 10 a.m. on 18 September. All my musical instruments are with me in my house. You can have a look when you come.' Feluda turned it over to take a quick look at the address: Minerva Hotel, Central Avenue, Calcutta 13. Then he glanced at the bottle of blue-black ink kept on the small table next to the bed. The letter did seem to have been written with the same ink.

Mr Dasgupta sat down on the bed, with an impatient air. Mr Samaddar asked him another question. 'What did you and my uncle discuss that morning?'

'Well, I had come to know about Radharaman Samaddar

only after I read an article by him that was published in a magazine for music lovers. So I wrote to him, and came here on the 18th as requested. There were two instruments in his collection that I wanted to buy. We discussed their prices, and I made an offer of two thousand rupees for them. He agreed, and I started to write out a cheque at once. But he stopped me and said he'd much rather have cash. I wasn't carrying so much cash with me, so he told me to come back the following Wednesday. On Tuesday, I read in the papers that he'd died. Then I had to leave for Dehra Dun. I got back the day before yesterday.'

'How did he seem that morning when you talked to him?' Mr Samaddar asked.

'Why, he seemed all right! But perhaps he had started to think that he wasn't going to live for long. Some of the things he said seemed to suggest that.'

'You didn't, by any chance, have an argument, did you?'

Mr Dasgupta remained silent for a few seconds. Then he said coldly, 'Are you holding *me* responsible for your uncle's heart attack?'

'No, I am not suggesting that you did anything deliberately,' Mr Samaddar returned, just as coolly. 'But he was taken ill just after you left, so . . . .'

'I see. I can assure you, Mr Samaddar, your uncle was fine when I left him. Anyway, it shouldn't be difficult for you to make a decision about my offer. I have got the money with me,' he took out his wallet, 'here's two thousand in cash. It would help if I could take the two instruments away today. I have to return to Dehra Dun tomorrow. That's where I live, you see. I do research in music.'

'Which two do you mean?'

Mr Dasgupta rose and walked over to one of the instruments hanging on the wall. 'This is one. It's called khamanche, it's from Iran. I knew about this one, but hadn't seen it. It's quite an old instrument. And the other was—'

Mr Dasgupta moved to the opposite end of the room and

stopped before the same instrument Sadhan had been playing with. 'This is the other instrument I wanted,' he said. 'It's called melochord. It was made in England. It is my belief that the manufacturers released only a few pieces, then stopped production for some reason. I had never seen it before, and since it's not possible to get it any more, I offered a thousand for it. Your uncle agreed to sell it to me for that amount.'

'Sorry, Mr Dasgupta, but you cannot have them,' said Feluda firmly. Mr Dasgupta wheeled around, and cast a sharp look at us all. Then his eyes came to rest on Feluda. 'Who are you?' he asked dryly.

'He is my friend,' Mr Samaddar replied, 'and he is right. We cannot let you buy either of these. You must appreciate the reason. After all, there is no evidence, is there, that my uncle had indeed agreed to sell them at the price you mentioned?'

Mr Dasgupta stood still like a statue, without saying a word. Then he strode out of the room as quickly as he could.

Feluda, too, rose to his feet, and walked slowly over to the instrument Mr Dasgupta had described as a khamanche. He didn't seen perturbed at all by Mr Dasgupta's sudden departure. The instrument looked a little like the small violins that are often sold to children by roadside hawkers, although of course it was much larger in size, and the round portion was beautifully carved. Then he went across to the melochord, and pressed its black and white keyboard. The sweet notes that rang out sounded like an odd mixture of the piano and the sitar.

'Is this the instrument you had heard your Dadu play?'
'Maybe.'

Sadhan seemed a very quiet and serious little boy, which was rather unusual for a boy of his age.

Feluda said nothing more to him, and moved on to open the almirah once more. He took put a sheaf of papers from a drawer, and asked Mr Samaddar, 'May I take these home? I think I need to go through them at some length.'

'Oh yes, sure. Is there anything else . . . ?'

'No, there's nothing else, thank you.'

When we left the room, I saw Sadhan staring out of the window, humming a strange tune. It was certainly not from a Hindi film.

Chapter 3

'What do you think, Mr Mitter?' asked Mr Samaddar on our way back from Bamungachhi. 'Is there any hope of unravelling this mystery?'

'I need to think, Mr Samaddar. And I need to read these papers I took from your uncle's room. Maybe that'll help me understand the man better. Besides, I need to do a bit of reading and research on music and musical instruments. Please give me two days to sort myself out.'

This conversation was taking place in the car when we finally set off on our return journey. Feluda had spent a lot of time in searching the whole house a second time, but even that had yielded nothing.

'Yes, of course,' Mr Samaddar replied politely.

'You will have to help me with some dates.'

'Yes?'

'When did Radharaman's son Muralidhar die?'

'In 1945, twenty-eight years ago.'

'How old was his son at that time?'

'Dharani? He must have been seven or eight.'

'Did they always live in Calcutta?'

'No, Muralidhar used to work in Bihar. His wife came to live with us in Calcutta after Muralidhar died. When she passed away, Dharani was a college student. He was quite bright, but he began to change after his mother died. Very soon, he left college and joined a theatre group. A year later, my uncle moved to Bamungachhi. His house was built in—'

'—1959. Yes, I saw that written on the main gate.'

*

Radharaman Samaddar's papers proved to be a collection of old letters, a few cash memos, two old prescriptions, a catalogue of musical instruments, produced by a German company called Spiegler, musical notation written on pages torn out of a notebook, and press reviews of five plays, in which mention of a Sanjay Lahiri had been underlined with a blue pencil.

'Hm,' said Feluda, looking at the notation. 'The handwriting on these is the same as that in Surajit Dasgupta's letter.' Then he went through the catalogue and said, 'There's no mention of a melochord'; and, after reading the reviews, remarked, 'Dharanidhar and this Sanjay Lahiri appear to be the same man. As far as I can see, although Radharaman refused to have anything to do with his grandson, he did collect information on him, especially if it was praise of his acting.'

Feluda put all the papers away carefully in a plastic bag, and rang a theatre journal called *Manchalok*, to find out which theatre group Sanjay Lahiri worked for. It turned out that the group was called the Modern Opera. Apparently, Sanjay Lahiri did all the lead roles. Feluda then rang their office, and was told that the group was currently away in Jalpaiguri. They would be back only after a week.

We went out after lunch. I had never had to go to so many different places, all on the same day! Feluda took me first to the National Museum. He didn't tell me why we were going there, and I didn't ask because he had sunk into silence and was cracking his knuckles. This clearly meant he was thinking hard, and was not to be disturbed. We went straight to the section for musical instruments. To be honest, I didn't even know the museum had such a section. It was packed with all kinds of instruments, going back to the time of the *Mahabharat*. Modern instruments were also displayed, although there was nothing that might have come from the West.

Then we went to two music shops, one in Free School Street, and the other in Lal Bazaar. Neither had heard of anything called melochord. 'Mr Samaddar was an old and valued customer,' said Mr Mondol of Mondol & Co. which had its shop in Lal Bazaar (Feluda had found one of their cash memos among Radharaman's papers yesterday). 'But no, we never sold him the instrument you are talking about. What does it look like? Is it a wind instrument like a clarinet?'

'No. It's more like a harmonium, but much smaller in size. The sound it gives out is a cross between a piano and a sitar.'

'How many octaves does it have?'

I knew the eight notes—sa re ga ma pa dha ni sa—made one octave. The large harmoniums in Mondol's shop had provision for as many as three octaves. When Feluda told him a melochord had only one octave, Mr Mondol shook his head and said, 'No, sir, I don't think we can help you. This instrument might well be only a toy. You may wish to check in the big toy shops in New Market.'

We thanked Mr Mondol and made our way to College Street. Feluda bought three books on music, and then we went off to find the office of *Manchalok*. We found it relatively easily, but it took us a long time to find a photograph of Sanjay Lahiri. Finally, Feluda dug out a crumpled photo from somewhere, and offered to pay for it. 'Oh, I can't ask *you* to pay for that picture, sir!' laughed the editor of the magazine. 'You are Felu Mitter, aren't you? It's a privilege to be able to help you.'

By the time we returned home after stopping at a café for a glass of lassi, it was 7.30 p.m. The whole area was plunged in darkness because of load shedding. Undaunted, Feluda lit a couple of candles and began leafing through his books. When the power came back at nine, he said to me, 'Topshe, could you please pop across to your friend Poltu's house, and ask him if I might borrow his harmonium just for this evening?'

It took me only a few minutes to bring the harmonium. When I went to bed quite late at night, Feluda was still playing it.

I had a strange dream that night. I saw myself standing before a huge iron door, in the middle of which was a very large hole. It was big enough for me to slip through; but instead of doing that, Feluda, Monimohan Samaddar and I were all trying to fit a massive key into it. And Surajit Dasgupta was dancing around, wearing a long robe, and singing, 'eight-two-o-nine-one! Eight-two-o-nine-one!'

Chapter 4

Mr Samaddar had told us he'd give us a call the following Wednesday. However, he rang us a day earlier, on Tuesday, at 7 a.m. I answered the phone. When I told him to hold on while I went to get Feluda, he said, 'No, there's no need to do that. Just tell your cousin I'm going over to your house straightaway. Something urgent's cropped up.'

He arrived in fifteen minutes. 'Abani Sen rang from Bamungachhi. Someone broke into my uncle's room last night,' he said.

'Does anyone else know how to operate that German lock?' Feluda asked at once.

'Dharani used to know. I'm not sure about Abani Babu—no, I don't think he knows. But whoever broke in didn't use that door at all. He went in through the small outer door to the bathroom. You know, the one meant for cleaners.'

'But that door was bolted from inside. I saw that myself.'

'Maybe someone opened it after we left. Anyway, the good news is that he couldn't take anything. Anukul came to know almost as soon as he got into the house, and raised an alarm. Look, are you free now? Do you think you could go back to the house with me?'

'Yes, certainly. But tell me something. If you now saw Radharaman's grandson, Dharani, do you think you could

154

recognize him?'

Mr Samaddar frowned. 'Well, I haven't seen him for years, but . . . yes, I think I could.'

Feluda went off to fetch the photo of Sanjay Lahiri. When he handed it over to Mr Samaddar, I saw that he had drawn a long moustache on Sanjay's face, and added a pair of glasses with a heavy frame. Mr Samaddar gave a start. 'Why,' he exclaimed, 'This looks like—!'

'Surajit Dasgupta?'

'Yes! But perhaps the nose is not quite the same. Anyway, there *is* a resemblance.'

'The photo is of your cousin Muralidhar's son. I only added a couple of things just to make it more interesting.'

'It's amazing. Actually, I did find it strange, when Dasgupta walked in yesterday. In fact, I wanted to ring you last night and tell you, but I got delayed at the press. We were working overtime, you see. But then, I wasn't absolutely sure. I hadn't seen Dharani for fifteen years, not even on the stage. I'm not interested in the theatre at all. If what you're suggesting is true . . . .'

Feluda interrupted him, 'If what I'm suggesting is true, we have to prove two things. One—that Surajit Dasgupta doesn't exist in real life at all; and two—that Sanjay Lahiri left his group and returned to Calcutta a few days before your uncle's death. Topshe, get the number of Minerva Hotel, please.' The hotel informed us that a Surajit Dasgupta had indeed been staying there, but had checked out the day before. There was no point in calling the Modern Opera, for they had already told us Sanjay Lahiri was out of town.

On reaching Bamungachhi, Feluda inspected the house from outside, following the compound wall. Whoever came must have had to come in a car, park it at some distance and walk the rest of the way. Then he must have jumped over the wall. This couldn't have been very difficult for there were trees everywhere, their overgrown branches leaning over the compound wall. The ground being totally dry, there were no

footprints anywhere.

We then went to find Anukul. He wasn't feeling well and was resting in his room. What he told us, with some difficulty, was this: mosquitoes and an aching head had kept him awake last night. He could see the window of Radharaman's bedroom from where he lay. When he suddenly saw a light flickering in the room, he rose quickly and shouted, 'Who's there?' But before he could actually get to the room, he saw a figure slip out of the small side door to the bathroom and disappear in the dark. Anukul spent what was left of the night lying on the floor of his master's bedroom.

'I don't suppose you could recognize the fellow?' Mr Samaddar asked.

'No, sir. I'm an old man, sir, and I can't see all that well. Besides, it was a moonless night.'

Radharaman's bedroom appeared quite unharmed. Nothing seemed to have been touched. Even so, Feluda's face looked grim. 'Moni Babu,' he said, 'you'll have to inform the police. This house must be guarded from tonight. The intruder may well come back. Even if Surajit Dasgupta is *not* Sanjay Lahiri, he is our prime suspect. Some collectors are strangely determined. They'll do anything to get what they want.'

'I'll ring the police from next door. I happen to know the OC,' said Mr Samaddar and went out of the room busily.

Feluda picked up the melochord and began inspecting it closely. It was a sturdy little instrument. There were two panels on it, both beautifully engraved. Feluda turned it over and discovered an old and faded label. 'Spiegler,' he said. 'Made in Germany, not England.' Then he began playing it. Although he was no expert, the sound that filled the room was sweet and soothing. 'I wish I could break it open and see what's inside,' he said, putting it back on the table, 'but obviously I can't do that. The chances are that I'd find nothing, but the instrument would be totally destroyed. Dasgupta was prepared to pay a thousand rupees for it, imagine!'

Despite his splitting headache, Anukul got up and

brought us some lemonade again. Feluda thanked him and took a few sips from his glass. Mr Samaddar returned at this moment. 'The police have been informed,' he told us. 'Two constables will be posted here from tonight. Abani Babu wasn't home. He and Sadhan have gone to Calcutta for the day.'

'I see. Well, tell me, Moni Babu, who—apart from yourself—knew about Radharaman's habit of hiding all his money?'

'Frankly, Mr Mitter, I realized the money was hidden only after his death. Abani Babu next door is aware that we're looking for my uncle's money, but I'm sure he hasn't any idea about the amount involved. If it was Dharani who came here disguised as Dasgupta, he may have learnt something that morning before my uncle died. In fact, I'm convinced Dharani had come only to ask for money. Then they must have had a row, and—' Mr Samaddar broke off.

Feluda looked at him steadily and said, '—and as a result of this row, your uncle had a heart attack. But that didn't stop Dharani. He searched the room before he left. Isn't that what you're thinking?'

'Yes. But I know he didn't find any money.'

'If he had, he wouldn't have returned posing as Surajit Dasgupta, right?'

'Right. Perhaps something made him think the money was hidden in one of those two instruments.'

'The melochord.'

Mr Samaddar gave Feluda a sharp glance. 'Do you really think so?'

'That's what my instincts are telling me. But I don't like taking shots in the dark. Besides, I can't forget your uncle's last words. He did use the word "key", didn't he? You are certain about that?'

Mr Samaddar began to look unsure. 'I don't know . . . that's what it sounded like,' he faltered, rubbing his hands in embarrassment. 'Or it could be that my uncle was talking pure nonsense. It could have been delirium, couldn't it? Maybe the word "key" has no significance at all.'

I felt a sudden stab of disappointment at these words. But Feluda remained unruffled. 'Delirium or not, there is money in this room,' he said. 'I can smell it. Finding a key is not really important. We've got to find the money.'

'How? What do you propose to do?'

'Just at this moment, I'd like to go back home. Please tell Anukul not to worry, I don't think anyone will try to break in during the day. All he needs to do is not let any stranger into the house. There will be those police constables at night. I must go back and think very hard. I can see a glimmer of light, but unless that grows brighter, there's nothing much I can do. May I please spend the night here?'

Mr Samaddar looked faintly surprised at this question. But he said immediately, 'Yes, of course, if that's what you want. Shall I come and collect you at 8 p.m.?'

'All right. Thank you, Moni Babu.'

*

'First of all, my boy, write down the name of the dead man.'

Feluda was back in his room, sitting on his bed. I was sitting in a chair next to him, a notebook on my lap and a pen in my hand.

'Radharaman Samaddar,' I wrote.

'What's his grandson called?'

'Dharanidhar Samaddar.'

'And the name he uses on the stage?'

'Sanjay Lahiri.'

'What's the name of the collector of musical instruments who lives in Dehra Dun?'

'Surajit Dasgupta.'

'Who's Radharaman's neighbour?'

'Abani Sen.'

'And his son?'

'Sadhan.'

'What were Radharaman's last words?'

'In my name . . . key . . . key.'

'What are the eight notes in the sargam?'

'Sa re ga ma pa dha ni sa.'

'Very well. Now go away and don't disturb me. Shut the door as you go. I am going to work now.'

I went to the living room and picked up one of my favourite books to read. An hour later, I heard Feluda dialling a number on the telephone extension in his room. Unable to contain myself, I tiptoed to the door of his room and eavesdropped shamelessly.

'Hello? Can I speak to Dr Chintamoni Bose, please?'

Feluda was calling the heart specialist who had accompanied Mr Samaddar the day Radharaman died. I returned to the living room, my curiosity satisfied. Ten minutes later, there was the sound of dialling again. I rose once more and listened at the door.

'Eureka Press? Who's speaking?'

This time, Feluda was calling Mr Samaddar's press. I didn't need to hear any more, so I went back to my book.

When our cook Srinath came in with the tea at four, Feluda was still in his room. By the time I had finished my tea and read a few more pages of my book, it was 4.35. I was now feeling more mystified than ever. What on earth could Feluda be doing, puzzling over those few words I'd scribbled in a notebook? After all, there wasn't anything in them he didn't know already. Before I could think any further, Feluda opened his door and came out with a half-finished Charminar in his hand. 'My head's reeling, Topshe!' he exclaimed, a note of suppressed excitement in his voice. 'Who knew it would take me so long to work out the meaning of a few words spoken by a very old man at his deathbed?'

In reply, I could only stare dumbly at Feluda. What he had just said made no sense to me, but I could see that his face looked different, which could simply mean that the light he had seen earlier was now much stronger than a glimmer.

'Sa dha ni sa ni . . . notes from the sargam. Does that tell you anything?'

'No, Feluda. I've no idea what you're talking about.'

'Good. If you could catch my drift, one would have had to assume your level of intelligence was as high as Felu Mitter's.'

I was glad of the difference. I was perfectly happy being Feluda's satellite, and no more.

Feluda threw his cigarette away, and picked up the telephone once again.

'Hello? Mr Samaddar? Can you come over at once? Yes, yes, we have to go to Bamungachhi as soon as we can . . . I think I've finally got the answer . . . yes, melochord . . . that's the important thing to remember.'

Then he replaced the receiver and said seriously, 'There is a risk involved, Topshe. But I've got to take it, there is no other choice.'

Chapter 5

Mr Samaddar's driver was old, but that didn't stop him from driving at eighty-five kilometres per hour when we reached VIP Road. Feluda sat fidgeting, as though he would have liked to have driven faster. Soon, we had to reduce our speed as the road got narrower and more congested. However, only a little while later, it shot up to sixty, despite the fact that the road wasn't particularly good and it had started to get dark.

There was no one at the main gate of Radharaman's house. 'Perhaps it's not yet time for those police constables to have arrived,' Feluda remarked.

We found Sadhan in the garden with his airgun.

'Why, Sadhan Babu, what are you killing in the dark?' Feluda asked him, getting out of the car.

'Bats,' Sadhan replied promptly. There were a number of bats hanging from the branches of a peepal tree just outside the compound.

The sound of our car had brought Anukul to the front door. Mr Samaddar told him to light a lantern and began unlocking the German lock. 'I'm dying to learn how you solved the mystery,' he said. I could understand his feelings, for Feluda hadn't uttered a single word in the car. I, too, was bursting with curiosity.

Feluda refused to break his silence. Without a word, he

stepped into the room and switched on a powerful torch. It shone first on the wall, then fell on the melochord, still resting peacefully on the small table. My heart began to beat faster. The white keys of the instrument gleamed in the light, making it seem as though it was grinning from ear to ear. Feluda did not move his arm. 'Keys . . .' he said softly. 'Look at those keys. Radharaman didn't mean a lock and a key at all. He meant the keys of an instrument, like a piano, or—'

He couldn't finish speaking. What followed a split second later took my breath away. Even now, as I write about it, my hand trembles.

At Feluda's words, Mr Samaddar suddenly sprang in the air and pounced upon the melochord like a hungry tiger on its prey. Then he picked it up, struck at Feluda's head with it, knocked me over and ran out of the door.

Feluda had managed to raise his arms in the nick of time to protect his head. As a result, his arms took the blow, making him drop the torch and fall on the bed in pain. As I scrambled to my feet, I heard Mr Samaddar locking the door behind him. Even so, I rushed forward, to try and push it with my shoulder. Then I heard Feluda whisper, 'Bathroom.' I picked up the torch quickly, and we both sped out of the small bathroom door.

There was the sound of a car starting, followed by a bang. A confused babel greeted us as we emerged. I could hear Anukul shouting in dismay, and Abani Sen speaking to his son very crossly. By the time we reached the front door, the car had gone, but there was someone sitting on the driveway.

'What have you done, Sadhan?' Mr Sen was still scolding his son furiously. 'Why did do you that? It was wrong, utterly wrong—!'

Sadhan made a spirited reply in his thin childish voice, 'What could I do? He was trying to run away with Dadu's instrument!'

'He's quite right, Mr Sen,' Feluda said, panting a little. 'He's done us a big favour by injuring the culprit, though in the future he must learn to use his airgun more carefully.

Please go back home and inform the police. The driver of that car must not be allowed to get away. Tell them its number is WMA 6164.'

Then he walked over to the figure sitting on the driveway and, together with Anukul, helped him to his feet. Mr Samaddar allowed himself to be half pushed and half dragged back into the house, without making any protest. A pellet from Sadhan's airgun had hit one corner of his forehead. The wound was still bleeding.

The melochord was still lying where it had fallen on the cobbled path. I picked it up carefully and took it back to the house.

*

Feluda, Mr Sen, Inspector Dinesh Gui from the Barasat police station and I were sitting in Radharaman's bedroom, drinking tea. A man—possibly a constable—stood at the door. Another sat huddled in a chair. This was our culprit, Monimohan Samaddar. The wound on his forehead was now dressed. Sadhan was also in the room, standing at the window and staring out. On a table in front of us was the melochord.

Feluda cleared his throat. He was now going to tell us how he'd learnt the truth. His watch was broken, and one of his arms was badly scraped. He had found a bottle of 'Dettol' in the bathroom, and dabbed his arm with it. Then he had tied a handkerchief around his arm. If he was still in pain, he did not show it.

He put his cup down and began speaking. 'I started to suspect Monimohan Samaddar only from this afternoon. But I had nothing to prove that my suspicions weren't baseless. So, unless he made a false move, I could not catch him. Fortunately, he lost his head in the end and played right into my hands. He could never have got away, but Sadhan helped me in catching him immediately . . . . Something he told me about working late on Monday first made me suspicious, not at the time, but later. He said he got very late on Monday evening because he had to work overtime. This was odd since a friend of mine lives in the same area where his press is, and I have often heard him complain that they have long power cuts, always starting in the evening and lasting until quite late at night. So I rang the Eureka Press, and was told that no work had been done on Monday evening because of prolonged load shedding. Moni Babu himself had left the press in the afternoon, and no one had seen him return. This made me wonder if a man who had told me one lie hadn't also told me another. What if Radharaman's last words were different from what I'd been led to believe? I remembered he wasn't the only one present at the time of his death. I rang Dr Chintamoni Bose, and learnt that what Radharaman had really said was, 'Dharani . . . in my name . . . key . . . key.' It was Dharani's name that Moni Babu had failed to mention. Dharani was, after all, Radharaman's only grandchild. He was still fond of him. If there were good reviews of his performance, Radharaman kept those press cuttings. So it was only natural that he should try to tell his grandson—and not his nephew—the secret about his money. I don't think he'd even recognized his nephew. Nevertheless, it was his nephew who heard his last words. He could make out that Radharaman was talking about his hidden money. But he couldn't find a key anywhere, so he decided to come to me, the idea being that I would find out where the key was, and Moni Babu would grab all the money. Nobody knew if there was a will. If a will could not be found, everything Radharaman possessed would have gone directly to Dharani. In any case, I doubt very much if Radharaman would have considered leaving anything to his nephew. It is my belief that he wasn't particularly fond of Moni Babu.'

Feluda stopped. No one spoke. After a brief pause, he continued, 'Now, the question was, why did Moni Babu lie to me about working late on Monday? Was it because he spent Monday evening indulging in some criminal activity, which meant that he needed an alibi? Radharaman's room was broken into that same evening. Could the intruder have been Moni Babu himself? The more I thought about it, the more likely did it seem. He was the only one who could use the combination lock, go into the room, unbolt the bathroom door, then come out again and lock the main door to the bedroom. That small bathroom door was most definitely bolted from inside when I saw it during the day. No cleaner could have come in after we left since it's not being used at all. I suspect Moni Babu had worked out what his uncle had meant by the word "key", so he'd come back in the middle of the night to steal the melochord. Am I right?'

All of us turned to look at Mr Samaddar. He nodded without lifting his head. Feluda went on, 'Even if Moni Babu could get away with stealing the melochord, I am positive he could never have decoded the rest of Radharaman's message. I stumbled on the answer only this evening, and for that, too, I have to thank little Sadhan.'

We looked at Sadhan in surprise. He turned his head and stared at Feluda solemnly. 'Sadhan,' Feluda said, 'tell us once again what your Dadu said about music and people's names.'

'Those who have melody in their names,' Sadhan whispered, 'are bound to have melody in their voices.'

'Thank you. This is merely an example of Radharaman's extraordinary intelligence. "Those who have melody in their names," he said. All right, let's take a name. Take Sadhan, for instance. Sadhan Sen. If you take away some of the vowels, you get notes from the sargam—sa dha ni sa ni. When I realized this, a new idea struck me. His last words were "in my name . . . key". Could he have meant the keys on the melochord that corresponded with his own name? Radharaman—re dha re ma ni. Samaddar—sa ma dha dha re. Dharanidhar was a singer, too; and he had melody in his name as well—dha re ni dha re. What a very clever idea it was, simple yet ingenious. Radharaman was obviously interested in mechanical gadgets. That German combination lock is an example. The melochord was also made in Germany, by a company called Spiegler. It was made to order, possibly based on specifications supplied by Radharaman himself. It acted as his bank. Thank goodness Surajit Dasgupta hadn't walked away with it, although I'm sure Radharaman would have emptied its contents before handing it over. Maybe he didn't feel the need for a bank any more. Maybe he knew he didn't have long to live . . . . I learnt two other things. Surajit Dasgupta is a genuine musician, absolutely passionate about music and instruments. The few books on music I have read in the last two days mentioned his name. I was quite mistaken in thinking it was Dharani in disguise. Dharani is truly away in Jalpaiguri, he hasn't the slightest idea of what's going on. What we have to do now is see if there is anything left for him to inherit. He wants to form his own group, according to an interview published in *Manchalok*. So I'm sure a windfall would be most welcome. Topshe, bring that lantern here.'

I picked up the lantern and brought it closer to the melochord. Feluda placed it on his lap. 'It's had to put up with some rough handling today,' he said, 'but it was designed so well that I don't think it was damaged in any way. Now let's see what Radharaman's brain and German craftsmanship has produced.' Feluda began pressing the keys that made up Radharaman's full name—re dha re ma ni sa ma dha dha re. A sweet note rang out with the pressing of every key. As Feluda pressed the last one, the right panel slid open silently. We leant over the instrument eagerly, to find that there was a deep compartment behind this panel, lined with red velvet, and packed with bundles of hundred rupee notes.

Sheer amazement turned us into statues for a few moments. Then Feluda began pulling out the bundles gently. 'I think we have at least fifty thousand here,' he said. 'Come on, Mr Sen, help me count it.'

A bemused Abani Sen rose to his feet and stepped forward. The light from the lantern fell on Feluda's face and caught the glint in his eye. I knew it wasn't greed, but the pure joy of being able to use his razor-sharp brain once more, and solve another mystery.

The Gold Coins of Jehangir

Chapter 1

'Hello, can I speak to Mr Mitter, please?'

'Speaking.'

'Namaskar. My name is Shankarprasad Chowdhury. I live in Panihati. You don't know me, but I am calling you to make a special request.'

'Yes?'

'I'd like you to visit my house here in Panihati. It is by the Ganges. It's about a hundred years old and is called Amaravati. Locally it's quite well-known. I'm aware of the kind of work you do, and that you're normally accompanied by your cousin and your friend, so I'm inviting all three of you. Do you think you could come next Saturday, say around ten in the morning? You could stay the night and go back the following morning.'

'Are you in trouble of some kind? I mean, you said you knew about my profession, so I wonder . . . ?'

'Yes, why else would I need to seek your help? But I'm not going to talk about it on the phone. I think you'll enjoy staying in my house. You'll be well looked after—I can guarantee that—and you'll get a chance to exercise your brain.'

'Well, I must confess I am free this weekend.'

'In that case, please say yes. But I must mention something else.'

'What is it?'

'There will be a few other people here. I don't want them to know who you are—at least, not right away. There's a special reason for this.'

'You mean we should come in disguise?'

'No, no, that will not be necessary. After all, you're not a film star, so I don't think the others are familiar with your appearance. All you need do is choose yourselves three different roles. I can even suggest what roles you might play.'

'Yes?'

'My great-grandfather Banwarilal Chowdhury was a strange man. I'll tell you about him when we meet, but you could pretend you have come to collect information about him to write his biography. In fact, I really think it's time his biography was written.'

'Very well. What about my friend, Mr Ganguli?'

'Do you have a pair of binoculars?'

'Yes.'

'Then why don't you turn him into a bird-watcher? I get plenty of birds in my garden. That'll give him something to do.'

'All right; and my cousin could be the bird-watcher's nephew.'

'Good idea. So I'll see you on Saturday, at around ten?'

'Yes, I'll look forward to that. Thank you and goodbye!'

Feluda put the phone down and repeated the whole conversation to me. He ended by saying, 'Some people speak with such genuine warmth and sincerity that it becomes impossible to turn down their request. This Mr Chowdhury is such a man.'

'But why should you even think of turning him down? From what he told you, there's a case waiting in Panihati for you. Surely you have to think of earning some money, at least occasionally?'

Over the last couple of months, Feluda had refused to accept a single case. He did this often after a spate of great activity, during which he might have had to work on more than one case. Then he would take some time off and spend his days studying different subjects. His current passion was the primitive man. He found an article by an American scientist called Richard Leaky in which it was suggested that the actual process of evolution took far longer than is generally believed. This got Feluda terribly excited. He paid five visits to the museum, went three times to the National Library and once to the zoo.

'Do you know what the latest theory says?' he told me once. 'It says man came from a particular species of apes called the "killer ape". That's why there is an inherent tendency towards violence in man.'

The chances of encountering violence in Panihati seemed remote, but I knew Feluda would welcome the opportunity to get out of Calcutta for a couple of days. In fact, we all enjoyed short trips to neighbouring towns.

We left for Panihati on Saturday morning in Lalmohan Babu's Ambassador. His driver being away, Feluda took his place. 'What a responsibility you've thrust upon me, Felu Babu,' Lalmohan Babu remarked as we set off. 'A birdwatcher? Me? I've never seen anything except crows and sparrows where I live. What use are these binoculars to me, and these two books you have told me to read?' The two books in question were Salim Ali's *Indian Birds* and Ajoy Hom's *The Birds of Bengal*.

'Don't worry,' Feluda reassured him. 'Just remember a crow is *Corvus splendens*, and a sparrow is *Passer domesticus*. But you needn't try to learn the Latin names of all the birds you might see—that'll only make you stutter. All you need do is throw in ordinary English names like drongo, tailor-bird or jungle babbler. If even that is difficult, just keep peering through your binoculars. That'll do.'

'I see. And what about a new name for me?'

'You are Bhabatosh Sinha. Topshe is your nephew. His name is Prabeer. And I am Someshwar Roy.'

We reached Mr Chowdhury's house in Panihati at five minutes to ten. The Gurkha at the gate opened it as he saw our car approach. Feluda drove gently up a cobbled driveway. The house was huge, and it had a massive compound. Whoever designed it must have been impressed by English castles, for the general pattern of the house reminded me instantly of pictures of castles I had seen. There was a garden on one side in which grew a number of flowers. It had a greenhouse in one corner, behind which an orchard began.

Mr Chowdhury was waiting for us at the door. 'Welcome to Amaravati!' he said, smiling, as we got out. He appeared to be about fifty, was of medium height and had a clear complexion. He was dressed in a pyjama-kurta and carried a cheroot in one hand.

'My cousin Jayanta arrived yesterday. I've told him everything, but he's not going to tell the others who you really are. I trust him entirely,' said Mr Chowdhury.

'Very well. But are the others already here?'

'No, I'm expecting them in the evening. Please come in; you can have a little rest, and we can talk more comfortably inside.'

We went in and sat on a wide veranda that overlooked the river. It was beautiful. I noticed a few steps going down to the edge of the water. It appeared to be a private bathing ghat.

'Is that ghat still in use?' Feluda asked.

'Oh yes. My aunt lives here, you see. She bathes in the Ganges every day.'

'Does she live alone?'

'No, no. I've been living here for the last couple of years. I work in Titagarh. That's closer from here than from my house in Calcutta.'

'How old is your aunt?'

'Seventy-eight. Our old servant Ananta looks after her. She's more or less in good health, except that she's lost most of her teeth and has had to have cataracts removed from both her eyes. Besides, she's turned a little senile—she can no longer remember names, she complains of not having eaten even after she's been fed, sometimes she gets up in the middle of the night to crush paan leaves for herself, for she can't chew on paan any more . . . you know, that kind of thing. She suffers from insomnia, too. If she gets two hours sleep every day, she's lucky. She could have stayed in Calcutta, but after my uncle died, she decided to come and live here.'

A bearer brought tea and sweets on a tray. 'Please help yourselves,' Mr Chowdhury invited. 'Lunch is going to be delayed. I think you'll like the sweets. You don't get this kind in Calcutta.'

'Thank you,' Feluda replied, picking up a steaming cup from the tray. 'Well, Mr Chowdhury, you know who I am. It'll help if you told me who you are and what you do. I hope you don't mind?'

'No, no, of course not. I asked you to come here simply to tell you a few things, didn't I? Very simply, I am a businessman. A successful businessman, as you can see.'

'Has your family always had a business?'

'No. This house was built by Banwarilal Chowdhury, my great-grandfather.'

'The same man whose biography I am supposed to be writing?'

'That's right. He was a barrister. He used to practise in Rampur. In time, he became quite wealthy and came to Calcutta. Then he decided to move here and had this house built. In fact, he died in this house. My grandfather, too, was a barrister, but his passion for gambling and drinking ate heavily into his savings. It was my father who started a business and eventually strengthened our financial position again. I simply carried on what my father had started. Things at present are not too bad. I only feel sorry to think about the possessions of Banwarilal that my grandfather sold to settle his gambling debts.'

'What about your cousin?'

'Jayanta did not join me in my business. He works for an

engineering firm. I believe he earns quite well, but of late he's started to play poker in his club. Clearly our grandfather's blood runs in his veins. Jayanta is five years younger than me.'

I noticed that Feluda had switched on the mini cassette recorder that we had brought back from Hong Kong. It was now so much easier to record what a client told us.

'Well, that covers my relatives. Let me tell you something about a few other people,' Mr Chowdhury added.

'Before you do that,' Feluda interrupted, 'please allow me to ask a question. Although it's almost gone, I can see traces of a white tika on your forehead. Does that mean—?'

'Yes, it's my birthday today. My aunt put that tika.'

'Oh, I see. Is that why you've invited your friends this evening?'

'There will be only three people. I had invited them last year to celebrate my fiftieth birthday. I had no wish to invite people again on my birthday this year. But there's a special reason why I had to.'

'And what is that?'

Mr Chowdhury thought for a minute. Then he said, 'If you will be so kind as to come with me to my aunt's room upstairs, I can explain things better.'

We finished our tea and rose. The staircase going up was through the drawing room. I was greatly impressed by the beautiful old furniture, the chandeliers, the carpets and the marble statues that filled the large drawing room.

'Who else lives on the first floor apart from your aunt?' asked Feluda, quickly climbing the stairs.

'My aunt's room is at one end. I have a room at the other. When Jayanta visits us, he, too, sleeps in a room on my side of the building.'

We crossed the landing and entered Mr Chowdhury's aunt's room. It was a big room, but only sparsely furnished. Through one of its open doors came a fresh cool breeze. The river must lie on that particular side. An old lady was sitting on a mat by the side of the open door, prayer beads in her hand.

Next to her on the mat was a hand-grinder, a few paan leaves in a container and a big fat book. It must be either the *Ramayana* or the *Mahabharat*, I thought. The old lady glanced up and peered at us through thick lenses.

'I have a few visitors from Calcutta,' Mr Chowdhury informed her.

'So you decided to show them this ancient relic?' asked his aunt.

We went forward to touch her feet. 'It's very good of you to have come,' she said. 'There's no point in telling me your names. I couldn't remember even a single one. Why, I often forget my own! It doesn't matter, I suppose, my days are numbered, anyway. I only have to wait for the end . . . .'

'Come this way, please.'

We turned as Mr Chowdhury spoke. The old lady went back to her prayer beads, mumbling under her breath.

Mr Chowdhury led us to the opposite end of the room where there was a huge chest. He took out a key from his pocket and began unlocking it. 'What I am going to show you now,' he said, 'belonged once to my great-grandfather. Many of his clients in Rampur were Nawabs, who often gave him expensive gifts. In spite of his son having sold most of them, what remains today is not insignificant. Take a look at these!'

He picked up a small velvet bag and turned it over on his palm. A number of gold coins slipped out. 'These are said to have been used by Jehangir,' said Mr Chowdhury. 'A sign of the zodiac is engraved on each.'

'But you've only got eleven pieces here. Surely there are twelve zodiac signs?'

'Yes. One of the coins is missing.'

We exchanged puzzled glances. Missing? Why was it missing?

'But there are other interesting objects as well,' Mr Chowdhury continued. 'Look, there's this golden snuff box from Italy. It's studded with rubies. There's a goblet made of jade, also studded with rubies and emeralds, and a large collection of rings and pendants made of precious stones. I will show you those in the evening when the others are here.'

'You keep the key to this chest, don't you?' Feluda asked.

'Yes. There is a duplicate which is kept in my aunt's wardrobe.'

'But why haven't you kept this chest in your own room?'

'My great-grandfather used to live in this room. It was he who had placed the chest in this corner. I saw no reason to remove it. Besides, we have very reliable guards at the gate and my aunt spends most of her time in this room. So it's quite safe to leave it here.'

We returned to the veranda downstairs. Feluda switched on his recorder again and asked, 'How does a single coin happen to be missing?'

'That's what I want to talk to you about. You see, last year on my birthday, I had invited three people. One of them was my business partner, Naresh Kanjilal. The second guest was Dr Ardhendu Sarkar. He lives here in Panihati. The third was Kalinath Roy, an old friend from school. I had lost touch with him completely. He contacted me after thirty-five years. Each one of these guests had heard of my great-grandfather's possessions, but none had seen any of them. That evening, I told Jayanta to take out the little bag of gold coins and bring it down to the drawing room. He did so, and I spread all twelve out on a table. We were bending over these to get a better look when suddenly, there was a power cut. Mind you, this was nothing unusual. One of the bearers brought candles in less than two minutes, and I put the coins back in the chest. Rather foolishly, I did not count them then for it never occurred to me that one might go missing. The next day, when it did dawn on me that counting the pieces might be a good idea, it was too late. My guests had left, and the coin showing the sign of cancer had vanished.'

'Are you sure you yourself had put the coins away?'

'Oh yes. But just think of my predicament, Mr Mitter. The three outsiders were all my guests. I have known my business partner for twenty-five years. Dr Sarkar is a well-known doctor here; and Kalinath is an old friend.'

'But are they totally honest? Do you happen to know that for a fact?'

'No, and that's why I'm so utterly confused. Take Kanjilal, for instance. Many businessmen are often dishonest in their dealings, but I've seen Kanjilal lie and cheat without the slightest qualm. It disturbs me very much. He knows this and often laughs at me. He says I should give up my business and become a preacher.'

'And the other?'

'I don't know too much about the doctor. He treats my aunt occasionally for rheumatism, that's all. But Kalinath . . . he makes me wonder. He rang me one day purely out of the blue, and said the older he was getting, the more inclined was he becoming to look back. He missed his childhood friends, so he wanted to come and see me.'

'Did you recognize him easily after all these years?'

'Yes. Besides, he talked of our years in school at great length. There's no doubt that he is my old classmate. What worries me is that he never tells me what he does for a living. I have asked him many times, but all he has ever said is that he, too, is a businessman. I don't know any other detail. He's a talented enough person—very jolly and cheerful, and clever with his hands. He knew magic in school and, in fact, is even now quite good at showing sleight of hand.'

'But your cousin was also in the room, surely?'

'Yes. He wasn't standing anywhere near the table, though. He had seen the coins before, so he wasn't interested. If anyone stole it, it must have been one of the other three.'

'What did you do when you realized one of the coins had gone?'

'What could I do? Anyone else would have reported the matter to the police and had these people's houses searched. But I couldn't do this. I've played bridge with them so often. For Heaven's sake, I have always treated them as my friends!

179

How could I suddenly turn around and call one of them a thief?'

'Does that mean you did nothing at all, and so none of them realizes he might be under suspicion?'

'That's right. In the last twelve months, I've met them on many occasions, but they've all behaved absolutely normally. Not one of them ever appeared uncomfortable in my presence. Yet, I know that one of them must be the culprit.'

We all fell silent. What a strange situation it was! But what was one supposed to do now?

Feluda asked the same question a few seconds later. 'I have a plan, Mr Mitter,' Mr Chowdhury replied. 'Since none of these people think I suspect them, I have invited them again to look at some of the other valuable possessions of Banwarilal. For the last few weeks, we've been having a power cut on the dot of seven every evening. Today, I shall place these objects on the same table a few minutes before seven. When the lights go off, I expect the thief would not be able to resist the temptation to remove something else. The total value of these pieces would be in the region of five million rupees, Mr Mitter. If something does get stolen this time, you can stop pretending to be a writer and start an investigation immediately.'

'I see. What does your cousin have to say about all this?'

'He didn't know anything about my plan until last night. He got quite cross at first. He said I should have gone to the police a year ago, and that it was too late now for you to do anything.'

'May I say something, Mr Chowdhury?'

'Yes, certainly.'

'The thief simply took advantage of your mild and easygoing nature. Not too many people would have hesitated to accuse one of their guests of stealing, if they were as sure of their facts as you seem to be.'

'I know. That's really why I sought your help. I know you will be able to do what I couldn't.'

180

Chapter 2

We had lunch a little later. Mr Chowdhury's cook produced an excellent meal, including hilsa from the Ganges cooked in mustard sauce. We met Mr Chowdhury's cousin, Jayanta, at the dining table. He seemed a most amiable man, not very tall but well-built.

'I'm going to rest for a while,' said Mr Chowdhury after lunch. 'Please feel free to do what you like. I'll meet you at tea time.'

We decided to explore the grounds with Jayanta Babu.

On the western side of the house was a wall with pillars that went right up to the river. A slope began where the wall ended, leading to the river-bank. Jayanta Babu took us to see the garden. He was passionately fond of flowers, roses in particular. He spoke at some length on the subject. I learnt for the first time that there were three hundred types of roses.

On the northern side was another gate. Most people in the house used this gate to go out if they wanted to go to the main town, Jayanta Babu told us. There was another flight of steps on this side, also going down to the river. 'My mother—the old lady you met this morning—uses these stairs when she goes to bathe in the river,' said Jayanta Babu.

We came back to our room after a few minutes. Jayanta Babu went to the greenhouse to look at his orchids. We had been given two adjoining rooms on the ground floor. There were three other rooms across the passage. Presumably, those were meant for the other three guests.

Lalmohan Babu took one look at the large, comfortable bed and said, 'Hey, I feel like having a nap, too. But no, I must read those books you gave me.'

'Feluda,' I said when he'd gone, 'have you thought about the plan this evening? Even if there *is* a power cut at seven, what happens if the thief does not steal anything this time? How will you catch him?'

'I can't. At least, not without studying all three people carefully. Anyone with a tendency to stealing would have a subtle difference in his behaviour. It shouldn't be impossible to spot it if I watch him closely. Don't forget that a thief is a criminal, no matter how polished and sophisticated his appearance might be.'

Soon, the sound of two cars stopping outside the front door told us that the guests had arrived. Mr Chowdhury came to fetch us himself when tea had been laid out on the veranda, and introduced us to the others.

Dr Sarkar lived within a mile, so he had come walking. About fifty years old, he had a receding hairline and specks of grey in his hair. But his moustache was jet black.

Naresh Kanjilal was tall and hefty. He was dressed formally in a suit. 'I am very glad you've decided to write Banwarilal's biography,' he said to Feluda. 'I've often told Shankar to have this done. Banwarilal was a remarkable man.'

Kalinath Roy turned out to be a fun-loving man. He was carrying a shoulder bag, possibly containing equipment for magic. He smiled as he met Lalmohan Babu and said, 'Who knew a bird-watcher would go carrying an egg in his pocket?' Then he quickly slipped a hand into Lalmohan Babu's pocket and brought out a smooth white stone egg. 'What a pity!' he said, shaking his head regretfully. 'I was planning to have it fried!'

It was decided that after dinner, Mr Roy would hold a

small magic show for us.

It had started to get dark. The last few rays of the sun shone on the water. A cool breeze rose from the river. Mr Kanjilal and Mr Roy went for a walk. Lalmohan Babu had been fidgeting for some time. Now he rose to his feet with the binoculars in his hand and said, 'I thought I heard the cry of a paradise flycatcher. Let me see if the bird is anywhere around.' I looked at Feluda as Lalmohan Babu went out busily; but, seeing that Feluda had kept a perfectly straight face, I managed to stop myself from bursting into laughter.

Dr Sarkar took a sip from his cup and turned to Mr Chowdhury. 'Where is your cousin? Is he still roaming in his garden?'

'You know how he feels about his flowers.'

'True. But I told him to wear a cap if he were to spend long hours out in the sun. Has he taken my advice?'

'Do you think Jayanta would ever take a doctor's advice? You know him better than that, don't you?'

Feluda was watching the doctor covertly, a Charminar in his hand.

'How is your aunt?' Dr Sarkar asked.

'Not too bad. But she was complaining of having lost her appetite. Why don't you pay her a visit?'

'Yes, I think I'll do that. Excuse me.'

Dr Sarkar got up and went upstairs. Jayanta Babu returned from the garden as soon as he left, grinning broadly.

'Why, what's so amusing?' Mr Chowdhury asked.

Jayanta Babu poured himself a cup of tea and turned to Feluda, still grinning. 'Your friend is trying desperately to pass himself off as a bird-watcher. I found him in the garden peering through his binoculars, looking dead serious.'

Feluda laughed. 'Well, virtually everyone present here will have to do a certain amount of acting today, won't he? Your cousin's plan has a heavy element of drama in it, don't you think?'

Jayanta Babu stopped smiling.

'Do you approve of my cousin's plan?' he asked.

'Why, don't you?'

'No, not in the least. The thief, I am sure, is far too clever to fall for something so obvious. You think he doesn't know we've discovered that a gold coin is missing?'

'Yes, Jayanta, you're quite right,' replied Mr Chowdhury, 'but I still want to give it a try. Call it simply a whim, if you like, or the result of reading too many detective novels.'

'Do you want to take out every single object from the chest?'

'No, no, just the snuff box and the goblet. They're both in an ivory box. Dr Sarkar is with your mother right now. You must go to her room the minute he returns and get me those two things. Here's the key.'

Jayanta Babu took the key with marked reluctance.

Dr Sarkar returned in five minutes. 'Your aunt is just fine,' he said happily. 'I left her on the veranda, eating rice and milk. She's going to be around for quite some time, Mr Chowdhury. She is in pretty good health.'

Jayanta Babu left without a word. 'Why are you still sitting around?' Dr Sarkar asked Feluda. 'Let's go out and get some fresh air. You'll never get such clean air in Calcutta.'

All of us got up and went down the steps. I spotted Lalmohan Babu behind a marble statue in the garden, still peering through the binoculars.

'Did you find the paradise flycatcher?' Feluda asked him.

'No. But I think I saw a jungle babbler.'

'Lalmohan Babu, it is now time for the birds to return to their nests. In a few minutes, you won't be able to find anything except perhaps an owl.'

There was no sign of either Naresh Kanjilal or Kalinath Roy. Where had they gone? Could they be in the orchard behind the greenhouse?

'Hey, Naresh, where are you hiding?' called Mr Chowdhury. 'And Kalinath, where have *you* got to?'

'I saw one of them go into the house,' said Lalmohan Babu.

'Which one?'

'I think it was the magician.'

But Lalmohan Babu was wrong. It was Naresh Kanjilal who emerged from the house, not Kalinath Roy. 'The temperature drops very quickly the moment the sun goes down,' he said upon seeing us, 'so I'd gone inside to get my shawl.'

'Where's Kalinath?'

'Why, he left me as soon as we reached the garden. He said he'd learnt a new trick to turn old, wilted flowers into fresh new ones, so . . . .'

Mr Kanjilal could not finish speaking. He was interrupted by Mr Chowdhury's old servant, Ananta, who came rushing out of the house, shouting and waving madly. 'Why, Ananta, whatever's the matter?' Mr Chowdhury asked anxiously.

'Come quickly, sir. It's Jayanta Babu. He fell . . . upstairs . . . he's lying on the stairs, unconscious.'

Chapter 3

Each one of us sped upstairs without a word. We found Jayanta Babu lying just outside his mother's room on the landing , about three feet away from the threshold. He had hurt the back of his head. Blood had oozed out on the floor,to form a small red pool.

Dr Sarkar was the first to reach him. He sat down by Jayanta Babu and quickly took his pulse. Feluda joined him a second later. He was looking grave, and frowning deeply.

'What do you think?' asked Mr Chowdhury in a low voice.

'His pulse is faster than it should be.'

'And that wound on his head?'

'He must have got it as he fell. I got tired of telling him to wear a cap when working in the sun.'

'Concussion—?'

'It's impossible to tell without making a proper examination. The trouble is, I didn't bring my medical kit today. I think he should be removed to a hospital right away.'

'That's not a problem. I have a car.'

Feluda helped the others in carrying Jayanta Babu to the car. He remained unconscious. Kalinath Roy met us on the staircase.

'I had stepped into my room just for a second to take some

186

medicine—and this happened!' he exclaimed.

'Shall I come with you?' asked Mr Chowdhury as Dr Sarkar got into the car.

'No, there's no need to do that. I'll give you a ring from the hospital.'

The car left. I felt very sorry for Mr Chowdhury. What an awful thing to happen on one's birthday. Besides, now his plan wouldn't work, either.

We went into the drawing room and sat down. But Feluda sprang to his feet almost immediately and went out of the room with a brief 'I'll be back in a minute'. He returned soon enough, but I couldn't tell where he'd gone. Mr Chowdhury continued to speak normally, even going so far as to tell his guests a few stories about his great-grandfather. But clearly it wasn't easy for him to remain calm and cheerful, when he must have been feeling anxious about his cousin.

Dr Sarkar rang an hour later. Jayanta Babu had regained consciousness and was feeling better. He would probably come back home the next day.

This piece of news helped everyone relax, but the chief purpose of our visit seemed to have been defeated. Mr Chowdhury made no attempt to bring out any objects from the chest and, in fact, after declining his offer to show us films on video, we returned to our room soon after dinner. The magic show also got cancelled.

As soon as we were back in our room, Lalmohan Babu asked the question I had been dying to ask for a long time.

'Where did you disappear to when we were all in the drawing room?'

'I went to Mr Chowdhury's aunt's room.'

'Why? Just to see how she was doing?' Lalmohan Babu sounded sceptical.

'Yes, but I also pulled at the handle of that chest.'

'Oh? And was it open?'

'No. I don't think Jayanta Babu got the chance to open it. He seemed to have fallen on the floor *before* he got to the room.'

'But where's the key?' I asked.

'I don't think Mr Chowdhury thought of looking for it. Everything happened so quickly.'

I opened my mouth to speak, but at this moment, Mr Chowdhury himself came into the room. 'I am so sorry about everything,' he said, 'but thank goodness Jayanta is feeling better. This happened once before. Sometimes his blood pressure drops alarmingly.'

'What else did Dr Sarkar say?'

'That's what I came to tell you. I didn't want to say anything in front of the others. You see, I'd forgotten all about the key. Now, the doctor tells me Jayanta hasn't got it. Perhaps it slipped out of his pocket as he fell.'

'Did you look for it?'

'Oh yes, I looked everywhere on the landing, the stairs and even outside the front door. That key has vanished.'

'Never mind. You have a duplicate, don't you?'

'Yes, but that's not the point. The mystery hasn't been solved, has it? That's what's worrying me. I couldn't even give you the chance to exercise your brain!'

'So what? *I* wouldn't consider this visit entirely fruitless. I've seen this beautiful house and enjoyed your wonderful hospitality. That's good enough for me, Mr Chowdhury.'

Mr Chowdhury smiled. 'It's very kind of you to say so, Mr Mitter. Anyway, I shall now bid you good-night. Your bed tea will arrive at six-thirty, and breakfast will be served at eight.'

Lalmohan Babu spoke in a whisper when Mr Chowdhury had gone. 'Could this be a case of attempted murder?' he asked. 'After all, both Mr Kanjilal and Mr Roy had gone into the house.'

'Surely murder was unnecessary to get what they wanted? All they had to do was make sure Jayanta Babu was unconscious.'

'What do you mean?'

'Just that. How long would it take, do you think, to

remove a key from the pocket of an unconscious man, unlock the chest, take what was needed and then slip the key back where it had been found?'

I hadn't thought of this at all.

'If that is the case,' I said, 'then we have two suspects instead of three—Kanjilal and Roy.'

'No,' Feluda shook his head, 'it's not as simple as that. If someone else had struck him unconscious, Jayanta Babu would have said so the minute he opened his eyes in the hospital. He didn't. Besides, his mother was in the room throughout. Surely she'd have said something if anyone other than a family member started to open the chest? I could pull at the handle only because her back was turned for a second.'

I didn't know what to say. So I went to bed, though I couldn't go to sleep. Feluda was still pacing in the room. What was keeping him awake, I wondered. After a few minutes, Lalmohan Babu returned from his own room.

'Have you looked out of the window?' he asked. 'I have never seen things bathed in moonlight like this. It's a crime to stay indoors on such a night!'

'Yes, you are right,' Feluda began moving towards the door. 'Let's go out. If you must turn into a poet in the middle of the night, you should have witnesses.'

Outside, Amaravati and its surroundings were looking more beautiful than they had done during the day. A thin mist covered everything on the other side of the river. The reflection of the moon shimmered in the dark, rippling water. The sound of crickets in the distance, the smell of hasnuhana, and a fresh breeze combined together to give the atmosphere a magical quality. Feluda looked at the nearly full moon and remarked, 'Man may have landed there, but who can ever take away the joy of sitting in moon-light?'

'There's a terrific poem about the moon,' declared Lalmohan Babu.

'Written, no doubt, by that man who was a teacher in your Athenium Institution?'

'Yes. Baikuntha Mallik. No one in our foolish, miserable country ever gave him his due, but he's a great poet. Listen to this one. Tapesh, listen carefully.'

We had been talking in soft tones. But now, Lalmohan Babu's voice rose automatically as he began to recite the poem.

'O moon, how I admire you!
    A silver disc one day,
    or half-a-disc as days go by,
    or a quarter, or even
    just a slice, oh my,
    like a piece of nail, freshly cut,
    lying in the sky.
After that comes the moonless night,
    there's no trace of you.
As you, my love, are hidden from sight,
    untouched by moonlight, too!'

Lalmohan Babu stopped and, unaware that I was trying desperately hard not to laugh, said seriously, 'As you can see, Tapesh, the poem is actually addressed to a lady.'

'Well, certainly your recitation has caused a lady to come out of her room,' Feluda observed, staring at the balcony on the first floor. This balcony was attached to Mr Chowdhury's aunt's room. The old lady, clad in her white sari, had stepped out of her room and was standing on the balcony, looking around. She remained there for about a minute. Then she went back inside.

We turned towards the river and sat on the steps of the ghat for more than half an hour. Finally, Feluda glanced at his watch and said, 'It's nearly one o' clock. Let's go.' We rose, and stopped still as a strange noise reached our ears.

Thud, thud, clang! Thud, thud, clang!

Slowly, we climbed the steps of the ghat and made our way back to the house.

'Is someone digging a s-secret p-passage?' Lalmohan

190

Babu whispered.

My eyes turned towards the old lady's room. That was where the noise appeared to be coming from. A faint light flickered in it.

Thud, thud, thud, thud, clang, clang!

But another light was on in one of the rooms in the far end. I could actually see someone through the open window. It was a man, talking agitatedly. A few seconds later he went out of the room.

'Mr Kanjilal,' Feluda muttered, 'in Mr Chowdhury's room.'

'What could they have been talking about so late at night?'

'I don't know. Perhaps it was something to do with their business.'

'Why, couldn't you sleep, either?'

All of us started as a new voice spoke unexpectedly. Then I noticed the magician, Kalinath Roy, coming out of the shadows.

That strange noise hadn't stopped. Mr Roy raised his head and looked at the open window of the old lady's room. 'Have you figured out what's causing that noise?' he asked.

'A hand grinder?' said Feluda.

'Exactly. Mr Chowdhury's aunt often wakes in the middle of the night and decides to crush paan leaves in her grinder. I've heard that noise before.'

Mr Roy took out a cigarette from his pocket and lit it. Then he shook the match slowly until it went out, and gave Feluda a sharp, knowing look.

'Why do you suppose a private investigator had to be invited to act as Banwarilal's biographer?' he asked casually. I gasped in astonishment.

So did Lalmohan Babu. Feluda laughed lightly. 'Oh, I'm glad someone recognized me!' he said.

'There's a lot that I know, Mr Mitter. I've been through so much that my eyes and ears have got accustomed to staying open at all times.'

Feluda looked steadily at him. 'Will you come to the point, Mr Roy? Or will you continue to speak in riddles?'

'How many people have you met who can speak their minds openly? Most people do not want to open their mouths. Unfortunately, I am one of them. You are the investigator, it is your job to speak openly and reveal all. But let me tell you one thing. You can forget about using your professional skills here in Shankar's house. Do spend a few days here, if you like, have fun and enjoy yourself. But if you meddle in things that don't concern you, you'll get into trouble.'

'I see. Thanks for your advice.'

Kalinath Roy went back into the house.

'It seems he knows something vital,' Lalmohan Babu observed.

'Yes, but that's not surprising, is it? After all, he was here last year. He may have seen something.'

'Or maybe Mr Roy himself is the thief?' I said. 'Don't you remember what Mr Chowdhury said about his sleight of hand?'

'Precisely,' Feluda nodded.

Chapter 4

I woke at six-thirty the following morning as my bed-tea arrived. But Feluda appeared to have risen long before me.

'I've been for a walk. Went to see the town,' he told me.

'What did you see?'

'Oh, a lot of things. The main thing is that now I'm convinced our visit isn't going to be a waste of time.'

Lalmohan Babu entered the room at this moment and declared that he hadn't slept so soundly for a long time.

'I think the old lady upstairs also slept well last night. She got up much later than usual this morning,' Feluda remarked.

'How on earth do you know that?'

'Ananta told me. He said she was late for her visit to the river. Normally she goes to the ghat at six every morning.'

The three of us were sitting on the veranda. Mr Chowdhury joined us in ten minutes. He'd had his bath, and looked quite fresh.

'I'm afraid I've been recognized,' Feluda told him. 'Your old classmate knows who I am.'

'What!'

'Yes. You were right about him. He knows much more than he lets on.'

'So should I tell everyone else the truth, do you think?'

'Yes, but if you do that, you'll also have to tell them why

I am here. I mean, your secret can no longer remain a secret, can it?'

Mr Chowdhury began to look worried and unhappy. But before he could say anything, Mr Kanjilal and Mr Roy appeared together. Almost in the same instant, a car tooted outside the front door. Feluda, Lalmohan Babu and I went with Mr Chowdhury to see who had arrived. The other two remained on the veranda.

A black Ambassador with a red cross painted on one side was standing outside. Dr Sarkar and Jayanta Babu got out and came walking towards us. The wound on Jayanta Babu's head was now dressed. Some of his hair had had to be shaved for this purpose. 'I am so very sorry,' he said to his cousin. 'I ruined your birthday, didn't I? Actually, my blood pressure—'

'Yes, Mr Chowdhury is aware of the details,' Dr Sarkar cut in. 'You're fine now, and there is no cause for concern. But no more roaming in the sun for you.'

'You'll stay for a cup of tea, won't you?' invited Mr Chowdhury.

'Yes, a cup of tea would be very nice, thank you.'

'Where are the others?' asked Jayanta Babu.

'They're on the veranda.'

Dr Sarkar and Jayanta Babu went off to join the others. Mr Chowdhury was about to follow them, but Feluda's words stopped him. 'Wait, Mr Chowdhury, there's something we need to do before we go back to the veranda,' Feluda said. There was something in his tone that made Mr Chowdhury look up in surprise.

'What is it?'

'You said your aunt had the duplicate key to the chest in her room. Would she give it to us now?'

'Yes, certainly if I asked her for it. But—'

'I need to open it and see what's inside. Yes, now.'

Without another word, Mr Chowdhury led us upstairs. We found his aunt getting ready to go for her bath.

'What!' Mr Chowdhury exclaimed. 'How did you manage

to get so late today?'

'God knows. I just overslept. This doesn't happen very often, of course, but sometimes . . . I don't know . . . .'

'I need the duplicate key to the chest.'

'Why? What have you done with yours?'

'I can't find it,' said Mr Chowdhury, a little helplessly. His aunt opened her wardrobe, and found a large bunch of keys which she handed to him silently. Then she left the room.

Mr Chowdhury went to open the chest. For some odd reason, Feluda stopped for a second to pick up the hand grinder from the floor and inspect it briefly.

'Oh my God, I don't believe this!'

Startled by Mr Chowdhury's scream, Lalmohan Babu dropped the book by Salim Ali he had been carrying under his arm.

'That little bag of gold coins and the ivory box have both disappeared, I take it?' Feluda asked calmly. Mr Chowdhury swallowed, unable to speak.

'Lock up your chest again, Mr Chowdhury, and then let's go downstairs. The time has come to reveal the truth. Please tell the others who I really am, and also tell them that I would be asking them a few questions.'

Mr Chowdhury pulled himself together with a supreme effort, and we trooped down to join the other guests on the veranda.

'I'd like to tell you something,' began Mr Chowdhury, and spoke briefly about what had happened on his previous birthday and what he had discovered only a few minutes ago.

'I could never have imagined that one of my close associates would do such a thing in my own house,' he finished, 'but there is no doubt at all that a gold coin was stolen last year, and now other things are missing. I am therefore asking Mr Mitter, who is a well-known investigator, to make a proper investigation. He would now like to ask you a few questions. I hope you will be good enough to answer them honestly.'

No one spoke. It was impossible to tell what each one of them was thinking. Feluda addressed his first question to Dr Sarkar. It came as a complete surprise to me.

'Dr Sarkar, how many hospitals are there in Panihati?'

'Only one.'

'Does that mean that was where you took Jayanta Babu last night and that was where you rang from?'

'Why do you ask?'

'I'm asking this question because I went to that hospital this morning. Jayanta Babu hadn't been taken there.'

Dr Sarkar laughed. 'But I never said I was calling from the hospital, did I, Mr Chowdhury?'

'Well then, where *were* you calling from?'

'From my house. Jayanta Babu regained consciousness in the car, which meant that his injury was not as serious as I'd thought and there was no concussion. So I decided to take him to my house to keep him under observation overnight.'

'All night. Now let me ask Jayanta Babu something. You took a key from your cousin yesterday. Was it still in your hand when you fell?'

'Yes, but I wouldn't know what happened to it afterwards.'

'It should have fallen somewhere on the landing, or in the vicinity of where you were found lying. But no one could find it.'

'So? How am *I* responsible for that? Why don't you stop beating about the bush, Mr Mitter, and tell us what you really mean?'

'One more question, and then I'll speak my mind, I promise you. Dr Sarkar, are you aware of a substance called alta?'

'Yes, isn't it a red liquid women use on their feet? I know my wife does, occasionally.'

'And you're also aware, aren't you, that at one glance it would be difficult to tell the difference between alta and blood, especially if the light was poor?'

196

Dr Sarkar cleared his throat and nodded.

'Very well. I shall now tell you all what I really think.'

Feluda paused. All eyes were fixed upon him.

'It is my belief,' he continued, 'that Jayanta Babu didn't lose consciousness at all. He only pretended to do so. He was in league with Dr Sarkar, because it was necessary for both of them to leave the house.'

'Nonsense!' shouted Jayanta Babu. 'Why should we do that?'

'So that you could return in the dead of night.'

'Return?'

'Yes. You came in through the smaller gate on the northern side, and crept up to your mother's room.'

'That's too much! If I did that, wouldn't my mother have got to know? Are you aware that she doesn't get more than two hours sleep every night?'

'Yes, I do know she's an insomniac. But what if she had been giving something to make her sleep? What if Dr Sarkar had dropped something into her bowl of milk and rice? A strong sleeping pill, perhaps?'

Neither Dr Sarkar nor Jayanta Babu said anything. Both were beginning to lose their colour and look uncomfortable.

'You had to come back,' Feluda went on, 'because this time you couldn't afford to get things wrong. You *had* to ruin Mr Chowdhury's plan for the evening and get back into the house much later to steal. The theft might not have been discovered for a long time. But you had lost the key you had been carrying, so you had to use the duplicate kept in your mother's wardrobe. While you were doing this, you suddenly heard my friend reciting poetry, and got a bit nervous. You obviously hadn't realized that others in the house were awake, and strolling outside. So you decided to wrap yourself in one of your mother's white saris and come out on the balcony, simply so that we could see a figure and assume it was your mother. Then you went back inside and started to use the hand grinder in the hope that that would make your act more convincing. My suspicions were aroused even then, for you were banging an empty grinder. If it had had paan leaves in it, it would have made a different noise.'

'So what are you accusing me of?' Jayanta Babu asked, making a brave attempt to sound casual. 'That I pretended to be unconscious? Or that I tampered with my mother's food? Or that I stole back into her room and opened the chest?'

'Ah, you admit doing all these things, do you?'

'That doesn't mean a thing, does it? None of these is a punishable offense. Why don't you speak of the real event?'

'Because there isn't only one event to speak of, Jayanta Babu, there are two. Let me deal with them one by one. The first is the theft that occurred a year ago.'

'And what do *you* know about it? For Heaven's sake, you weren't even there!'

'No. But there were others. Someone happened to be standing right next to the thief. He'd have seen everything.'

Mr Chowdhury spoke this time. He sounded greatly distressed. 'What are you saying, Mr Mitter? If someone saw it happen . . . why, surely he'd have told me?'

Instead of giving him a reply, Feluda suddenly turned to face Kalinath Roy. 'What trouble were you talking about, Mr Roy, when you told me to keep away from this case?'

Kalinath Roy smiled. 'Revealing an unpleasant truth can always lead to trouble, can't it, Mr Mitter? Just think of poor Shankar. I only wanted to spare his feelings.'

'You needn't have bothered,' Mr Chowdhury said crossly. 'If you know anything abut this case, Kalinath, come clean. Never mind about my feelings. We've wasted enough time.'

'He couldn't tell you what he'd seen, Mr Chowdhury,' Feluda said before Mr Roy could utter another word, 'for that would have meant a great deal of financial loss for him. And that was why he didn't want me to catch the thief, either. You see, he's been milking the thief dry these past twelve months.'

'What! Blackmail?'

'Yes, Mr Chowdhury, blackmail. But what Mr Roy didn't

know was that the thief had an accomplice. He had noticed only one person remove that gold piece. But I think it was his constant demands for money that forced the thief to think of stealing a second time. And so—'

'No!' cried Jayanta Babu, a note of despair in his voice. 'You're wrong. There was nothing left to be stolen. Banwarilal's other valuable possessions had already gone! That chest is empty.'

'Does that mean none of my allegations are false or baseless? You admit—?'

'Yes! But who . . . who stole the other stuff last night? Why don't you tell us?'

'I will. But before that I want a full confession from you. Go on, tell us, Jayanta Babu, did you and Dr Sarkar get together last year and steal one of the twelve gold coins of Jehangir?'

'Yes. I admit everything. Mr Mitter's absolutely right.'

Feluda quietly took out his mini cassette recorder and passed it to me.

'I . . . I can only beg for forgiveness,' Jayanta Babu continued, casting an appealing glance at his cousin. Dr Sarkar sat with his head in his hands.

'Dr Sarkar has still got that gold coin,' Jayanta Babu added. 'We'll return it to you. We . . . we were both badly in need of money. But when we tried to sell the first coin, we realized the whole set would fetch a price a hundred times more, so . . . .'

'So you decided to remove the remaining eleven pieces?'

'Yes. But we were not the only ones capable of stealing. Anyone who can blackmail . . . .'

'. . . can well be a thief? True. But Mr Roy did not steal anything from that chest.'

'How do you mean?'

'The remaining coins and other objects were removed by Pradosh Mitter.'

As everyone gaped in silence, Feluda left the veranda and went to his room. When he returned, he had the little bag of coins and the ivory box in his hands. 'Here you are, Mr Chowdhury,' he said, 'your great-grandfather's possessions are all safe and intact. You'll find the rings and pendants, too, in that box.'

'But how . . . ?'

'I began to smell a rat, you see, when I found alta on the floor instead of blood, and there was no sign of the key. So I was obliged to pick your pocket, Jayanta Babu, when I helped the doctor to carry you to the car. Thank goodness you had kept the key in your right pocket. I couldn't have taken it if it had been in the other one. The others came and sat down in the drawing room after you'd gone. I took this opportunity to rush upstairs, open the chest and take everything away. I could tell they were no longer safe in your mother's room. Luckily, she was already asleep, so she didn't see me open the chest . . . . Well, here's your key, Mr Chowdhury. Now you must decide what you want to do with the culprits. I have finished my job.'

*

On our way back to Calcutta, Lalmohan Babu made us listen to another poem by Baikuntha Mallik. We heard him in silence, without offering any comments on its poetic merits. It was called 'Genius', and it went thus:

> The world has seen some amazing men,
>   Who knows of what stuff is made
>   their brain?
>
> Shakespeare, Da Vinci,
> Angelo, Einstein,
>   I salute you all,
>   each hero of mine!

The Mystery of Nayan

Chapter 1

Feluda had been quiet and withdrawn for many days. Well, *I* say he was withdrawn. Lalmohan Babu had used at least ten different adjectives for him, including distressed, depressed, lifeless, listless, dull, morose and apathetic. One day he even called him moribund. Needless to say, he didn't dare address his remarks directly to Feluda. He confided in me, but like him, I had no idea why Feluda was behaving so strangely.

Today, quite unable to take it any longer, Lalmohan Babu looked straight at Feluda and asked, 'Why do you seem to preoccupied, Felu Babu? What's wrong?'

Feluda was leaning against a sofa, his feet resting on a small coffee table. He was staring at the floor, his face grim. He said nothing in reply to Lalmohan Babu's question.

'This is most unfair!' Lalmohan Babu complained, a trifle loudly. 'I come here only to have a good chat, to laugh and to spend a few pleasant moments with you both. If you keep behaving like this, I'll have to stop coming. Do give us at least a hint of what's on your mind. Who knows, maybe I can help find a remedy? You used to look pleased to see me every day. Now you just look away each time I enter your house.'

'Sorry,' said Feluda softly, still staring at the floor.

'No, no, there's no need to apologize. I am concerned about you, that's all. I really want to know why you're so upset.

Will you tell me, please?'

'Letters,' said Feluda, at last.

'Letters?'

'Yes, letters.'

'What letters? What was written in them that made you so unhappy? Who wrote them?'

'Readers.'

'Whose readers?'

'Topshe's. Readers who read the stories Topshe writes, all based on the cases I handle. There were fifty-six letters. Each one said more or less the same thing.'

'And what was that?'

'Feluda's stories do not sound as interesting as before, they said. Jatayu can no longer make people laugh. Topshe's narrative has lost its appeal, etc etc.'

I knew nothing about this. Feluda received at least six letters every day. But I'd never bothered to ask what they said. His words surprised me. Lalmohan Babu got extremely cross.

'What do they mean? *I* can't make people laugh? Why, am I a clown or what?'

'No, no. That's not what they mean. No one tried to insult you. They just . . . ' Lalmohan Babu refused to be pacified.

'Shame on you, Felu Babu!' he said, standing with his back to Feluda. 'I am really disappointed. You read all these stupid letters, you stored them away, and you let them disturb you so profoundly. Why? Why didn't you just throw them away?'

'Because,' Feluda replied slowly, 'these readers have given us their support in the past. Now if they tell me the Three Musketeers have grown old much before their time, I cannot ignore their words.'

'Grown old?' Lalmohan Babu wheeled around, his eyes wide with anger and amazement. 'Tapesh is only a young boy, you are as fit as ever. I know you both do yoga regularly. And I . . . why, I managed to defeat my neighbour in an arm wrestle only the other day! He is seventeen years my junior. Now is that a sign of old age? Doesn't everyone grow older with time?

And doesn't age add to one's experience, improve one's judgement, sharpen one's intelligence, and ... and ... things like that?'

'Yes, Lalmohan Babu, but obviously the readers haven't found any evidence of all this in the recent stories.'

'Then that itself is a mystery, isn't it? Do you think you can find an answer to that?'

Feluda put his feet down on the floor and sat up straight.

'It's a wonderful thing to be popular among readers. But such popularity and fame often demand a price. You know that, don't you? Don't your publishers put pressure on you?'

'Oh, yes. Tremendous pressure.'

'Then you should understand. But at least your stories and your characters are entirely fictitious. You can create events and people to satisfy your readers. Topshe cannot do that. He has to rely on what really happens in a case. Now, although I admit truth can sometimes be stranger than fiction, where is the guarantee that all my cases would make good stories? Besides, you mustn't forget that Topshe's readers are mainly children between ten and fifteen. I have handled so many cases that may well have had the necessary ingredients for a spicy novel, but in no way were they suitable for children of that age.'

'You mean something like that double murder?'

'Yes. That one was so messy that I didn't let Topshe anywhere near it, although he is no longer a small child and is, in fact, quite mature for his age.'

'Does that mean Tapesh hasn't been choosing the right and relevant cases to write about?'

'Perhaps, but he is not to be blamed at all. The poor boy has to deal with impatient and unreasonable publishers. He doesn't get time to think. But even that is not the real problem. The real problem is that it is not just children who read his stories. What he writes is read by parents, uncles, aunts, grandparents, and dozens of other adults in a child's family. Each one of them has a particular taste, and a particular requirement. How on earth can all of them be satisfied?'

'Then why don't you give Tapesh a little guidance? Tell him which cases he should write about?'

'Yes, I will. But before I do that, I'll have to have a word with the publishers. They ought to be told that a Feluda story will be ready for publication only if a suitable case comes my way. If it doesn't, too bad. They'll just have to give the whole thing a miss occasionally, and hold their horses. They're hardcore businessmen, Lalmohan Babu. Their only concern is sales figures. Why should they worry about my own image and reputation? I myself will have to take care of that.'

'And your readers? All those who wrote those awful letters to you? Shouldn't you have a word with them as well?'

'No. They're not fools, Lalmohan Babu. What they have said is neither unfair nor incorrect. Now, if Topshe can provide what they expect from him, they'll stop feeling disappointed in me.'

'Hey, what about *me*?'

'And you, my dear friend. We complement each other, don't we? You've been with us throughout, ever since our visit to Jaisalmer. Why, I don't suppose any of our readers could think of me without thinking of you, and vice versa!'

This finally seemed to mollify Lalmohan Babu. He turned to me and said seriously, 'Be very careful in choosing your stories, Tapesh.'

'It's going to be quite simple, really,' Feluda said to me. 'Don't start writing at all until I give you the go-ahead. All right?'

'All right,' I replied, smiling.

Chapter 2

I made this long preamble to show my readers that I am going to write about the mystery of Nayan with full approval from Feluda. In fact, even Lalmohan Babu seemed to agree wholeheartedly.

'Splendid! Splendid!' he said, clapping enthusiastically. 'What a good idea to write about Nayan! Er . . . I hope my role in it is going to remain the same? I mean, you do remember all the details, don't you?'

'Don't worry, Lalmohan Babu. I noted everything down.'

But where should I start?

'Start with Tarafdar's show. That really was the beginning, wasn't it?' Feluda said.

Mr Sunil Tarafdar was a magician. His show was called 'Chamakdar Tarafdar'. Magicians were growing like mushrooms nowadays. Some of them were serious about their art, but the stiff competition made many of them fade into oblivion. Those who stayed on had to maintain a certain standard. Feluda had once been interested in magic. In fact, it was I who had revealed this a long time ago. As a result, many up and coming magicians often invited Feluda to their shows. I accompanied Feluda to some of these, and was seldom disappointed.

Sunil Tarafdar was one of these young magicians on the way up. His name had started to feature in newspapers and journals a year ago. Most reports spoke favourably about him. Last December, he turned up in our house one morning and greeted Feluda by touching his feet. Feluda gets terribly embarrassed if anyone does this, so he jumped up, saying, 'No, no, please don't do that . . . there's no need . . .' Mr Tarafdar only smiled. He was a young man in his early thirties, tall and slim. He sported a thin, carefully trimmed moustache.

'Sir,' he said, straightening himself, 'I am a great fan of yours. I know you are interested in magic. I am going to hold my next show in Mahajati Sadan on Sunday. I have had three tickets reserved for you in the front row. The show begins at 6.30 p.m. I'll be delighted if you come.'

Feluda did not say anything immediately. 'I am inviting you, sir,' Mr Tarafdar continued, 'because the last item in my show is going to be absolutely unique. I am very sure no one has ever shown anything like this on stage before.'

Feluda agreed to go. Lalmohan Babu arrived at 5.30 in his green Ambassador the following Sunday. We chatted for a while over a cup of tea, and left for Mahajati Sadan at six. We got there just five minutes before the show was to start. The hall was packed. Obviously, the large advertisement that had appeared in the press recently had worked. We found our seats in the front row. 'Did you see the ad in the paper?' asked Lalmohan Babu.

'Yes,' Feluda replied.

'It said something about a totally new attraction . . . something called "Jyotishka". What could it be?'

'I don't know, Lalmohan Babu. Just be patient, all will be revealed shortly.'

The show began on the dot of six-thirty. I saw Feluda glance at his watch as the curtain went up, raise his eyebrows and smile approvingly. Punctuality was something he felt very strongly about. He had obviously given Mr Tarafdar a bonus point for starting on time.

The few items we saw in the first half of the programme were, sadly, nothing out of the ordinary. It also became obvious that apart from a costume made of brocade, Sunil Tarafdar had not been able to pay much attention to glamour and glitter in his show, which was unusual for a modern magician.

The show took a different turn after the interval. Mr Tarafdar came back on the stage and began to hypnotize people from the audience. Very soon, it was established beyond any possible doubt that hypnotism was indeed his forte. Certainly, *I* had never seen anyone with such skill. The applause he got was defeaning.

But then, Mr Tarafdar made a sudden false move. He turned towards Feluda and said, 'I would now request the famous sleuth, Mr Pradosh Mitter, to join me on the stage.'

Feluda rose, pointed at Lalmohan Babu and said politely, 'I think it would be a better idea to have my friend join you instead of me, Mr Tarafdar. Having me on the stage might lead to difficulties.'

But Mr Tarafdar paid no attention. He smiled with supreme confidence and insisted on Feluda going up on the stage. Feluda obeyed, and it became clear in a matter of minutes why he had warned about difficulties. The magician tried his utmost to hypnotize Feluda and turn him into a puppet in his hands, but failed miserably. Feluda remained awake, alert and in full control of his senses. In the end, Mr Tarafdar turned to the audience and said the only thing he could possibly say to save the situation.

'Ladies and gentlemen,' he declared, 'you have just witnessed what tremendous powers Mr Mitter is in possession of. I have no regret at all in admitting defeat before him!'

The audience burst into applause again. Feluda came back to his seat. 'Felu Babu,' Lalmohan Babu remarked, 'your entire physiology is different from other men, isn't it?' Before Feluda could respond to this profound observation, Mr Tarafdar announced his last item. The unique, hitherto unseen and unheard of 'Jyotishka' turned out to be a good-looking boy of about eight. What he performed a few minutes later took my breath away.

Mr Tarafdar placed a chair in the middle of the stage and invited the boy to sit down. Then he took the microphone in his hand. 'Ladies and gentlemen,' he said, 'this child is called Jyotishka. He, too, is in possession of a highly remarkable gift. I admit I have nothing to do with his power, it is entirely his own. But I am proud to be able to present him before you.' Then he turned to the boy. 'Jyotishka, please look at the audience.'

Jyotishka fixed his gaze in front of him.

'All right. Now look at that gentleman on the right . . . the one over there, wearing a red sweater and black trousers. Do you think he's got any money in his wallet?'

'Yes, he has,' the boy replied in a sweet, childish voice.

'How much?'

'Twenty rupees and thirty paisa.'

The gentleman slowly took out his wallet and brought out its contents.

'My God, he's absolutely right!' he exclaimed.

'Well, Jyotishka,' Mr Tarafdar went on, 'he has got two ten-rupee notes. Can you tell us the numbers printed on them?'

'11 E 111302; and the other is 14 C 286025.'

'Oh my goodness, he's right again!' the gentleman stood with his mouth hanging open. The hall began to boom with the sound of clapping.

'Any one of you can ask him a question,' said Mr Tarafdar when the noise subsided a little. 'All you have to remember is that the answer to your question must be in numbers. But I must warn you that Jyotishka finds this exercise quite strenuous, so I will allow only two more questions this evening.'

A young man stood up. 'I came here in a car. Can you tell me its number?'

Jyotishka answered this correctly and added, 'But you

210

have another car. And the number of that one is WMF 6232.'

Mr Tarafdar picked out another boy from the audience.

'Did you sit for an exam this year?' he asked.

'Yes, sir. Class X,' the boy replied.

'Jyotishka, can you tell us how much he got in Bengali?'

'Yes. He got eighty-one. In fact, he got the highest marks in Bengali this year.'

'Yes, that's right! But how did you guess? Who told you—?'

The boy's remaining words were drowned in thunderous applause.

'We must go backstage and thank Tarafdar,' Feluda said.

Mr Tarafdar was sitting in front of a mirror, removing his make-up when we found him. He beamed as he saw us.

'How did you like my show? Tell me frankly, sir.'

'Two of your items were truly remarkable. One was your hypnotism, and the other was this child. Where did you find him?'

'He used to live in Nikunjabihari Lane, near Kalighat. His real name is Nayan. I found the name Jyotishka for him. Please don't tell anyone else.'

'No, of course not,' said Feluda. 'But how exactly did you come to know about him?'

'His father brought him to me, in the hope that Nayan's power with numbers might help add to their family income. They're not very well off, as you can imagine.'

'Oh, I'm sure Nayan would have no problem at all in making money. Does he not live with his father any more?'

'No. I have kept him in my own house. A private tutor has been arranged for him, and I've had a doctor work out his diet. He is going to be well looked after, I assure you.'

'Yes, but that would mean spending a lot of money on him, wouldn't it?'

'Yes, I am aware of that. But I also realize Nayan is a gold mine. If initially I have to borrow from friends to raise enough funds, I wouldn't mind doing that because I know I can recover whatever they lend me, in no time.'

'Hmm . . . but ideally, you ought to look for a sponsor.'

'You're right. I *will* contact the right people, in due course . . . just give it a little time.'

'All right. There are only two things I'd like to say, and then we'll leave you in peace. One—make sure you do not lose this gold mine. You really must keep an eye on that boy, at all times. And second, did I see journalists sitting in the second row during your show?'

'Yes. Eleven journalists and reporters came to see the show this evening. They're all going to write about it next Friday. I don't think there's any cause for concern there, at least not until the full story gets printed.'

'Very well. But please remember that if there are any enquiries made regarding Nayan, or if someone wants to meet him, or anything suspicious happens, I am here to help you.'

'Thank you very much, sir. And . . . er . . .'

'Yes?'

'Please call me Sunil, Mr Mitter.'

Chapter 3

To my surprise, Sunil Tarafdar rang us on Tuesday. Surely the press reporters were not going to report anything for another couple of days?

Feluda spoke briefly on the phone, then told me what had happened.

'The news has spread, you see, Topshe,' he said. 'After all, eight hundred people saw his show on Sunday. A lot of them must have talked about Nayan. Anyway, the upshot was that Tarafdar got four telephone calls. Each one of these four people are wealthy and important, and they all want to talk to Nayan. Tarafdar asked them to come after nine tomorrow morning. Each one will be given fifteen minutes, and they've been told three other people will be present at the interview—that's you, me and Lalmohan Babu. Ring him now and tell him.'

'I will, but who are these four people?'

'An American, a businessman from north India, an Anglo-Indian and a Bengali. The American is supposed to be an impresario. Tarafdar wants us to be around because he's not sure he can handle the situation alone.'

When I rang Lalmohan Babu, he decided to come over at once.

'Srinath!' he yelled as he came in and sat down in his favourite couch. Srinath was our cook. He appeared with fresh tea in just a few minutes.

'What's cooking, Felu Babu?' Lalmohan Babu asked with a grin. 'Do I smell something familiar?'

'You are imagining things, my friend. Nothing's happened yet for anything to start cooking.'

'I've been thinking about that boy constantly. What an amazing power he's got, hasn't he?'

'Yes. But these things are entirely unpredictable. One day, without any apparent reason, he may lose this power. If that happens, there won't be any difference left between Nayan and other ordinary boys of his age.'

'Yes, I know. Anyway, we're going to Tarafdar's house tomorrow morning, right?'

'Yes, but let me tell you something. I am not going in my professional capacity.'

'No?'

'No. I will simply be a silent spectator. If anyone has to talk, it will be you.'

'Hey, you really mean that?'

'Of course.'

'Very well, Felu Babu. I shall do my best.'

*

Mr Tarafdar lived in Ekdalia Road. His house must have been built over fifty years ago. It had two storeys and a small strip of a garden near the front gate. An armed guard stood at the gate. Mr Tarafdar had clearly taken Feluda's advice. The guard opened the gate on being given Feluda's name. As we made our way to the main door, Feluda said under his breath, 'Within two years, Tarafdar will leave this house and move elsewhere, you mark my words.'

A bearer opened the door and invited us in. We followed him into the drawing room. The room wasn't large, but was tastefully furnished. Sunil Tarafdar arrived a minute later, accompanied by a huge Alsatian. Feluda, I knew, loved dogs. No matter how large or ferocious a dog might be, Feluda simply couldn't resist the temptation to stroke its back. He did the same with this Alsatian.

'He's called Badshah,' Mr Tarafdar informed us. 'He's twelve years old and a very good watchdog.'

'Excellent. I *am* please to see your house so well-protected. Well, here we are, fifteen minutes before the others, just as you'd asked.'

'Thank you, Mr Mitter. I knew you'd be punctual.'

'Did you take this house on rent?'

'No, sir. My father built it. He was a well-known attorney. I grew up in this house.'

'Aren't you married?'

'No.' Mr Tarafdar smiled. 'I am in no hurry to get married. I must get my show established first.'

The same bearer came in with tea and samosas. Feluda picked up a samosa and said, 'I am not going to utter a single word today. This gentleman will do the talking. You do know who he is, don't you?'

'Certainly!' Mr Tarafdar exclaimed, raising his eyebrows. 'Who doesn't know the famous writer of crime thrillers, Lalmohan Ganguli?'

Lalmohan Babu acknowledged this compliment with a small salute, thereby indicating openly that he thought modesty was a waste of time.

Feluda finished his samosa and lit a Charminar.

'I'd like to tell you something quite frankly, Sunil,' he began. 'I noticed an absence of showmanship in your performance. A modern magician like yourself mustn't neglect that particular aspect. Your hypnotism and Nayan are both remarkable, no doubt, but today's audience expects a bit of glamour.'

'I know that, sir. I did not have enough resources to add glamour to my show. But now I think that lapse is going to be remedied.'

215

'How?'

'I have found a sponsor.'

'What! Already?'

'Yes. I was about to tell you myself. I don't think I need worry any more about money—at least, not for the moment.'

'May I ask who this sponsor is?'

'Excuse me, sir, but he wants to keep his identity a secret.'

'But how did it happen? Are you allowed to tell me that?'

'Why, yes, by all means, sir. What happened is that a relative of this sponsor saw Nayan on the stage on Sunday, and told him about it. My sponsor rang me the same evening and said he'd like to see Nayan immediately. I told him to come at 10 a.m. the following morning. He arrived right on time, and met Nayan. He then asked him a few questions, which, of course, Nayan answered correctly. The gentleman stared at him for a few seconds, quite dumbfounded. Then he seemed to pull himself together and gave me a fantastic proposal.'

'What was it?'

'He said he'd bear all the expenses related to my show. In fact, he's going to form a company called "Miracles Unlimited". I am going to perform on behalf of this company, although no one is going to be told who its owner is. I will get all the credit if my shows are successful. My sponsor will keep the profit. Nayan and I will both be paid a monthly salary. The figure he quoted was really quite generous. I accepted all these terms for the simple reason that it removed a major worry at once—money!'

'But didn't you ask him why he was so interested?'

'Oh yes. He told me rather a strange story. Apparently, this man has been passionately interested in magic since his childhood. He had taught himself a few tricks and had even bought the necessary equipment. But before he could take it up seriously, his father found out what he was doing, and was furious. My sponsor was afraid of his father for he had always been very stern with him. So, in order to please his father, he gave up magic and began to do something else to earn his living. In time, he became quite wealthy, but he couldn't forget his old passion. "I have earned a lot of money," he said to me, "but that has not satisfied my soul. Something tells me this young child will bring me the fulfilment I have craved all my life." That was all, Mr Mitter.'

'Have you actually signed a contract?'

'Yes. I feel so much more relieved now. He's paying for Nayan's tutor, his doctor, his clothes and everything else. Why, he's even promised to pay for me to go and have a show in Madras!'

'Really?'

'Yes. You see, I got a call from a Mr Reddy from Madras, just a few minutes before my sponsor arrived. A south Indian gentleman who lives in Calcutta had seen my show on Sunday and rung Mr Reddy to tell him about it. Mr Reddy owns a theatre. He invited me to go to Madras and perform in his theatre. I said I needed time to think about it. But in just a few minutes my sponsor arrived. When he heard about Mr Reddy's invitation, he told me I shouldn't waste time thinking, and should cable Mr Reddy at once, accepting his offer. All expenses would be paid.'

'But surely you'll have to account for what you spend?'

'Of course. I have a close friend called Shankar who acts as my manager. He'll take care of my accounts. He's a most efficient man.'

A bearer turned up and announced that a foreigner had arrived with a Bengali gentleman. I glanced at my watch. It was only a few seconds past 9 a.m.

'Show them in,' said Mr Tarafdar.

Lalmohan Babu took a deep breath. Feluda remained silent.

The American who entered the room had white hair, but the smoothness of his skin told me he wasn't very old. Mr Tarafdar rose to greet him, and invited him to sit down.

'I am Sam Kellerman,' said the American, 'and with me is Mr Basak, our Indian representative.' Mr Basak, too, was offered a seat.

Lalmohan Babu began his task.

'You are an impresoria—I mean, impresario?'

'That's right. People in America are very interested in India these days. The *Mahabharat* has been performed as a play, and has also been made into a movie, as I'm sure you know. That has opened new avenues for your heritage.'

'So you are interested in our culture?'

'I am interested in that kid.'

'Eh? You take an interest in young goats?'

I had been afraid that this might happen. Lalmohan Babu obviously didn't know Americans referred to children as 'kids'.

Mr Basak came to the rescue. 'He is talking of Jyotishka, the boy who appears in Mr Tarafdar's show,' he explained quickly.

'What exactly do you want to know about him?' Mr Tarafdar asked.

'I want,' Mr Kellerman said slowly and clearly, 'to present this boy before the American people. Only in a country like India could someone be born with such an amazing power. But before I make any final decision, I'd like to see him and test him for myself.'

'Mr Kellerman is one of the three most renowned impresarios in the world,' Mr Basak put in. 'He's been doing this work for more than twenty years. He's prepared to pay handsomely for this young boy. Besides, the boy will get his own share regularly from the proceeds of every show. All that will be mentioned in the contract.'

Mr Tarafdar smiled. 'Mr Kellerman,' he said gently, 'that wonder boy is a part of my own show. The question of his leaving me does not arise. I am shortly going to leave for a tour of south India, starting with Madras. People there have heard of Jyotishka and are eagerly looking forward to his arrival. I am sorry, but I must refuse your offer, Mr Kellerman.'

Kellerman's face turned red. After a brief pause, he said

a little hoarsely, 'Is it possible to see the child at all? And to ask him a few questions?'

'That's no problem,' said Mr Tarafdar and told a bearer to bring Nayan.

Nayan arrived a few seconds later, and went and stood by Mr Tarafdar's chair. He looked no different from other ordinary boys, except that his eyes held a quiet intelligence. Mr Kellerman simply stared at him for a few moments.

Then he said, without removing his eyes from the boy, 'Can he tell me the number of my bank account?'

'Go on, Nayan, tell him,' Mr Tarafdar said encouragingly.

'But which account is he talking about?' Nayan sounded puzzled. 'He's got three accounts in three different banks!'

Kellerman's face quickly lost its colour. He swallowed hard before saying, in the same hoarse voice, 'City Bank of New York.'

'12128-74,' said Nayan promptly.

'Jesus Christ!' Kellerman's eyes looked as though they would pop out of their sockets any minute. 'I am offering you twenty thousands dollars right now,' he said, turning to Mr Tarafdar. 'He could never earn that much from your magic shows, could he?'

'I've only just started, Mr Kellerman. I shall travel with Nayan all over my country. Then there's the rest of the world to be seen. People anywhere in the world would love a magic show, and you've just seen what Nayan is capable of doing. How can you be so sure we'll never earn the kind of money you're talking about on our own merit?'

'Does he have a father?'

'Does that matter? Nayan is in my care, officially *I* am his guardian.'

'Sir,' Lalmohan Babu piped up unexpectedly, 'in our philosophy, sir, to make a sacrifice is more important than to acquire a possession!'

Mr Basak rose to his feet. 'You are letting a golden opportunity slip through your fingers, Mr Tarafdar,' he said,

219

'Please think very carefully.'

'I have.'

Mr Kellerman was now obliged to take his leave. He glanced once at Mr Basak, who took out his visiting card from his pocket and handed it to Mr Tarafdar. 'It's got my address and telephone number. Let me know if you change your mind.'

'Thank you, I will.'

Mr Tarafdar went to see them off. Nayan went back with the same bearer.

'Basak is a clever man,' Feluda remarked, 'or he wouldn't be an American impresario's agent. And he must be wealthy, too. He was reeking of French aftershave, did you notice? But there was a trace of shaving cream under his chin. I don't think he's an early riser. He probably had to shave in a hurry this morning simply to keep his appointment with us.'

Chapter 4

'Well, that's one down. Let's see how long the second one takes. He should be here any minute now.' Mr Tarafdar said. The doorbell rang in a couple of minutes. A man in a dark suit was ushered in. 'Good morning,' greeted Mr Tarafdar, rising. 'I'm afraid I didn't quite catch your name on the telephone. You must be . . . ?'

'Tiwari. Devkinandan Tiwari.'

'I see. Please have a seat.'

'Thank you. Have you heard of T H Syndicate?'

Lalmohan Babu and Mr Tarafdar looked at each other in silence. Clearly, they had not. Feluda was obliged to open his mouth.

'Your business has something to do with imports and exports, right? You have an office in Pollock Street?''

'Yes, that's right,' Mr Tiwari said, looking a little suspiciously at Feluda.

'These three people are my friends. I hope you won't mind talking to me in their presence?' Mr Tarafdar asked.

'Oh no, not in the least. All I want to do, Mr Tarafdar, is ask that young chap a question. If he can give me the correct answer, I shall be eternally grateful.'

Nayan was brought back into the room. Mr Tarafdar laid a hand on his back and said kindly, 'I'm sorry, Nayan, but you

have to answer another question. All right?' Nayan nodded.
Mr Tarafdar turned to Mr Tiwari. 'Go ahead, sir. But please
remember the answer to your question must be in numbers.'

'Yes, I know. That is precisely why I've come.' Mr Tiwari
fixed his eyes on Nayan. 'Can you tell me the combination of
my chest?'

Nayan stared back, looking profoundly puzzled.

'Listen, Jyotishka,' said Feluda quickly, before anyone
else could speak, 'perhaps you don't understand what Mr
Tiwari means by a combination. Let me explain. You see, some
chests and cupboards don't have ordinary locks and keys.
What they have is a disc attached to the lid or on the door that
can be rotated. An arrow is marked on the disc, and around it
are written numbers from one to zero. A combination is a series
of special numbers meant for a particular chest or a cupboard.
If you move the disc and bring the arrow to rest against the
right numbers, the chest opens automatically.'

'Oh, I see,' Nayan said, nodding vigorously.

Lalmohan Babu suddenly asked a pertinent question.

'How come you don't know the combination of your own
chest?'

'I knew it . . . in fact, I had known it and used it to open
my chest a million times over the last twenty-three years. But,'
Mr Tiwari shook his head regretfully, 'I am getting old, Mr
Tarafdar. My memory is no longer what it used to be. For the
life of me, I cannot remember the right numbers for that
combination. I had written it down in an old diary and I have
spent the last four days looking for it everywhere, but I
couldn't find it. It's gone . . . vanished.'

'Didn't you ever tell anyone else what the number was?'

'I seem to remember having told my partner—a long time
ago—but he denies it. Maybe it's my own memory playing
tricks again. After all, one doesn't go about giving people the
details of a combination, does one? Besides, this chest is my
personal property, although it's kept in my office. I don't keep
any money or papers related to our business in it. It only has

the money—my own personal money, you understand—that I don't keep in my bank . . . . I tell you, Mr Tarafdar, I was getting absolutely desperate. Then I heard about this wonder boy. So I thought I'd try my luck here!' He brought his gaze back on Nayan.

'6438961,' Nayan said calmly.

'Right! Right! Right!' Mr Tiwari jumped up in excitement and quickly took out a pocket diary to note the number down.

'Do you know how much money there is in that chest?' asked Mr Tarafdar.

'No, I couldn't tell you the exact figure, but I think what I have is in excess of five lakhs,' Mr Tiwari said with a slight smile.

'This little boy could tell you. Would you like to know?'

'Why, yes! I am curious, naturally. Let's see how far his power can go.'

Mr Tarafdar looked at Nayan again. But, this time, Nayan's reply did not come in numbers.

'There's no money in that chest. None at all,' he said.

'What!' Mr Tiwari nearly fell off his chair. But then he began to look annoyed. 'Obviously, Mr Tarafdar, this prodigy is as capable of making mistakes as anyone else. However, I'm grateful he could give me the number I really needed. Here you are, my boy, this is for you.' Mr Tiwari offered a slim package to Nayan.

'Thank you, sir,' said Nayan shyly, as he took it.

Mr Tiwari left.

'Open it and see what's inside,' Feluda said to Nayan. Nayan took the wrapper of, revealing a small wrist watch.

'Hey, that's very nice of Mr Tiwari!' Lalmohan Babu exclaimed. 'Wear it, Nayan, wear it!'

Nayan put it round his wrist, looking delighted, and left the room.

'I think Mr Tiwari is in for a rude shock,' Feluda remarked when Nayan had gone.

'I bet he'll suspect his partner when he discovers the

223

money's missing—unless, of course, Nayan really made a mistake this time?' Lalmohan Babu said. With a shrug, Feluda changed the subject.

'How are you travelling to Madras? By train or by air?' he asked Sunil Tarafdar.

'It'll have to be by train. I have far too much luggage to go by air.'

'What about security for Nayan?'

'Well, I am going to be with him throughout our journey, so I don't think that's a problem. When we get to Madras, I will be joined by my friend, Shankar. We'll both look after Nayan.'

Feluda started to speak, but was interrupted by the arrival of another gentleman, also attired in a formal suit and tie.

'Good morning. I am Hodgson. Henry Hodgson. I made an appointment with—'

'Me. I am Sunil Tarafdar. Please sit down.'

Mr Hodgson sat down frowning and casting looks of grave suspicion at us. He was obviously a Christian, but I couldn't make out which part of India he came from. Perhaps he had lived in Calcutta for a long time.

'May I ask who all these other people are?' he asked irritably.

'They are very close to me. You may speak freely in front of them. I did tell you they would be present,' Mr Tarafdar said reassuringly.

'Hmm.' Mr Hodgson continued to frown. Why was he in such a bad mood?

'A friend of mine happened to see your show last Sunday,' he said at last. 'He told me about your wonder boy. I didn't believe him. I don't even believe in God. Therefore I have no faith in the so-called supernatural powers some people are supposed to possess. But if you bring that boy here, I'd like to talk to him.'

Mr Tarafdar hesitated for a few seconds before asking his

bearer to call Nayan once more. Nayan reappeared in a minute.

'So this is the boy?' Mr Hodgson looked steadily at Nayan. Then he said, 'We have horse races every Saturday. Did you know that?'

'Yes.'

'Well, can you tell me which horse won the third race last Saturday? What was its number?'

'Five,' replied Nayan instantly.

Mr Hodgson's demeanour changed at once. He stood up and began pacing restlessly, his hands thrust in his pockets.

'Very strange! Oh, how very strange!' he muttered. Then he stopped abruptly and faced Mr Tarafdar. 'All I want is this,' he said, 'I will come here once a week to learn the number of the horse that will win the following Saturday. I shall be frank with you, Mr Tarafdar. Horse races are a passion with me. I've lost a great deal already, but that cannot stop me. If I lose some more, however, my creditors will have me sent to prison. So I want to be absolutely definite that I back only the winning horse. This boy will help me.'

'How can you be so sure? What makes you think that he will?' Mr Tarafdar asked coldly.

'He must, he must, he must!' cried Mr Hodgson.

'No, he must not!' Mr Tarafdar returned firmly. 'This boy's powers must not be misused. There's no use arguing with me, Mr Hodgson. I am not going to change my mind.'

Mr Hodgson's face seemed to crumple. When he spoke, his voice shook.

'Please,' he begged, folding his hands, 'let him at least tell me the numbers for the next race. Just this once.'

'No help for gamblers, no help for gamblers!' said Lalmohan Babu, speaking for the first time since Mr Hodgson's arrival.

Mr Hodgson turned to go. His face was purple with rage.

'I have never seen such stupid and stubborn people, damn it!' he exclaimed and strode out.

'What a horrible man!' Lalmohan Babu wrinkled his nose.

'We've certainly met some weird characters today,' Feluda remarked. 'Mr Hodgson was smelling of alcohol. I caught the smell, I suppose, because I was sitting close to him. His financial resources have clearly hit rock bottom. I noticed patches on his jacket—the sleeves, in particular. *And* he travelled this morning by bus, not by taxi or the metro rail.'

'How do you know that?'

'Someone trod on his foot and left a partial impression of his own shoe on his. This can happen only in a crowded bus or a tram.'

Feluda's powers of observation bordered on the supernatural, too, I thought.

A car came and stopped outside the main gate. All of us automatically looked at the door.

'Number four,' said Feluda.

226

Chapter 5

A minute later, a strange creature was shown in: a smallish man in his mid-sixties, clad in a loose and ill-fitting yellow suit, a green tie wound rather horrifically round his throat, a beard that stood out like the bristles of an old brush and a moustache that reminded me of a fat and well-fed caterpillar. His eyes were abnormally bright, and he carried a stout walking-stick.

He looked around as he entered the room and asked in a gruff voice, 'Tarafdar? Which one of you is Tarafdar?'

'I am. Please sit down,' Mr Tarafdar invited.

'And these three?' The man's eyes swept over us imperiously.

'Three very close friends.'

'Names? Names?'

'This is Pradosh Mitter, and this is his cousin, Tapesh. And over there is Lalmohan Ganguli.'

'All right. Now let's get to work, to work.'

'Yes, what can I do for you?'

'Do you know who I am?'

'You only mentioned your surname on the phone, Mr Thakur. That's all I know.'

'I am Tarak Nath Thakur. TNT. Trinitrotolvene—ha ha ha!'

Mr Thakur roared with laughter, startling everyone in the

227

room. I knew TNT was used in making powerful explosives. But what was so funny about it?

Mr Thakur did not enlighten us. Feluda asked him a question instead.

'Does an exceptionally small dwarf live in your house?'

'Kichomo. A Korean. Eighty-two centimetres. The smallest adult in the entire world.'

'I read about him in the papers a few months ago.'

'Now the Guinness Book of Records will include his name.'

'Where did you find him?' Lalmohan Babu asked.

'I travel all over the world. I have plenty of money. I got it all from my father, I've never had to earn a penny in my life. Do you know how he made his money? Perfumes, he ran a thriving business in perfumes. Now a nephew of mine looks after it. *I* am a collector.'

'Oh? What do you collect?'

'People and animals. People from different countries and different continents. People who have some unique trait in them. I've just told you about Kichomo. Besides him, I have a Maori secretary who can write simultaneously with both hands. He's called Tokobahani. I have a black parrot that speaks three different languages, a Pomeranian with two heads, a sadhu from Laxmanjhoola who sits in the air—quite literally, six feet from the ground, and . . .'

'Just a minute, sir,' Lalmohan Babu interrupted. Tarak Nath Thakur reacted instantly. He raised his stick over his head and shouted, 'You dare interrupt me? *Me*? Why, I—'

'Sorry, sorry, sorry,' Lalmohan Babu offered abject apologies. 'What I wanted to know was whether all these people in your collection stay in your house totally voluntarily?'

'Why shouldn't they? They're well-fed, well-paid and kept in comfort, so they're quite happy to live where I keep them. You may not have heard of me or my collection, but hundreds of people elsewhere in the world have. Why, only

228

the other day, an American journalist interviewed me and published an article in the *New York Times* called "The House of Tarak".'

'That's all very well, Mr Thakur,' put in Mr Tarafdar, 'but you still haven't told me why you're here.'

'You mean I must spell it out? Isn't it obvious? I want that boy of yours for my collection ... what's his name? Jyotishka? Yes, I want Jyotishka.'

'Why? He's being very well looked after here, he's happy and content. Why should he leave me and go and live in your queer household?'

Mr Thakur stared at Sunil Tarafdar for nearly a minute. Then he said slowly, 'You wouldn't speak quite so recklessly if you saw Gawangi.'

'What is Gawangi?' asked Lalmohan Babu.

'Not what, but who,' Mr Thakur replied. 'He's not a thing, but a man. He comes from Uganda. Nearly eight feet tall, his chest measures fifty-four inches and his weight is 350 kgs. He could beat the best of Olympic heavy weight champions hollow, any day. Once he spotted a tiger in the jungles of Terai that had both stripes and spots. A perfectly unique specimen. He managed to knock it unconscious with a shot of a tranquillizer. Then he carried that huge animal for three and a half miles. That same Gawangi is now my personal companion.'

'Have you,' asked Lalmohan Babu, with considerable courage, 'reintroduced the old system of slavery?'

'Slavery?' Mr Thakur almost spat the word out. 'No, sir! When I first saw Gawangi, he was facing a totally bleak future. He came from a good family in Kampala, Uganda's capital. His father was a doctor. It was he who told me that Gawangi had reached the height of seven and a half feet even before he'd turned fifteen. He couldn't go out anywhere for little urchins threw stones at him. He'd had to leave school because his classmates teased and taunted him endlessly. His height and his size were a constant source of embarrassment to him.

229

When I met him, he was twenty-one, spending his days quietly at home, worrying about his future. He would have died like that, had I not rescued him from that situation and brought him with me. He found a new life with me. Why should he be my slave? I look upon him like a son.'

'All right, Mr Thakur, we believe you. But even so, I cannot allow Jyotishka to go and join your zoo.'

'You say that even after being told about Gawangi?'

'Yes. Your Gawangi has nothing to do with my decision.'

For the first time, Mr Thakur seemed to lose a little bit of his self-assurance. I heard him sigh. 'Very well,' he said, 'but can I at least see the boy?'

'Yes, that can be easily arranged.'

Nayan returned to the room. Mr Thakur looked him over, scowling.

'How many rooms does my house have?' he asked abruptly.

'Sixty-six.'

'Hm . . . .'

Mr Thakur slowly rose to his feet, gripping the silver handle of his walking-stick firmly with his right hand.

'Remember, Tarafdar, TNT does not give up easily. Goodbye!'

None of us spoke for a long time after he left. At last, Lalmohan Babu broke the silence by saying, 'Felu Babu, number four is quite an important number, isn't it? I mean, there are the four seasons, and four directions, most of our gods and goddesses have four arms, then there are the four Vedas . . . I wonder what these four characters might be called?'

'Just call them FGP—Four Greedy People. Each was as greedy as the other. But none of them got what they wanted. I must praise Sunil for that.'

'No, sir, there's no need for praise. I only did what struck me as very simple. Nayan is my responsibility. He lives in my house, he knows me and I know him. There's no question of passing him on to someone else.'

'Good. All right, then. It's time for us to leave, I think.'

We stood up.

'There's just one thing I'd like to tell you before I go,' Feluda added. 'No more appointments with strange people.'

'Oh no, sir. I've learnt my lesson! This morning's experience was quite enough for me.'

'And please remember, if Nayan needs my protection, I am always there to do what I can. I've already grown rather fond of that boy.'

'Thank you, sir, thank you so much. I'll certainly let you know if we need your help.'

Chapter 6

It was Thursday. We had spent the previous morning with the Four Greedy People. Things were now getting exciting, which was probably why Lalmohan Babu had turned up at 8.30 today instead of 9 a.m.

'Have you seen today's papers?' Feluda asked him as soon as he came in.

'I'm afraid not. A Kashmiri shawl-walla arrived early this morning and took such a lot of time that I never got the chance. Why, what do the papers say?'

'Tiwari opened his chest, and discovered it was empty.'

'Wha-at! You mean young Nayan was right, after all? When was the money stolen?'

'Between 2.30 and 3 one afternoon. At least, that's what Mr Tiwari thinks. He was in his dentist's chamber during that time. His memory is now working perfectly. Apparently, he had opened the chest two days before the theft and found everything intact. The money was indeed in excess of five lakhs. Tiwari suspects his partner, naturally, since no one else knew the combination.'

'Who is his partner?'

'A man called Hingorani. The 'H' in T H Syndicate stands for Hingorani.'

'I see. But to tell you the truth, I'm not in the least

interested in Tiwari or his partner. What amazes me is the power that little boy has got.'

'I have been thinking about that myself. I'd love to find out how it all started. Topshe, do you remember where Nayan's father lives?'

'Nikunjabihari Lane. Kalighat.'

'Good.'

'Would you like to go there? We might give it a try—my driver is familiar with most alleyways of Calcutta.'

As it turned out, Lalmohan Babu's driver did know where Nikunjabihari Lane was. We reached there in ten minutes. A local paanwalla showed us Nayan's house. A rather thin gentleman opened the door. Judging by the towel he was still clutching in his hand, he had just finished shaving.

'We are sorry to disturb you so early,' Feluda said pleasantly. 'Were you about to leave for your office? May we talk to you for a minute?'

'Yes, of course. I don't have to leave for another half-an-hour. Please come in.'

We walked into a room that acted as both a living room and a bedroom. There was no furniture except two chairs and a narrow bed. A rolled-up mattress lay on it.

'Let me introduce myself. I am Pradosh Mitter, and this is my cousin, Tapesh, and my friend Lalmohan Ganguli. We came to find out more about Nayan. You see, we've come to know him and Tarafdar recently. What a remarkable gift your child has been blessed with!'

Nayan's father stared at Feluda, open awe in his eyes. 'You mean you are *the* Pradosh Mitter, the investigator? Your pet name is Felu?'

'Yes.'

'Oh, it is such a privilege to meet you, sir! I am Ashim Sarkar. What would you like to know about Nayan?'

'I am curious about one thing. Was it Tarafdar's idea that Nayan should stay with him, or was it yours?'

'I shall be honest with you, Mr Mitter. The suggestion was

first made by Mr Tarafdar, but only after he had seen Nayan. I had taken my son to see him.'

'When was that?'

'The day after I came to know about his power with numbers. It was the second of December.'

'Why did you decide to take him to Tarafdar in the first place?'

'There was only one reason for that, Mr Mitter. As you can see, I am not a rich man. I have four children, and only a small job in a post office. My salary gets wiped out long before a month gets over. I have no savings. In fact, I haven't been able to put Nayan in a school at all. When I think of the future of my family, it terrifies me. So when I realized Nayan had a special power, I thought that might be put to good use. It may sound awful, but in my situation, anyone would welcome the chance to earn something extra.'

'Yes, I understand. There's nothing wrong with what you did. So you took Nayan to see Tarafdar. What happened next?'

'Mr Tarafdar wanted to test Nayan himself. So I told him to ask him any question that might be answered in numbers. Tarafdar said to Nayan, "Can you tell me how old I am?" Nayan said, "Thirty-three years, three months and three days." Tarafdar asked two more questions. Then he made me an offer. If I allowed him to take Nayan on the stage with him, he'd pay me a certain amount of money regularly. I agreed. Then he asked me how much I expected to be paid. With a lot of hesitation, I said, "A thousand rupees." Tarafdar laughed at this and said, "Wrong, you're quite wrong. Nayan, can you give us the figure that's in my head?" And Nayan said immediately, "Three zero zero zero." Mr Tarafdar kept his word. He's already paid me an advance of three thousand rupees. So when he suggested that Nayan should stay in his house, I couldn't refuse him.'

'Was Nayan happy about going and living with a virtual stranger?'

'Yes, surprisingly enough. He agreed quite happily, and

now seems to be perfectly content.'

'One more question, Mr Sarkar.'

'Yes?'

'How did you first learn about his power?'

'It happened purely out of the blue. One fine morning he just woke up and said to me, "Baba, I can see lots of things . . . they're running helter-skelter, and some are jumping up and down. Can you see them, too?" I said, "No, I can see nothing. What are these things, anyway?" He said, "Numbers. They're all numbers, from nine to zero. I've a feeling if you asked me something that had anything to do with numbers, these crazy ones would stop dancing around." I didn't believe him, of course, but thought a child ought to be humoured. So I said, "All right. What is that big fat book lying in that corner?" Nayan said, "That's the *Mahabharat*." I said, "Yes. Now can you tell me how many pages it's got?" Nayan smiled at this and said, "I was right, Baba. All the numbers have gone away. I can see only three, standing still. They are nine, three and four." I picked up the *Mahabharat* and looked at the last page. It said 934.'

'I see. Thank you very much, Mr Sarkar. I haven't got any more questions. We're all very grateful to you for giving us your time.'

We said namaskar, came out of the house and got into our car.

We returned home to find two visitors waiting for us. One of them was Sunil Tarafdar. I did not know the other.

'Sorry,' said Feluda hurriedly. 'Have you been waiting long?'

'No, only five minutes,' said Mr Tarafdar. 'This is my manager, Shankar Hublikar.'

The other gentleman rose and greeted us. He seemed to be of the same age as his friend. His appearance was neat and smart. 'Namaskar,' said Feluda, returning his greeting. 'You are from Maharashtra, aren't you?'

235

'Yes, that's right. But I was born and brought up here in Calcutta.'

'I see. Please sit down.' We all did. 'What brings you here this morning?' Feluda asked Mr Tarafdar.

'It's something rather serious, I'm afraid.'

'What do you mean?'

'We were attacked last night by a giant.'

My heart skipped a beat. Was he talking about Gawangi?

'Tell us what happened.'

'I got up this morning as usual at 5.30 to take my dog Badshah for a walk. I came downstairs to collect him, but had to stop when I reached the bottom of the stairs.'

'Why?'

'The floor was covered with blood, and someone's footprints went from there right up to the front door. I measured these later. Each was sixteen inches long.'

'Sixt . . .?' Lalmohan Babu choked.

'And then?'

'There is a collapsible gate at my front door, which stays locked at night. That gate was half open, the lock was broken, and outside that gate was lying my chowkidar, Bhagirath. The bloody footprints went past him up to the main compound wall. Well, I washed Bhagirath's head with cold water and brought him round. He began screaming, "Demon! Demon!" the minute he opened his eyes and nearly fainted again. Anyway, what he then told me was this: in the middle of the night, he happened to be standing just outside the collapsible gate, under a low power bulb that's left on all night. Bhagirath looked up at a sudden noise and, in the semi-darkness, saw a huge creature walking towards him. It had obviously jumped over the wall, for outside the main gate was my armed guard, who had not seen it. Bhagirath told me he had once been to the zoo and seen an animal called a "goraila". This creature, he said, looked very much like a "goraila", except that it was larger and more dangerous. I couldn't learn anything more from Bhagirath because one look at this "demon" made him

236

lose consciousness.'

'I see,' said Feluda, 'the demon then presumably broke open the collapsible gate and got inside. Your Badshah must have attacked him after that and bitten his leg, which forced him to run away.'

'Yes, but he didn't spare my Badshah, either. Badshah's body was found about thirty feet from the main gate. This horrible creature had wrung his neck and killed him.'

The only good thing about this whole gruesome story, I thought, was that TNT had failed in his attempt. Nayan, thank God, was still safe.

Feluda fell silent when Mr Tarafdar finished his tale. He simply sat staring into space, frowning deeply.

'What's the matter, Mr Mitter?' Mr Tarafdar said impatiently. 'Please say something.'

'The time has come to act, Sunil. I can no longer sit around just talking.'

'What're you thinking of doing?'

'I have decided to accompany you and Nayan—all over south India, wherever you go, starting with Madras. He's in grave danger, and neither you nor your friend here could really give him the protection he needs. I must do my bit.' Mr Tarafdar smiled for the first time.

'I can't tell you how relieved I feel, Mr Mitter. If you now start working in your professional capacity, I will naturally pay your fee and all expenses for the three of you to travel together. I mean, my sponsor will meet all costs.'

'We'll talk about costs later. Which train are you taking to Madras?'

'Coromandel Express, on 19 December.'

'And which hotel are you booked at?'

'The Taj Coromandel. You'll travel by first class AC. Just let me have your names and ages. Shankar will make the reservations.'

'Good,' said Feluda. 'If you have any problems, let me know. I know a lot of people in the railway booking office.'

Chapter 7

Mr Tarafdar and his friend left at a quarter to ten. Just five minutes after they'd gone, Feluda received a phone call that came as a complete surprise. He took it himself, so at first we had no idea who it was from. He spoke briefly, and came back to join us for a cup of tea.

'I checked in the directory,' he said, raising a cup to his lips, 'there are only two such names listed.'

'Look, Felu Babu,' Lalmohan Babu said, a little irritably, 'I totally fail to see why you must create a mystery out of every little thing. Who rang you just now? Do you mind telling us simply, without making cryptic remarks?'

'Hingorani.'

'The same Hingorani we read about this morning?'

'Yes, sir. Tiwari's partner.'

'What did he want?'

'We'll find that out when we visit him in his house. He lives in Alipore Park Road.'

'Have you made an appointment?'

'Yes, you ought to have realized it while I was speaking to him. Obviously, you were not paying enough attention.'

'I heard you say, "five o' clock this evening",' I couldn't help saying. This annoyed Lalmohan Babu even more. 'I don't listen in on other people's telephone conversations, as a matter of principle,' he declared righteously. But he was much mollified afterwards when Feluda asked him to stay to lunch, and then spent the whole afternoon teaching him to play scrabble. This did not prove too easy, since it turned out that Lalmohan Babu had never done a crossword puzzle in his life, while Feluda was a wizard at all word games, and a master at unravelling puzzles and ciphers. But Lalmohan Babu's good humour had been fully restored; he didn't seem to mind.

We reached Mr Hingorani's house five minutes before the appointed time.

There was a garage on one side of his compound in which stood a large white car. 'A foreign car?' asked Lalmohan Babu.

'No, it's Indian. A Contessa,' Feluda replied.

A bearer stood at the front door. He looked at Lalmohan Babu and asked, 'Mitter sahib?'

'No, no, not me. This is Mr Mitter.'

'Please come with me.'

We followed him to the drawing room. 'Please sit down,' said the bearer and disappeared. Lalmohan Babu and I found two chairs. Feluda began inspecting the contents of a book case.

A grandfather clock stood on the landing outside. Mr Hingorani entered the room as the clock struck five, making a deep yet melodious sound. Mr Hingorani was middle-aged, thin and perhaps ailing, for there were deep, dark circles under his eyes. We rose as he came in. 'Please, please be seated,' he said hurriedly. We sat down again.

Mr Hingorani began talking. I noticed that the strap of his watch was slightly loose, as it kept slipping forward when he moved his arm.

'Have you read what's been published in the press about T H Syndicate?' he asked.

'Yes indeed.'

'My partner's gone totally senile. At least, I can't think of any other explanation. Nobody in his right mind would behave like this.'

'We happen to know your partner.'

'How?'

Feluda explained quickly about Tarafdar and Nayan. 'Mr Tiwari went to Sunil Tarafdar's house to meet Jyotishka,' he added, 'and we happened to be present. That little wonder boy told him the right numbers for the combination and said there was no money in the chest.'

'I see . . . .'

'You told me on the phone you were being harassed. What exactly has happened?'

'Well, you see, for well over a year Tiwari and I hadn't been getting on well, although once we were good friends. In fact, we were classmates in St Xavier's College. We formed T H Syndicate in 1973, and for a few years things worked out quite well. But then . . . our relationship started to change.'

'Why?'

'The chief reason for that was Tiwari's memory. It began to fail pretty rapidly. At times, he couldn't even remember the simplest of things, and it became very difficult to have him present during meetings with clients. Last year, I told him I knew of a very good doctor who I thought he should see. But Tiwari was most offended at my suggestion. That was when our old friendship began to disintegrate. I was tempted to dissolve the partnership, but stayed on because if I hadn't, the whole company would have had to close down. Still, things might have improved, but . . . but Tiwari's recent behaviour really shook me. He came straight to me when he found his chest empty and said, "Give me back my money, this minute!"'

'Is it true that he had once told you what numbers made up the combination?'

'No, no, it's a stinking lie! He kept his own money and personal papers in that chest. There was no reason for him to have told me the combination. Besides, he seems to think that I stole his money while he was at his dentist's. Yet, I can prove that I was miles away during that time. As a matter of fact, I had gone to visit a cousin who'd had a heart attack, in the Belle

240

Vue clinic at 11 a.m. and I returned at half past three. Tiwari, however, doesn't believe me and has even threatened to set goondas on me if I don't return his money. He's lost his mind completely.'

'Do you have any idea as to who might have stolen the money?'

'To start with, Mr Mitter, I don't believe there's been a theft at all. Tiwari himself must have kept it elsewhere or spent it on something that he's now forgotten. I wouldn't put it past him, really. Have you ever heard of anyone who forgets the numbers of his own combination lock, having used it for over twenty years?'

'I see what you mean. Let's now come to the point, Mr Hingorani.'

'Yes, you wish to know why I called you here, don't you?'

'That's right.'

'Look, Mr Mitter, I need protection. Tiwari himself might be forgetful, but I'm sure his hired hooligans would never forget their task. They'd be cunning, clever and ruthless. Now, protecting a client from criminals does form a part of a private detective's job, does it not?'

'Yes, it does. But I have a problem. You see, I am going to be away for about five weeks. So I cannot start my job right away. Do you think you can afford to wait until I get back?'

'Where are you going?'

'South India, starting with Madras.'

Hingorani's eyes began shining. 'Excellent!' he said, slapping his thigh. 'I was going to go to Madras, in any case. Someone told me of a new business opportunity there. I've stopped going to our local office here, you see. After the way Tiwari insulted me, I just couldn't face going back there. But obviously, I can't stay at home all my life. So I thought I'd try and find out more about the offer in Madras. Are you going by air? We could all go together, couldn't we?'

'We are travelling by train, Mr Hingorani. In fact, I am going simply in order to protect somebody else—a little boy of eight. He's the child called Jyotishka who helped Tiwari.

241

Three different men want to use him for their own purpose. Mr Tarafdar and I must ensure no one gets near him and puts his power to misuse.'

'Of course. But why don't you kill two birds with one stone?'

'How do you mean?'

'If you start working for me, I'll pay you your fee as well. So you can keep an eye both on me and Jyotishka.'

Feluda accepted this offer. But he gave a word of warning to Mr Hingorani. 'I'll do my best, of course, but please remember that may not be sufficient. You yourself must be very careful indeed in what you do and where you go.'

'Yes, naturally. Where will you be staying in Madras?'

'Hotel Coromandel. We'll reach there on the 21st.'

'Very well. I'll see you in Madras.'

We left soon after this. On our way back, I said to Feluda, 'I noticed two empty spaces on the wall in the drawing room, rectangular in shape. It seemed as though a couple of paintings had once hung there.'

'Good observation. They had probably been oil paintings.'

'And now they are missing,' Lalmohan Babu remarked. 'Could that have any special significance, do you think?'

'It's obvious that Mr Hingorani got rid of them.'

'Yes, but why? What does it imply?'

'It can have a thousand different implications, Lalmohan Babu. Would you like a list?'

'I see. You are not treating this matter very seriously, are you?'

'I see no reason to. I've noted the fact and stored it away in my memory. It will be retrieved, if need be.'

'And what about this second case you have just taken on? Will you be able to manage both?'

Feluda did not reply. He looked out of the window of our car with unseeing eyes and began muttering under his breath. 'Doubts . . .' I heard him say, 'Doubts . . . doubts . . . .'

Chapter 8

Many of the leading papers next morning carried reports of Tarafdar's forthcoming visit to Madras. His first show there would be held on 25 December, they said.

Feluda had gone to have a haircut. When he returned, I showed him the reports. 'Yes, I've already seen them,' he said, frowning. 'Clearly, Sunil Tarafdar couldn't resist a bit of publicity. I rang him before I left to give him a piece of my mind, but he refused to pay any attention to what I said. He told me instead how important it was for him to make sure the media took notice of what he was doing. When I pointed out that those three people would now come to know about Nayan's movements and that wasn't desirable at all, he said quite airily that they wouldn't dare do anything now, not after the way he'd handled them the other day. I put the phone down after this since he obviously wasn't gone to change his mind. But this means my job is going to get a lot more difficult and I have to be ten times more alert. After all, *I* know Nayan is still in danger.'

A car stopped outside and, a few seconds later, someone rang the bell twice. This had to be Lalmohan Babu. He was late today. It was almost ten-thirty.

'Have I got news for you!' he said as he walked in, his eyes wide with excitement.

243

'Wait!' Feluda said, smiling a little. 'Let me guess. You went to New Market this morning, right?'

'How do you know?'

'A cash memo of Ideal Stores in New Market is peeping out of the front pocket of your jacket. Besides, that big lump in your side pocket clearly means that you bought a large tube of your favourite toothpaste.'

'All right. Next?'

'You went to a restaurant and had strawberry ice cream—there are two tiny pink drops on your shirt.'

'Shabash! Next?'

'Naturally, you didn't go into a restaurant all alone. You must have run into someone you knew. *You* didn't invite him to have an ice cream. He did. I am aware that you don't have a single close friend—barring ourselves—with whom you'd want to go to a restaurant. So presumably, this person was someone you met recently. Now, who could it be? Not Tarafdar, for he's far too busy. Could it be one of the four greedy people? Well, I don't think it was Hodgson. He hasn't got money to waste. TNT? No, he wouldn't travel all the way to New Market to do his shopping. That leaves us with—'

'Brilliant, Felu Babu, absolutely brilliant! After a long time, you've shown me today that your old power of deduction is still intact.'

'Was it Basak?'

'Oh yes. Nandalal Basak. He told me his full name today.'

'What else did he tell you?'

'Something rather unpleasant, I'm afraid. Apparently, Basak added ten thousand dollars to their original offer. But even so, Tarafdar refused. That naturally annoyed Basak very much. He said to me, "Go tell your snoopy friend, Mr Ganguli, Nandalal Basak has never been defeated in his life. If Tarafdar does a show in Madras, he'll have to drop the special item by that wonder boy. We'll see to it!"'

My hands suddenly turned cold not because Basak's words meant that he had recognized Feluda, but because there was a hidden menace behind his words that I didn't like at all.

'That accounts for Basak,' said Feluda coolly. 'Tiwari is out of the picture. So we now have to watch out for Tarak Nath Thakur and Hodgson.'

'Tarak Nath cannot do anything by himself. It's Gawangi we have to deal with.'

Feluda started to speak, but was interrupted by the door bell. I could hardly believe my eyes when I opened the door. Never before had I seen telepathy work so quickly. TNT himself stood outside.

'Is Mr Mitter in?'

'Come in, Mr Thakur,' Feluda called. 'So you've worked out who I really am?'

'Of course. And I also know who this satellite of yours is,' TNT said, turning to Lalmohan Babu. 'You are Jatayu, aren't you?'

'Yes.'

'I had once thought of keeping *you* in my zoo, do you know that? After all, in the matter of writing absolute trash, you're quite matchless, I think. *Hullabaloo in Honolulu* . . . ha ha ha!'

The sound of his loud laughter boomed out in our living room. Then he looked at Feluda again. 'So we're meeting once more in Madras, I think?'

'Have you made up your mind about going there?'

'Oh yes. And I won't be alone. My Ugly from Uganda will accompany me, of course. Isn't that marvellous? Sounds just like the title of one of your books, doesn't it, Mr Jatayu?'

'Are you going by train?' Feluda asked.

'I have to. Gawangi couldn't fit into a seat in an aircraft.'

Mr Thakur burst into a guffaw again. Then he rose and began walking towards the front door. 'There's only one thing I'd like to tell you, Mr Mitter,' he threw over his shoulder. 'In some situations, brain power can't possibly be a match for muscle power. Your intelligence may be thousand times stronger than Gawangi's, but if it came to a physical combat,

he'd win with both his hands tied behind his back. Goodbye!'
Mr Thakur disappeared as suddenly as he had appeared.
I'd love to see this Gawangi in person, I thought.

Chapter 9

There was no sign of either Gawangi or TNT on the train. Our journey to Madras proved to be totally eventless.

'I fail to see,' Lalmohan Babu remarked on our way to the hotel, 'why Madras is clubbed together with cities like Delhi, Bombay and Calcutta. Why, any small town in Bengal is more lively than this!'

In a way, he was right. The roads were so much more quiet than the streets of Calcutta. But they were wide, smooth and devoid of potholes. There weren't many skyscrapers, either; nor were there any traffic jams. I began to like the city of Madras. Heaven knew why Lalmohan Babu was still looking morose. However, he cheered up as we entered the brightly lit lobby of our hotel. He looked around a few times, then nodded approvingly and said, 'Beautiful. Hey, this *is* quite something, isn't it?'

We had already decided that we'd spend the first three days just seeing the sights. Nayan and Mr Tarafdar would, of course, accompany us. 'We've seen the Elephanta caves, Ellora and the temples of Orissa,' said Feluda. Now we ought to visit Mahabalipuram. That'll show us a different aspect of architecture in India. Have a look at the guide book, Topshe. You'll enjoy things much better if you're already aware of certain points of interest.'

Since it was already dark, we did not venture out in the evening. In fact, each one of us felt like an early night, so we had dinner by 9 p.m. and went to bed soon after that. The next morning, Feluda said as soon as we were ready, 'Let's go and find out what Sunil and Nayan are doing.'

Unfortunately, we had been unable to get rooms on the same floor. Ours was on the fourth, while Nayan's was on the third. We climbed down a flight of stairs and pressed the bell outside room 382. Mr Tarafdar opened the door. We found Shankar Hublikar in the room, and another gentleman. But there was no sign of Nayan.

'Good morning, Mr Mitter,' said Tarafdar with a big smile, 'meet Mr Reddy. He is the owner of the Rohini Theatre, where I am going to have my first show in Madras. He says there's a tremendous interest in the local public. There have been a lot of enquiries and he thinks the tickets will sell like . . . .'

'Where's Nayan?' Feluda interrupted a little rudely.

'Being interviewed. A reporter from the *Hindu* arrived a little while ago to take his interview. This will mean more publicity for my show.'

'Yes, but where is this interview taking place?'

'The Manager himself made arrangements. There's a conference room on the ground floor . . . .'

Feluda darted out of the room even before Tarafdar had finished speaking, I followed Feluda quickly, Tarafdar's last words barely reaching my ears, ' . . . told him no one should go in . . . .'

We rushed down the stairs without waiting for the lift. Feluda kept muttering under his breath. I caught the words 'fool' and 'imbecile', which I realized were meant for our magician.

A passing waiter showed us where the conference room was. Feluda pushed open the door and marched in. There was a long table, with rows of chairs around it. Nayan was sitting in one of them. A bearded man sat next to him, jotting something down in a notebook. Feluda took this in and, a second later, strode forward to grab the reporter and pull at his beard. It came off quite easily. Henry Hodgson stood staring at us.

'Good morning,' he grinned, without the slightest trace of embarrassment.

'What was he asking you?' Feluda asked Nayan.

'About horses.'

'All right, Mr Mitter, have me thrown out,' said Hodgson, still grinning. 'I have already got the numbers of all the winning horses in every race for the next three days. I shouldn't have a care in the world for many years to come. Good day, sir!'

Mr Hodgson slipped out. Feluda flopped down on a chair, clutching his head between his hands. Then he raised his face and looked straight at Nayan. 'Look, Nayan,' he said somewhat impatiently, 'if anyone else tries talking to you, from now on, just tell them you're not going to utter a word unless I am present. Is that understood?'

Nayan nodded sagely.

'There is one consolation, Feluda,' I ventured to say. 'At least Hodgson's not going to bother us again. He'll now go back to Calcutta and put his last few pennies on horses.'

'Yes, that's true, but I am concerned at Tarafdar's totally irresponsible behaviour. A magician really ought to know better.'

We took Nayan back to Tarafdar's room. 'Did you want publicity, Sunil?' Feluda said sarcastically. 'You'll get it in full measure, but not in the way you'd imagined. Do you know who was taking Nayan's interview?'

'Who?'

'Mr Henry Hodgson.'

'What! That bearded—?'

'Yes, it was that bearded fellow. He's got what he wanted. Didn't I tell you Nayan wasn't out of danger? If Hodgson could follow us to Madras, why shouldn't the others? Now, look, if you want Nayan to remain safe, you've got to do as I tell you. Or else don't expect any help from me.'

'Y-yes, sir!' Mr Tarafdar muttered, scratching his neck and looking somewhat shamefaced.

'Leave the publicity to Mr Reddy,' Feluda continued. 'Neither you nor your friend Shankar should go anywhere near reporters from the press. Many genuine reporters will want interviews and information. You must learn to stay away from them. Your main priority should be Nayan's safety because—remember—if your show is successful, it will be because of *his* power and what he does on the stage, not because of any publicity you might arrange for yourself. Do I make myself clear?'

'Yes, sir. I understand.'

Over breakfast, we told Lalmohan Babu about Hodgson's visit. 'Good, good!' he exclaimed, attacking an omelette. 'I was afraid things would go quiet in Madras. I'm glad something like this has happened. It all adds to the excitement, don't you think?'

We returned to our room to get ready to go out. It had been decided that we'd go to the snake park today. An American called Whitaker had created it and, by all accounts, it was certainly worth a visit. Just as we were about to leave, the doorbell rang. Lalmohan Babu had already joined us in our room. Who could it be?

I opened the door to find Mr Hingorani. 'May I come in?' he asked.

'Of course, please do,' Feluda invited.

Mr Hingorani came in and took a chair. 'So far, so good!' he said with a sigh of relief. 'I don't think Tiwari knows I'm here. I left without a word to anyone.'

'Good. But I hope you're being careful. There's something I really must stress, Mr Hingorani. If anyone rings your doorbell, you must always ask who it is, and open the door only if the person who answers is known to you.' Before Mr Hingorani could say anything, our own doorbell rang again. This time, it was Tarafdar and Nayan.

'Come in,' said Feluda.

'Is this that famous wonder boy?' Mr Hingorani asked.

Feluda smiled. 'Is there any need to introduce these two people to you?'

'What do you mean?'

'Mr Hingorani, you have appointed me for your protection. You ought to have realized that if a client doesn't come clean with his protector, the protector's job becomes much more difficult.'

'What are you trying to say?'

'You know that very well, but you're pretending you don't. But then, you're not the only one who did not tell me the whole truth.'

Feluda looked at Mr Tarafdar, who stared blankly. 'Very well, since neither of you will open your mouth, allow me to do the talking.' Feluda was still looking at Mr Tarafdar. 'Sunil, you said you had got a sponsor from somewhere. My guess is that your sponsor is none other than Mr Hingorani here.'

At this, Mr Hingorani jumped up in sheer amazement. 'But how did you guess?' he cried. 'Are you a magician, too?'

'No, my guess had nothing to do with magic. It was simply the result of keeping my eyes and ears open.'

'How?'

'When we'd gone to see Sunil's show, Nayan had told someone from the audience the number of his car. It was WMF 6232. I saw the same number on your white Contessa. It wasn't too difficult to guess that the young man in the audience was someone from your family, and that he had told you about Jyotishka.'

'Yes, yes. It was Mohan, my nephew.' Mr Hingorani still seemed bemused.

'Besides,' Feluda went on, 'when we went to your house the other day, I noticed quite a few books on magic in your book case. This could only mean—'

'Yes, yes, yes!' Mr Hingorani interrupted. 'When my father found out about my interest in magic, he destroyed all my equipment, but not my books. I managed to save those, and have still got them.'

I glanced at Mr Tarafdar. He was looking extremely uncomfortable. 'Don't blame Sunil,' Mr Hingorani added. 'It was I who asked him to keep my name a secret.'

'But why?'

'There is an important reason. You see, my father is still alive. He's eighty-two, but quite strong and alert for his age. He lives in Faizabad in our old ancestral home. If he finds out that I've got involved with magic and magicians, then even at this age, he's very likely to cut me out of his will.'

'I see.'

'When Mohan told me about Jyotishka, I decided almost immediately to finance his show. By then it was pretty obvious to me that Tiwari and I would soon have to part company, and I'd have to find a new source of income. So I met Tarafdar the next day and made a proposal, which he accepted. Two days later, Tiwari came to me to accuse me of stealing. I just couldn't take it any more. I wrote to Tiwari the following morning, and told him that I was unwell, and that my doctor had advised me a month's rest. I stopped going to my office from the next day.'

'That means you were going to travel to Madras, in any case, to see Tarafdar's show?'

'Yes, but what I told you about my life being in danger is absolutely true, Mr Mitter. I would have had to seek your help, anyway.'

'What about the new business opportunity in Madras you mentioned?'

'No, that was something I just made up. It isn't true.'

'I see. So I've been appointed to protect you from Tiwari's hoodlums, and to save Nayan from three unscrupulous men. We can arrange for one of us to be present with Nayan at all times. But you must tell me what you're going to do to make my job a little easier.'

'Well, I promise to do as I'm told. I have visited Madras

252

many times before. So I don't have to go sight-seeing. Tarafdar's manager can keep me posted about sales figures, once the show starts. In other words, there's no need for me to step out of my room; and most certainly I'm not going to open the door to anyone I don't know.'

'Very well. All right then, Mr Hingorani, I suggest you go back to your room and stay in it. It's time for us to leave.'

All of us rose. 'Come along, Nayan Babu,' said Jatayu, offering his hand. Nayan took it eagerly. He and Jatayu had clearly struck up a friendship.

Chapter 10

We didn't spend very long in the snake park, but even a short visit showed us what a unique place it was. It seemed incredible that a single individual had planned the whole thing. I saw every species of snake that I had read about, and many that I didn't know existed. The park itself was beautifully designed, so walking in it was a pleasure.

No untoward incident took place during our outing on the first day. The only thing I noticed was that Lalmohan Babu tightened his hold on Nayan's hand each time he saw a man with a beard. 'Hodgson has gone back to Calcutta, I'm sure,' I said to him.

'So what?' he shot back. 'How can you tell Basak won't try to appear in a disguise?'

We were strolling along a path that led to an open marshy area. To our surprise, we discovered that this area was surrounded by a sturdy iron railing, behind which lay five alligators, sleeping in the sun. We were watching them closely and Lalmohan Babu had just started to tell Nayan, 'When you're a bit older, my boy, I'll give you a copy of my book *The Crocodile's Crunch*,' when a man wearing a sleeveless vest and shorts turned up, carrying a bucket in one hand. He stood about twenty yards away from the railing and began taking out frogs from the bucket. He threw these at the alligators one by one, which they caught very neatly between their jaws. I watched this scene, quite fascinated, for I had never seen anything like it before.

We returned to our hotel in the evening, all safe and sound. None of us knew what lay in store the next day. Even now, as I write about it, a strange mixture of amazement, fear and disbelief gives me goose-pimples.

*

The guidebook had told me Mahabalipuram was eighty miles from Madras. The roads were good, so we expected to get there in two hours. Shankar Babu had arranged two taxis for us. Nayan insisted on joining us instead of Mr Tarafdar as Jatayu had started telling him the story of his latest book, *The Astounding Atlantic*. I sat in the front seat of the car, Nayan sat between Jatayu and Feluda in the back.

It soon became clear that we were travelling towards the sea. Although the city of Madras stood by the sea, we hadn't yet seen it. Two hours and fifteen minutes later, the sea came into view. A wide empty expanse stretched before us, and on the horizon shimmered the dark blue ocean. The tall structures that stood out on the sand were temples.

Our taxi stopped next to a huge van and a luxury coach. A large number of tourists—most of them American—were getting into the coach, clad in an interesting assortment of clothes, wearing different caps, sporting sunglasses in different designs, and carrying bags of every possible shape and size. We stopped and stared at them for a minute. 'Big business, tourism!' proclaimed Lalmohan Babu and got out of the car with Nayan.

Feluda had never visited Mahabalipuram before, but knew what there was to see. He had already told me everything was spread over a vast area. 'We cannot see it all in a day, at least not when there's a small child with us. But you, Topshe, must see four things—the shore temple, Gangavataran, the Mahishasurmardini Mandap and the Pancha Pandava caves. Lalmohan Babu and Nayan can go where they like. I have no idea what Shankar and Sunil wish to do. They don't seem at all interested in temples or sculpture.'

We began walking together.

'All this was built by the Ballabhas, wasn't it?' asked Lalmohan Babu.

'Not Ballabhas, Mr Ganguli,' Feluda replied solemnly. 'They were Pallavas.'

'Which century would that be?'

'Ask your young friend. He'll tell you.'

Lalmohan Babu looked faintly annoyed at this, but did not say anything. I knew Mahabalipuram had been built in the seventh century.

We went to take a look at the shore temple first. Noisy waves lashed against its rear walls. 'They certainly knew how to select a good spot,' Lalmohan Babu remarked, raising his voice to make himself heard. On our right was a statue of an elephant and a bull. Next to these were what looked like small temples. 'Those are the Pandava's chariots,' Feluda said. 'You'll find one that looks a bit like a hut from a village in Bengal. That's Draupadi's chariot.'

Gangavataran made my head reel. Carved in relief on the face of a huge rock was the story of the emergence of Ganges from the Himalayas. There were animals and scores of human figures, exquisite in every detail.

'All this was done by hand, simply with a chisel and hammer, wasn't it?' Lalmohan Babu asked in wonder.

'Yes. Just think, Lalmohan Babu. There are millions of carved figures like these, to be found in temples all over our country. It took hundreds of years to finish building these temples; dozens and dozens of craftsmen worked on them. Yet, nowhere will you find a single stroke of the hammer that's out of place, or a mark made by the chisel that doesn't fit in. If something goes wrong with a figure of clay, the artist may be able to correct his mistake. But a single mark on a piece of rock would be permanent, absolutely indelible. That is why it always takes my breath away when I think of how totally perfect these ancient artists' skill had been. God knows why modern artists have lost that sense of perfection.'

Mr Tarafdar and Shankar Babu had gone ahead. 'You may as well go and see the two caves I told you about,' Feluda said to me. 'I am going to look at these carvings more closely, so I'm going to take a while.'

I took the guidebook from Feluda and looked at the map to see where the caves were located. 'Look, Lalmohan Babu,' I said, pointing at two dots on the map, 'this is where we have to go.' But it was not clear whether Lalmohan Babu heard me, for he had already resumed his story about the Atlantic and started to walk away. I followed him, and soon found a path that went up a small hill. According to the plan, I was supposed to go up this path. The noise of the waves was a lot less here. I could hear Lalmohan Babu's voice quite clearly. Perhaps his story was reaching its climax.

I found the Pancha Pandava cave. Before I could go in, I saw Lalmohan Babu and Nayan come out and walk further up the same path. Neither seemed even remotely interested in the astounding specimens of sculpture all around.

I took a little time to inspect the carvings. The figures of animals were surprisingly life-like. Even in thirteen hundred years, their appearance hadn't changed. When I stepped out of the cave, two things struck me immediately. The sky had turned grey, and the breeze from the sea was stronger. There was no noise except the steady roar of the waves and an occasional rumble in the sky.

The Mahishasurmardini Mandap stood in front of me. Since Lalmohan Babu had come in the same direction, he should have been in there, but there was no sign of either him or Nayan. Could he have walked on without going into the mandap at all? But why would he do that? There was nothing worth seeing on the other side. Suddenly, I felt afraid.

257

Something must have happened. I came out quickly and began running, almost without realizing it. Only a few seconds later, a new noise reached my ears—and froze my blood.

'Ha ha ha ha ha ha!'

There could be no mistake. It was TNT's laughter.

I turned a corner sharply, and my eyes fell on a horrible sight. A colossal black figure, clad in a red and white striped shirt and black trousers, was walking rapidly away, carrying Lalmohan Babu and Nayan, one under each arm. I could now see for myself why Mr Tarafdar's chowkidar had called him a demon.

Under any other circumstances, I would have been petrified. But now there was no time to lose. 'Feluda!' I yelled and began sprinting after the black giant. If I could attach myself to one of his legs, perhaps that would slow him down?

I managed to catch up with him eventually and lunged forward to grab his leg. He let out a sharp yelp of pain, which could only mean that my hands had landed on the same spot where Badshah had bitten him. But in the next instant, I found myself being kicked away. Two seconds later, I was lifted off the ground and placed under the same arm which held Nayan. My own legs swung in the air like a pendulum. I was held so tightly that, very soon, I began to feel as though I'd choke to death. Lalmohan Babu, too, was crying out in pain.

But TNT was still laughing. Out of the corner of my eye, I saw him raise his stick in the air, making circular movements, and heard him shout like a maniac, 'Now do you see what I meant? How do you find Gawangi, eh?'

I would have told him, but at this moment, events took a dramatic turn. Two men emerged from behind TNT. One of them was leaning forward and walking strangely, taking long, measured steps. He was also swaying his arms from side to side.

Mr Tarafdar! And his friend, Shankar Hublikar.

I knew what Mr Tarafdar was trying to do. I had seen him make the same gestures on stage, when he hypnotized people.

He continued to move forward, his eyes fixed on our captor. By this time, TNT had seen both men. He charged at Tarafdar, his stick still raised high. Shankar Hublikar snatched it from his hand.

Gawangi slowed down. He suddenly seemed unsure of himself. I saw TNT tear at his hair and shout at him; but I couldn't understand a word of the language he spoke.

Mr Tarafdar and Gawangi were now facing each other. With an effort, I managed to turn my head and look up at Gawangi's face. What I saw took me by surprise again. His eyes were bulging, his jaw sagged and I could see all his teeth. I had never seen a human face like that.

Then, slowly, the huge arms that were carrying us began to lower themselves. A few moments later, I felt solid ground under my feet, and realized that Lalmohan Babu and Nayan had also landed safely.

'Go back to your car,' Mr Tarafdar spoke through clenched teeth. 'Let me deal with this, then we'll find ours.'

The three of us turned and began running back towards the caves. I saw TNT sit down on the sand, his face between his hands.

We found Feluda still looking at Gangavataran. The sight of three figures rushing forward madly made him guess instantly what had happened. He ran quicker than us and opened the doors of our taxi. Luckily, the driver had not left his seat.

All of us jumped in.

'Turn back!' shouted Feluda. 'Go back to Madras, fast!'

Only one of us spoke as our car started to speed towards the city. It was Nayan.

'That giant has forty-two teeth!' he said.

Chapter 11

We were having a most enjoyable lunch in the dining room called Mysore in our hotel. It specialized in Moghlai cuisine. Lalmohan Babu had offered to pay for this meal, as a token of thanks to Mr Tarafdar for having saved his life. Tarafdar and Shankar Babu had rejoined us in the hotel.

'But how did Gawangi find you in the first place?' Feluda asked Lalmohan Babu.

'Don't ask me, Felu Babu! What happened was this: I was totally engrossed in telling my story, and Nayan was hanging on to every word. We kept going into and coming out of caves and mandaps, without really taking anything in. In one of these, suddenly I saw a statue of Mahishasur. I was about to come out after just one glance, when my eyes fell on another statue, painted black from head to toe, except that its torso was covered with red and white stripes. It was massive, and it was horrible. I was staring at it, quite puzzled by this deviation from all the other sculptures in the complex and wondering if it might perhaps be a statue of Ghatotkach—I mean, there *were* characters from the *Mahabharat* strewn about, weren't there?—when the statue suddenly opened its eyes. Can you imagine that? The monster had actually been sleeping while standing up! Anyway, he lost not a second when he opened his eyes and saw us. Before either of us could get over the

260

shock, he'd picked us up and was striding ahead. Well, I think you know the rest.'

'Hm. Gawangi might be physically exceptionally strong, but I'm sure he's actually quite simple. Thank Heavens for that, or Sunil would have found it a lot more difficult to hypnotize him.'

'Yes, you're right,' Mr Tarafdar said. 'We'd no idea, of course, that we'd been followed. You see, Shankar is interested in Ayurved. He'd heard somewhere that a herb called Sarpagandha could be found in Mahabalipuram. So we'd gone to look for it. In fact, we even found it and were returning feeling quite jubilant, when we saw Gawangi and Thakur.'

'Sarpagandha? Isn't that given to people with high blood pressure?' Feluda asked.

'Yes,' Shankar Babu replied. 'Sunil's pressure tends to climb up occasionally. I wanted the herb for him.'

Lalmohan Babu threw a chicken tikka into his mouth. 'Felu Babu,' he said, munching happily. 'We managed without your help today. Perhaps you're not going to be needed any more!'

Feluda ignored the jibe and said, 'What is more important is that Gawangi and Thakur's efforts failed.'

'Yes. We're now left with only Basak.'

Mr Reddy, who had arrived just before lunch and had been persuaded to join us (although he ate only vegetarian food), spoke for the first time. 'Tell you what, Mr Tarafdar,' he said gently. 'I suggest you don't go out anywhere else today. In fact, you should rest in the hotel tomorrow as well. After today's events, I really don't think you should run any more risks with that boy. After all, your show begins the day after tomorrow and we're sold out completely for the first couple of days. If anything happened to Nayan, every single person would want his money back. Where do you think we'd stand then?'

'What about security during the shows?'

'I have informed the police. Don't worry, that's been taken care of.'

Mr Reddy had indeed worked very hard to arrange good publicity for the show. We had seen large posters and hoardings on our way back from Mahabalipuram which showed Mr Tarafdar in his golden costume and introduced Nayan as 'Jyotishkam—the Wonder Boy'.

'We've all got to be a lot more vigilant,' Feluda said. 'I must apologize both to you, Mr Reddy, and to Sunil for not taking better care of Nayan. Those statues and carvings in Mahabalipuram simply turned my head, you see, or else I wouldn't have allowed Nayan to get out of my sight.'

We finished our meal and left the dining room. Nayan went back with Mr Tarafdar since Jatayu had finished his story. Feluda, Lalmohan Babu and I returned to our room, and barely five minutes later, came the second surprise of the day.

Feluda was in the middle of telling Jatayu, 'I must now think of retirement, mustn't I? I ought to put you in charge, I think. I'm sure you'll make a very worthy successor—' and Lalmohan Babu was grinning broadly, thoroughly enjoying being teased, when the telephone rang. Feluda broke off, spoke briefly on the phone, then put it down.

'I have no idea who he is. But he wants to come up and see us. He rang from the lobby. So I told him to come. Mr Jatayu, please take over.'

'What!' Lalmohan Babu gasped. 'What do you mean?'

'*You* said my days were over. Let's see how well you can manage on your own.' The bell rang before Lalmohan Babu could utter another word. I opened the door to find a middle-aged gentleman, of medium height, sporting a thick black moustache, although his hair was thin and grey. He walked into the room, glanced first at Feluda and then at Lalmohan Babu, and said, 'Er . . . which one of you is Mr Mitter?'

Feluda pointed at Lalmohan Babu and said coolly, 'He is.'

The man turned to face Lalmohan Babu, with an outstretched hand. Lalmohan Babu pulled himself together, and gave him a manly hand-shake. I remembered Feluda had once said to him, 'A hand-shake is a Western concept. Therefore, if you must shake hands with someone, do so as a Westerner would—a firm grip, and a smart shake.' Perhaps, like me, he had recalled these words for I saw him clutch the other gentleman's hand tightly and give it a vigorous shake. Then he withdrew his hand and said, 'Please sit down, Mr—?'

The man sat down on a sofa. 'I could tell you my name, but that wouldn't mean anything to you,' he said. 'I have been sent here by Mr Tiwari. I have known him for many years. But that isn't all. You see, I am a private detective, like yourself. The company called Detecnique, for which I work, moved from Calcutta to Bombay more than twenty years ago. That is why I never got round to meeting you before, although I did hear your name. Pardon me, Mr Mitter, but I am a little surprised. I mean, you don't *look* like an investigator . . . in fact, this gentleman here is more . . .' he glanced at Feluda.

'He is my friend, Lalmohan Ganguli, a powerfully outstanding writer,' Lalmohan Babu announced solemnly.

'I see. Anyway, let me tell you why I'm here.' He took out a photograph from his pocket. I could see from where I was standing that it was a photo of Mr Hingorani.

'You are working for this man, aren't you?'

Feluda's face remained impassive. Lalmohan Babu's eyebrows rose for a fleeting second, but he said nothing. We were under the impression that no one knew about Mr Hingorani and us. How had this man found out?

'If that is the case, Mr Mitter,' continued our visitor, 'then I am your rival, for I am representing Tiwari. I contacted him when I read about his case in a newspaper. He was delighted, and said he needed my help. I agreed, and left for Calcutta immediately. The first thing I did on reaching Calcutta was ring Hingorani. His nephew answered the phone and said no one knew where his uncle had gone. Then I checked with Indian Airlines and found his name on the passenger list of a Calcutta-Madras flight. It became clear that he had fled after Tiwari's threats. So I went to his house, and met his bearer. He told me that three days ago, three visitors had been to the house. One of them was called Mr Mitter. This made me suspicious, and I looked up your number in the telephone directory. When I rang you, I learnt that you, too, had left for Madras. I put two and two together and decided to discover where you were staying. So here I am, simply to tell you what the latest situation is. You do admit, don't you, that Hingorani appointed you to protect him?'

'Any objections?'

'Many.'

Nobody spoke for a few seconds. Feluda kept smoking, blowing out smoke rings from time to time, his face still expressionless.

'Do you know what developments have taken place regarding Tiwari's case?' our visitor asked.

'Why, has anything been reported in the press?'

'Yes. Some new facts have come to light, that open up a totally different dimension. Are you aware what kind of a man you're protecting? He is a thief, a liar and a scoundrel of the first order.' The man raised his voice and almost shouted the last few words. Lalmohan Babu gulped twice and, despite a heroic effort, failed to hide the anxiety in his voice.

'H-how do you kn-know?'

'Tiwari found irrefutable evidence. Hingorani's ring—a red coral set in gold—was found under the chest. It had rolled to the far end, which was why no one saw it at first. A sweeper found it eventually. Everyone in the office recognized the ring. Hingorani had worn it for years. This is my trump card, Mr Mitter. This will finish your client.'

'But when the theft took place, Mr Hingoraj—no, I mean Hingorani, was visiting his cousin in a hospital.'

'Nonsense. He stole into the office at two in the morning to remove the money. He had to bribe the chowkidar to get in. How do I know? I know because the chowkidar made a full confession to the police. Hingorani paid him five hundred rupees. Tiwari told me he could now remember perfectly when and how he'd told his partner about the combination. It was nearly fifteen years ago. Tiwari had suffered a serious attack of hepatitis. He thought he'd die, so he called Hingorani and gave him the number.'

'But why should Hingorani steal his partner's personal money?'

'Because he was nearly bankrupt, that's why!' our visitor raised his voice again. 'He had started to gamble very heavily. He used to travel to Kathmandu pretty frequently and visit all the casinos. He lost thousands of rupees at roulette, but that did nothing to make him stop. Tiwari tried to warn him. He paid no attention. In the end, he'd begun to sell his furniture and paintings. When even that didn't bring him enough, he thought of stealing Tiwari's money.'

'Well, what do you intend to do now?'

'I will go straight to his room from here. It is my belief that he's brought the stolen money with him. Tiwari is such a kind man that he's offered not to take any action against Hingorani as long as he gets his money back. I am going to pass his message to Hingorani, and hope that he will then come to his senses and return the money.'

'What if he doesn't?'

Our visitor's lips spread in a slow, cruel smile. 'If he doesn't,' he said with relish, 'we'll have to think of a different course of action.'

'You mean you'll use force? But that's wrong, that's unlawful! Why, you are a detective, aren't you? Your job is to expose criminals, not to break the law yourself!'

'Yes, Mr Mitter. But there are detectives, and detectives. I believe in playing things by ear. Surely you know that the dividing line between a criminal and a good sleuth is very, very thin?' He rose. 'Glad to have met you, sir. Good day!' he said, shaking Lalmohan Babu's hand again. Then he swiftly went out.

The three of us sat in silence after he'd gone. Then Feluda spoke. 'Thank you, Lalmohan Babu. The advantage in staying

265

silent is that one gets more time to think. I now realize that Mr Hingorani has recently lost a lot of weight. He's been ailing for sometime, perhaps with diabetes, I don't know. Anyway, the point is that that's why the strap of his watch became loose, and so did his ring. When it slipped off his finger and rolled under the chest, he didn't even notice it.'

'What! You mean what that man just said was true? You're prepared to believe him?'

'Yes, I am. A lot of things that were unclear to me before have now become crystal clear. But that man was wrong about one thing. Hingorani did not steal Tiwari's money to settle his gambling debts. One look at Nayan had told him his financial worries were over. He took the money simply to create the Miracles Unlimited Company, and to support Tarafdar.'

'Won't you go and talk to Hingorani now?'

'No, there's no need. That man from Detecnique will do all the talking. And Hingorani will return Tiwari's money, if only to save his own life. He has no future left as Tarafdar's sponsor.'

'But that means—?'

'Stop it right there, Lalmohan Babu. I do not know what that means, or what all the future implications are. Give me time to think.'

Chapter 12

Lalmohan Babu and I went for a walk in the evening by the sea. Heaven knew what lay in store for Mr Hingorani, but perhaps Nayan was safe for the moment. As a matter of fact, I thought, if Hingorani managed to produce just enough money to pay for his first show—that is, after he'd paid Tiwari back—then everything would be all right. Once people had actually seen what Nayan was capable of, the money would come rolling in and Mr Hingorani would be able to manage quite well.

However, Lalmohan Babu was most annoyed when I told him my theory. 'Tapesh, I am shocked!' he said sternly. 'That man is a criminal. He's stolen a lot of money from his partner. How can you feel happy about the same man making use of Nayan?'

'I am not happy about it, Lalmohan Babu. There is enough evidence against Hingorani to put him in prison right away. But if Tiwari is willing to forgive him, why should either you or I mind if he just gets on with his life?'

'I mind because that man's a gambler. I have no sympathy for gamblers.'

I said nothing more. A little later, Lalmohan Babu seemed to calm down and suggested we stop somewhere for a quick coffee. I was feeling thirsty, too; so we found a café near the beach and went in. It was fairly crowded, but we managed to find a table. 'Two cold coffees, please,' I said to the waiter. A minute later, two tall glasses with straws landed in front of us. Both of us bent our heads slightly to take a sip through the straw.

'Did you speak to your snoopy friend?' asked a voice. Lalmohan Babu choked. I raised my eyes quickly to find Mr Nandalal Basak standing by our table, dressed in a garish shirt. 'Tell your friend, and Tarafdar,' he added, when Lalmohan Babu stopped spluttering, 'that Basak doesn't let grass grow under his feet. He may well have his show on the 25th, but that wonder boy will never get the chance to appear on stage. I can guarantee that.'

Without waiting for a reply, Mr Basak walked out of the café and disappeared from sight. It was already dark outside, so I couldn't see where he went. We paid for our coffee and took a taxi back to the hotel. We reached it in half-an-hour, to find the lobby absolutely packed with people. Right in the middle of the lobby was a huge pile of luggage. Obviously, several large groups of tourists had arrived together.

We made our way to the lift as quickly as we could and pressed number 4. When we reached our room, we realized someone else was in the room already, for Feluda was speaking to him with a raised voice, sounding extremely cross.

He opened the door a few seconds after I rang the bell, and began shouting at us. 'Where the hell have you two been? What's the point in having you here, when I can't ever find you when you're needed?'

Rather embarrassed, we went into the room and found Mr Tarafdar sitting on the sofa, looking as though the world had come to an end.

'What . . . what happened?' Lalmohan Babu faltered.

'Ask your magician.'

'What is it, Sunil?' Mr Tarafdar did not reply.

'He's bereft of speech,' Feluda said, his voice sounding cold and hard, 'so perhaps *I* should tell you what happened.'

He lit a Charminar and inhaled deeply. 'Nayan's gone. Been kidnapped. Can you believe that? How will anyone ever be able to trust me again? Didn't I *tell* you he mustn't step out of your room? Didn't I say so a thousand times? But no, he had to go out with Shankar to the hotel bookshop, when the whole place is crawling with strangers.'

'And then?' I could hear my own heartbeats.

'Go on, Tarafdar, tell them the rest. Or do I have to spend my life speaking on your behalf?' I had very seldom seen Feluda so totally livid with rage.

Mr Tarafdar finally raised his face and spoke in a whisper. 'Nayan was getting fed up of being couped up in the room. He kept badgering Shankar all day to take him out to buy a book. So Shankar went out with him in the evening, only as far as the hotel shopping arcade, and found the bookshop. Nayan chose two books, and passed them to the lady at the cash till. Shankar was watching her make the bill and wrap the books up, when she suddenly said, "That boy . . . where is that boy?" Shankar wheeled around to find Nayan had vanished. He looked for him everywhere. But . . . but there was no sign of him. There were so many people there, such a lot of pushing and jostling . . . who would have noticed a little boy of eight?'

'When did this happen?'

'That's the beauty of it!' Feluda shouted again. 'All this happened an hour and a half ago. But Sunil decided to inform me barely ten minutes before you arrived.'

'Basak,' Lalmohan Babu said firmly. 'Nandalal Basak did this. No doubt about it, Felu Babu. Absolutely none.'

'How can you be so sure?'

I explained about our encounter with Mr Basak. Feluda's frown deepened.

'I see. This is what I'd been afraid of. He must have spotted you in that café soon after he'd had Nayan removed from this hotel.'

'Where is Shankar?' Lalmohan Babu asked.

'He's gone to the police station,' Mr Tarafdar replied.

'But informing the police alone isn't going to solve your problem, is it? You'll have to tell your sponsor and Mr Reddy. Do you think they'll still be prepared to go ahead with your show, even without Nayan? I doubt it!'

'Well, then . . . who's going to tell Hingorani?' Lalmohan Babu asked.

'Not our hypnotist here,' Feluda said. 'He hasn't got the nerve. He's already asked me to do it, since he's afraid Hingorani will throttle him to death, on the spot.'

'All right,' Lalmohan Babu held up a hand, 'neither of you need tell Hingorani. We will. Tapesh, are you ready?'

'Yes, of course.'

'Very well,' Feluda said slowly, 'You two can go and give him the bad news. Go at once. He's in room 288.'

We took the staircase to go down to his room and rang the bell. Nothing happened. 'These bells don't work sometimes,' Lalmohan Babu told me. 'Press it hard.' I did, three times in a row. No one opened the door. So we went down to the lobby once more and rang room 288 from a house telephone. The phone rang several times, but there was no answer. Puzzled, we went to the reception.

'Mr Hingorani must be in the room for his key isn't here,' said the receptionist.

'But . . .' Lalmohan Babu grew agitated, 'he may be sleeping, right? We need to check, see? Very important for us to see him. Now. No duplicate key?' Something in the way he spoke must have impressed the receptionist. Without another word to us, he asked a bell-boy to take a duplicate key and come with us. This time, we took the lift to go up to the second floor. The bell-boy unlocked the door and motioned us to go in.

'Thank you,' said Lalmohan Babu and pushed the door open. Then he took a few steps forward, only to spring back again and run straight into me.

'H-h-h-h-ing!' he cried, looking ashen.

By this time, I, too, had seen it. It made my heart jump into my mouth, and my limbs began to go numb.

Mr Hingorani was lying on his back, although his legs stretched out of the bed and touched the floor. His jacket was unbuttoned and, through the gap, I could see a red patch on his white shirt, from the middle of which rose the handle of a dagger.

Someone had left the TV on, but the sound had been switched off. People talked, laughed, cried, moved and jumped on the screen, in absolute silence. Strange bluish shadows, reflected from the TV screen, danced endlessly on Mr Hingorani's dead face.

Chapter 13

There seemed little doubt that Mr Hingorani had been killed
by the man from Detecnique. The police surgeon put the time
of death between 2.30 and 3.30 p.m. Our visitor had left our
room at 2.45 and had told us that he would go straight to see
Hingorani. It was obvious that Mr Hingorani had refused to
return Tiwari's money, and so Mr Detecnique had decided to
kill him. The police found only sixty-five rupees in a drawer
and a handful of coins. The only luggage in the room was a
suitcase, partly filled with clothes. If indeed Mr Hingorani had
carried lakhs of rupees with him, he'd have put it in a briefcase.
There was no sign of a briefcase anywhere.

Feluda spoke to the police and gave them a description of
the man from Detecnique. 'I couldn't tell you his name,' he
said, 'but if he's taken the money, he'll pass it on to
Devkinandan Tiwari of T H Syndicate in Calcutta. I think your
colleagues there ought to be informed.'

Mr Reddy had heard of the double tragedy, and was now
sitting in our room. I had expected him either to throw a fit, or
have a heart attack. To my amazement, he remained quite calm
and began to discuss how the magic show might still go ahead,
even without Nayan.

'Suppose you concentrate more on your hypnotism?' he
said to Tarafdar, 'I will get leading personalities—politicians,

film stars, sportsmen—on the opening night. You can hypnotize each one of them. How about that?'

Mr Tarafdar shook his head sadly. 'It's very kind of you, Mr Reddy. But I can't spend the rest of my life performing on your stage. I have to move on, but who will treat me with such kindness in other cities? The word has spread, everyone will expect Nayan on my show. Most theatre managers are ruthless businessmen. They wouldn't dream of giving me a chance. I am finished, Mr Reddy.'

'Did Hingorani pay you anything at all?' Feluda asked.

'Yes, he paid me a certain sum before I left Calcutta. It was enough to cover our travel and stay here. Tomorrow, he was supposed to pay me another instalment. You see, he believed in astrology. Tomorrow, he'd told me, was an auspicious day.'

Mr Reddy looked sympathetically at Mr Tarafdar.

'I can see what you're going through. You can't possibly perform in your present state of mind.'

'It isn't just me, Mr Reddy. My manager, Shankar, is so upset that he's taken to his bed. I can't manage without him, either.'

The police had left half-an-hour ago. A murder enquiry had been started. Every hotel and guest-house in the city was going to be asked if they'd had a visitor in the recent past who fitted the description Feluda had given. Hingorani's nephew, Mohan, had been contacted. He was expected to arrive the next day. The police had removed the body.

Feluda himself was going to make enquiries about Nayan and try to find him. 'I am relying solely on you, Mr Mitter,' Mr Reddy said, rising. 'I can postpone the show for a couple of days. Find our Jyotishkam in these two days. Please!'

Mr Reddy left. A minute later, Mr Tarafdar said, 'I think I'll go back to my room. I'll wait for two more days, as Mr Reddy suggested. If Nayan can't be found, I'll just pack my bags and go back to Calcutta. What else can I do? Will you stay on in Madras?'

'Well, obviously I cannot stay here indefinitely. But I'm

not going to go back without getting to the bottom of this business. Why should anyone pull the wool over our eyes and be allowed to get away with it?'

'Very well,' said Mr Tarafdar and went out. Feluda took a long puff at his Charminar, and then muttered a word I had heard him use before: 'Doubts ... doubts ... doubts ....'

'What are you feeling doubtful about?' Lalmohan Babu asked.

'To start with, Hingorani had been told not to open his door to a stranger. How did Mr Detecnique manage to get in? Did Hingorani know him?'

'He may have. Is that so surprising?'

'Besides, Feluda, why are you thinking only of Hingorani's murder? Isn't finding Nayan more important?'

'Yes, Topshe. I am trying to think of both Hingorani and Nayan ... but somehow the two are getting entangled with each other in my mind.'

'But that's pure nonsense, Felu Babu! The two are totally separate incidents. Why are you allowing one to merge with the other?'

Feluda paid no attention to Lalmohan Babu. He shook his head a couple of times, and said softly, 'No signs of struggle ... absolutely no signs of struggle ....'

'Yes, that's what the police said, didn't they?'

'Yet, it wasn't as though the man had been murdered in his sleep.'

'No, of course not. Have you ever heard of anyone going to bed fully dressed, without even taking off his socks and shoes?'

'People do sometimes, if they are totally drunk.'

'But this man hadn't been drinking. At least, not in his room. He might have gone out, of course, and returned quite sozzled.'

'No.'

'Why not?'

'Because the TV had been left on. And there was a

half-finished cigarette in the ash-tray, which means someone had rung the bell while he was in the room, smoking and watching television. He stubbed his cigarette out, switched off the sound of his TV, and opened the door.'

'But surely he'd have wanted to know who it was before opening the door?'

'Yes, but if it was someone he knew, he would naturally have let him in.'

'Then you must assume he knew this man from Detecnique. What he probably didn't know was that Mr Detecnique was a merciless killer.'

'That still doesn't make sense. Why didn't Hingorani resist him when he took out a large knife and attacked him?'

'*I* don't know, Felu Babu! You must find out the reason, mustn't you? If you can't, we'll have to admit you've lost your touch and Tapesh's readers have every right to complain. Where is your earlier brilliance, sir? Where is that razor sharp—?'

'Quiet.'

Lalmohan Babu had to stop in mid-sentence. Feluda was no longer looking at us. His eyes were fixed on the blank wall, his brows creased in a deep frown. Lalmohan Babu and I stared at him for a whole minute without uttering a single word. Then we heard him whisper, 'Yes . . . yes . . . I see . . . I see. But why? Why? Why?'

'Would you like to be left alone for a few minutes, Felu Babu?' Lalmohan Babu asked gently.

'Yes. Thank you, Mr Jatayu. Half-an-hour. Just leave me alone for half-an-hour.'

We came away quietly.

Chapter 14

'Shall we go down to the coffee shop?' I suggested tentatively.

'Hey, that's exactly what I was going to suggest myself,' Lalmohan Babu replied, looking pleased.

We found an empty table in the coffee shop. 'We could have some sandwiches with a cup of tea,' Lalmohan Babu observed. 'That'll help us kill more time.'

'Two teas and two plates of chicken sandwiches, please,' I told the waiter. I was hungry, but food didn't seem all that important just now. Feluda had obviously seen the light. Whether it was only a glimmer, or whether he'd solved the whole mystery, I didn't know. But I began to feel elated.

Lalmohan Babu found another way of killing time. He started to tell me the story of his next book. As always, he had already decided on the name. 'I am going to call it *The Manchurian Menace*. It will mean reading up on China and the Chinese way of life, although my book will have nothing to do with modern China. It will be set during the time of the Mandarins.'

Soon, we finished our tea and sandwiches. Lalmohan Babu finished his story, but even so we had about ten minutes to spare.

'What should we do now?' he asked as we came out in the lobby.

'Let's go to that bookshop,' I said. 'After all, it's become a sort of historic place, hasn't it, since that's where Nayan was seen last?'

'Yes, you're right. Let's go and have a look. Who knows, they might even have displayed copies of my books!'

'Er . . . I don't think so, Lalmohan Babu.'

'Well, no harm in asking, is there?'

There was only one lady in the shop, sitting behind a counter. She was both young and attractive.

'Excuse me,' said Lalmohan Babu, walking straight up to her.

'Yes, sir?'

'Do you have crime novels for . . . for . . . youngsters?'

'In which language?'

'Bengali.'

'No, sir, I'm afraid we don't keep books written in Bengali. But we have lots of books for children in English.'

'I know. Today—in fact, this afternoon—a friend of mine bought two books from this shop for a young boy.'

The lady gave him a puzzled glance. 'No, sir,' she said.

'Eh? What do you mean?'

'I would have remembered, sir, if someone had bought two children's books today. I haven't sold a single one over the last four days.'

'What! But he said . . . maybe some other lady . . . ?'

'No, sir. I handle the sales alone.'

Lalmohan Babu and I looked at each other. I looked at my watch and said, 'Half-an-hour's up!' Lalmohan Babu grabbed my hand. 'Let's go,' he said, dragging me out with him. He paused for a second at the doorway, turned his head and threw a 'Thank you, Miss!' at the lady, then broke into a run to catch a lift.

'How very odd!' he exclaimed, pressing a button. I said nothing, for I simply didn't feel like talking.

The few seconds it took us to reach our room seemed an eternity.

'Feluda!' I said, as we burst in.

'Felu Babu!' said Jatayu, simultaneously.

'One at a time,' Feluda replied sternly.

'Let me speak,' I went on breathlessly. 'Shankar Babu did not go to the bookshop!'

'That's stale news, my boy. Do you have anything fresh to deliver?'

'You mean you knew?'

'I did not sit around doing nothing. I went to the bookshop nearly twenty minutes ago. I spoke to Miss Swaminathan there, and then went to find you to give you the news. But when I saw you were busy gobbling sandwiches, I came away.'

'But in that case—?' I began. Feluda raised a hand to stop me. 'Later, Topshe,' he said, 'I'll hear you out later. Tarafdar rang me from his room just now. He sounded pretty agitated, so I told him to come straight here. Let's see what he has to say.'

The bell rang. I let Mr Tarafdar in.

'Mr Mitter!' he gave an agonized cry. 'Save me. Oh God, please save me!'

'What's happened now?'

'Shankar. Now it's Shankar! I went to his room a few minutes ago, and found him lying unconscious on the floor. I can't believe any of this any more . . . is there going to be no end to my problems?'

The reply that came from Feluda was most unexpected. 'No, Sunil,' he said casually, 'this is just the beginning.'

'What is that supposed to mean?' Mr Tarafdar croaked.

'My meaning is simple enough, I think. You're still pretending to be totally innocent. You should stop the act now, Sunil. The game's up.'

'I do not understand you at all, Mr Mitter. You are insulting me!'

'Insulting you? No, Sunil. All I'm doing is speaking the truth. In five minutes, I'm going to hand you over to the police. They're on their way.'

'But what did I do?'

'I'll tell you gladly. You are a murderer and a thief. That's what I told the police.'

'You have gone mad. You don't know what you're saying.'

'I am perfectly aware of what I'm saying. Mr Hingorani would never have opened his door to a stranger. He did *not* know that man from Detecnique; and that man didn't know him, either, which was the reason why he had brought a photo of Hingorani with him, just to make sure he spoke to the right man. So we can safely assume that Hingorani did not let him get inside his room. But you, Sunil? He knew you well enough. There was no reason for him to keep you out, was there?'

'You are forgetting one thing, Mr Mitter. Remember what the police said? There were no signs of struggle. If I took out a knife and tried to kill him, do you think he would have let me, without putting up a fight?'

'Yes, he would, under a special circumstance.'

'What might that be?'

'It is your own area of specialization, Sunil Tarafdar. Hypnotism. You hypnotized Hingorani before you killed him.'

'Do stop talking nonsense, Mr Mitter. Hingorani was my sponsor. Why should I bite the hand that fed me? Why should I destroy the only man who was prepared to support me? You . . . you make me laugh!'

'All right then, Mr Tarafdar. Laugh while you can, for you'll never get the chance to laugh again.'

'Are you trying to imply that I lost my mind after Nayan was kidnapped? That a sudden attack of insanity made me—'

'No. According to your own story, Nayan went missing in the evening. And Hingorani was killed between 2.30 and 3.30 p.m.'

'You are still talking pure drivel. Try to calm down, Mr Mitter.'

'I can assure you, Sunil Tarafdar, I have seldom felt more

279

calm. Allow me now to give you a piece of news. I went to the
hotel bookshop, and spoke to the lady there. She told me no
one bought children's books in the last four days, and most
certainly no small boy was seen in the shop today.'

'She . . . she lied to you!'

'No, she didn't but you clearly are. You have been telling
lies all day, as has your friend, Shankar Hublikar. He might
come to his senses after being hit with a heavy porcelain
ash-tray, but *you* . . . .'

'What! *You* hit Shankar with an ash-tray? Is that what
knocked him unconscious?'

'Yes.'

'But why?'

'He conspired with you. He helped you to hide your
motive for murder.'

The bell rang again.

'That will be Inspector Ramachandran. Bring him in,
Topshe.'

Inspector Ramachandran walked in and looked
enquiringly at Feluda. Mr Tarafdar turned to him before
Feluda could open his mouth. 'This man here says I killed
Hingorani,' shouted Mr Tarafdar, 'but he cannot show a
motive.'

'It isn't just murder,' Feluda said icily, 'you are also being
accused of stealing. The five lakhs that Hingorani had brought
with him is now in your own possession. You were going to
support yourself with that money, weren't you?'

'Why? Why would I do that?'

'Because,' Feluda spoke slowly, 'Hingorani refused to pay
you another paisa. There was no reason for him to continue to
support you; not after he learnt what had happened to Nayan.'

'Wh-what happened to Nayan?'

Feluda turned to me. 'Topshe, open the bathroom door.
Someone's hiding in there.'

I opened the door, and to my complete bewilderment,
found Nayan standing there. He came out slowly and stood

by Feluda's chair.

'Shankar had had him locked in his bathroom. He wasn't kidnapped at all. I went to Shankar's room the minute I got the whole picture. He denied my allegations, of course, so I had to knock him out in order to rescue Nayan. Are you still going to harp on the motive for murder, Mr Tarafdar? Very well then, Nayan will tell you.'

Mr Tarafdar opened his mouth, but no words came. His hands trembled.

'Nayan,' said Feluda, 'how many years do you think Mr Tarafdar will have to spend in prison?'

'I don't know.'

'Why not? Why can't you tell?'

'I cannot see numbers any more.'

'Not at all?'

'No. I told you, didn't I? Every single number disappeared this morning, when I woke up. They just didn't come back again. So I told Mr Tarafdar and Shankar Babu, and then . . . then they locked me up.'

Mr Tarafdar sat very still. No one spoke. Only the inspector moved forward swiftly.

Robertson's Ruby
(Feluda's Last Case)

Satyajit Ray began writing this novella in 1991, aiming for publication in the annual issue of the *Desh* magazine the following year. Although his health started to fail rapidly, he managed to finish it, despite the fact that by then he was finding it difficult even to hold a pen in his hand and write steadily. In early 1992, he was taken to hospital for what everyone thought to be a routine check-up. He told the editor of *Desh* that the first draft of the novella was ready, but he would revise it and make necessary changes when he returned home. No one knew, of course, that that was not to be. Satyajit Ray died in hospital in April 1992.

'Robertson's Ruby'—Feluda's last case—was published posthumously in October the same year.

Chapter 1

'Do the words "Mama-Bhagney" mean anything to you?'
Feluda asked Jatayu.

I knew what he meant, but looked curiously at Lalmohan
Babu to hear his reply.

'Uncle and nephew?' he asked.

'No, a mere translation of the words won't do. We all
know "mama" means uncle and "bhagney" is nephew. What
do the words remind you of?'

'To be honest, Felu Babu, I haven't the slightest idea what
you're talking about. Your questions always startle me. *You*
tell me what you mean.'

'Have you seen the film *Abhijaan*?'

'Yes, but that was years ago. Why does that—oh, yes, yes!'
Jatayu's eyes lit up. 'Now I do remember. Rocks, aren't they?
There is a small, flat rock balanced on top of a bigger rock. It
seems as though one little push would make the smaller one
jiggle and dance. It's Uncle giving his nephew a piggy-back,
isn't it?'

'Right. That's what the locals say. But can you remember
which district it's in?'

'No.'

'It's in Birbhum. I have never been there. Have you?'

'No, sir.'

'Shameful, isn't it? You are a writer, Lalmohan Babu. Never mind what you write, or who reads your books. You ought to have visited the area in which Tagore spent so many years of his life.'

'The thing is, you see, I have often wanted to go there, but somehow couldn't manage it. Besides, how can Tagore possibly provide any inspiration to someone who writes stuff like *Shivers in the Sahara*?'

'Yes, but Birbhum isn't famous only because of Santiniketan. There are the hot springs of Bakreshwar, there's Kenduli where the poet Jaydev was born, there's Tarapeeth where the famous Tantrik Bama Khepa used to live, there's Dubrajpur which has those funny rocks we were just talking about, apart from endless temples made of terracotta.'

'Terracotta? What's that?'

Feluda frowned. Lalmohan Babu's ignorance often turned Feluda into a schoolteacher. 'It's a mixture of Latin and Italian,' he said. 'Terra is a word meaning soil; and cotta is burnt. It refers to statues and figures made with clay and sand, and baked in fire, like bricks. There are many temples in Bengal that have work done in terracotta, but the best and the most beautiful are in Birbhum. If you didn't know about these, Lalmohan Babu, I'm afraid there's very little that you've learnt about your own state.'

'Yes, I see that now. Forgive me, Felu Babu. Kindly excuse my ignorance.'

'And yet, a European professor has done such a lot of research in this subject. It's really most impressive. I assume you don't read anything but the headlines in newspapers, so obviously you've missed the article published in today's *Statesman*. The name of this professor has been mentioned in this article. He was called David McCutcheon.'

'Which article do you mean?'

'"Robertson's Ruby".'

'Right, right! I did see it, and the colour photograph of the ruby, too. But just as I'd begun to read it, you see, my dhobi turned up, and then I forgot all about it.'

'The writer of that article, Peter Robertson, is visiting India at present. He appears to be very interested in India and Indians. McCutcheon's work and what he wrote about the temples of Birbhum made Robertson want to see them. He wants to go to Santiniketan, too.'

'I see. But what's this about a ruby?'

'There's a story behind it. An ancestor of Peter Robertson called Patrick had fought in the mutiny against the sepoys. Although he was in the Bengal regiment, he happened to be in Lucknow when the mutiny ended and the British won. He was only twenty-six at the time. He joined some of the other British officers who barged into the palace of a nawab and looted whatever they could lay their hands on. Robertson found a huge ruby which he brought back to England with him. In time, it became a family heirloom for the Robertsons, and people began to refer to it as "Robertson's Ruby". Only recently, someone found a diary Patrick Robertson had kept in his old age. No one had been aware of its existence so far. In it, he apparently expressed deep regret at what he had done as a young man, and said that his soul would find ultimate peace only if someone from his family went back to India and returned the ruby to where it had come from. Peter Robertson has brought it with him. He'll give it to an Indian museum before he returns to England.'

Lalmohan Babu remained silent for a few minutes when Feluda finished his story. Then he said, 'Kenduli has a big mela every winter, doesn't it?'

'Yes. A large number of bauls come to it.'

'When does it start?'

'As a matter of fact, it has started already this year.'

'I see. Which is the best way to go?'

'Do you really want to go to Birbhum?'

'Very much so.'

'Well, then, I suggest you ask your driver to take your car straight to Bolpur. We'll go the same day by the Santiniketan

Express. We should reach Bolpur in less than three hours. This train stops only at Burdwan. We need to book rooms for ourselves at the tourist lodge.'

'Why should we go by train?'

'Because this train is different from all the others. It has a first class compartment called the Lounge Car. It's huge, like the ones they had years and years ago, furnished with settees, tables and chairs. Travelling in it will be an experience none of us should miss.'

'Oh, I quite agree. Perhaps I ought to inform Shatadal.'

'Who is Shatadal?'

'Shatadal Sen. We were together in school. Now he lives in Santiniketan, a Professor of History in Vishwa Bharati. He was a brilliant student. I could never beat him.'

'You mean you were a brilliant student yourself?'

'Why, is that so difficult to believe about a man who is the most popular writer of thrillers in Bengal?'

'Well, your present IQ—' Feluda broke off, adding, 'Yes, by all means inform your friend.'

It took us a few days to make all the arrangements. A double and a single room were booked in the Bolpur Tourist Lodge. We packed our woollens carefully, since we knew Santiniketan would be a lot cooler than Calcutta. I found the book by David McCutcheon and quickly leafed through it before we left. It was amazing how a foreigner had collected such detailed information about something my own country possessed, but of which I knew virtually nothing.

The following Saturday, Lalmohan Babu's driver left early with his green Ambassador. We reached Howrah at 9.30 a.m.

'My right eye has been twitching for the last two days. Is that a good sign?' asked Lalmohan Babu.

'I wouldn't know. You know very well I don't believe in such superstitions,' Feluda retorted.

'I had begun to think this might be an indication that we're heading for another mystery, another case,' Lalmohan Babu confided, 'but then I thought Tagore couldn't possibly have any connection with crime, could he? You're right, Felu Babu. If we're going to visit Bolpur, there's no chance of getting mixed up in funny business.'

Chapter 2

Lalmohan Babu claimed afterwards that what happened later was related directly to his twitching eye. 'A coincidence, Lalmohan Babu, that's all it was,' Feluda told him firmly.

The Lounge Car of the Santiniketan Express was large enough to hold twenty-five people. But when we boarded the train, we discovered there were only seven others including two foreigners. Both were white. One was clean shaven with blond hair; the other had a thick beard. Long, dark hair rippled down to his shoulders. Something told me one of them was Peter Robertson. Ten minutes after the train started, I found that I was right.

The three of us were sitting together on a sofa. I had never travelled in such a comfortable carriage. Feluda leant back and lit a Charminar. At this moment, the man with the blond hair, who happened to be sitting close by, stretched out a hand and said, 'May I—?'

Feluda passed him his lighter and said, 'Are you going to Bolpur?'

The man lit his own cigarette and returned the lighter to Feluda. Then he said, smiling and proffering his hand, 'Yes. My name is Peter Robertson and this is my friend, Tom Maxwell.'

Feluda shook his hand, and then introduced us. 'Was it

your article that I read the other day?' he asked.

'Yes. Did you like it?'

'Oh yes. It was a very interesting article. Have you already handed that ruby to a museum?'

'No, it's still with us. But we've spoken to the curator of the Calcutta museum. He said he'd be very pleased to accept it if he gets the go-ahead from Delhi. Once that is confirmed, we'll hand it over to him officially.'

'You have an Indian connection, I know. Does your friend?'

'Yes. Tom's great-great-grandfather was the owner of an indigo factory in Birbhum. The British stopped growing indigo in India when the Germans found a way of producing it artificially and began selling it cheap. That was when Tom's ancestor, Reginald Maxwell, returned to Britain. Tom and I were both bitten by the travel bug. We've travelled together quite often. He's a professional photographer. I teach in a school.'

Tom was sitting with a leather bag resting at his feet. That must contain his camera and other equipment, I thought.

'How long will you be in Birbhum?'

'About a week. Our main work is in Calcutta, but we'd like to see as many temples as we can in Birbhum.'

'There are many other things in Birbhum besides temples that are worth seeing. Maybe we could see them together? Anyway, going back to your article, hasn't there been any feedback from your readers?'

'Oh my God, yes! The *Statesman* began receiving dozens of letters within a couple of days. Some of them were from old Maharajas, some from wealthy businessmen, or collectors of rare jewels. But I had made it quite plain in my article that I wasn't prepared to sell it. You know, I had it valued in England before I came here. I could have sold it there, had I so wished. I was offered up to twenty thousand pounds.'

'You have the stone with you right here?'

'Tom's got it. He's a lot more careful than I am. Besides,

he's got a revolver that he can use, if need be.'

'May we see the ruby, please?'

'Of course.'

Peter looked at Tom. Tom picked up his leather bág and took out a small blue velvet box from it. He passed it to Feluda. Feluda opened it slowly, and all three of us gave an involuntary gasp. Not only was the stone large and beautifully cut, but its colour was such a deep red that it was really remarkable. Feluda held the ruby in his hand for a few seconds, turning it around and looking at it closely. Then he returned it to Tom, saying, 'It's amazing! But there's something else I'd like to see, if I may. Will you show me your revolver, please? You see, I know something about fire arms.' He handed one of his visiting cards to Peter.

'Good Heavens!' Peter exclaimed. 'You're a private investigator, are you? I'm glad we've met. If we have problems we might have to seek your help.'

'I hope it won't come to that, but a lot depends on you, Mr Maxwell, for the ruby is with you for safe-keeping.'

Tom Maxwell said nothing in reply. He just took out his revolver and showed it to Feluda. It was not a Colt like Feluda's.

'Webley Scott,' Feluda said, looking at it. Then he added, 'May I ask you something?'

'Of course,' said Tom, speaking for the first time.

'Why do you need to keep a revolver with you?'

'My work takes me to all kinds of places, some of which are remote and dangerous. I've taken photographs of tribal people in jungles. Not all tribes are friendly, I can tell you. Having a revolver makes my job a lot easier. I once killed a black Mamba snake in Africa with this very revolver.'

'Have you been to India before?'

'No, this is my first visit.'

'Have you started taking photos?'

'Yes, I've taken some of a poor and congested area of Calcutta.'

'You mean a slum?'

'Yes, that's right. I like taking pictures of people and places that are totally different from anything I've known or anything I'm familiar with. The stranger or more alien the subject, the better I find it to photograph. Poverty is, for instance, I think, far more photogenic than prosperity.'

'Photo—what?' Lalmohan Babu whispered.

'Photogenic. Something which looks good when photographed,' Feluda explained.

Lalmohan Babu gave me a sidelong glance and muttered softly, 'Does he mean to say that a hungry, starving man is more photogenic than a well-fed one?'

Tom didn't hear him. 'I will take photographs here in India with the same idea in my mind,' he added. I found his words and his attitude rather peculiar. Peter was undoubtedly a lover of India, but his friend's views appeared to be devoid of any feelings or sympathy. How long would they remain friends, I wondered.

The train stopped at Burdwan. We called a chaiwalla to have tea from small earthen pots. Tom Maxwell took photos of the chaiwalla.

Soon, the train pulled in to Bolpur station. The sight of dozens of rickshaws outside the main gate made Tom want to stop for photos again, but this time Peter was firm and said they mustn't waste time.

We had to hire four rickshaws for ourselves and our luggage. Peter and Tom were also booked at the tourist lodge. By the time we reached it, it was ten minutes past 1 p.m.

Chapter 3

Lalmohan Babu's friend, Shatadal Sen, had come to the station to meet us. He accompanied us back to the lodge. A man of about the same age as Lalmohan Babu, he seemed to know him pretty well. After a long time, I heard someone call him 'Lalu'.

We sat chatting in the lobby before going to our rooms.

'You're expecting your car at three, did you say?' Mr Sen asked. 'You can come to my house when your car gets here. Anybody in Pearson Palli will show you my house. I'll take you to see the complex at Uttarayan.'

'Thank you. May we bring two foreign visitors with us?' Feluda asked.

'Yes, of course. They'd be most welcome.'

Mr Sen left. We moved into our rooms. I was struck immediately by the peace and quiet of our surroundings. This should do Feluda a lot of good. He had just finished solving two complex cases of murder and fraud. He needed a break.

A little later, we found Peter and Tom in the dining hall. Feluda told them of our plan for the evening. Peter seemed delighted, but Tom didn't say anything. 'By the way,' said Peter, 'I received a call from a businessman in Dubrajpur. That's not far from here, I gather. He got his son to call me since his spoken English, his son said, isn't all that good. Anyway, he said he'd heard about my ruby and wanted to buy it. When

I told him I would never sell it, he said that was fine, but he'd like to see it once, so would I be kind enough to visit his house? I agreed.'

'What is this man called?'

'G. L. Dandania.'

'I see. When do you have to meet him?'

'At ten tomorrow morning.'

'May we go with you?'

'Certainly. In fact, I'd be quite grateful for your company. You could act as an interpreter, couldn't you? After we finish our business with Dandania, we could go and have a look at the terracotta temples in Dubrajpur and Hetampur. McCutcheon wrote about those.'

'There are many other things in Dubrajpur worth seeing. We could look at those, too, if we have the time,' Feluda told him.

Lalmohan Babu's driver arrived with the car at 3.45 p.m. 'I stopped for lunch in Burdwan,' he said, 'and I don't think I need a rest. If you want to go out, sir, I can take you any time.'

We left for Mr Sen's house almost immediately. Only a few minutes later, we found ourselves in Uttarayan. Peter said he had never seen a building like it. 'It looks like a palace out of a fairy tale!' he exclaimed. Then we went to Udichi and Shyamali, which were as beautiful. Tom, I noticed, did not take out his camera even once, possibly because there was no evidence of poverty anywhere.

Lalmohan Babu looked at everything with great interest. In the end, however, he shook his head sadly and said, 'No, sir, in a serene atmosphere like this, I could never think up a plot for a thriller. I'd need to go back to Calcutta to do so.'

On our way back, Peter and Tom got into a rickshaw. 'Someone told us there's a tribal village near here. Tom would like to take some pictures,' Peter said. They were obviously off to a Santhal village. We waved them off and returned to the lodge, where we spent the rest of the evening playing antakshari.

'Look, I nearly forgot!' said Mr Sen before taking his leave. 'Lalu, I brought this book for you—*Life and Work in Birbhum*. It was written by a priest a hundred years ago. He was called Reverend Pritchard. It's full of interesting information. You must read it.'

'I certainly will, even if your friend doesn't. Thank you, Mr Sen,' said Feluda.

*

We finished breakfast by eight-thirty the next day. Dubrajpur was only twenty-five kilometres away. Mr Dandania's son had given us excellent directions, and told us that theirs was the largest house in the area.

We arrived a little before ten o'clock at a large house with a very high boundary wall. The name plate on the tall iron gate said 'G L Dandania'. A chowkidar quickly opened the gate for us. He had clearly been warned about our visit. Our car passed through the gate and the long driveway, before coming to a halt at the front door.

A young man in his mid-twenties was tinkering with a scooter just outside the door. He left the scooter and came forward to greet us as we got out of our car. 'My name is Peter Robertson,' said Peter, shaking his hand. 'You must be Kishorilal.'

'Yes, I am Kishorilal Dandania. My father would like to see you. Please come with me.'

'Can my other friends come, too?'

'Of course.'

We followed Kishorilal through a courtyard, up a flight of stairs, past a couple of rooms before he finally stopped outside the open door of their drawing room.

'Should we take off our shoes?' asked Feluda.

'No, no, there's no need.'

The drawing room was large, furnished partly with sofas

and chairs. One end was covered by a thick mattress. Mr G. L. Dandania sat in one corner of the mattress, leaning on a bolster. A pale, thin man with a huge moustache that looked quite incongruous. Besides him in the room was another man of about fifty, wearing grey trousers and a brown jacket. He stood up as we entered. Peter looked at the thin man with the moustache and folded his hands.

'Namaste,' he said. 'Mr Dandania, I presume?'

'Yes, and this is my friend, Inspector Chaubey,' replied Mr Dandania.

'How do you do? Meet my friend, Tom Maxwell. And here are my other friends, Mr Pradosh Mitter, Lalmohan Ganguli and Tapesh.'

'Glad to meet you all. Please be seated. Kishori, *inke liye mithai aur sharbat mangwao* (send for sweets and sherbet for them).'

Kishori disappeared and returned in a few moments. 'I realize you made an appointment to see Mr Robertson,' Feluda said when we were all seated. 'If you have any objection to our presence, we shall leave the room.'

'No, no, please don't worry. All I want to do is take a look at that ruby. Your presence makes no difference to me.'

Tom spoke unexpectedly. 'May I take some pictures?'

'What pictures?'

'Of this room.'

I noticed for the first time that there were innumerable pictures of Hindu gods and goddesses hanging on the walls. It reminded me of Maganlal Meghraj's room in Benaras.

'*Theek hai.*'

'He says you may,' Feluda translated.

'*Lekin pehle woh cheez to dikhaiye.*'

'He wants to see the ruby first.'

'I see.'

Tom Maxwell brought out the blue velvet box from his leather bag. Then he opened the lid and passed it to Mr

Dandania. For some strange reason, my heart suddenly started to flutter.

Mr Dandania held the ruby in his hand and stared at it for a few seconds, his face impassive, before passing it to his friend, Inspector Chaubey. Chaubey glanced at it with open admiration in his eyes, then handed it back to Dandania.

'What price in England?' Mr Dandania asked.

'Twenty thousand pounds,' Peter replied.

'Hm. *Dus lakh rupaye ....*' He put the ruby back in its box and returned it to Maxwell. '*Hum denge dus lakh,*' he added.

'He says he'll pay you a million rupees for it,' Feluda said obligingly.

'But surely he knows that's out of the question? I'm not here to sell it.'

Mr Dandania switched to English again, thereby revealing that he could understand and speak it well enough.

'Why not?' he asked.

'Because my ancestor wanted it to return to India. I came simply to fulfil his wish. The last thing I want to do is set a price on it and give it to someone else for money. It will go to the Calcutta museum, and that's that!'

'You are being foolish, Mr Robertson. In a large museum like that it will simply lie in a corner gathering dust. People will forget all about it.'

'And if I sold it to you? Would it not lie hidden in a chest somewhere, totally out of sight?'

'Nonsense! Why should I allow that to happen? I'd open a private museum of my own, like the Salar Jung in Hyderabad. Ganesh Dandania Museum. Your ruby will get special attention. Everyone will see it. I will put up a plaque outside its case, explaining its history. It will include your own name.'

Before Peter could reply, a bearer came in with sweets on a large plate and glasses of sherbet. We began helping ourselves. Only Tom Maxwell dropped a tablet in his glass before drinking from it.

298

'*Inko kahiye yehan ke paani ko shudh karne ki zaroorat nahin hai,*' said Mr Dandania, glaring. I looked at Feluda with interest, to see how he might tell Tom there was no need to purify the water; but Feluda only smiled and said nothing.

It took us only a few minutes to finish the sweets.

'Well?' Mr Dandania said in his deep voice. Like his moustache, his voice came as a surprise.

'Very sorry, Mr Dandania,' said Peter. 'I told you before I wouldn't sell it under any circumstances. I showed it to you only because you'd made a special request.'

Inspector Chaubey spoke suddenly. 'Look, Mr Robertson,' he said, 'whether or not you wish to sell the ruby is your business. What concerns me is that your friend is roaming around with that ruby in his bag. I don't like this at all. If you like, I can arrange to send a constable with you wherever you go. He'll be in plain clothes, you won't even realize he's with you. But he'll be able to ensure your safety.'

'No,' Tom Maxwell said firmly. 'I am quite capable of taking care of it, thank you. Should anyone try to steal it, I'd know how to deal with him. I can use a gun myself, and I can do without any help from the police.'

Inspector Chaubey gave up. 'Very well. If you are so utterly confident of yourself, there is nothing more to be said.'

'How long are you here for?' Mr Dandania asked.

'Another five days, I should think.'

'All right. Please think this over, Mr Robertson. Think carefully, and come to me again in two days.'

'OK. Thinking can't hurt, can it? I'll consider your proposal very seriously, and let you know what I decide.'

'Good,' Mr Dandania replied, looking grave, 'and goodbye.'

Chapter 4

'Unbelievable! This is really incredible, isn't it?' Lalmohan Babu whispered. I found myself in full agreement. All that stretched before our eyes was an ocean of rocks. Stones and boulders of various shapes and sizes lay scattered on the ground, covering a total area of at least one square mile. Some lay flat, others on their side. Some were huge—as high as three-storeyed buildings—but others were relatively small. A few had large cracks running right across, possibly the result of an earthquake hundreds of years ago. It might have been a scene from prehistoric times. If a dinosaur had peeped out from behind a boulder, I would not have been surprised.

This was one of the sights Dubrajpur was famous for. We had already seen the well-known pair called 'Mama-Bhagney'. Soon after leaving Ganesh Dandania's house, Feluda had suggested we saw these famous rocks. Inspector Chaubey, who had accompanied us, agreed that it was a good idea. Peter seemed absolutely overwhelmed. 'Fantastic! Fantastic!' I heard him mutter more than once. Tom, too, seemed a lot happier. I saw him smile for the first time, possibly because he had found a new subject for photography. Right now, he was sitting atop a huge rock, running a fine comb through his beard. How he had got there, I could not tell.

'Tell me,' said Peter, 'how come there are so many stones

lying around at this particular spot, when there are no mountains or hills nearby? Isn't there a story or a legend behind this?'

Before Feluda could say anything, Lalmohan Babu piped up most unexpectedly. 'Do you know of the god Hanuman?' he asked.

'I have heard of him,' Peter said, smiling.

'Well, when Hanuman was flying through the air with Mount Gandhamadan on his head, some rocks from the mountain fell here in Dubrajpur.'

'How interesting!' Peter nodded.

Feluda gave Jatayu a sidelong glance and said under his breath, 'You just made that up, didn't you?'

'No, sir!' Jatayu protested loudly. 'I heard that story from the manager of the lodge this morning. Everyone in this region believes in it. Why should I have made it up?'

'Because, my friend, the story *I* read in my guide book is different. According to it, it was Ram who had dropped these stones here accidentally, when he was gathering stones to build a bridge across the ocean.'

'I don't care what you've read, Felu Babu! I think my story is much better.' Lalmohan Babu walked away in a huff.

By this time, Tom had climbed down from his rock and joined us. Now he was looking a little bored. Perhaps the stones and rocks weren't photogenic enough for him. His real chance came a few minutes later when we made our way to an old and well-known Kali temple. This was probably the first time he was seeing Hindu devotees having a puja in a temple. His camera didn't stop clicking.

This seemed to upset Inspector Chaubey. 'Look, Mr Maxwell,' he said, 'people here don't like to see photographs taken of religious rituals. You'll have to be a little more discreet.'

'Why?' Tom shot back angrily. 'I am not doing anything illegal or unethical. I am merely taking photos of a public event, openly in front of everyone.'

'Yes, but people can sometimes be extremely sensitive. A foreigner may well find our customs and traditions strange and difficult to accept. Some may object to his taking photos back home, misrepresenting our values and ideas.' Maxwell started to protest again, but this time Peter looked at him sternly, which made him shut up.

*

By the time we finished seeing all the sights of Dubrajpur, we were all quite thirsty. So we found a roadside tea stall and sat down at two of the long benches that were placed outside.

Inspector Chaubey sat between Feluda and me. 'I realized who you were the minute I heard your name,' I heard him say to Feluda, 'but I didn't say anything since I thought you might not wish to reveal your profession to all and sundry.'

'You were absolutely right.'

'Are you here on holiday?'

'Yes, purely.'

'I see.'

'You are from Bihar, aren't you?'

'Yes. But the last five generations of my family had lived here in Birbhum. By the way, has that boy called Maxwell got an Indian connection?'

'Yes. His great-great-grandfather used to own an indigo factory here. I think his name was Reginald Maxwell.'

'I see. My own grandfather used to talk about a Mr Maxwell, who was also a factory owner. Although he had lived many years ago, his name had not been forgotten. From what little I have seen of Tom Maxwell, it is obvious that this other Maxwell was his ancestor.'

'How is it obvious?'

'Reginald Maxwell hated Indians. He was unbelievably cruel to his workers. Tom Maxwell seems to have inherited his arrogance. But Mr Robertson seems just the opposite. He's clearly genuinely fond of this country.'

Feluda made no reply. We had finished our tea. Peter and Tom joined us, and we set off for Hetampur, which was famous for its terracotta temples. The carvings on these enthralled Peter, particularly that of a European lady, on a temple wall. It was two hundred years old, we were told. Tom wasn't interested in temples or carvings. He began taking photos of a child being given a bath by its mother at a tubewell.

Just before getting back into our car to return to the tourist lodge, Feluda turned to Inspector Chaubey to bid him goodbye. 'You seemed to know Dandania pretty well,' he said. 'What sort of a man is he?'

'Very clever. I know him, but I certainly do not regard him as a friend. He tries to keep himself in my good books. He's involved in a lot of shady dealings, so he thinks if he knows someone in the police it might help. I go to his house occasionally, but I keep my eyes and ears open. If I catch him doing anything wrong, I shall not spare him. But he *is* extremely wealthy. He could quite easily buy that ruby for ten lakhs.'

'Does his son look after his father's business?'

'Kishori? No, he doesn't really want to. He wants to start something of his own. Ganesh is fond of his son. I think he'll agree in the end and let Kishori go his own way.'

'I see.'

'Oh, by the way, what are your plans for tomorrow?'

'We might go to see the mela in Kenduli.'

'Are you all planning to go together? I mean, would Robertson and Maxwell go with you?'

'Yes, why?'

'I would like you to keep an eye on Maxwell, Mr Mitter. His behaviour worries me.'

'Very well, Inspector. I'll do my best.'

We returned to the lodge in Bolpur a little before 2 p.m. Soon after our return, two men turned up to meet Peter and Tom. One of them was Aradhendu Naskar, a well-known businessman from Calcutta. The other was called Jagannath Chatterjee, a historian who had specialized knowledge of the temples in Birbhum. Both had read Peter's article in the *Statesman* and decided to meet him. Peter said he'd be very grateful for Mr Chatterjee's help, and asked him to stay in touch. Mr Chatterjee agreed happily.

Mr Naskar took much longer. 'What can I do for you?' Peter asked politely, shaking his hand.

Mr Naskar pulled up a chair and sat down, facing Peter. 'First of all, I want you to confirm one thing.'

'Yes?'

'Is it really true that you have come here to fulfil the wish of your ancestor? I mean, are you visiting because of what he wrote in his diary more than a hundred years ago?'

'Absolutely.'

'You mean you really and truly believe that his soul will find ultimate peace if you return that ruby to India?'

'I don't think what *I* believe is of any relevance,' Peter replied dryly. 'You sound as though you're interested in buying the ruby. I am not going to sell it, Mr Naskar.'

'Have you had it assessed in your country?'

'Yes, it's worth twenty thousand pounds.'

'I see. May I see it, please?'

Tom took it out of his bag without a word and passed it to Mr Naskar. Mr Naskar held it between his thumb and forefinger and turned it to catch the light. Then he turned to Peter and said, rather unexpectedly, 'Neither of you appears to be well off.'

'We're not, Mr Naskar; nor are we greedy.'

'However,' Tom spoke suddenly, 'we don't always think alike.'

'What do you mean?' Mr Naskar raised his eyebrows. Peter answered before Tom could say anything. 'What he means is that we've had a difference of opinion in this matter. Tom doesn't mind selling the ruby, but I do. It is, after all, my property, not his. So you needn't pay any attention to him at all.' I looked at Tom. He scowled in silence.

'Anyway,' said Mr Naskar, 'I am going to be here in Santiniketan for the next three days. I'll stay in touch with you. You can't get rid of me that easily, Mr Robertson. I'm prepared to give you twelve lakhs. My collection of precious stones is well-known, all over the country. I can't see why you're refusing such a splendid chance to earn good money. I hope you'll change your mind in due course.'

'Perhaps I should tell you something, Mr Naskar. I've already had an offer for this ruby.'

'Who made it?'

'A businessman in Dubrajpur.'

'Dandania?'

'Yes.'

'How much did he offer you?'

'Ten lakhs. But who's to tell his offer won't go up?'

'All right. I know Dandania quite well. I'll manage him.'

'Very well, Mr Naskar. Goodbye!'

'Goodbye!'

Mr Naskar left at last. We rose and went into the dining hall. I was starving.

Chapter 5

The fair at Kenduli was being held at a temple built two hundred and fifty years ago, by the Maharani of Burdwan.

We had arrived together in Lalmohan Babu's car. His driver was given the day off. Feluda drove. Lalmohan Babu and I sat next to him. Peter, Tom and Jagannath Chatterjee sat at the back.

A large group of bauls had gathered under a huge banyan tree. One of them was playing his ektara and singing. Mr Chatterjee began explaining the history of the place and the details of the carvings. I noticed, to my surprise, that many of the figures carved on the walls and pillars of the temple were figures from the *Ramayana* and *Mahabharat*. Peter was listening to Mr Chatterjee with rapt attention. Tom had disappeared. Mr Chatterjee stopped after a while and ambled off in a different direction. Feluda seized this opportunity to ask Peter the question that had been bothering me since yesterday. 'Is everything all right between Tom and you? He's been behaving rather oddly, hasn't he? I don't like it, Peter. Can you really trust him?'

'Yes, I think so. I've known him for twenty-two years. We went to the same school and college. He was fine back home but I've noticed a few changes in him since our arrival in India. Sometimes he behaves as though the British are still the rulers here. Besides, back in England he didn't seem interested in selling the ruby at all. Now, he's not averse to the idea of filling his pockets.'

'Is he in need of money?'

'In a way, yes. You see, he wants to travel all over the world, taking photos everywhere, particularly where he can see stark poverty. At this moment, neither of us has the kind of money we'd need to travel so widely. But if we sold that ruby, then there would be no problem.'

'What if he sold it without telling you?'

'No, I'm sure he would not betray my trust completely. I've been speaking to him sternly and seriously since yesterday, trying to make him see reason. I think he'll come round before long.'

Feluda looked around for Tom. But still there was no sign of him.

'Do you know where he's gone?'

'No, I'm afraid not. He didn't tell me.'

'I am beginning to get a nasty suspicion.'

'What do you mean?'

'Look over there. Can you see smoke rising from the river-side? That means there's a cremation ground. Could he have gone there to take photos? We ought to go and find out.'

We left at once, making our way through groups of bauls. The river bank lay just beyond, sloping gradually to lead to the water.

Here was the cremation ground. A corpse lay on a burning pyre.

'Look, there's Tom!' cried Peter.

Tom was standing a few yards away from the pyre, getting his camera and various lenses out of his bag.

'He is doing something utterly foolish,' Feluda said. Almost instantly, his words were proved right. Four young men were sitting near the pyre. One of them saw what Tom was about to do. He ran forward, snatched the camera from Tom's hands and threw it on the sand.

And Tom? Tom took a step forward, curling his right hand into a fist. It landed on the young man's nose a second later. He fell on the ground, clutching his nose. When he removed his hand, we could all see it was smeared with blood.

Feluda did not waste another moment. Before either the first young man or his friends could move, he strode across and placed himself between Tom and the others. 'Please,' he said, raising his hands placatingly, 'please forgive my friend. He is new to our country, and he hasn't yet learnt what he should or shouldn't do. It was very wrong of him to have tried to take a photo of a pyre. I'll explain everything to him, and he won't repeat this mistake, I promise you. But please let him go now.'

To my surprise, one of the young men came forward and quickly touched Feluda's feet.

'What . . . what are you doing?'

'You are Felu Mitter, aren't you? *The* Pradosh Mitter? The famous—?'

'Yes, yes,' Feluda said hurriedly, 'I am Felu Mitter, I am an investigator and this gentleman here is my friend. Please will you forgive him and let him go?'

'All right, sir, never mind. No problem,' said the three men, staring at Feluda with a mixture of awe and admiration. Getting recognized, I thought, was no bad thing, after all.

But the injured man, who had by now risen to his feet, was not so easily impressed. 'I shall pay you back, sahib,' he spoke clearly. 'I'll settle scores with you before you go back. Just remember that. No one lays a hand on Chandu Mallik and gets away with it!'

None of us said anything to him. We turned around to go back. Tom's camera appeared undamaged. But he himself seemed totally taken aback by this sudden development. Perhaps this would teach him to be more careful, I told myself.

We had lunch back in the tourist lodge, and were sitting in the lounge when Inspector Chaubey turned up. 'I came to find out how you were doing,' he said, 'and I can tell there's something wrong.'

'You're quite right, Inspector,' Feluda replied, and briefly explained what had happened. 'Does the name Chandu Mallik mean anything to you?' he asked.

'Oh yes. He's a notorious goonda. He's been to prison at least three times. If he has threatened to settle scores, we cannot just laugh it off.'

Tom had gone back to his room. Peter was sitting with us.

'Mr Robertson,' the Inspector said, 'only you can do something to help.'

'How?'

'Talk to your friend. Tell him he must learn to control his temper. India became independent forty-five years ago. No Indian today would accept from a Britisher the kind of behaviour Mr Maxwell has shown.'

'I suggest *you* tell him that,' Peter said a little sadly. 'I can't think straight. Tom is behaving so strangely I feel I don't know him at all. He's just not listening to me any more. If you talk to him, maybe that'll work?'

'Very well, I'll do as you say. But must you let him keep you ruby? Why don't you take it back?'

'I have a problem, Inspector. I am extremely forgetful and absent-minded. Tom isn't. The ruby is really much safer in his custody. Besides, despite everything, I'm convinced he won't sell it without telling me.'

We rose and went to find Tom in his room. Peter did not come with us.

He was sitting in a chair, deep in thought, a half-finished cigarette dangling from his lips. The door was open. He looked up as we arrived, but did not rise to greet us. Inspector Chaubey took the second chair. Feluda, Lalmohan Babu and I sat on the bed.

'Are you trying to put pressure on me?' asked Tom.

'No. We have come to plead with you,' said the Inspector very politely.

'What for?'

'Mr Maxwell, you are free to think what you like about the country you're visiting and its people. But please do not show your feelings so openly.'

'Who are you to tell me how I should behave? I will do exactly as I please. I have seen in the last couple of days just how backward your country is. You haven't moved an inch in forty-five years. Your farmers are still using animals to till the land. I have seen dozens of men in Calcutta pulling rickshaws. Millions sleep on footpaths. And you dare call yourselves civilized? I know you wish to hide these disgraceful facts from the rest of the world, but I won't let you. I *will* take photographs of the real India and expose the depths of your hypocrisy to the whole world.'

'You are making a grave error, Mr Maxwell. You can't just talk of India's poverty and harp on our shortcomings. Why, haven't you seen the progress we have made? We've explored outer space, we've started producing everything one might need to live in comfort, from clothes to cars to electronics—just name it! Why should you let your eyes stay focused on only one single negative aspect of our culture? Nobody's denying there's poverty in our country, and there's exploitation. But is everything in your own country totally above reproach, Mr Maxwell?'

'Don't compare your country with mine, Mr Chaubey! You talk of India's independence? That whole business is a bloody farce. I'll get my camera to prove it. You *need* someone to rule over you, just as my ancestors did all those years ago. That's what you deserve. My great-great-grandfather was absolutely justified in doing what he did.'

'What do you mean?'

'He owned an indigo factory. Once he kicked one of his servants to death.'

'What!'

'Yes. It was his punkha-puller. I have heard how terribly hot and stuffy this place can get in the summer. Well, one night in the summer, my ancestor, Reginald Maxwell, was sleeping in his bungalow. The punkha-puller was doing his job. But a little later he fell asleep. Reginald Maxwell woke in the middle of the night, feeling hot and sticky and covered with mosquito bites. He came out of his room and found the punkha-puller fast asleep. Wild with rage, he kicked him hard in the stomach. As it happened, he was wearing heavy boots. The punkha-puller never woke up after that. His body was removed in the morning. That, sir, was the right treatment. Today I wanted to take photos of your awful system of burning corpses. I wanted to show the people of my country how you treat your dead. But a local hoodlum came to threaten me. Yes, I punched his nose because he asked for it. I have no regrets. None at all.'

After a few moments of silence, Inspector Chaubey said slowly, 'Mr Maxwell, there is only one thing I'd like to say. The sooner you leave this country, the better. Your staying here will simply mean more trouble, not just for our poor country, but also for yourself. Surely you realize that?'

'I have come here to take photos. I will not leave until I have finished my job.'

'But that's not the real reason why you're here, is it? You came chiefly to return the ruby to India, didn't you?'

'No. That was Peter's wish. I think he is being very stupid about the whole thing. I'd be a lot happier if he sold it.'

Chapter 6

We were back in our room after dinner, chatting idly, when Lalmohan Babu suddenly announced that he must return to his room.

'Why? What's the hurry?' Feluda asked.

'It's that book Shatadal gave me. You know, the one written by Rev Pritchard called *Life and Work in Birbhum*. It's absolutely gripping. In fact, there's mention of the story we just heard from Maxwell about a punkha-puller being kicked to death.'

'Really?'

'Yes. This happened towards the end of the nineteenth century. Reginald Maxwell killed his servant, but no one punished him for doing so . . . . The punkha-puller was called Hiralal. His wife had died, but he had a little boy. When Rev Pritchard heard about the murder, he rushed to Maxwell's house, and found the orphan boy. He brought the child back with him and began looking after him as though he was his own. The child was called Anant Narayan. Eventually, he became a Christian and was put in a missionary school. Now I am dying to find out what happened next. So if you'll excuse . . . .'

Someone knocked on the door. I found Peter standing outside.

'May I come in?'

'Of course.'

Feluda rose. Lalmohan Babu, who was about to leave, changed his mind and sat down again. Peter looked extremely unhappy. Something serious must have happened.

'What's the matter, Peter?' Feluda asked.

'I have decided to sell the ruby.'

'What! Why? Oh, do sit down, Peter. Tell us what happened.'

Peter sat down. 'I don't want to lose an old friend. Tom is totally obsessed with the idea of selling that ruby. His dream is to travel all over the world, and that dream can come true if the ruby is sold. I thought things over, and felt there was no point in giving it away to a museum. After all, how many people would really get to see it, tell me? So I thought . . . ' his voice trailed away.

Feluda frowned. After a short pause, he said, 'Well, it's your decision. Who am I to say anything? I *am* disappointed, but it's really none of my business, is it?'

'When do you want to sell it?' Lalmohan Babu asked.

'I've just spoken to Dandania. He made the first offer, so I think I should go back to him. He told me to meet him the day after tomorrow at ten.'

'I thought your return to India would result in a historic event,' Feluda said sadly, 'but now all one would get to see would be a simple commercial transaction.'

'I am very sorry,' said Peter, and left.

We sat in silence, feeling terribly deflated and let down.

*

We had planned to visit Bakreshwar the following morning. We'd just finished our breakfast and reached the lounge, when Mr Naskar arrived in his car.

'Good morning,' he said, coming in to the reception area.

313

'Good morning.'

'Would you like to see a Santhal dance this evening? A dance has been arranged in the Phulberey village. It should be worth seeing, especially as there's going to be a full moon tonight.'

'Who has arranged it?'

'The local people, for a group of Japanese tourists. I've come to invite all of you to dinner at my place this evening. If you're interested in seeing the dance, I can .take you there myself, after dinner. The village is only two miles from my house.'

'Does your invitation include Peter and Tom?' Feluda asked.

'Yes, yes, of course. All five of you are invited.'

'Thank you very much. When would you like us to arrive?'

'About eight, if that's all right. Should I send my car?'

'There's no need. We can quite easily go in ours. There shouldn't be any problem.'

'Very well. I shall look forward to seeing you later. Good day!'

*

Bakreshwar turned out to be a place that hadn't bothered to step out of primitive times. There were rows of old temples, behind which stood several large trees. Most of these were banyan trees. Huge roots hung down from these and clung to the temple walls. Nearly every temple had its own pond. Jagannath Chatterjee, who had accompanied us again, told us what each pond was called. Peter stopped at one called 'Soubhagya Kunda', and went in for a swim. Someone had told him what 'soubhagya' meant. So he laughed as he came up and said, 'This should bring me good luck!'

There were scores of beggars near the temples. Tom took

out his camera and soon found several people with special photogenic features.

Half an hour after our return to the tourist lodge, Inspector Chaubey rang Feluda. 'Did you know there's going to be a Santhal dance later today?' he asked.

'Yes, Mr Naskar told us. In fact, we're going to have dinner at his place this evening. He's offered to take us to the dance afterwards. We should reach there by 10 p.m.'

'Good. I hope to get there by half past ten, so I guess that's where we shall meet tonight.'

Mr Naskar had given us very good directions. We found his house without any problem. It was a fairly large house with two storeys and a carefully maintained garden. Mr Naskar came out to greet us as we got out of our car, and then took us straight to his drawing room. A bearer came in with drinks almost immediately.

'You stay here alone, don't you?' Feluda asked, picking up a cold drink from a tray.

'Yes, but I have a lot of friends. We normally arrive in groups to spend a few days here. This time, I came alone.' Mr Naskar suddenly turned to Lalmohan Babu. 'I had heard of Mr Mitter, but I don't think I got your name—?'

'Most people don't know his real name,' Feluda answered. 'He writes crime thrillers under a pseudonym. Millions know him simply as Jatayu. His books are immensely popular.'

'Yes, yes, now that you mention . . . why, I've read some of your books, too! *Shaken in Shanghai* was one, wasn't it?' Lalmohan Babu smiled politely. 'I don't like serious books at all,' Mr Naskar continued. 'All I ever read are thrillers. What are you writing now?'

'Nothing at this moment. I'm here simply on a holiday. My latest book was published only a couple of months ago. *Dumbstruck in Damascus* it was called.'

'Another best seller?'

315

'Well . . . four thousand copies have been sold already, heh heh.'

Mr Naskar smiled and turned to Peter. 'Have you thought any more about my proposal?' he asked, coming straight to the point.

'I've decided to sell the ruby.'

'That's excellent.'

'But not to you.'

'Are you selling it to Dandania?'

'Yes, since his was the first offer I received.'

'No, Mr Robertson. You will sell your ruby to me.'

'How is that possible, Mr Naskar? I've told Dandania already. My mind is made up.'

'I'll tell you how it's going to be possible. You don't believe me, do you? All right, let's get someone totally impartial to explain things. Mr Ganguli!'

'Y-yes?' Lalmohan Babu looked up, startled.

'Do you mind stepping forward and standing here on this rug?'

'M-me?'

'Yes. I want you as you have no interest in the ruby, and you've got a pleasant, amiable nature.'

'What has that to do with anything?'

'Don't be afraid, Mr Ganguli. You'll come to no harm, I promise you. The thing is, you see, I haven't yet told you of a special skill that I acquired years ago. I can hypnotize people, and get them to give me correct answers to vexing questions. The reason for this is that when a person's been hypnotized, he temporarily loses the ability to make things up and tell lies. This ability, that comes naturally to most people, is replaced by an extraordinary power. A hypnotized person always tells the truth. I'll soon prove this to you.'

Before Lalmohan Babu got a chance to protest, Mr Naskar caught him by his shoulders and dragged him to stand on a rug in the middle of the room. Then he switched off all the lights and took out a small red torch from his pocket. I glanced

316

at Feluda, but found him watching the scene with an impassive face. I knew he sometimes quite enjoyed it if anyone involved Lalmohan Babu in a bit of harmless fun.

Mr Naskar switched on the torch and shone it on Lalmohan Babu's face, moving it slowly. 'Look at this carefully, Mr Ganguli,' he whispered, 'and forget everything else. You are about to become a totally different person . . . a new man with a special magical power to tell the truth . . . that no one knows but you . . . just you . . . yes, yes, yes, yes . . . .'

Lalmohan Babu's eyes soon began to look glazed. He stared into space unseeingly. His mouth fell open. Mr Naskar stopped moving the torch, but did not switch it off. After a few seconds of silence, he asked his first question.

'What is your name?'

'Mr Know All, alias Lalmohan Ganguli, alias Jatayu.'

Mr Know All? I had never heard anyone call him that!

'How many people are present in this room?'

'Six.'

'Are they all Indian?'

'No, there are two Englishmen among them.'

'What are their names?'

'Peter Robertson and Tom Maxwell.'

'Where in England do they come from?'

'Lancashire.'

'How old are they?'

'Peter is thirty-four years and three months. Tom's age is thirty-three years and nine months.'

'Why are they visiting India?'

'Peter wants to return Robertson's Ruby to India.'

'Who has actually got the ruby?'

'Tom Maxwell.'

'What is the future of this ruby?'

'It will be sold.'

'To Ganesh Dandania?'

'No.'

'But he's already made an offer, hasn't he?'

317

'Yes, but he'll go back on his word. He'll now offer only seven lakhs for it.'

'And Peter won't sell his ruby to him. Is that what you're saying?'

'Yes.'

'Then who will he sell it to?'

'Ardhendu Naskar.'

'For how much?'

'Twelve lakhs.'

'Thank you, sir.'

Mr Naskar switched the torch off and shook Lalmohan Babu gently. I saw him give a start. By the time Mr Naskar came back to his chair after turning the lights back on again, Lalmohan Babu was once more his normal self.

'Well, Mr Robertson?' Mr Naskar asked.

'That was most impressive,' Peter replied.

'Now do you believe me?'

'I don't know what to think.'

'You needn't think at all. I am in no great hurry. Go and see Dandania tomorrow. Sell your ruby for seven lakhs, if you so wish. However, should you change your mind, my own offer of twelve lakhs still stands.'

Peter was spared the necessity of making a reply by the arrival of Mr Naskar's cook. 'Dinner has been served,' he announced.

We rose and made our way to the dining room.

Chapter 7

We left for Phulberey after a most sumptuous meal. By the time we got there, it was a quarter past ten. A crowd had gathered in a large open field. Not many of them were Santhals; obviously, people from towns nearby had arrived to see the dance. The full moon and torches that burnt here and there made it possible to see everything clearly.

Inspector Chaubey emerged from the crowd. 'You'll find many other familiar figures here,' he informed us.

'Why, who else has turned up?'

'I saw Kishorilal and Chandu Mallik. And that gentleman who's an expert on Birbhum.'

'Jagannath Chatterjee. Well, that's good news. When is the dance going to start?'

'Any minute now. Look, the dancers are all standing together.'

Feluda spotted Peter. 'Don't get lost, Peter,' he called. 'If we don't stay relatively close to each other, going back together won't be easy.'

I saw Tom getting his camera ready with a flash gun. Mr Naskar, too, was holding a small camera in his hand. 'Do you have a studio of your own?' he asked Tom.

'No. I am not a studio photographer. I take photographs while I travel. I only do freelance work. My photos have been printed in several magazines and journals. In fact, this assignment in India is being paid for by the *National Geographic*.'

The drums began to roll. All of us moved forward to get a better view. About thirty women, dressed in their traditional costume and jewellery, were standing in a semi-circle, holding hands and swaying gently to the rhythm of the music. Two men playing flutes sat with the drummers. The drummers wore bells around their ankles.

Lalmohan Babu came and stood by my side. 'Now my left eye is twitching. Heaven knows what's in store,' he muttered.

'Getting hypnotized didn't have any adverse effects on you, I hope?' I asked.

'No, no. It's been an amazing experience, you know. I can't remember even a single word that I spoke.'

In the light of a torch, I saw Chandu Mallik smoking a bidi and moving slowly in the direction of the dancers. But no. It was not the dancers he was interested in. He had seen Tom, and was sneaking up to him.

'We must keep an eye on him, Lalmohan Babu,' I whispered.

'Yes, you're quite right.'

But Tom had moved from where he had been standing to a different spot, possibly to get a better angle. Were all photographers restless like him?

Chandu Mallik came and stood in front of us. He was frowning. His hands were stuffed into his pockets. Then he moved on in a different direction. Our group dispersed gradually. Lalmohan Babu and I stayed together, trying to spot the others for we were all supposed to re-group once the dance was over. There was Feluda in the distance. Chaubey had been standing next to him even a moment ago, but now I couldn't see him. Mr Naskar was busy clicking; I saw his camera flash more than once. The dancers were still swaying with a slow and easy grace.

Suddenly, I saw Kishorilal approaching Peter. What was

he going to tell him? Curious, I left Lalmohan Babu and moved forward to hear their conversation.

'Good evening,' Peter said to Kishorilal. 'Our appointment tomorrow still stands, I hope?'

'Oh yes.'

'Your father's not likely to change his mind, is he?'

'No, sir. His mind is made up.'

'Good.'

Kishorilal left. Jagannath Chatterjee took his place.

'Hello, Mr Chatterjee,' greeted Peter. 'I'm glad I've run into you. Will you please explain to me the purpose of this dance? I mean, does this signify anything?'

'Why, certainly,' Mr Chatterjee came closer and began explaining various aspects of tribal culture. I returned to rejoin Lalmohan Babu.

Feluda was now standing near a burning torch. I saw him light a cigarette. The first dance came to an end, and the second one began. The rhythm of this one was much faster, and a group of singers joined the drummers. The dancers increased their pace to match the rhythm, bending and straightening their bodies, their feet rising and falling in a uniform pattern.

'Very exciting,' remarked Lalmohan Babu.

Mr Naskar passed us by, camera in hand. 'How do you like it?' he asked, but moved on without waiting for an answer.

Feldua saw us and walked across.

'Why, Felu Babu,' Lalmohan Babu asked, 'why are you frowning even on a joyous occasion like this? Those drummers are really playing well, aren't they?'

'Yes, but there's something not quite right over here. I feel distinctly uneasy. Have you seen Tom Maxwell?'

'I saw him a few minutes ago. But I don't know where he went.'

'We must find him,' said Feluda and moved to the left.

'Your cousin needs our help, I think,' Lalmohan Babu said to me and leapt forward to follow Feluda, dragging me with him. In a few seconds, we found ourselves behind the dancers.

The crowd was thinner here. I could see Chandu Mallik and Kishorilal roaming about. Where was Tom?

There was Peter, standing alone and looking around. 'Have you seen Tom?' he asked Feluda.

'No, we've been looking for him, too.'

'I don't like this at all.'

Peter moved off in one direction to look for Tom. We went to the other side. Feluda soon got lost in the crowd. The music and the dancing were getting faster every minute, but there was no time to stop and enjoy it. Feluda reappeared suddenly. 'Chaubey? Have you seen him?' he asked anxiously.

'No. Why, Feluda, what's—?'

But he was already a few steps ahead of us, calling, 'Inspector Chaubey! Inspector Chaubey!'

Chaubey must have been standing somewhere close by, for only a minute later, he and Feluda came out of the crowd and began hurrying away.

'What's the matter?' Lalmohan Babu asked, struggling to keep pace with them.

'Maxwell,' Feluda replied briefly.

We broke into a run. Feluda stopped abruptly near a tree. A torch was burning about ten feet away. In its light, we saw Tom Maxwell lying on the ground. His camera and his bag containing other equipment were lying on the grass beside him.

'Is he . . . is he dead?' Chaubey asked, breathing hard.

'No,' Feluda replied, bending over Tom and taking one of his wrists between his fingers, 'I can feel his pulse. He is not dead . . . at least, not yet.'

Chaubey took out a small torch from his pocket and shone it on Tom's face. His eyes seemed to flicker for a second. Feluda shook him by his shoulders.

'Tom! Maxwell!'

At this moment, another figure tore through the crowd and came up panting. It was Peter. 'What's the matter with Tom? My God, is he . . . he's not . . . ?'

322

'No, he's just unconscious. But I think he's coming round.'

Tom had begun to stir. Now he opened his eyes, wincing. 'Where does it hurt?' Feluda asked urgently. With an effort, Tom raised a hand to indicate a spot at the back of his head.

In the meantime, Peter had picked up his bag and looked inside. He glanced up, the pallor on his face clearly visible even in the semi-darkness.

'The ruby is gone!' he cried hoarsely.

*

We returned to Mr Naskar's house with Tom. When told about the theft, Mr Naskar's face became a study in fury and disappointment.

'You should be happy!' he snapped. 'You got what you wanted, didn't you? Robertson's Ruby came back to India all right, though now you'll never be able to go on that world tour.'

One Dr Sinha from the neighbourhood was called to examine Tom.

'There is a swelling on his head where he was struck. Someone attacked him with a heavy object,' Dr Sinha said.

'Could this blow have killed him?' Peter wanted to know.

'Yes, if his attacker had hit him harder, your friend might well have been killed. But that did not happen, so please don't dwell on it. Give him an ice-pack which will help the swelling to subside. If the pain gets very bad, take a pain-killer, Mr Maxwell. There's nothing else to be done at this moment. Don't worry, though. You'll recover soon enough.'

Chaubey opened his mouth when Dr Sinha had gone.

'Mr Maxwell,' he said, 'you didn't actually get to see who attacked you, did you?'

'No, I didn't.'

'I wonder what his motive was. To steal the ruby? But not too many people knew the ruby was with Tom Maxwell, and not Peter Robertson. In fact, the only people who knew this fact were Mr Mitter, Mr Ganguli, Tapesh, Kishorilal, Jagannath Chatterjee, Mr Naskar and myself.'

'What are you saying, Inspector?' Mr Naskar protested. 'I would have got that stone, anyway. Why should I do something absurd like this? Why, for Heaven's sake, Tom might have been killed! Would I risk being charged with murder when all I had to do was just wait for another day?'

'It's no use arguing, Mr Naskar. You are a prime suspect. What Mr Ganguli said when he was supposedly hypnotized is of no consequence. After all, there was no guarantee that his words would come true, was there? There was every chance of that ruby being sold to someone else. We all know it was no ordinary ruby, and you are no ordinary collector. So why shouldn't I assume that you tried to get there first, *without* paying a paisa for it?'

'Nonsense! Nonsense!' said Mr Naskar, just a little feebly.

'Apart from yourself, there's Kishorilal to be considered,' Chaubey went on. 'His father was going to buy it, but that would not have been of any use to Kishori. He knew its value, and he knew where to find it. So if he found Maxwell alone, he might simply have given in to temptation, who knows? . . . A third suspect is Chandu Mallik. He had already threatened to settle scores with Tom. But did he know about the ruby? I don't think so. If he did find it, it must have been by accident. After knocking Tom down, he might have slipped his hand into his bag to look for money, and come across the ruby. This possibility cannot be ruled out . . . Then there is Jagannath Chatterjee. He knew about the ruby and where it was kept. Pure greed might have prompted him to remove it.'

'You have left out one important suspect, Inspector,' Feluda said.

'Who?'

'Peter Robertson.'

'What!' Peter jumped to his feet.

'Yes, Peter. You had wanted to hand over the ruby to the

museum in Calcutta. Your friend opposed the idea. You agreed to sell it because you didn't want to lose your friend. But who's to say you didn't change your mind? What if you went back to your original decision and found a way of getting the ruby back without risking your friendship with Tom?'

Peter stared at Feluda, rendered speechless for the moment. Then he raised his arms over his head and said slowly, 'There is a very simple way to find out if I'm the culprit. If I did indeed take the ruby back, I would still have it with me, wouldn't I? I mean, I have been with all of your throughout since we found Tom. So search me, Inspector Chaubey. Come on, search me!'

'Very well,' said Chaubey and searched Peter thoroughly. He found nothing.

'All right, Inspector,' Feluda said. 'Since you took the trouble to search Peter, I think you should do the same for each one of us.' Chaubey seemed to hesitate. 'Come along now, Inspector, there is no reason to leave us out,' Feluda said again. This time, Chaubey stepped forward and searched everyone in the room, including me. Still he didn't find the ruby.

'Mr Robertson,' he asked, 'would you like me to carry out an official investigation?'

'Of course!' Peter said firmly. 'I want that ruby back at any cost.'

Chapter 8

Tom seemed a lot better in the morning. He was still in pain, but the swelling had gone down and, hopefully, in a couple of days he'd recover completely.

But he couldn't get over the shock of having lost the precious ruby. 'I never thought I'd have to leave that stone here with an unknown criminal,' Peter kept saying.

'Oh, why didn't we sell it to Dandania the first day?' moaned Tom time and again. It was difficult to tell who was more sorry at the loss.

Inspector Chaubey came to our room around 11 a.m.

'I've just been to see Tom,' he said.

'Tom's doing fine. Have *you* made any progress?' Feluda asked.

'One of the suspects has had to be eliminated from my list.'

'Really?' Who?'

'Kishorilal.'

'Why?'

'Well, I happen to know Kishori pretty well. It's not like him to do anything so reckless. Besides, his father has recently bought him a plastics factory. Kishori has been going there regularly. Dandania, I know, keeps a careful eye on his son. If Kishori stole that ruby simply to sell it and make a packet for himself, his father would most certainly come to know, and then there would be hell to pay. So Kishori is out.'

'I see. What about Chandu Mallik?'

'As far as I can make out, Maxwell was attacked at around a quarter to eleven last night. Chandu had left the dance before that and was sitting with friends having a drink in a small shop. There are several witnesses who'd vouch for him. I've already spoken to most of them. That rules out Chandu, too.'

'And the others?'

'I searched Naskar's house this morning. I didn't find the ruby, of course, but that doesn't mean a thing. He could easily have hidden it somewhere else. But I have started to think Jagannath Chatterjee is our best bet.'

'Why do you say that?'

'He claims to be an authority on Birbhum. But he's lived here only for the last three years. My guess is that he's no expert at all. All his information probably comes from a guide book for tourists. Besides, I discovered he'd been arrested for fraud in Burdwan where he used to live before. He's a criminal, Mr Mitter. I'm convinced he's our man. Did you know he was charging a fee for his services? Yes, sir. Mr Robertson paid him a hundred rupees each time he met him!'

'No, I did not know that. Have you searched his house?'

'No, but I will this afternoon, though I don't think a search will yield anything. What I have to do is speak to him sternly and put the fear of God in him. Anyway, aren't *you* going to do anything?'

'No. Any action you as a police officer may take will have a lot more effect, I think. But I'll keep my eyes and ears open, naturally, and will let you know if I notice anything suspicious. Oh, by the way, what about the fifth suspect I mentioned?'

'You mean Peter Robertson?'

'Yes. I have a feeling Peter would now accept the loss of an old friendship, if need be. What is important to him is that his ancestor's wish be fulfilled. He's changed his mind about selling that ruby. I know he has.'

'Yes, you said so last night, didn't you? I remembered your words, Mr Mitter, and I searched Peter Robertson's room only a few minutes before I came here. Need I tell you there was no sign of the ruby?'

Feluda made no reply. Inspector Chaubey rose. 'I'll come and see you again in the evening,' he said and left.

'A most complicated case,' Feluda sighed. 'Five suspects . . . all strewn in five different places. What can I do from here? The police have certainly got the upper hand this time.'

'Come on, Felu Babu, you're not even trying. Tell us who you really suspect,' said Lalmohan Babu.

'Out of these five?'

'Yes.'

'I had ruled out Kishorilal for the simple reason that he didn't strike me as the type who'd resort to violence to get what he wanted. He hasn't got the courage it would take to knock someone out, steal something from his bag and run away, especially when there were so many people about.'

'What about Chandu Mallik?'

'Chandu might have hit Maxwell—he's quite capable of having done that—but how could he have known that the ruby was in his bag? No, Chandu did not do it. Mr Naskar? It's difficult to imagine him getting into a messy business like this. There was absolutely no need for him to go to such lengths; not with the kind of money he's got.'

'There's something I don't understand at all,' Lalmohan Babu confessed.

'What is it?'

'Do people always speak the truth when they're hypnotized?'

'What is the truth you're supposed to have spoken?'

'Why, didn't I tell you all how old Peter and Tom were, and that they came from Lancashire? They never mentioned it to me, so how did I know? Mind you, *I* don't remember having said it, but Tapesh says I did.'

'Both those facts had been mentioned in that article in the *Statesman*. Even if you didn't read the whole thing, Lalmohan Babu, your memory had somehow absorbed those details, and it came out when you were asked a specific question. Everything else you said has already been proved to be quite incorrect. So please don't go around thinking you had acquired any extraordinary powers at any time.'

'All right, Felu Babu, point taken. But do you agree with Inspector Chaubey? Was it Jagannath Chatterjee?'

'Who else could it be? It's such a pity the whole thing had to end so tamely, but . . .' Feluda couldn't finish his sentence. Someone knocked on the door.

It turned out to be Tom Maxwell, looking rather grim. Feluda offered him a chair, but he shook his head.

'I haven't come to sit down and chat with you,' he said.

'I see.'

'I am here to search your room and your friend's.'

'But we were all searched yesterday. Wasn't that good enough for you?'

'No. You were searched by an Indian policeman. I have no faith in him.'

'Do you have a warrant? Surely you're aware that you cannot search anyone's room without a proper warrant?'

'You mean you won't let me—?'

'No, Mr Maxwell. Neither my friend nor I will let you go through our things. Inspector Chaubey searched each one of us yesterday, in your presence. You'll have to be satisfied with that.'

Tom made an about-turn without another word and strode out of the room.

'Just imagine!' Lalmohan Babu exclaimed. 'I have been on so many cases with you, Felu Babu, but I've never ended up as one of the suspects!'

'Put it down to experience, Mr Ganguli. It's good to have all sorts of experiences, isn't it?'

'Yes, that's true. But are you going to spend all your time indoors?'

'I'll go out if I feel like it. Right now all I want to do is think, and I can do that very well without stirring out of my room. But that's no reason why you and Topshe shouldn't go out. There's a lot still left to be seen.'

'Very well. Let's go and get hold of Shatadal. He may be able to make some useful suggestions. Tell you what, Felu Babu. I'll leave that book with you, the one that Shatadal lent me. Read it. You'll get a lot of information about Tom Maxwell's ancestor. And if you wish to learn about how indigo was grown and what the British did with it, this book will tell you that, too.'

'Thank you, Lalmohan Babu. I should love to read your book.'

We left soon after this, leaving Feluda to go through what Rev Pritchard had written. Shatadal Sen happened to be free, and offered to take us to see a village by the river Kopai, which Tagore used to watch and admire. I had seen villages and rivers before, but there was something about Kopai and the village called Goalpara that touched my heart and lifted my spirits instantly.

Lalmohan Babu went a step further and began reciting poetry.

'My favourite poet, Baikuntha Mallik, visited Santiniketan, you see, and wrote quite a few poems on its natural beauty,' he told me, 'Listen to this:

'O Kopai, thin you might be,
        but you're fast.
May your beauty forever last,
        you are a pleasure to see.

Rice fields lie by your sides,
        nature's bounty in them hides,
etching pictures in my memory.
        Kopai, you are a pleasure to see.'

330

Chapter 9

Inspector Chaubey returned to our room at 5 p.m. The announcement he made wasn't altogether unexpected, but nevertheless we were all somewhat taken aback.

'The mystery is cleared up,' he said. 'I was right. Jagannath Chatterjee took the stone. When I searched his house, I didn't find it at first; but a few threats from the police can often work wonders, as they did in this case. Chatterjee broke down and confessed in the end. He even returned the stone to me. Do you know where he'd hidden it? In a flower-pot!'

'Have you brought it here?'

'Yes, naturally.'

Chaubey took it out of his pocket. It lay on his palm, glowing softly under the light. It felt strange to look at it.

'How very odd!' Feluda exclaimed.

'What's odd?'

'Chatterjee might well be a thief, but somehow I can't see him lifting a heavy object and striking someone with it. He wouldn't have the nerve, Inspector. He doesn't look the type.'

'Don't judge anyone by his looks, Mr Mitter.'

'Yes, you're right. My own experience has taught me just that. And yet . . .' Feluda broke off, frowning.

'Shall we go now and return this stone to its owner?' Chaubey asked.

'Yes, let's do that.'

We left our room and made our way to Peter's. Peter himself opened the door. Tom was with him.

'Well, Mr Robertson,' said Chaubey, 'I have a little gift for you.'

'A gift?'

Silently, Chaubey handed the ruby back to Peter. Peter's mouth fell open.

'I don't believe this! Where—how—?'

'Never mind all that, Mr Robertson. Just be happy that you've got it back. Mr Maxwell, I hope you'll now agree that the Indian police aren't altogether stupid and incompetent. Anyway, now you must decide what you want to do with it.'

Peter and Tom had both risen to their feet. Now they sank back into their chairs. Peter said softly, 'Good show, Inspector. Congratulations!'

'Thanks. May I now take your leave?' asked Chaubey.

'I . . . I don't know how to thank you!' Tom spoke unexpectedly.

'You don't have to. That the thought of saying thanks crossed your mind is good enough for me. Goodbye!'

*

'What are you thinking, Felu Babu?' Lalmohan Babu asked over breakfast the next day.

'There is something wrong . . . somewhere . . .' muttered Feluda absent-mindedly.

'I'll tell you what's wrong. For the first time, the police caught the criminal before you. The Inspector won, Felu Babu, and you lost. That's what's wrong.'

'No. The thing is, you see, I cannot believe that the case is over, and there's nothing for me to do.'

Feluda grew preoccupied again. Then he said, 'Topshe, why don't you and Lalmohan Babu go for a walk? I need to be alone. I need to think again.'

'We can sit in my room. Come on, Tapesh.'

'I don't like this, Tapesh, my boy,' Lalmohan Babu said, offering me a chair in his room. 'We got such a good opportunity to solve a mystery, and yet it just slipped through our fingers. Maybe it's because my left eye was twitching? No, I mean seriously, is your cousin all right? He looked tired, as though he hadn't slept very well.'

'He sat up late reading the book you gave him. I don't know what time he went to bed, but he was up at five this morning to do his yoga.'

'Topshe!' called Feluda from outside. His voice sounded urgent. Why had he followed us? Was anything wrong?

I opened the door quickly. Feluda rushed in and said, 'We have to go and see Chaubey, immediately.'

'What happened?'

'I'll tell you later.'

'OK.'

We were both ready to go out in just a few seconds.

'To Dubrajpur,' said Feluda to the driver. 'We need to find the police station there.'

This was not difficult. Our car went straight to the police station and stopped before the main gate. The constable on duty looked up enquiringly as we got out. 'May we see Inspector Chaubey?' Feluda asked.

'Yes, please come this way.'

Chaubey was in his room, going through some files. He looked up with a mixture of pleasure and surprise.

'Oh, what brings you here?'

'There is something we need to talk about.'

'Very well. Please sit down. Would you like a cup of tea?'

'No, thanks. We've just had breakfast.'

'I see. So what can I do for you?'

'There's just one thing I'd like you to tell me.'

'Yes?'

'Are you a Christian?'

Chaubey raised his eyebrows. Then he smiled and said, 'Why do you suddenly need to know that, Mr Mitter?'

'There's a reason. Are you?'

'Yes, I am a Christian. But how did you guess?'

'Well, I saw you eat with your left hand, more than once. At first I paid no attention, but later it struck me as odd since Hindus—unless they're left-handed—prefer, using their right hands to eat. I wondered if you were a Christian, but didn't ask at the time for I didn't realize it might have a special significance. I think I now know what it means.'

'Really? So what does it signify, Mr Mitter? You didn't come all this way just to tell me you'd guessed my religion, did you?'

'No. Allow me to ask you another question.'

'Go ahead.'

'Who was the first in your family to become a Christian?'

'My grandfather.'

'What was his name?'

'Anant Narayan.'

'What was his son called?'

'Charles Premchand.'

'And his son?'

'Richard Shankar Prasad.'

'That's you, isn't it?'

'Yes.'

'Was your great-grandfather called Hiralal?'

'Yes, but how did you—?'

Chaubey had stopped smiling. He only looked amazed and bewildered.

'It was the same Hiralal who used to pull the punkha for Reginald Maxwell. Am I right?'

'Yes, but you have to tell me how you learnt all this.'

'From a book written by a Rev Pritchard. He took charge of Anant Narayan after Hiralal's death, made him a Christian and helped him build a new life and find new happiness.'

'I didn't know there was such a book!'

'Indeed there is, though it's not easily available.'

'But if you know all that, you must have . . . .'

'What?'

'You must know . . . .'

'What, Inspector? What should I know?'

'Why don't you tell me yourself, Mr Mitter? I would find it extremely awkward to say anything myself.'

'All right,' said Feluda slowly, 'I'll tell you what happened. You grew up hearing tales of Reginald Maxwell's cruelty. You could never forget that he was responsible for your great-grandfather's death. But there was nothing you could do about it. However, when you heard Reginald's great-great-grandson Tom was here and saw that Tom had inherited Reginald's arrogance and hatred for Indians in full measure, you . . . .'

'Stop, Mr Mitter! Please say no more.'

'Does that mean I am right in thinking that it was *you* who struck Tom at the dance, just because you felt like settling old scores? And then you took the stone so that the suspicion fell on the others?'

'Yes, Mr Mitter, you are absolutely right. Now you must decide how I ought to be punished. If you wish to report the matter—'

'Inspector Chaubey,' Feluda suddenly smiled, 'I wish to do no such thing. That is what I came to tell you.'

'What!'

'Yes, sir. I thought the whole thing over and realized that had I been in your shoes, I'd have done exactly the same. In fact, I think Tom's behaviour called for something much worse than what you did to him. Relax, Inspector. Nobody's going to punish you.'

'Thank you, Mr Mitter, thank you!'

*

335

'Which one of your eyes is twitching now, Mr Know All Ganguli?'

'Both, Felu Babu, both. They're dancing with joy. But we mustn't forget one thing.'

'I know what you mean.'

'What do I mean?'

'We mustn't forget to thank your friend Shatadal Sen.'

'Correct. If he hadn't lent us that book—'

'—we couldn't have solved this case—'

'—and Jagannath Chatterjee would have remained a criminal.'

'At least in our minds.'

'Yes. To Mr Sen's house, please driver, before you take us back to the lodge.'

*

Robertson's Ruby eventually went to the Calcutta museum. Needless to say, Feluda played an important role in the actual transfer. He pointed out to Peter that Tom was simply being greedy. If he could get sponsorship from a famous journal like the *National Geographic*, he couldn't, by any means, be lacking in funds.

Tom Maxwell did his best to influence his friend's decision again, but this time Peter was adamant.

Patrick Robertson's last wish was finally fulfilled.